THE SEA
ELEPHANTS

THE SEA ELEPHANTS

SHASTRI AKELLA

FLATIRON
BOOKS
NEW YORK

THE SEA ELEPHANTS. Copyright © 2023 by Shastri Akella.
All rights reserved. Printed in the United States of America.
For information, address Flatiron Books,
120 Broadway, New York, NY 10271.

www.flatironbooks.com

Designed by Michelle McMillian

Library of Congress Cataloging-in-Publication Data

Names: Akella, Shastri, author.
Title: The sea elephants / Shastri Akella.
Description: First edition. | New York : Flatiron Books, 2023.
Identifiers: LCCN 2022054326 | ISBN 9781250867056 (hardcover) |
    ISBN 9781250867254 (ebook)
Subjects: LCGFT: Novels.
Classification: LCC PS3601.K43 S43 2023 | DDC 813/.6—dc23/
    eng/20230209
LC record available at https://lccn.loc.gov/2022054326

Our books may be purchased in bulk for promotional, educational,
or business use. Please contact your local bookseller or the Macmillan
Corporate and Premium Sales Department at 1-800-221-7945, extension 5442,
or by email at MacmillanSpecialMarkets@macmillan.com.

First Edition: 2023

10 9 8 7 6 5 4 3 2 1

For Nana and Amma. Kamu and Akka.
My sentences are an expression of gratitude for you.

For my found family: Subhadra, Andrew, Sabina,
Parker, Edie, Spencer, Freddie, Grace, Moira, Kritika, Prayathna,
Sagari, Bükem, Daniel, and Callum.
Without you, *The Sea Elephants* wouldn't exist, nor would I.
Thank you for welcoming me into your homes and lives
and teaching me how to thrive.

PART I

1989–1990

ARRIVAL

My father left the country the year my sisters were born. He returned six months after I watched them drown in the Bay of Bengal.

My sisters' funeral dinner was scheduled to coincide with the day of his arrival. Some relatives came over that morning to participate in the ritual. When I got back home from school, I found them sitting cross-legged in the foyer: fifteen women, the henna on each left palm drying to a russet circle of mangoes and leaves. The air tingled with excitement. And I understood. My father was here.

At dusk, we all filed into our backyard. I was still in my school uniform. We formed a circle around a priest. He read aloud a Ganesha hymn, and we chanted after him. We sat down cross-legged. In front of each of us was a banana leaf that held a heap of lemon rice surrounded by small pools of lentils, aloo-gobi, mango chutney, and yogurt. We started eating in the light of paper lanterns that ran from Ma's window past the well to the outhouse, their amber bellies glimmering against the slowly darkening sky. The lighthouse on the banks of the Bay of Bengal swept its illuminated arm across the evening at nine-second intervals.

I avoided looking at my parents. The priest stood in our midst and watched us eat. He rubbed his potbelly and grinned at anyone who made eye contact with him. I didn't want to be grinned at, I certainly didn't want to grin back, so I looked away from him as well.

Suddenly, Ma called out my name. "Shagun? Where are you?"

The conversations around us were suspended.

"Shagun?" she called again.

The woman to my left hollered, "Your son's here."

Ma dropped her head a little, leveled her eyes with mine, and asked, "Why won't you respond when I call you, son?"

I cupped a palm around my ear and leaned toward her.

"This is your father," Ma announced.

That was how, at the age of sixteen, I met the man who made me. His face was owlish, his hair salt-and-pepper. He had the build of a banyan; he dwarfed Ma who sat next to him.

Some guests started to clap their hands to their thighs. All their bangles jingled.

Ma swept an arm my way and said to my father, "Your son. A Mathur obviously."

Laughter spilled from everyone's mouths. And some food.

The conversations around us resumed. Ma kept shaking her head to brush aside the two locks of hair that kept falling onto her forehead. He blushed when he tucked them behind her ear, and my neck went hot.

After dinner, an aunt took me up the stairs and to my father. He was sitting on my mother's bed. I clasped my hands and stood before him with my head bowed.

"Ay-hay, look at him," she said, "feeling nervous to meet Daddy. That's so cute."

She laughed and clapped the back of my head. She closed the door as she left.

"You're not to call me that," my father said.

My throat ached. I wanted to gulp down a bottle of water.

"No Daddy-Papa business. You'll call me Pita-jee," he said. "Now come here."

He held my head in cupped palms. He thumbed my eyebrows, ran a knuckle down my cheek, turned me around, placed his palm on my back, turned me again. He studied me slowly, head to toe, until his little lashes met.

"Are you asleep?" I asked. "Should I go?"

He laughed with his eyes closed and his shoulders shook. He picked me up, his sixteen-year-old, and put me on his lap. Four of his shirt buttons were open. He smelled of something pleasant and foreign. He pressed his cracked lips to my forehead, then opened his eyes. They were hazel like mine. The edges of his mouth curved downward.

Downstairs, Ma and our visitors sang bhajans as they cleaned the backyard and the kitchen, their voices punctuated by the dull clang of metal pans, by the mop's wet slurp on the floor.

It was a mild October day so my uniform didn't reek of dried perspiration; that felt like a small consolation. I leaned into my father and wrapped tentative hands around his shoulders. A hug would bring our reunion to its end, I thought, and he'd let me slip off his lap and go back to my room.

Instead, he pressed me to himself. He smothered my face against the wiry hair on his chest. His stubble scraped my forehead. He scrubbed my arms ferociously. His throat, as he cleared it, rumbled against my forehead. His embrace felt less like an act of affection, more like a punishment. Punishment for what I'd done.

I panicked and pressed my forearms to his chest and tried to place some distance between my body and his. When his tight grip frustrated my attempts, I raised my head and bit his ear.

He sucked in a sharp breath. With a hand on my arm he pried us apart. He nursed his ear, but discreetly. He pretended to relieve an itch. Then the power went out.

"Who's your favorite god?" he asked, in the dark.

"What?"

"Boys should like Hanuman," he said, placing me down. "Hanuman makes you good at cricket and maths. Did you know?"

I didn't, my silence said.

"That's why you need a father," he said as he struck a match. "To teach you things."

He lit a candle, let me out, and closed the door. He stood at the window that faced the hallway. I watched him as I passed him by, his face streaked in shadows and candlelight.

I walked down the stairs in the dark. The voices of the women became clearer. They were in the middle of a song about Krishna. My mother's favorite god. Some of their words now muffled by the sloshing of a bucket being drawn up the well. They were bathing in our backyard.

I remembered the myths that Ma would read to my sisters and me when we had our nightly power outage. We finished dinner and cleaned the kitchen by 8:00 P.M. and gathered around her, a ritual put on hold only during Exams Week. She held one of her books in the still light of a lamp fueled by kerosene and I'd watch her lips move in the dull lick of the flame. She always ended her readings with a question. "So what's the moral of that story, hmm?" she'd ask, closing her book. Or: "What happens to greedy children?"

I entered the kitchen. I opened the cupboard where Ma kept her books stacked horizontally, took out *The Dravidian Book of Seas and Stargazing, Volume 1,* and carried it to my room. I sat by the window and, in the light of a nearly full moon, opened to the first page.

Once upon a time, the gods took away the first ancestor of the sea elephants, coveting him for his exceptional beauty—tusks blue, body ivory. The trauma of that original separation haunts every sea elephant thereafter and even when they sing, their songs contain five notes or fewer, the full octave missing from their music. Only the soul of a drowned child makes their suffering manageable. So their patriarch comes ashore every so often, steals a child, and brings it back with him. He spares no effort to make the child feel at home: the seabed becomes the child's playground, the sea's life-forms in all their throbbing colors its playthings. The child forgets, over time, its mortal family and frolics about in its aquatic home. Until it is time for it to reincarnate. Then it disappears. Like a flame snuffed by wind. And the patriarch resurfaces, maddened by an old grief, in search of another child.

When Ma first read it to us, Mud had exclaimed, "What's the moral of that story? If you're a god, you can do whatever you like?"

Ma shook her head piously. "Sometimes it's hard to understand God's way."

Mud scoffed. "What rubbish. Sometimes gods behave like spoiled brats. Just admit it."

"Enough with that kind of talk," Ma chided. "It's getting late, go change and go to sleep."

That night, in the dark, I said to Mud, "Ma didn't have an answer to your question, so she shut you up and sent us packing to bed."

Mud giggled, so did Milk. They'd found a flaw: in a story written by a wise sage and read by Ma—in the gods themselves. It became thereafter my sisters' favorite tale.

Their critique of the gods didn't put an end to Ma's storytelling sessions. Their deaths did.

I heard the women come inside. The darkness trilled with the music of their anklets. They left a trail of smells: Lifebuoy soap, Gokul talcum powder.

I lay down in Milk's bed, covered myself in Mud's sheet, and looked across the room at my bed, unrumpled, as though I were a son who hadn't come home in a while. I heard the women spread their sleeping mats in the living room. They put out their lamps. Darkness stepped forward and claimed the house. A pair of footsteps strode lightly up the stairs.

I got out of bed, sidled into the foyer, and went up half the stairs on all fours. My parents stood outside Ma's room. A candle burned inside the room; it cast on them a pale glow. A breeze whistled. The light flickered. Their shadows quivered. They surged forward, the sides of their bodies glued together. I couldn't see their faces. They went into the room and closed the door. The window that faced the upstairs hallway slowly darkened.

The yodel of a cow reached me as I crawled up the remaining steps and down the corridor. I kneeled near the window and set my chin on the ledge.

A dark figure, outlined by moonlight, moved on the bed. A grunt floated my way, then a moan. My nose sweated against the window, my breath steamed its glass.

The lighthouse briefly dazzled the darkness. In its passing light, his tongue glittered. In the next burst of light, he pressed his lips to her neck, and in the next, her fingers were in his hair. Her hair lay coiled under his chest.

I waited until the jerking of his hips quickened. Then I counted up to three and pounded the window once with my forehead and stepped away. I heard a gasp and a scream that was stifled. I moved swift and weightless as a shadow along the corridor, down the stairs. I knew he wouldn't get to the door without slipping on his pajamas. And, so long as he didn't see me, he wouldn't ask me the next morning if it was I who'd wilted his pleasure; even in their private conversations, Ma and Pita-jee would chalk up the aberrant sound to a trick of the wind, a quirk of our old house, a prank by a ghost. I could count on the collective pretense that keeps families safely in their orbits.

As I lay back in Milk's bed, hearing the door above open, then close, I asked myself a question: How could a father come home six months after his daughters died, show no sign of grief, and seek instead his bodily pleasure? Even over dinner he seemed too preoccupied with his wife to mourn for his children.

But he wouldn't be here if my sisters were still here, I reminded myself. If I hadn't, with one reckless decision, caused them to drown.

My sisters on a boat that seesawed away from the shore. Milk's eyes squeezed shut, Mud's meeting my gaze. Never before had I seen a thing so animal on a human.

I sat up with a gasp. I fell asleep only when, in a slowly expanding pool of daylight, my world's reassuring forms resurfaced.

In the morning, our guests followed Pita-jee, Ma, and me into the empty living room. The white sari Ma wore, recently starched, hung stiffly down her shoulder and crackled like eggshells when she walked. Together my parents unhooked the pictures of my sisters from the Wall of the Living, to the left, and hung them on the Wall of the Dead, to the right. Ma lit an earthen lamp under their frames and their eyes gleamed.

My sisters were fourteen when their lives ended. They were identical twins. When they were disgusted, it was easy to tell them apart: Milk's lips slackened, Mud puckered her mouth. When they were scared, they collapsed into one. Like an image and its double that formed when I looked at the world squint-eyed.

On the Wall of the Living were two black squares where their photos once hung.

That afternoon our guests packed their bags and left.

DEODORANT DAYS

Our home had no furniture. We had a delivery of rentals the next day. A cane sofa for six rupees a day, a coffee table for two. Big names in our small town, all men, sat on the sofa and welcomed Pita-jee back: the Krishna temple treasurer, the police chief, the local court's judge, the mayor's son, the dairy farm owner. Among others. I was obliged to be part of these meetings (my parents insisted). I had to wear a button-down (Pita-jee insisted) and dust Gokul talcum powder in my armpits (Ma insisted).

My home had rarely contained anyone other than my sisters, me, and our mother. The homes of my friends, on the other hand, were dynamic spaces, frequented by friends, by extended family, at times for an evening, at times for longer, staying over to see our town's rustic beaches. It took my father's return to erase the demarcation between our home and the world. Where were these so-called important men all those years before? As if without Pita-jee our family was not worth their acknowledgment. They said my father was the native who'd returned to his soil; they said he was the son reunited with his motherland.

Pita-jee said to one of our guests, a banker, "Tell Shagun about Rohit-jee."

"Are you sure?" he asked, somewhat uncertain.

"He's growing up, he should know," Pita-jee said. "Start from the beginning."

"Your father, me, and Rohit-jee met at a religious studies group," he said.

"The Hanuman Satsang," Pita-jee added. "Every week I went until I left for London."

"One day, quite recently, Rohit-jee got some troubling news. His son had fallen in love with a Dalit. Rohit-jee sent four young men, fellow members of the Hanuman Satsang, to maim the boy." The banker rubbed the elbow of his right arm. "They told the girl that if she didn't keep her distance, they would go for his leg next."

"I know that story," I said.

Pita-jee and our guest gasped like Bollywood parents.

"Rohit-jee's youngest—Rusty—is my classmate," I said. "Everyone knows."

"You are not to play with him," Pita-jee said.

"Serves Rohit-jee right, after what he did to you," our guest said as he looked at Pita-jee.

"What did he do?" I asked.

Our guest exchanged with Pita-jee a glance, and Pita-jee replied, "Not the point."

"Rohit-jee didn't attack the girl, see?" our guest added hastily. "Who cares about the lowlife anyway? She was just trying to eat up the caste chain."

"It's our children we must fix," Pita-jee concurred.

"So you would do that to me?" I asked Pita-jee.

"But you look just like your father—I bet you have his values too," our guest said. "You'll do no wrong, nothing that merits punishment."

My body responded to his observation about my resemblance to Pita-jee: the sweat under my arms thickened, releasing the sweet aroma of Ma's talcum powder. Pita-jee sniffed a couple of times and frowned at me.

"Go do your studies," he said. Happy to be dismissed, I returned to my room.

The next day, when I was getting ready for school, Pita-jee came into my room and said, "From now on you'll use my deodorant. No more smelling like ladies."

I took it and saw that it was caked with two strands of his underarm hair.

"It's Old Spice," he said. "Go on. Try it."

He stood with his fists on his hips and watched me, so I slipped it under my shirt and ran it under one arm then the other and then looked at it. His hair strands were no longer stuck to its sticky surface. I found them, after he left my room, under my left arm, glued to my skin. I nearly vomited my breakfast. I picked each strand off and deposited it in the dustbin.

My father brought a statue of Hanuman the following Tuesday and placed it next to Ma's statue of Krishna. Every morning thereafter, he entered the prayer room, clad in a shawl and silk dhoti. He smeared turmeric on his Brahmin thread and chanted aloud the forty verses Tulsidas had penned in the deity's praise. Hanuman loves Tuesdays and Saturdays, he claimed, and on those days he insisted that Ma and I join his performance.

He insisted as well on family dinners. As we sat cross-legged on the kitchen floor, he described at length the buildings he'd constructed in and around London: cooling towers, pellet plants, bridges. During Sunday dinners the radio sat next to him and played Bollywood songs from the 1950s. One day, there was a problem with the reception. All we heard was static and snatches of the refrain, which ended with the exclamation, "Oh really!"

"When are you leaving?" I asked Pita-jee, interrupting him as he spoke (again) about how geometry and bravery are critical to success in the construction industry.

"What do you mean?" he asked.

"Your London office," I said. "When do they need you back? You've been here a month."

"I told you already," he said. "You must listen properly when I speak."

"He quit his job," Ma said.

"I'll look for something local, but after you start eleventh grade," he said. "We'll have plenty of time together next summer. Isn't that nice?"

The static on the radio dimmed and I heard a line in a man's voice. "The whole town's been gossiping about us, my dear." The woman replied, "Oh really!"

"Why quit now?" I asked. "Why not six months back?"

He opened his mouth. Ma held his hand. "Not now," she said.

"Why are you always hiding things from me?" I asked.

"Give us some time," Ma said.

"You always say that. How much time do you *want*?" I asked. "Give me a deadline."

Ma looked at me with a mixture of sympathy and desperation. "Your father—" she began several times but never finished her sentence. She started to cry and the radio went bonkers: a loud screech, then the woman exclaimed, "Oh really! Oh really! Oh really! Oh really! Oh really!"

"This is nonsense," I said, turning the radio off.

"Don't be like that," said Ma, sniffling, turning it on again. "Your father likes this show."

"But it's not even a song," I said and got up to go. "Maybe it's a cheap radio."

"Shagun," Pita-jee said. "You will not disrespect your food."

A crazed look entered his eyes. I sat back down and lowered my head.

"Now say sorry to your food," he said.

"It's okay," Ma said.

He grabbed her wrist and pressed it hard to the floor. She made a slight hissing sound. I looked at my plate and said, "Sorry."

"Why must you respect your food?" he asked.

I didn't know. He let Ma's hand go. He turned the radio off.

"Because food is the gift of god," he said. "Which god?"

I shook my head, my gaze still fixed on the food.

"Brahma," he said. "And who is Brahma?"

"The creator of our universe," I said, recollecting one of Ma's stories.

"Good boy."

We resumed eating. When all of our plates were empty, Ma washed her hands and took the utensils to the countertop, where she emptied them into smaller bowls and covered them.

"Mop the floor," she said to me as she wiped her hands dry with the edge of her sari.

After she left the kitchen, I looked out the open window, at the tree that stood in our forecourt. An ancient banyan. It held the treehouse like its spectacular canopy. Some nights my sisters and I stole out of the house and into the treehouse where we playacted Ma's stories.

"My father got that made," my father said behind me. "Isn't it a beauty?"

I played the cursed prince in that treehouse, I wanted to say, and my sisters dressed me up in a makeshift sari: Mud wrapped her chunni around my waist, Milk threw hers across my shoulder.

"Are you done with your homework?" Pita-jee asked. "Come play cricket with me."

"Don't start," I said.

"Being with ladies, you've become like a lady," he said. "No man will be your friend."

I looked at him bug-eyed. "I'm so scared I think I'm going to fart."

To my surprise, he laughed.

"Listen," he said. "Be gentle with your mother."

"That's rich coming from you."

"We've been through a lot. You don't know."

"And whose fault is that?"

He got up, washed his hand in the kitchen sink, and went upstairs.

As I mopped the floor—one of Mud's chores that I'd inherited—I remembered Ma's failed attempts to complete statements that she began with "your father." As if I were taking an English quiz and tasked with fill-ing in the blanks, with the appropriate action verbs, with identifying nouns.

She did eventually finish her statement and tell me why Pita-jee didn't come home when his daughters died, why Ma allowed my sisters and me to enter her room only on our birthdays. But all that came later. The boy that I was lived in the middle of my story.

The next day, I went to Ma's room, *The Dravidian Book of Seas and Star-gazing, Volume 1,* tucked under my arm, an unlit candle in one fist, a matchbox in my pocket. I stood at the entrance to her room and asked her if I could read to her. I didn't hear her walk up to the door, so I was startled when she opened it and appeared before me.

"Tune in to the local 93.1 at seven P.M.," she said. She held out a radio. "Take it."

I didn't ask her why, but I did as she directed and found out that 7:00 to 8:00 P.M. was *Storytime with Amar Sethi*. The lights went off just as the story ended, and I was plunged into darkness. The radio to which she'd outsourced storytelling felt like a wall Ma had erected to hold me at a distance from her and Pita-jee. I slipped a hand into my pocket and played with the matchbox. The silence filled with the rustle of matches.

FURNITURE

We didn't celebrate Diwali that year because there was a death in the family. The temple priest didn't want to deny us the blessings of Krishna, the festival's patron deity, so he offered to come over the day after the festival to give us a portion of the temple feast.

October's northeast monsoons arrived on time that year and it rained all morning on the day of the priest's visit. The furniture that Pita-jee rented to host him had arrived wet: the rickshaw driver had covered the sofa with two layers of plastic, but the slashing rain left on the backrest a patch of dampness. By afternoon, a smell like that of a wet dog had filled the hall.

The downpour was heavier the next day. A man, who appeared to be in his twenties, came and informed us that the rickshaw driver had refused to drive the furniture back in such heavy rain. I watched him from the window of my room, through curtains of beadlike raindrops.

"We won't pay extra," Ma said to him as he stood under the awning. "It was smelling when the guest came." She left him standing outside.

He stood with his back pressed to the door and waited out the rain. Each time the wind lashed rainwater onto his face, he ran a hand over his nose and lips.

When I opened the door, he stumbled but swiftly found his footing. He turned to face me. His shirt was glued to his body. Water had turned the fabric sheer. His belly button was visible. I offered him a fresh towel. He took it, scrubbed his head vigorously, and sponged his face slowly. He kept his lips stiff to keep them from shivering.

"You want tea?" I asked.

He raised an eyebrow. "Tea sounds nice."

I arranged four tie biscuits on a saucer, poured him the cup of milk tea that Ma had brewed for Pita-jee, and came back out. He sat down on the porch and I shut the door behind us and sat next to him. He brought the glass to his lips. He held some tea in his mouth before he gulped it.

"Ginger and cinnamon," he said.

"Correct," I said and clapped, like he had solved a puzzle. He smoothly tilted his head and brought a hand to his forehead in imitation of a court salute. He dipped one biscuit then another in the steaming cup of chai and munched on them once they softened.

Everything about him transfixed me: the day-old stubble that dotted his jaw, his thick eyelashes, his Adam's apple, which pitched against his throat as he spoke about the college he went to, the sea he saw when he opened the window of his dorm room, his engineering roommate. He went swimming on Thursdays. Why Thursdays? I wondered later. He was the son of the man who rented us this furniture. He studied in a neighboring state. He was here on Diwali vacation.

"Happy Diwali," I said, and held out my hand. He shook it. His hands, oddly, had diluted remnants of color: green on his palm, some of his fingertips purple. As if he celebrated Diwali with Holi colors, not firecrackers.

A dull creak drew my attention away from him. Pita-jee closed the gate and lumbered toward us. He was returning from his daily constitutional. He never skipped it. Come rain, come heat wave. He never changed his route. To the sea, on the beach sand, three kilometers, then back. He never asked me to join him.

He held his umbrella at a tilt against the rain. The wind flattened its skin like it was a cheek on a window. We stood up to let him pass. The boy stepped to the left of the door, and I was about to move to the right. In the last moment, when Pita-jee was almost upon us, I stepped to my left as well, toward the boy. I stood very close to him, my back brushing his chest. Pita-jee stood there, looking from him to me.

"Give me your umbrella," I said, wanting him to go away. "I'll bring it in when it's dry."

Behind me, the boy said, as he patted my shoulder, "Smart chap."

"You know my son," Pita-jee said. He leaned toward me, his face, wet perhaps from the rain, close enough that I could smell his onion breath. "Why so serious?"

He looked to the emptied teacup, to the saucer on which two biscuits remained, then he opened the door, stepped in, and said, "Oh, I forgot, the umbrella. Put it out for me, boy."

I gripped the umbrella that he held across the threshold. He didn't let go of it. His face was covered in shadow. But his eyes, pearl-hard, were fixed on me. Then, he released the umbrella and closed the door.

"You want to go?" the boy asked.

"Do you?" I asked.

He sat down on the porch, chuckling, and I wanted to be that sound in his throat, to be that decibel that corresponded so precisely to his pleasure. He picked up a biscuit and bit into it.

"When will you come again?" I asked, sitting next to him.

"I don't come here often."

"Not even to meet your parents?"

"Things change when you grow up. It's how it is. You'll see."

He placed a hand on my shoulder, and I tensed.

"Relax," he said, and he squeezed my shoulder, turning it supple again. He removed his hand and I cursed my body for clamming up in response to the touch I craved.

He hummed a song I didn't know as we watched the rain drench the landscape. My forehead broke into sweat and I worried that I'd start to smell like Old Spice.

At last, the downpour turned to a drizzle before ending. The earth around us lay stilled. The treehouse basked in an afterglow.

"I better go," he said, placing the half-eaten biscuit back on the saucer.

He rose, stretched his hands, and rotated his clenched fists. He picked up his umbrella and shook it. A hundred water droplets leaped from its surface.

I said, "I'm going to get out of here as well."

"Janab, please tell me you aren't running off to try your luck in Bollywood."

"That's genius. How did you know?"

"If there's a reward on your head, I'll come after you," he said, wagging a finger at me.

"I'll tell you where to find me if you split the reward with me."

"Deal."

"I'll apply to boarding schools," I said, wanting to impress upon him that I was following in his footsteps.

He smiled and held out his hand. My hand found its way to his. My palm and fingers drowned again in his grasp. The back of his hand was lined with hair. Curly, soft, black.

I watched him walk out the gate. He looked at me and winked. Residual rainwater trickled down his neck. He turned left onto Lawson Street and was gone. The air held the fragrance of wet mud. I pocketed his partially eaten biscuit.

"You gave him Pita-jee's tea," Ma said when I came into the kitchen.

She was sautéing onions that sizzled and paled against the black iron pot. I was about to leave the cup and the saucer in the sink.

"Not here," Ma cried. "You know that!"

The kitchen sink was reserved for vessels used by our family and those of the upper caste. I left the cup and saucer in the outdoor wash area. I hadn't learned his name. I called him Furniture and made up stories about him.

When I came home from school three days later, the living room had a cane sofa set: one two-seater and two singles separated by a coffee table. Pita-jee sat next to Ma. She had the formal bearing of a guest, her head politely lowered, her body upright, her hands arranged on her knees.

"Come join us, Shagun," Pita-jee called.

The curtains were drawn. The afternoon sunlight came flooding in through the windows. It burned into the glass top of the coffee table, a blinding glare.

"How do you like this furniture?" he asked.

I shrugged. "Who's coming home now?"

"This isn't rented," he said.

With her eyes fixed on the floor, Ma said, "Your father got us new furniture. Nice, no?"

"When he doesn't have a job?"

"I did it for you," Pita-jee said. "For your roka."

"My what?"

"When a boy comes of age, when he gets into senior secondary that is, we promise him to a girl from a good family. Once you get a job, you'll honor our promise."

I stared at him disbelievingly.

"That's how your ma and I met," he said. "When her parents visit—the parents of your future wife—we don't want them to think we're not well off. Let them see we even have our own furniture."

I sat down with a hand pressed to my forehead.

"So," Pita-jee said. "Now that that's been decided, let's eat."

The moment he left the room, I asked Ma, "You're not going to say anything?"

She looked up. I wondered if it hurt her neck to keep her head lowered that long.

"Do as your father says," she said, her throat moist, her left temple red.

She joined Pita-jee in the kitchen. After a moment, he hollered, "Get here right now, Shagun, or you can forget about lunch."

I went to my room and lay down. My parents' murmurs reached me. Then came the metallic sounds of pots unlidded, then came the food smells: the turmeric of rasam, the coriander of aloo-gobi, the freshness of steamed rice. I was starving, but I closed my eyes and refused my body's hunger. Furniture's face came to mind, refreshing all the feelings that had passed through me when he placed his hand on my shoulder. Could my desire be suppressed? Could I make peace with the future Pita-jee decided for me? Would he start training me for my life as a husband with lessons on cricket and the ways of a man? When my sisters turned fourteen, I remembered Ma started preparing them to be housewives. Give it four, at most five, years, she liked to remind them. Ma drew a list of household chores for them: Mud mopped the kitchen after dinner; three days a week, Milk woke up at 5:00 A.M. to give the dhobi our laundry.

I remembered Milk telling Mud and me what the dhobi told her: ships brought gora sahibs to our town every monsoon. A horse carriage, he said, takes them from the port to old cottages where they spend a week or two. He told Milk that he knew the timetable of the carriage, the days and times it was scheduled to pick up its clients.

And so at the appointed hour, given to us by our dhobi like a gift, we stood at the junction where our alley met Lawson's Street. When we saw the carriage clatter toward us, we were surprised, as if it were an unexpected sighting. It rushed past us, a blur of wind, wood, and horse, and we chased after it through the fish basti, Mud and Milk upfront, I a step behind. At the port we clambered up on a boat parked on the beach and stood on its rim: this slight elevation, my sisters were convinced, offered a better look of the new arrival, his suit his dress shirt his lovely reddened face, his laced boots his socks his pale plump ankles as he stepped off the ship and walked down the gangplank.

For all of one season, it was our favorite game: standing at the junction at the time the dhobi recommended, bounding to the port, watching those men from atop a beached boat. They started to replace the gods in our playacting game: with her face plastered with powder, Mud pretended to be an Englishman and walked stiffly across the treehouse as if it were the gangplank; Milk, who pretended to be an Indian girl in love with him, watched from one corner, doe-eyed and sighing. Mud serenaded Milk with Bollywood songs, the Hindi words replaced with their English counterparts. I complained that I felt left out of their game.

"Don't be sad, Shagun, my boy," Mud said in a lousy British accent, her voice deepened to sound like a man's. "Give me your sister's hand, and I'll find you a nice English lass."

"I don't care for girls," I said.

"That's what all lads say," Milk observed.

I accused Milk of acting out of character: Since when did Indian girls say "lads"?

"The ones with English husbands listen and learn," she replied.

Only Ma knew about the role I'd played in the fatal turn our games had taken. She promised not to tell anyone that I had set in motion the sequence of steps that claimed my sisters' lives.

"Come eat, child," Ma said to me now, standing outside my room.

"I told you to let him be," Pita-jee said. I couldn't see him.

"No," Ma snapped, looking at him, wherever he stood. "Don't tell me how to treat my child."

"He's no child," Pita-jee said. "I can see that now."

A charged silence followed. Ma didn't look away. Then came the sound of footsteps stomping up the stairs.

"Come," Ma said, holding her hand out to me.

In the kitchen, she sat next to me as I ate ravenously. "Slowly," she said, running her hand through my hair, her bangles jingling in my ear. I ached for the original order to be restored: Ma and my sisters the kings of this household, I their subject.

After my parents fell asleep, I went into the prayer room, and pressed Furniture's biscuit, the side tattooed with his teeth, into the bowl of vermillion. When I picked it up, a dusting of the sacred powder clung to it, a rich orange. It was the wedding cake made for Furniture and me, I imagined. And I realized, in that moment, with unerring clarity, that I could not get married to a girl.

IN RUSTY'S FOOTSTEPS

Rohit-jee's son was the captain of the middle school cricket team. He had inherited his mother's light skin; he had his father's name, Rohit, but went by Rusty. I never spoke to him. I was tempted to the day Pita-jee forbade it, but I decided to pursue the possibility in earnest after my father sprung upon me his plans for my roka, my marriage, my ruin.

When I saw Rusty enter our school counselor's office, I conjured up a pretext to approach him, and during lunch break, when he sat under the school banyan, surrounded by his devotees, I walked over to him. He looked up, his brown eyes bronzed by sunlight. The conversation, that I caught only a strain of as I neared them, stopped. They were sensitive to the rhetoric of his gaze, his body language. Momentarily, I was caught up in the aura that surrounded him. Then, I began introducing myself.

"I know who you are," he interrupted.

I almost thanked him. Then I saw his face.

"Can I talk to you?"

"We're talking," he said, and the other boys leaned forward.

"The counselor told me to ask you," I lied.

"What about?"

"Senior secondary," I said. "Where are you applying? She wanted me to ask you."

It was a calculated risk. Mid-November was when we began applying to senior secondary. The local one, or ones at a distance.

"Kali sent you to me?" He guffawed.

Our school counselor's name was Fatima. He called her Kali because she was dark-skinned and because, as he had once announced, he wanted to "make the Muslim chick a Hindu" by giving her a Hindu name.

"Can you believe that, boys?" he said, resting his elbow on a boy's shoulder, biting his thumb. "I meet her once and she's a fan."

One boy clapped his shoulder. One released a lewd grunt.

"Meet her after final period," a third boy said.

"She'll take you home, bro," said a fourth.

A fifth stood up and jerked his hips. The sixth named the act: bumping uglies. They had all earned participation points for the afternoon. They laughed, as if relieved. Rusty looked at me. I panicked and joined them in their laughter.

"It's a boarding school," he said. "To answer your question. Only because Kali sent you. Let no one say Rusty doesn't know how to treat his girls right."

Applause followed. As it died down, I asked, "Where?"

"Doesn't matter," Rusty said. "Your dad can't afford it. Not after what happened."

What did he mean? A hot wind blew against our bodies. A boy stuffed his face with a spoonful of mushy yogurt rice. He chewed with his lips wide open and, as blobs of spittle and yogurt spilled from his mouth, he looked at me and said, "You smell good."

I met Fatima that afternoon in her office, a clean, minimal space, adorned only with a framed photo of her with her sister and parents.

"I want to apply to a boarding school," I said. "The one Rusty is applying to."

"You couldn't find yourself a better role model?" she asked, shaking her head. "That's all the way in Doon. It takes two days to get there by train. Are your parents okay with that?"

I couldn't tell my parents. Pita-jee would prohibit me from applying, I suspected, so he could keep me here and pledge me off like cattle to a girl's family.

Her expression shifted. As though my silence was a response she'd heard.

"They don't charge an application fee," she said. "We'll include a scholarship form."

I devoted the next fortnight to preparing my application material. I wrote many drafts of my scholarship essay. Fatima read each version and returned it with feedback: marking sentences I had to rewrite, making notes in the margins. After each revision, the number of statements that contained an "I" dwindled.

Once there were no more edits to be made, on a cold morning at the beginning of November, she assembled the material in order and slipped it into a manila envelope.

"How much will it cost to post?" I hesitantly asked.

"Don't worry about it," she said as she sealed the envelope.

I had a dream that night: Pita-jee and I were in Ma's room, the bed prepared in the fashion of a bridal night, covered in jasmine, end to end. Ma escorted into the room a bride whose face was concealed by a red veil. After Ma left, Pita-jee closed the door and made us sit on the bed next to each other. He looked from me to her and asked, "Who wants to go first?"

BRIEF TUTORIAL ON HOW
THE ADULT MALE PISSES

There was a tropical depression in the Bay of Bengal. Rain, unseasonal, ruined our roads. I went to school, took my first final exam, and came back, watchful of each step as I approached my house: the drainage overflowed, the one that ran by our alley's curb, a burbling black stream full of plastic bags, fish eyes, used diapers, drowned rats, onion skins. Would the road clear by my next exam? Our finals ran through the second week of May, each exam separated from the next by a two-day interval.

I woke up with a start, my bladder full. It was early: the clear sky blushed with the first glow of daylight. I went and used the outdoor toilet. Out of habit, I left the door open.

As I peed squatting, a white flash winked at some distance. An artificial light. And then another. When I finished, I pulled my shorts up and fled.

When I got to my room after my second exam, I saw some pictures on my bed. Pictures of me squatting and peeing. Unnaturally bright.

"Do you know why I took those pictures?" asked Pita-jee. He was sitting at my study.

Because you're a sick bastard, I wanted to say.

"Take these photos to school," he said. "Ask a boy friend what's wrong."

He stressed on *boy*. He separated it from *friend* by the length of a breath. He had, once again, that crazed look, the sort that, I felt, came to life on a butcher's face before he plunged his knife into an animal's chest.

"I'll iron you out, oh I will," he said, gesturing to the photos. "One day you'll thank me."

"And if you're dead by then?" I asked. "Will I thank your picture on the wall?"

"I was a teenager once," he said. "I know what you're doing."

He left the room. As I changed into my nightclothes, I imagined a man developing the film in his darkroom. The studio man doesn't notice the images at first: not as they emerge in a tray of liquid hydroquinone, not when he strings them up on a clothesline, not when he brings them to the front desk and cuts them, autopilot, each picture a perfect five-by-seven, ready to be inserted into photo albums. He distractedly eyes the image on top as he stuffs the lot into an envelope. The image registers in his head, after a lag. He pulls the photos out to confirm: yes, they are pictures of a boy squatting on a hole, his shriveled penis and balls reduced by distance to a wrinkled mass of flesh. When Pita-jee went to pick the photos up, did the studio man deliberate on the change to be returned, tapping one coin, then another as he appraised Pita-jee, wondering if he was a pedophile or if he received a monthly paycheck for photographing peeing boys? Did he try to see if the man before him resembled the boy whose image he'd birthed in the lab?

It continued to rain. Purple thunderbolts intermittently revealed the gray edges of swollen rainclouds. The power went out. I had to study for English. I lit a candle and went to the living room and turned Ma's radio on. It was *Storytime with Amar Sethi.*

Princess Kunti, beautiful and young, is blessed with a chant she may use to invoke any god of her choice. "Imagine that," the storyteller said, "you look at the heavens, point at a god, say 'That's who I want.' Like a spoiled child in a toy shop."

With no particular desire in mind, with nothing but the knowledge of the chant and the youthful impatience to put it to the test, she looks at the sun and invokes it. And he appears before her: the god who illuminates the world.

At that moment, the living room filled with electric purple. A deafening sound followed close on its heel. The windowpanes rattled in their frames. I squeezed my eyes shut. Then the steady drumbeat of rain returned. The curtains, scrunched tightly against the window, billowed again.

I got up, candle in hand, walked to the window, and pushed aside the curtain. In the windowpane, my reflected lips parted, my reflected fist slackened. The candle slipped from my hand. The wick, snuffed against the floor, released smoke and the smell of burned wax. A branch, sawed off the tree by the storm, had made a hole in the roof of our treehouse.

In the window, a little above me, a little to the right, appeared Pita-jee's reflection, his candle giving him a hazy halo. He went back into Ma's room and closed the door.

The radio storyteller continued his tale. I went into the prayer room and struck a match. Kunti spends a night with the sun god. I came out holding the alabaster statue of Hanuman in the crook of my arm. Kunti is impregnated with the sun's bastard. I marched up the stairs and flung the door open. It struck the wall and quivered. Pita-jee, who was lying down with his head in Ma's lap, sat up. The two candles on the nightstand dimmed then brightened.

Ma looked confused. When her gaze slid from my frowning face to the deity's smiling one, she started. "What's going on?"

Staring at my father, I said, "I hope I never grow up to be like you."

Kunti abandons her bastard boy by the banks of the Ganga, the storyteller said.

"Mud and Milk," I said. "Were you their father as well?"

His face crumpled.

"I get it. If you showed up right when they died, you'd have to be decent."

Thirty years later, Kunti's illegitimate son—fierce warrior, fine archer—is killed by her legitimate son. She casts his ashes in the currents of the Ganga.

I smirked. "But come six months later and you can get straight to bumping uglies."

Ma said, "From the way you're turning out, becoming him doesn't seem a bad option."

"Did I say something wrong? Oh. My mistake. Maybe he's going at it so hard because he wants a new kid—to, you know, replace the dead ones."

"And why are they dead, Shagun?" Ma asked.

"What's wrong with you," my father exclaimed, looking at her angrily.

I could tell from his reaction that she'd told him about the hand I had in my sisters' deaths. She'd promised me she'd keep it a secret.

I raised the statue of Hanuman above my head and flung it down. My parents got to their feet as Hanuman exploded into a hundred shards of painted alabaster.

Ma ran to the ruined god. She sank to the floor, collected a piece, and turned it over.

Kunti swims in the Ganga, her aged, sagging breasts speckled with her son's ashes.

Pita-jee charged toward me. Ma, still on the floor, leaned forward on her knees and extended her hand toward me.

"Go, Shagun," she said. "Run. Quickly."

I pulled the door as I left the room but not hard enough for it to close.

Between door and jamb I saw her fingers wrapped around his ankle. I raced down the corridor. I was at the mouth of the staircase when I heard Ma's door whistle open and hit the wall. I watched Pita-jee march toward me.

My chest went tight. I stood frozen. Enraptured by the crazed look that now filled his face. A hot rush of urine burned the inside of my flesh.

"Don't," Ma shouted, emerging into the corridor.

His heavy breathing reached me before he did. He raised both hands, as though asking me to stay away. His palms met my back and pushed.

I tumbled down the stairs, my elbows, my forehead, my hip striking the edge of one tread, then the next. I landed on my stomach. I pressed my forearms to the floor and tried lifting myself. Blood dripped from my forehead but made no sound on the floor. My jaw hurt. My vision swam.

I relinquished control to the oncoming tide of darkness.

THE UNEXPECTED GUEST

At first, I sensed only a soreness along my hips and a tightness in my back. When I moved, pain made its presence known, in my knees, in my forehead, which seemed to carry an enormous weight. I raised a hand and touched it.

"Let it heal," Ma said.

I was in my room, my bed. Ma sat next to me. I looked for and found him: he stood leaning against the door, his arms folded, his feet crossed. My whole body tensed.

"I did this for you," he said, when he found my eyes upon him.

"Please stop?" Ma snapped.

He continued, "Every sin has a price. You broke the statue of a god. You would've suffered anyway, sooner or later. Better it's now, you're young, your parents are here to nurse you back."

"You promised," Ma said, her voice raised, and he withdrew.

I did not see him for the rest of the day. I prepared for my exams as best as I could: I read for twenty or thirty minutes; when my head hurt, I lay down, slept for an hour, woke up, and continued my study. Ma brought my lunch to my room.

I awoke from my umpteenth nap that evening and heard murmurs from the living room. Ma was next to me on a chair. I unpeeled my blanket and swung my feet to the ground. I sat up with my palms pressed to the bed. Light blurred the edges of my vision. I watched Ma watching me as I took off my nightshirt and wiped my upper body with it. Her gaze went from my face to my chest. Then she looked away.

"You're growing up," she said.

"Don't remind Pita-jee," I said. "He'll have my roka today."

"I wish he and you could talk."

"I don't."

"There are things only he can tell you. Things only I could've spoken to your sisters about."

She looked out the window and her face filled with the light, like a face in an overexposed photograph.

I put on a button-down. Standing before the mirror, I unpeeled the gauze from my forehead. The flesh underneath was swollen and purple. Red cobwebs branched out from a deep cut.

"What are you doing?" Ma said.

I started to leave the room. My knee, hip, and back burned with each step I took. I turned and looked at Ma. She nodded slowly as she returned her attention to the window.

Our guest, I saw from some distance, was walking around the single-sofa, admiring it.

His face fell when I entered the living room. Pita-jee turned, and our eyes met. He traded the look of astonishment for a smile before he turned and faced our guest who sat down, rubbing his forehead as he looked at me.

"Pita-jee should tell you," I said as I sat next to my father.

"He fell down the stairs," Pita-jee said.

"My father pushed me," I said.

Our guest froze for a moment, his eyes wide. I laughed, and he joined his laughter to mine. My father was forced to laugh along with us. His Old Spice deodorant couldn't mask the stench of his sweat.

The night before the last exam, geography, my parents came into my room. Ma held out an envelope. Magpies Boys Senior Secondary and College, it said.

"Of course I didn't get in," I said, devastated, as if the blow had already been delivered.

"Learn to be positive," Pita-jee said. His tone seemed anything but positive.

"You got a full scholarship," Ma said.

"When were you going to tell us, Shagun?" said Pita-jee.

"Now come give your father a hug," Ma said.

He wrapped his arms around me, his body tensed with the expectation of a returned embrace. I raised my hands but held my palms inches away from his back.

"Rohit-jee's son is going to Magpies," I whispered in his ear. "We'll be best friends."

He stepped back. His face flushed.

"God be with you," Ma said, in the tone of an announcement.

She handed me the admission letter, and it was my sisters who filled my mind. I would miss them, I thought. As if they were still here.

I approached Rusty after the exam.

"What did you do? Break your head on our history textbook?" Rusty asked.

"It was Dad," I said.

His face beamed a sort of solidarity as he nodded. Satisfied that we now had something in common, a common enemy, I told him I got into Magpies.

"Ditto," he said. "Your old man's paying?"

"I don't need his money," I said, raising my head. "I got a full scholarship."

I waited for him to congratulate me.

"We were on the phone with them," he said. "Ask for bunk twenty-two. It's next to mine. You'll do my homework, obviously. Scholarship boy."

I blushed. He left and joined his friends.

I walked back home, feeling thrilled by my future's geometry: my bed parallel to Rusty's. I pictured waking one night and seeing him: fast asleep, bare-chested, his moonlit body hunched against the cold. I cover him and linger in the cloud of his heat and body odor, my hand clinging to one edge of the blanket. In his sleep, he welcomes the warmth by pressing my hand hard to his chest.

A tepid sea breeze met me as I turned into the lane to my house. The image of waves violently encircling a rock abruptly replaced the sensation of Rusty's tight grip.

Which film did you lift the blanket-covering idea from? Mud asked in my head.

Shameless Shagun, Milk chided.

I came home feeling chastened and smelling of dry sweat and sea salt. I read a story from a myth book retrieved from the kitchen and calmed myself.

I went to bed that night, wondering why it happened: Rusty's warm fingers on my wrist replaced by waves frothing over a rock. Daylight appeared in place of an answer, it sketched the few forms outside my window into hazy visibility: gate, tree, broken treehouse, road. I named them repeatedly, until the monotony of it drugged me to sleep.

That evening, Rohit-jee came to our home unannounced with Rusty and a box of sweets. It was the first time I remembered seeing him. He had the build of a reed and seemed older than Pita-jee, his hair white, his forehead thick with wrinkles.

"You have new furniture, I see," he said as he planted himself on the cane sofa. Pita-jee took one of the singles. Ma remained in her room.

"Can I bring you some water, uncle?" I asked him.

"What a well-behaved boy." Rohit-jee beamed. "Why don't you show Rusty your room?"

"That won't be necessary, Shagun," Pita-jee said, his eyes fixed on Rohit-jee. "Our guest is an important man. We don't want to detain him with unnecessary formalities."

Rohit-jee placed the box of sweets on the coffee table. He said, "Congratulations are in order. Shagun got into Magpies. Same as Rusty. No scholarship for my boy, though. You clearly have the smarter son."

"Rusty is better at sports," I said.

"Facts," Rusty said.

"My boy's not one for modesty," Rohit-jee said.

"It must run in the family," Pita-jee said.

Rohit-jee laughed. My father didn't. Rusty walked up to me.

"You showing me your room or what?" he asked.

As we left the room, Rohit-jee said, "Still upset about our deal gone south, aren't you?"

I stopped and turned. My father's back was to me. Rohit-jee had a small smile on his lips.

"What's wrong?" Rusty asked.

I shook my head. "Let's go."

A moment later, he was in my room. He sat on the bed and looked around.

"No posters," he observed. "Do you like movies, at least?" He leaned back, propping his torso up on his elbows.

"Big fan, especially Sridevi films," I said. "I loved her in *ChaalBaaz*."

In one supple move he got to his feet, clasped his hands, and said as he swayed his shoulders, "I loved her in *Chaalbaaz*."

He was mimicking me, exaggerating my feminine mannerisms.

He clapped my shoulder. "Come on, man," he said. "You can be better than that."

My father's abruptly raised voice broke in. "I would have, if you showed some decency. My wife—"

Rusty got up and closed the door.

"You know what they're talking about, right?" Rusty asked.

Before I could respond, he posed another question.

"What's up with the bunk bed?"

"My sisters used to sleep here," I said.

He grinned. "Your sisters were going to marry my brothers—that you must know."

The movement of my head as I shook it felt dumb to me. As if he'd given me a basic instruction, a "sit down" or "turn left" and I was unable to comprehend it. Pita-jee wanted Mud and Milk to marry Rusty's brothers, but he hated their father and warned me off Rusty. What was I missing?

"Your dad even paid dowry in full. To 'reserve' my brothers, see?"

"How old are your brothers again?"

"One's twenty-nine, and the fool who busted his hand for that Dalit bitch, he's thirty." He tilted his head. "I mean, guy to guy—we like them young, don't we?"

He winked. He walked to the dresser and opened its only drawer. He picked up a pink comb that had on its handle the word PRINCESS in gold lettering. He sniffed it, stuffed it into his pocket.

"That's my sisters'," I said.

"So now you don't need it, right?" he asked, walking up to me until our noses nearly touched. He emanated a woody smell. I shook my head. He took a step back. Only then did I look up and meet his brown eyes. He squeezed his nose between thumb and forefinger. He'll give it to a girl to impress her, I guessed. I complimented his smell.

"Dad's handwash," Rusty said. "Imported from London. He's real possessive about it. I asked him if I could use it before we got here and he warns, 'Only a smidge.' Mind you, the man has four extra bottles. Always."

He wanted to smell good because he's coming here to meet me, I thought. Rohit-jee called his name.

When we joined our fathers in the living room, Rohit-jee was standing and Pita-jee was still sitting down, and though we were behind him, I could tell he was breathing hard.

"Your father is upset I didn't come and see him sooner," Rohit-jee said. He walked up to me and patted my arm. "Such a well-behaved boy," he said again. "Pity you're not a girl or I would've asked for your hand for Rusty."

"Rohit," Pita-jee said, without the respectful "jee."

"Make sure your mother gets some of those sweets," Rohit-jee said to me. "The last time she visited us we couldn't show her our famous hospitality."

I escorted them to the door and, after bidding them goodbye, I came back in reluctantly, prepared for an earful from Pita-jee. But he wasn't in the living room, nor was the sweet box. The door to the room upstairs was closed.

I woke up the next morning feeling troubled by the fact that Rusty's behavior didn't upset me. We like them young.

I thought of Furniture—his jawline, where a stubble blossomed, his wrist on my shoulder—wanting to make him, once again, the subject of my ardor. But his beauty failed to move me. Rusty's wink animated my feelings, not Furniture's—Rusty's sweat-soaked forehead, not Furniture's rain-soaked face. Feeling defeated, humiliated, and exhilarated, I stood before the mirror and repeated my love for *ChaalBaaz*. I kept my shoulders stiff, my hands by my side. I imagined Rusty rewarding my revised body language with a grave nod of approval.

THE DRAVIDIAN BOOK OF SEAS AND STARGAZING, VOLUME 2

Pita-jee came into my room the next morning. I was in bed with my back against the headrest and my legs drawn up. He pointed to *The Dravidian Book of Seas and Stargazing, Volume 1*, which was spread open on my lap. His presence condensed all my attention around the fact that he'd fixed the marriage of my sisters, who were children, to adult men. How dare you, I repeatedly thought, until the phrase felt like an incantation—a curse. I frowned and looked fixedly at the page where words were black smudges that blurred into each other.

"There's a volume two of that book," he said.

In an alternate reality, I'd ask him to get me a copy, I'd tell him about the sea elephant stories his daughters and son playacted in the treehouse his father built. Instead I said, in the curtest voice I could muster, "I haven't seen it."

"It's hard to find a copy," he said.

"How come?" I asked, still not looking away from my book.

"It has a story that shows a god as less powerful than a sea elephant. They thought it might send a wrong message and started pulling the book out of circulation."

"Who's they?"

"Priests, the ruling class—it was a long time ago."

"So people like your Hanuman Satsang folk, just from a different time."

"Come, take a walk with me," he said.

I opened my mouth to decline his invitation. But I decided to go, resolving to find, in whatever inane conversation he wanted to conduct, a moment where I could hurt him by speaking the knowledge I had, thanks to Rusty.

It was a pleasant morning and we walked to the railway station in silence, still in our nightclothes. From there we followed the tracks until the buildings of our town gave way to farms and fields and, eventually, to what looked like an abandoned building.

"What are we doing here?"

He said, "When I accepted my job, fourteen years back, I knew I was going to be on probation for four years—which lasts, as I found later, a year if you're English, two if you're American or European. We get no leave during that time. At the end of four years, instead of turning me into a full-time employee they put me on a second round of probation."

"How come?"

"No explanation. Immigrants, especially the ones from the subcontinent, have so few rights. They increased my salary, so I didn't complain. I wasn't made permanent until my ninth year. After that, I could take three weeks of paid leave every two years."

"So not coming home after your tenth or twelfth year—that was your decision," I said.

He pointed to the building.

"I built that," he said. "It's a cement plant, no longer functional. But I never got to show you something I constructed and this is the closest at hand."

I looked at the chimney, which towered over the three stout buildings around it. Its mouth had blackened. There was a hole in the compound wall that surrounded the place.

"Why did they shut it down?" I asked, stuffing my hands into my pockets.

"I relate to the sea elephant stories," he said. "The patriarch has to leave his home, but in return the gods bless his family with comforts that last a lifetime."

"Leave his family?" I said. "It's not like he has a choice."

"He doesn't have a choice, yes."

A question surfaced to mind, one that Mud and Milk would've approved of. Why did humans have to pay, with the flesh and blood of one of their own, for an act of the gods?

"Your London job couldn't have been that bad," I said, "if it helped you pay for your daughters' dowry."

He turned to face me, his eyes wide with surprise at my knowledge of the secret that he'd kept from me.

"Daughters you hadn't met," I said. "Tell me. If they had refused to marry men twice their age, would you have pushed them down the stairs as well? That would've saved them marital issues later, yeah?"

His face was laid bare, his shame uncontainable by ideology.

Two nights later, Pita-jee announced he was returning to London. His former employer had assigned him to a construction project in the East End.

"They've hired me back eight months after I quit," he said over dinner. "Isn't that nice?"

Ma didn't speak until Pita-jee finished eating and left the kitchen.

"He got to live with us after years of staying away," she said. "I don't condone what he's done. But you don't tell your father to pay a price."

"What?" I snapped. "I didn't tell him to leave, okay?"

"You didn't have to in as many words."

"I'm gone soon," I said. "He might as well stay."

"That's not how it works, son. You're too young to know."

She put the dishes away as I mopped the floor. She said again, after she completed her chore, "There are things only a father can tell a son."

"What things?"

She looked at my chest. Then she shook her head and left the kitchen. As I continued mopping, I conjured up memories of standing next to

Pita-jee every Tuesday and Saturday as he worshipped Hanuman. What was his chest, concealed by a red shawl, like? Was it different from my own: a little fleshy on either side of the hard center? There was little I could recollect of those worship sessions other than the itch I felt to get away from them.

THE DEPARTURES BEGIN

On the last day of school, June 6, after all the final goodbyes, I felt rudderless, one way of life over, the other yet to start. I went to the school church, lit a candle, and sat down. Comforted by the fragrance of warm wax and frankincense, I looked at the cross and narrated the stories Ma used to read to Mud and Milk and me. That day, I told Jesus many Hindu myths.

In the hot months, April and May, I remembered, when soaring temperatures roasted our classroom, my sisters went to the school church after classes ended. They sought refuge in its cool stone walls and dim candlelight. They sat on the bench before the piano and drummed its ebony keys. They couldn't read the sheet-notes but they fixed their frowning faces on the pages anyway. Sometimes I joined them on that colonial-era bench.

Pita-jee left a month into my summer vacation. My bruise, by then, had left my forehead, leaving in its place a crescent scar that would take years to fade.

I sat on the porch steps as he packed his bag and Ma fried potato fritters for him to eat on the train. He came and sat down by my side. It was a humid day and the air was sticky.

He said, "Life doesn't end with senior secondary. There's college. There's life. If you want me to help, you'll have to follow my rules."

"Your rule being the roka," I said, and he nodded. "And if I don't need your money?"

His lip trembled and his breath turned heavy, as if saturated with something liquid.

He said, "The choice you're making, it'll ruin you, I swear it."

"What's that, a curse? A warning?"

"It's not," he said, raising his voice. Lowering it, he said, "You'll bring it on yourself."

"Is it a choice, who I am?"

"To be virtuous is the choice you make when your body tempts you to be otherwise."

"And if I don't, you'll do what Rohit-jee did to his son?"

He lifted his gaze, found the scar on my forehead. He tried to touch it. I leaned away from him. He withdrew his hand and rubbed his jaw. The noise of rolling luggage wheels approached us. He got up, took a few steps, stopped short.

"One day you'll know I loved you," he said.

He surged into the night, Ma next to him. She was going to see him off at the station. They got into an auto-rickshaw and left.

When I turned to go back inside, I saw that the broken branch had been removed from the treehouse. Its roof had been mended.

The next day I took Pita-jee's pictures of me to the backyard and burned them. When I followed the plumes of rising smoke, I saw Ma at the window, her elbows planted on the sill, her face stoic as she stared at me. It was at this window that Pita-jee brought the camera to his face. Did she know? I didn't want to know.

On the first Saturday of July, the postman came home with Pita-jee's money order and letter. When I was growing up, my mother always wore a bright cotton sari to receive her husband's letter, and pinned to her hair a string of fresh jasmine, her favorite flower. When the postman came to the house she sprang out of her room and plunged down the stairs, gathering the pleats of her sari in her hand, the newly bloomed jasmine flailing in her wake. It was her festival, my sisters and I would joke, and while the rest of us waited a year for Holi and Diwali, she got to celebrate her festival once every month. But for the first time that day in July, no shadow crossed the window of her room.

I took my father's mail and gave the postman a ten-rupee note.

Over dinner that night, I pushed Pita-jee's letter and his money across the floor, toward Ma, until my fingers touched her feet. Her whole body recoiled.

"Please give him ten rupees when he comes back," she said.

Please. She'd never used the word before. It left my ears raw. It took me a few seconds to register the *please,* to measure all that the *please* contained.

"I already did," I said.

"Thank you," said Ma. She stared at her food.

"Are you okay?"

"Finish eating, child," she said. "The food's getting cold."

On her way up, Ma paused at the staircase post, tilted her head toward the prayer room, and moved her lips slowly with her eyes closed. Then she plodded stiffly up the stairs, dabbing her eyes with the edge of her sari. I lowered my head to say *please* to my plate.

I called Rusty up the next morning and gave him my date of departure. "Let's take the train to Doon together," I suggested. But he was leaving early with his family. Together they'd go to a hill station. They'd take an empty suitcase along and fill it up with handspun sweaters for Rusty. Hill town sweaters are better, said his father, the man my father hated. I pictured Rusty's father standing next to him, listening to our conversation.

On Krishna's birthday, the eighth of August, Ma stood with me before the Wall of the Dead and prayed to our ancestors.

"Bless my son," she said, her palms pressed together, her eyes closed. "Look over him when he's away. Because I can't."

When she was done, she patted my back gently. Together we looked at the pictures of my sisters.

"You know I didn't want that to happen," I said.

"I know," she said, rubbing my back. "We don't have to talk about it."

I felt both stung and grateful. I wasn't surprised either. Silence replaced the conversations we should've had after the sea took my sisters, before Pita-jee's arrival, when he pushed me down the stairs. That was why she read to us, I thought: she bonded with us over those stories about the gods and their pastimes the way other mothers bonded with their kids over conversations.

After dinner, Ma left home to spend the night in the temple. She'd celebrate the birth of a god among humans. A clay baby Krishna would be passed from one devotee's hands to another's.

She came back moments after she left.

"Son, the temple oil, go bring it for me? I forgot." She smiled. "I'm getting old."

She kept the sacred oil in her room. For the first time I'd enter her space in her absence. Step upon careful footstep I climbed the stairs.

Her room was burnished to a dull gold by the lantern that burned on the windowsill. Its wick wavered, its light flickered to the beat of the sea breeze. There lingered in the air of the room the scent of her beloved jasmine. The flowers, both their sight and fragrance, evoked memories of her mother, she once told me. The space where the Hanuman statue had broken was circled with chalk. Inside the circle were three turmeric dots.

I opened her chest and found, next to the bottle of temple oil, a biscuit tin filled with pictures: my sisters and I playing hopscotch in the first rain of monsoon. Every monsoon. Until Mud and Milk died. I browsed the pictures backward. My sisters and I grew younger.

Also in the chest: neatly folded stacks of baby clothes. They were small. Impossibly so. How could anyone be that little? Under the clothes: envelopes fat with coins, inscribed with our names—money she'd pledged to different gods to secure our health, our well-being, our long lives.

"Shagun?" Ma said. I started. She was at the door.

I fished the bottle out and went to her. She gripped the bottle's neck but didn't take it. There was something in her eyes that sought expression. And, not then, when she took the bottle and left, but later, as I tried to sleep, I realized how uncharacteristic it was for her to forget anything—an article of worship, no less. No. She had not forgotten. She wanted me to enter her room, to see that I was loved despite what I had done to my sisters.

I was haunted, in her absence, by memories of all those occasions when she was present for my sisters and me: before she made dinner, she supervised our homework; as she ate with us, she asked over our day; before we slept, she read to us, her voice bringing the gods in our midst. Krishna, Rama, and Durga were not deities perched on pedestals but characters my sisters and I could become, calling them at will into our bodies and tongues. She remembered and asked after our wounds well after they'd turned to scars. Her efficiency was brisk but not cold. Only after Pita-jee came home was her absence complete.

I fell asleep but woke up when I heard the main door open. I knew from the smell in the air that the hour was still tender. I got up and looked out my window. Our foyer was filled with pale-blue light, a silhouette at its center. Ma closed the door and came inside in a cloud of frankincense. At the staircase, she paused, turned, and in what light there was, she found my face. She smiled.

In that morning hour, I'd like to think, we understood that we loved each other.

A GAME GONE WRONG

My train to Doon entered the bridge that ran over an inlet of the Bay of Bengal. From that height, the sea appeared still as a pond. As we rattled past the bridge's suspensions, and the metallic smell of damp iron filled my lungs, I watched my hometown diminish. I failed to find my house in what, at this distance, felt like a LEGO township, the buildings' gray backs turned to their shore, their windows no longer visible. And only then, with my geography rendered anonymous, was I able to recollect the day, the hour, of my sisters' deaths.

At 4:00 P.M., when our breath smelled of sambar and Horlicks, when a strip of sharp daylight brightened the edges of the overcast sky, Mud and Milk and I waited at the junction. When a buggy clattered down Lawson's Street—a whiplash in the air, a rumble of hoofs down the road—we turned right and picked our way through the fish basti. Snakehead mullets were on display that day. They twirled in the wind with their grinning mouths fixed to iron hooks. An old man slept cross-legged and erect before a basket of lobsters. A stray sniffed his shriveled arm, turned, and raised a leg.

It started to rain by the time we reached the port. We found no boat parked on the beach, but in the hustle and bustle surrounding us, between the many bodies running around with luggage and children, we

spotted a coracle perched precariously on the lip of the sea, its unan-
chored body round and shallow, nearly flat, the underlying rip currents
unable to get a grip on it and carry it away, its volatile movements dic-
tated by the rhythm of surface currents: on the crest of an arriving wave
it surged shoreward, on an ebbing wave it wobbled away.

I didn't want to brave the choppy sea, not in all that rain, to drag it
ashore for our amusement.

"It doesn't make a difference anyway," I said. "We can get just as good
a look from here."

"We're shorter than you," Milk explained. "We see better if we stand
on top of a boat."

"Just admit you're scared," Mud said.

"As if you aren't," I said.

"Speak for yourself," Mud said.

"Then go sit on that boat, why don't you?" I pointed to the coracle.
"Go on. Do it."

They looked from the unstable boat to each other.

"That's what I thought," I said, looking away.

With a whistle that sounded like a foghorn, my train left the bridge
behind. I got up and went to my bogie's door and opened it. My place of
birth had disappeared completely from sight, and the sea was reduced to
a blue brushstroke. I closed my eyes and breathed deep, grateful that the
air carried no coastal moisture.

The rain had become a downpour. Two sailors hurried toward hand-
drawn rickshaws followed by coolies in red shirts, their heads burdened
with boxes and bedding. A chain of cyclists drove effortlessly on the wet
beach sand, ringing their horns as they went along.

The buggy arrived. An Englishman walked toward it, a child in tow.
Only after he boarded his vehicle did I notice the tea man: the tinny
timpani of his spoon against his canister as he stood under a tin awning
drummed by rain.

"Chai, you want?" I asked. "My treat," I offered.

I stuffed a hand into my drenched trouser pocket to jingle some coins and show my sisters I wasn't lying. It was my peace offering: tea in lieu of the boat I didn't bring ashore.

There was no response from them, not even from Milk. I turned and didn't find them by my side. I looked about frantically. It was difficult to see through the curtain of raindrops. Eventually, I spotted them.

Where before the coracle wavered on the edge of land and sea, the weight of the twins, who now sat on it, allowed the sea's rip currents to gain purchase and carry it away from the shore.

I ran toward the waves. My sisters gripped the vessel's edges and shook their drenched faces. Their voices crying for help dimmed as they moved steadily away. Their clothes were glued to their hunched frames.

Had they gotten in the boat before pulling it ashore? They were trying to make the point that they weren't scared like me, I guessed, and they got themselves entangled in an incredibly dangerous situation. I resolved to give them a piece of my mind once they were by my side and safe. The thought of that future fight gave me a modicum of hope. But it was fleeting.

The boat's rear end rose under a bulging wave. My sisters lurched forward and their heads got dunked in the sea. The boat fell back flat when the wave passed. They sat up with dripping chins, open mouths, saltwater brows.

I ran into the turbulent waters. Retreating waves grabbed my ankles. I fell with a splash. Cold salt water stung my eyes. A wave rolled over my head. I was inside a roaring liquid womb. Every other sound muted.

Heaving my head out with a gasp, I scrambled back to the safety of land. The noises around me caught my attention. This was no desert island, I reminded myself. Adults often swam far into the sea, well beyond where the twins now precariously hovered.

I tore my way into the milling crowd, certain of finding help. I tugged at shirtsleeves and the edges of saris. Most passersby swatted my hand away. Some squinted at me as I spoke quickly and pointed at the sea. My words were drowned by the noise of the rain. So they flung coins at me and hurried away, seeking shelter. Legs ran helter-skelter. Someone knocked over the tea canteen. Someone knocked a cyclist into the sludge.

I returned to the shore and stood with my fists pressed to my chest, as if challenging the sea to a duel. The coracle had drifted farther away. I could barely make out their faces. The wind gathered speed. The waves rose higher.

My sisters' legs went knee-deep into the cold, churning waters. The coracle detached itself from their bodies and swiveled on. Their heads went underwater. Their hands shot into the air. Their trembling fingers sank out of view.

At the curve a hill, many hours after my departure, I saw my train's illuminated compartments rocking softly through the twilit darkness.

I wiped my cheeks, got up, and closed the bogie door. I went back to my berth and lay down. I fell asleep and woke up the next day feeling ashamed that I did.

PART II

1990–1991

TARGET MAN

The cab rumbled past the iron gates and came to a halt at a building on the far end of the mud road. Nailed above its entrance were oxidized copper letters: some had turned aquamarine, some green, together they read MAGPIES BOYS DO M.

An older-looking boy who stood with his foot pressed to the wall by the door plucked the cigarette smoking between his clenched teeth and smiled, lopsided. He scratched his neck, producing a sound like sandpaper on wood. His presence felt off to me. I didn't smile back.

The cabdriver took my suitcase out of the trunk, placed it on the curb, got back in, and started his vehicle. I said to him, in a low voice, with a hand to his window, "Can you wait?"

I gestured discreetly to the boy, and he nodded. I skipped up the few steps that there were, two at a time, and rattled a brass knocker.

"Why're you being so unfriendly?" the boy asked me.

I didn't reply. He flicked his cigarette and it fell next to my feet.

"Why don't you leave him alone?" the driver asked him.

He shrugged. "Just having some fun."

"Don't look to me like he's having fun."

Emboldened by the support, I kicked his still-smoking butt toward him.

"Oh, buddy," the boy said. He clicked his tongue. "No good."

A short man with a curled gray mustache and close-set eyes opened the door, glanced at my admission sheet, and, introducing himself as the warden, asked me to bring my luggage in.

"Thank you," I said to the driver as I picked my suitcase up.

I followed the warden through a musty corridor and up a stairwell to Level Two—"For eleventh graders," he clarified.

We entered a long cement-floored room lined with bunk beds, some of them a tangle of unmade blankets and skewed pillows, most still untouched, like mine, a bottom bunk by the window that offered a view of the forecourt. The copper statue of a British officer stood in a bare garden surrounded by a clutter of small angels.

The boy, I noticed with a start, was still down there, with his foot to the wall.

"Do college students also live here?" I asked, turning away from the window.

"No, they get off-campus housing," he said as he pressed into my palm a lapel pin embossed with the school emblem: a sun rising over an open book.

"There's an orientation that just started," he said. "It's about the history of this place. British history, I'll add. Gets boys more interested."

"Is that where the others are?" I asked.

"Those who're already here, yes. Most students come in tonight."

I showered and put on my uniform: beige trousers, cream shirt, black shoes. As I bounded out of the building, excited to meet Rusty at the orientation, the older boy stepped abruptly in front of me. I crashed into him. The lapel pin slipped from my hand and I nearly tipped over. He grabbed my waist and steadied me against his body.

I found my footing and wriggled against his hard chest, his firm thighs. He let go of me and I stepped back. My flesh throbbed where his fingers gripped me tight.

He said, "Where you are going? Your session is here. Go to the rooftop hall. Presonjeet didn't tell you—your warden? He's my friend."

I was unsettled by his tone, the abrupt turn it took into practical camaraderie. Don't trust him, my lizard brain warned.

"Presonjeet told you about the meal card?" he asked, picking up my fallen pin. When I shook my head, he said, "Oh-ho. Fellow's becoming old. Always forgetting stuff."

He explained where I could procure the card as he undid the lapel pin and needled it into my breast pocket. He snickered.

"What?" I snapped.

"Hey, watch it," he said. "I'm helping you out. You're welcome."

He pushed the needle out, pinned the lapel pin, and pointed to the roof. I scooted back indoors, happy to get away from him.

Rusty had the lower bed, like I did, in the opposite bunk. Viren slept above me. He and Rusty had gotten here around the same time, hours before the orientation; Viren lived close by, Rusty was holidaying with family not far from Magpies. They were friends already. Rusty wanted to be the captain of the eleventh-grade cricket team. Batting was his strength; Viren liked balling. Rusty pointed to the two pictures he'd pasted above his bed. Rohit-jee, his mother, his brothers.

"Where's your family?" he asked, pointing at the blank wall above my headrest.

"I didn't bring any," I said.

"Neither did I," Viren said. "You kick in your sleep? If I fall off my bed and land in Rusty's arms, we'll know whom to blame."

Rusty made a face, and we laughed. The warden came and turned the light off. We lay down and spoke in the dark.

"Where are you from, Shagun?" Viren asked, and I told him.

"We're from the same place," Rusty said. "I told you, dummy."

"You did?" Viren asked.

Rusty said, "Shagun, if you thought you had it bad in the daddy department, you should hear about Viren's dad. I mean, for starters, he sells murdered animals."

A pillow came flying at Rusty. In the dark I heard him grab it.

"This will be put to good use," Rusty said. "To stroke the sausage."

"No!" Viren yelled. I giggled nervously.

"Keep it quiet, will you?" someone said.

The remaining eleventh graders had come in that evening. They were from different parts of the country, the influence of their mother tongues apparent in the English they used when they spoke to each other.

"Shagun," Rusty said. "If my comment embarrassed you, well, this is who I am."

"I wasn't embarrassed, I promise," I said.

Rusty chuckled. When I first saw him, I thought him attractive. Now I was attracted to him. His cocky confidence turned that initial pause of observation to desire. I wanted to say something clever, exaggerate or embellish a fact of my life so he'd turn toward me, prop his head on a fist, and respond, "Say more." But anything I said in the grip of a new crush's fever would, I knew, make me look desperate or foolish. Or both. So I kept quiet.

I woke up thinking that for the first time in sixteen years I was waking up in a new place. I turned to wish Rusty good morning. But he wasn't there. Nor was anyone else. Next to my bed was a note: *We tried waking you, you were out like a light. Hurry! Class starts at 9. We're left. —Rusty.*

Surely he meant "we left"? I looked at my wristwatch. It was quarter to nine. I brushed and, without showering, changed into my uniform and ran out of the room, down the stairs, and across the mud road that separated the dorms from the school building.

None of the classrooms were numbered. How would I locate XI-A? It was five past nine. The classes had begun. Lectures on calculus and philosophy floated my way. I was sweating profusely. I took off my backpack and held it in my hand.

Someone clapped my back. I turned and saw it was the older boy from yesterday.

Bringing his thick arms to his hips, he said, "Why aren't you in class, boy?"

He pointed at the five white human outlines painted on the dark compound wall. They had bullet holes near the chest.

"That's where English soldiers once did target practice," he said. "Now that's where latecomers are punished. 'Go stand against Target Man,' teachers say. You want that or what?"

He snapped his fingers and, with a flick of his head, beckoned me to follow him. In that moment, what scared me more than the boy was the thought of being thrown out of class as Rusty watched. So I followed him down the corridor. He had directed me to my orientation yesterday, I told myself, and today he'll direct me to my classroom.

We were at the mouth of a cavernous staircase when he said, "Lucky for you, you found me. You're welcome."

"Thank you, Senior."

Without turning around he said, "Senior! I like. About time you show respect."

In the light of the naked bulb that dangled above the stairwell, he scratched his neck. We descended one flight of stairs after another until, six floors later, we reached what I thought might be the very bowels of the earth. To our left was a single, unlit room. The glass panes of the two open doors reflected the overhead tube light.

Pointing at the room with his thumb, he said, "Your class."

I stepped in, disbelievingly, inevitably. First, I felt the room's cold bite, then I saw the vapor gusts released by overhead air conditioners. I pressed my backpack to my chest. A pungent odor stung my nostrils.

The doors were pulled shut, a bolt latched. A sharp metallic clink. Senior's towering figure, silhouetted against the lit-up glass doors, stretched out a hand and punched a switch. Light from a naked bulb spilled a circle of light between us.

To my left and to my right were beds lined one next to the other, and lying on them, covered in white sheets up to their necks, were dead men. Here to be dissected. Where was the custodian?

With his hands on his hips, Senior said, "Your shirt. Get rid of it."

I felt light-headed. I squeezed my nose between forefinger and thumb.

His voice gulped the distance between us. "You deaf, bitch? Your shirt," he said.

If I looked him in the eye, I knew I wouldn't have the courage to defy him. So I turned away and shook my head.

His heavy footfalls brought him up close within a second. He curled his foot around my ankle and tugged. I fell facedown. He slapped the back of my head, grabbed both my arms, and turned me around. He sat on my crotch, wrenched the backpack out of my grip, and dumped it by my head. He untucked my shirt and opened its buttons. I shivered. He smirked. His teeth, coated in spit, shined like a knife's edge.

"Breasts!" he said.

I blinked at him, my head blank. With a quick, sharp slap on one of my cheeks then the other, he said, in a childish voice, "Poor baby, sweet boy, you don't understand? See."

He pulled his T-shirt over his head and thrust his trunk forward. Running his fingers over his smooth, flat chest, he said, "This is a man's chest."

He dug his clean fingernails into the small, soft masses of flesh capped by my nipples.

"This," he said, "this is girly stuff. Breasts."

He collapsed over me. His heavy body knocked out my breath. He opened his mouth and exhaled. His hot, nicotine breath singed my upper lip.

"I'm cold, Senior. Please," I said.

"Don't complain," he said. He wagged a forefinger in my face, and it swatted my nose. He spoke with a whoop, like a man to his dog. "Who's a good boy? Who's a good boy?"

He lowered his head. His wiry hair scratched my chin. I turned my head away.

A sharp, shooting pain—my small breasts, his teeth. "If you're bitten by a dog, you take sixteen injections in the chest," Mud once said. His veined, hard muscle moving over my trousered thigh as his rough palm moved up my arm and my neck and onto my mouth, sealing it, trapping my squeals in. Airtight. His guttural grunting. His teeth working my flesh. His muscle working my thigh.

Then at last his stillness. My trousers, drenched.

A memory came to me: your father should talk to you, Ma had said, the day after he'd pushed me down the stairs, her gaze sliding to my chest.

Senior brought his lips together and put his teeth away. He lifted his head up and clutched my jaw. In his black eyes I saw my face. The air smelled sour.

He picked up my hand and saw the time. Suddenly, he was in a rush. He zipped his trousers and unbolted the door. "Fast," he said as I buttoned up my shirt up and picked up my bag. As we ran up the stairs, we passed by two men in gray uniforms. The custodians, perhaps, back from a breakfast break: they spoke in drowsy voices, their breaths smelling of dhal.

Senior touched my shoulder when we came out. I flinched from the sight of his hand on my body in daylight. He pointed to the school: from afar it appeared to be one building, but it was two structures separated by a narrow passage.

"Left side for school boys," he said. "Right side for college chaps."

Releasing my shoulder, he said, "We'll meet again, you and I." He flashed a lopsided smile. "Your warden, Presonjeet. Why you think he let me smoke there? We're thick friends."

His forked fingers moved from his eyes to my chest.

I left him behind and entered the left wing. The classes here were named. At the end of the first floor I found XI-A. The teacher had his back to the class. The chalk creaked on the blackboard as he wrote out the formulas for Newton's laws. I walked quietly up to the last bench. My classmates eyed me, some discreetly, others openly.

I opened my notebook and leafed through its blank pages. A fist struck my desk. I stood up with a start. The teacher leaned forward. Scratched glasses concealed his eyes.

"Good morning, sunshine. Bright and early, are we?" he said.

The classroom exploded with laughter. I opened my mouth to apologize. I hoped, sincerely, that Rusty was in a different section.

The teacher raised his hand. My classmates fell quiet. "You snuck in and thought I won't notice? Smart boy."

Smart boy. Who's a good boy. Who's a good boy.

He said, "Are you mocking me?"

"No!" I cried. Had I spoken aloud?

"So I'm a liar, that's what you're saying. Never mind. Where's your book?"

Bending my knees, using the desk to hide Senior's stain, I held out my notebook.

"God help me. Where's your *text*book? And why are you giving me this? Would you prefer I write your notes for you while Your Royal Highness catches a few extra winks?"

"Sorry, Senior."

"What did you call me?"

More laughter. He grabbed my shoulder. "Go outside and stand against the wall!"

Stand against Target Man. A hole in Target Man's crotch. In that hole a centipede, getting out, getting inside my trouser, making its home in a new hole.

I threw up on the teacher's clean, ironed coat.

BITCH BAGS

An ayah took me to the campus doctor. As he examined me, I observed the sickroom. I don't want to see my classmates tonight, I thought, as he wrote my prescription.

I brought my hand to my stomach. "Can I stay here tonight?" I asked. "I don't feel well."

"Don't be silly," he said as he tore the notepad's top page and handed it over to the ayah. "Have one now and one tomorrow after breakfast and you'll be fit as a fiddle."

"Next time, hold two onions like this," the ayah said as we walked to the dispensary. She tucked her thin hands under her armpits. I was confused. She wiped her hands on the edge of her blue sari and continued, "Give it an hour or so. Your whole body will start burning. They'll let you stay in the sickroom."

If I went to the kitchen around three, she said, I wouldn't run into cooks.

"Second door to your left is the pantry," she said, running a hand down her scalp, as if to smooth down an errant strand, even though her gray-streaked hair was tamed with what smelled like castor oil and neatly combed into a long plait that reached her waist.

She stopped walking; so did I. She was tall and lowered her head to meet my eyes. Her smile exuded the touch of fresh, clean sheets. I felt, however momentarily, comforted.

In the forecourt garden, I lingered in the moon-shadow of the British officer's statue. In the first-floor dining hall, beyond a grilled window, boys sat at four long wooden tables, two for eleventh form, two for twelfth, and partook of their nighttime repast: toasted bread, sliced pineapple, and cow milk. When they finished, they pushed their chairs back and got up, a table at a time, beginning with eleventh form, and filed past the principal, who stood by the door wearing a severe look. The tables were mopped, the lights switched off. After waiting another hour, shivering in the eventide chill that, I'd soon come to know, was typical of hill towns, I tiptoed into the dorm and, hoping to see everyone fast asleep, opened the door to my room.

They were as awake as the tube lights that filled the room with a sickly white light. Boys who were my classmates snorted as I walked past them, piquing the curiosity of the rest. My classroom fiasco was passed from smiling mouths to willing ears, and for each step I took forward, the space behind me cracked open with whispers and laughter. I snapped open my suitcase and picked out fresh clothes. I looked up and saw Rusty staring at me with the expressionless eyes of a puppet.

In the bathroom, some boys stood before a mirror that extended from the ceiling to a granite stone platform that held three white basins. They wore towels around their waists and were bare-chested. Water trickled down their necks. They combed their hair, carefully setting it in place with their fingers. None of them, luckily, were from XI-A.

All six bathing cabins were occupied. A boy came and stood behind me, shirtless, towel-clad. As we waited for the baths to free up, he pointed to a wall where shirts and trousers hung from rusting nails.

"Hang your clothes there and wait wearing a towel," he said. "When a bath gets free, pop in."

He smiled wisely, happy to disburse his expertise of Magpies bathroom culture. My attention drifted to his chest. Flat as a slab of cheese. I turned to the mirror, the reflections of the boys it held. All flat-chested. The boy tapped my shoulder.

"Your shirt, brother. Open it," he said.

A spigot in one of the baths creaked as it was turned shut. The roar of running water was reduced to a trickle. The green door flew open and a boy stepped out, running his fingers vigorously through his wet hair. I ran in and shut the door.

"Weirdo," hollered the boy whose advice I hadn't followed.

I leaned against a wall and sank slowly down. I clamped a hand on my mouth and cried.

I came out when the bathroom was quiet, stood before the mirror, and took my shirt off. Not just the fat of a chubby boy but breasts. Breasts shaped like breasts. Not a woman's full breasts. Lemon-size breasts. A pubescent girl's breasts. Swollen man breasts.

I felt great anger, not for my anatomy but for my ignorance. I struggled and failed to recollect the bare chests of boys my age, but bare-chested men—the temple priest, Bollywood actors—I readily remembered. Did I imagine that, just as I would sprout the hair present on the chest of adults but not yet on mine, I would lose the breasts present on my chest but not theirs?

With cotton dipped in Dettol, I sponged the wounds on my chest, each a sequence of closely huddled teeth marks.

In a hurry to get out of the room, I noticed only now, I'd picked up a button-down and black trousers in place of my nightclothes. I wore them and left the bathroom as if I had an important midnight appointment to keep.

The lights in my room were off. Rusty was fast asleep. As were the other boys. Their snores swept the air like brooms. Moonlight trickled in through the window.

I lay down but couldn't sleep. Was Senior on his way to me now, the warden having given him the address to my bed? What if Rusty witnessed our congress? The bed creaked as I shifted restlessly, troubled by questions not partnered with answers.

Viren poked his head out. "Quiet. Be quiet. You too dumb to know 'quiet'?"

My disturbing his sleep was the pretext he used to express his true sentiment: we could no longer be friends even if last night's exchange suggested otherwise, not after how the classroom incident had positioned me in the minds of classmates whose favor he wished to curry. I didn't blame him. I had also lost, obviously, what chance there was for friendship, or something more, with Rusty. I had to keep things from getting worse.

I rested a hand across my chest. They simply could not know.

The teasing came in tides. They snuck up on me in groups of two or three and barked a gagging noise. I let them have their fun. I played along, in fact: I frowned at them, added a vehement "stop it." If they're kept entertained, I thought, they won't notice what else is wrong with me.

Rusty never partook of the teasing. He didn't tell them to stop. He didn't want to compromise his growing popularity, I guessed.

I walked up to him after trigonometry one day and tried talking. What followed resembled an unsuccessful Q&A: my questions, about how he liked school, the town, the people, banal but impassioned; his responses polite, indifferent, holding me at the kind of remove that an open insult couldn't.

I took to having early showers. Five in the morning, sometimes earlier. I stepped out of the shower, stood before the mirror, and strapped a belt around my chest, inserting the pin into the last hole and turning the belt to conceal the buckle under my arm. It was an uncomfortable arrangement that strained my breathing. But it kept my breasts from showing: when we walked back to the dorm against the wind; when we sweated in chemistry lab, heating test tubes over Bunsen flames; when, on long Wednesday afternoons, we studied the anatomy of cockroaches and frogs under the gaze of bottled sea creatures floating in formaldehyde. I shed the belt and changed into nightclothes before I slept. I slept after the rest.

Between classes I entered the bathroom with my head lowered against the boys who, I noticed, from the corner of my eye, stood against a wall and talked. I locked myself in a stall and, with a handkerchief, wiped the sweat off my chest so the belt didn't slip.

One Sunday, after two months of successfully concealing my flesh, I woke up late, so I took a shower late in the afternoon instead of early morning. I stepped out and froze: Rusty stood at a sink with a towel around his waist. He turned and saw me. I hastened back in and shut the door.

"What are you up to?" I asked.

"It's happening. Guess who's the new captain of the eleventh-grade cricket team?"

"Congratulations," I said.

"I'm meeting Prince at four," he said.

Prince was the name he gave our principal.

"So cleaning up a bit, nothing too fancy, of course, just splashing them hands and pits. That's plenty for Prince."

"You're doing him a favor, in fact," I said.

I strapped the belt around my chest, but before I could buckle it, it fell noisily to the floor.

"You're dressing in there? You'll get your clothes wet."

"Almost done." I slipped my shirt on, sans the belt, and buttoned up in a hurry, mismatching button to hole, so that one flap stood longer than the other.

"You're one shy boy, Shagun."

Sound accumulated in the distance: a tap was turned open; water hit the sink, then splashed against skin; his footsteps paddled toward my stall; his knuckles found the green door.

"Knock, knock," he said.

I threw the towel over one shoulder and opened the door.

"You're not supposed to open. You're supposed to say 'Who's there.'"

"Sorry?"

"It's a game. Let's do this again. Pretend the door is closed. Knock, knock."

"Who's there."

"Your master," he said, bringing his sleek-wristed hands to his slender waist.

I blinked at him, not knowing how to respond.

"Go on. Be a sport. Say, 'Yes, sir, how may I be of service today?'"

As if in a state of trance, I said what he asked me to, word for word.

"Hey, butler," he said, scratching his eyebrow. "I forgot my spare towel. Can't take this one off, can I?" He gestured to the towel wrapped around his waist and I laughed uneasily.

"But you have one right there."

I offered it to him.

"Come now. Be a good butler. Wipe me dry, boy."

With his forefinger he circled his upper body, then raised his hands. I balled the towel and blotted glistening droplets from his pale skin, starting with the notch of his neck, then drying his belly and chest.

"You're blushing?" Rusty guffawed. "I'm a boy. You're not a girl. It's just a game. Here, get my pits too."

I did as I was told. He said, "Sniff them for me, boy, see if they still smell."

I paused, uncertain, torn between temptation and reason, my eyes fixed on the thin strands of hair under his arms.

I stepped back and said, "You're all dry now."

He pressed one fist to the wall on my left and the other to the door on my right. He entered the stall. I stepped back. My heel struck the belt, forestalling further movement. He moved closer to me. I felt the heat his body radiated.

"You did your shirt wrong," he said.

He reached for the topmost button but gathered it in a fist. I pressed both my hands to his flat chest and pushed him. He fell heavily on the floor outside. I shut the door and locked it.

Rusty pounded the door. "Bloody open up."

"Sorry, Rusty. I didn't mean to push you."

"I won't ask again."

We bided our time on either side of the door. His sharp breathing was audible.

He punched the door. "Booby fucking faggot."

He spat on the floor and left. I waited, huddled against the door, one hand to the bolt.

When I returned to the room, clothes on, buttons corrected, belt intact, the room's energy appeared unaltered. No boy regarded me with renewed interest. My relief, that Rusty had told no one, was premature.

When he came back from his meeting with Prince, Rusty stood next to my bed and called my name out loud. The other boys stopped what they were doing and looked our way. I got off the bed and trembled in front of him.

"Our class puker has a dirty secret, boys," he announced.

"I don't," I said weakly.

"You're a liar now?" He took his voice up by a notch. "That's how ashamed you are about growing breasts, huh?"

A chorus of gasps followed. Boys shuffled to their feet.

"Then why grow them in the first place? Whose fault is it?" Still louder. "I asked you a question. Whose fault is it?"

"Mine," I said loudly, afraid he'd ask me to repeat myself.

"What do you mean, breasts," said Viren, leaping off his bed.

"Ask him," Rusty said.

With a triumphant smile he turned to the boys, who regarded him with faces feverish with admiration.

"Say, Shagun," Viren said. "Give us a sneak peek, yeah? Show us what you got in there."

A few boys blocked the space between my bed and Rusty's.

"Please," I said. "I need to use the bathroom."

"To grow your breasts?" a boy said, his face unseen, the comment provoking whistles and catcalls.

Rusty pulled my suitcase out from under my bed and flung it open. He picked clothes up by the fistful and threw them up in the air.

"What are you doing?" I cried.

"Don't squeal," he said. "Let him go, boys. We'll check his stuff to see if he's hiding lace bras and tampons."

Rusty continued digging through my suitcase, which was nearly empty. Viren stepped aside and, with a sweep of his hand, gestured toward my escape route. I took a few tentative steps, then crossed Viren. He flung his hand out and set his fingers to work.

"It's soft, but hard between," he yelped.

I tried to run. But Rusty was on me in a flash. He apprehended me, holding both my wrists behind me with one hand. Fingers flexed on flesh. Once, twice.

"He's worn a strap to keep his titties from showing," he said. "Save it. Now we all know, Bitch Bags."

There rose, in response to the title he accorded me, a chorus of whoops. My nose turned hot. To Rusty, I had thus far lacked materiality. Like air that makes its presence known only when it stirs against our skin. But now, in pushing him, I had made myself visible. He wanted to turn me into an example—to my classmates, but especially to me, most especially to himself—of what happened to those who displeased him.

When I returned to my room the next night, I saw Viren get off his bed and walk toward me. His head was lowered and he was frowning, as if lost in thought. But I knew he wanted to give my man breasts a squeeze: an animal twitch animated his fingers. I started to unbutton my shirt. When he was a few steps away, I flipped my shirt open and thrust my man breast toward him.

"Sick bastard," Viren said.

He raised his hands to push me away. My man breasts came in the way. We did a little dance: he stepped away from me, I toward him.

"You wanted a peek, Vixen, I mean Viren. Here, take it, take it."

Rusty stepped between us and kneed me in the nuts. I crumpled to the floor, howling, something between a howl of pain and a howl of laughter. "Rusty wants more than a peek, looks like."

He grabbed my jaw. "Listen, homo," he said as he raised his fist swiftly. I screamed shrilly. He let go of my jaw. He looked rattled. I crawled away from him and buttoned my shirt up.

The warden came in. "What's going on?" he demanded.

"Rusty hit me real hard, sir, down there, like," I said, pretend-crying.

"And when I said I'll complain, sir, he said he'll kick you there also because he says you and Prince—that's what he calls Principal, sir—you're both his little bitches."

Rusty opened his mouth to protest.

"Did you or did you not hit him?" the warden asked.

"I did, but—"

"Did you or did you not call Principal Sir 'Prince'?" I asked.

His devotees were looking at him. He couldn't possibly lie. "Yes, but—" he began.

The warden grabbed the nape of his neck with one hand and pushed his head down with the other. "Not a peep, Rusty. Let's take a walk."

Thereafter, instead of reaching for my man breasts, the boys flapped their shirts open and shoved their flat chests toward me. "This is a real man's chest," they'd say. Or, "Don't you wish you had this?" The first time that happened, the boy turned and looked at Rusty, and Rusty nodded and met my gaze and smirked.

I laughed and made snide remarks when faced with a flat chest: "So hairy! Your daddy a chimpanzee?" or, "Bony fellow. Mommy starve you as a baby?"

But Rusty did have his vengeance. In the face of the evidence that they were all normal, all the boys in my grade, I no longer needed to be told I was the weirdo. The taunt was baked into my perception of myself. I started to wear the belt again, I wore it pulled tight, to punish rather than conceal my man breasts. When confronted by mirrors, I lowered my gaze. And I welcomed the nights, for sleep was a chance to get away from myself.

THE CAULDRON HOURS

The results of our midterm exams were announced before winter break. In physics, biology, Hindi, and maths I had earned the highest score, and in chemistry, geography, and history, the second-highest score. In English I earned a mediocre score, a fact that Rusty didn't fail to bring up. Of course you suck at the language of posh people, he said. My classmates didn't come up to ask me for help with their weakest subject. I had hoped my success would forge a few friendships. Academic success was clearly not as important as avoiding the oddball with man breasts whom Rusty hated. But my teachers, even Mr. Sajid, whose coat I threw up on, commended my performance. Every teacher identified me as the grade topper, I was a scholarship boy for a reason, my teachers said. And for the first time since I came to Magpies, I received notoriety for good reasons.

During the five-week winter break, I stayed back in the dorm, as did a few other boys who lived far away. But we didn't mingle. Rusty wasn't in our midst. He went and met his family in Delhi and they went sightseeing: "First to the Pink City of Jaipur, then to the Taj Mahal," he'd announced with a flourish the day exams ended.

I went out exploring one afternoon. I left the dorm's backyard and entered the woods. There I saw a giant black cauldron on a plot cleared of trees but crowded with wild shrubs and weeds.

Our laundryman told me that the cauldron was once used to make large batches of broths for English travelers during the busy summer months, April through July. An underground pit, now sealed, was fed with logs of cedar that smoldered and released a smoke that smelled, he said, of pine and sandalwood.

I borrowed a ladder from the pantry, leaned it against the cauldron, and made my way up. Then, sitting on the thick iron rim, I picked the ladder up, leaned it on the inner wall, and descended, rung by rung, into a paler light.

Dry leaves, trapped inside, formed a bed that crunched when I lay down with my hands tucked under my head. The clear sky was speckled with flocks of birds, pheasants and finches, mynahs and bulbuls. At times their feathers, blue or green, ended their tapered descent on my body. I felt contained. Here, in my flesh.

On New Year's Eve, the boys who remained at Magpies for the break wore rented blazers and helped one another with ties inherited from fathers. They slipped on boots that they'd spent the better part of the morning scrubbing with old toothbrushes. They showed off their fake IDs to one another as they left. They each belonged, in their forged document, to a new state, they had a new birthday.

After they left, I picked up a thick blanket and went to lay down in the cauldron. When the clock struck midnight and 1990 came to be, I watched the fireworks that soared into the night in time to distant explosions and flared into circles of red and orange against the clear, starry sky. I clapped for them and felt sad for their evanescent lives. I fell asleep and awoke in the wee hours to the drunken songs of my classmates, muffled but audible, as they reentered the building. I pictured their bodies huddled together and trading heat as they walked through the cold night.

I corresponded with Ma regularly. I read and reread her letters in the cauldron, each filled with stories from her girlhood in Banaras: her best friend, a girl from Calcutta, the peda she brought home every Monday from the Baba Vishwanath temple. Ma belonged to the first generation of Indians with childhoods in independent India.

I waited for her letters to move through time and arrive at the sentence that began with "your father" and finally complete it.

It was in the cauldron that I read the book Ma sent me as a New Year's gift. Her copy of *The Dravidian Book of Seas and Stargazing*. That winter I performed the sea elephant stories in my dorm room on evenings when it was empty, when the boys who were straddlers like me went into town. Rusty's bed became the demon, the wicked cousin, the crooked uncle, it received a thorough thrashing; Viren's bed the traitor minister, the spineless prince, the soldier who flees the battlefield. I assigned roles to Mud and Milk and stood still when it was their characters' turn to speak. Sometimes I heard their voices, clear, unbleached.

My sisters and I once performed the story of the fallen prince, Arjuna, who angers a god and is cursed to be a woman for a year. I played him, Mud the god who curses him, Milk the god who cures him.

"Why is it a curse to become a woman anyway?" I inquired.

"So sad, the author died one million years ago and isn't here for your Q&A," Milk jibed.

"Big help he'd be," Mud scoffed. "As if *he* knows what a woman's curse is."

School reopened and the boys came back smelling of talcum powder, lemon pickles, mango chutney, and long hours spent on clean, sun-dried bedsheets. I went to the cauldron on Sunday afternoons only, when my classmates napped or went into town. I didn't want them to invade my territory. Despite my discretion, I was discovered one day.

I heard him walk up to the cauldron and around to the far side.

"Don't ask me to come in," he said. "We can be friends. But like this only."

I said, "When I'm in the cauldron?"

"And me outside. If you see me, you'll identify me in the dorm."

"And if I do, you'll lose your friends."

"You got it. So. Friends?" We exchanged a variation of a handshake. He tapped three times on the outside, I tapped three times on the inside, and that was how, early in that spring of 1990, I found my first and only friend at Magpies, a boy I never saw, only met across the iron curve of my cauldron.

He was from the state of Bihar. He told me about the vacations they took in the Ratnagiri hills where the Buddha preached the Lotus Sutra, the cricket games he played in the ruins of Nalanda. I told him about the seaside town where I grew up, the horse carriages that picked up foreign men at our port. I never told him that my sisters died.

He said, "I never saw the sea."

I said, "Who knows, maybe you'll live by the sea someday."

"I'll never leave Bihar. I have to be a cop when I grow up."

"*Have* to?"

"All the men in my family join the Bihar police. My father is the DSP in the state of Bihar."

"DSP—isn't that the highest ranking?" I asked.

"At the state level, yes. And my brother's a chief inspector in Madhuban, and in its neighboring province, my uncle holds the same position. It's practically the family business."

"You always have a choice."

With a piece of chalk I drew my friend's face. I drew many faces. Smiling, serious, thoughtful. Twenty faces in white on the cauldron's black interior. Each time he spoke to me from the other side of the cauldron I looked at one of the faces and associated it with it his voice.

I now performed for the statue of the British officer early on Sunday mornings. Around the hour of sunrise, as my classmates were fast asleep, I told him the stories I'd memorized, imitating the cadence of Amar Sethi, the raconteur I listened to on Ma's radio. The stone angels who surrounded him had chipped noses and broken penises.

One morning, after I finished my story, I heard applause. I started and turned and saw the ayah who'd taken me to the clinic after I threw up in class. She came and sat next to me.

"Sir Coxswain also claps for you," she said. "From hell, of course."

"You know his name?"

"Back when gora sahibs were here, my father worked as a janitor at

Regent Cinema. Their films came in special boxes. All the way from London. They dressed nicely on Fridays and went to the movies and ate tiny pastries."

"How do you know so much about them?"

"My father loved Englishmen. People found that odd but, well, it wasn't like the god-fearing locals did us any favors. We were only 'chamar' to them. Still are."

I felt Pita-jee's hands on the small of my back, pushing me down the stairs.

"God people did me no favors either," I said. "Don't know why I like these stories."

"How do you know them?"

"Ma read them to my sisters and me, and we performed them."

"Then stop associating them with nasties," she said, playfully spanking my arm.

I smiled. "Your father, he saw the Englishmen's movies too?"

"In snatches. When the sahibs or their wives went in and out." She slapped her thigh and cracked up. "He once saw a memsahib wearing a big gown that bounced when she walked."

"In the movie?"

"No. Outside. He was scared. He thought she was hiding something dangerous inside."

We laughed.

She said, "You heard of Manna? A street theater performs there for Ram Navami."

"But school's in session in April."

"Tell them you went to Manna for the weekend and caught something contagious so you stayed back. You know what to do if they check."

We each tucked our hands in our armpits and burst out laughing.

The next time I met my cauldron friend, I told him about Furniture. The tea he drank. His love for swimming on Thursdays. His infrequent homecomings. I concealed the vital part: the biscuit that my imagination had alchemized to a wedding cake. So I was surprised by his response.

"It's okay if you like him," he said.

"Why wouldn't it be okay?"

"You know what I'm saying."

He leaned forward and tapped the cauldron.

"Have you?" I asked, leaning forward. "You seem sure."

He didn't reply. I looked at one of his chalked faces that had a smile.

"You've done it!" I cried.

"Behave yourself. You're right, and it was special, and that's all you're getting."

There was a protracted silence. I pressed my ear to the cool iron wall and heard his shallow breathing. Had he fallen asleep? Then he spoke about putting things in a bag and going away somewhere.

"Someplace where we can be whatever we want," he said. "Won't that be nice?"

It was hard to disagree. That day I decided to go to Manna.

On the first Sunday of March, the ayah brought a cup of tea that she shared with me. She drank from the cup, I slurped from the saucer. It was flavored with cloves, I observed.

"Friday was payday," she said. "So I'm being fancy. Now stop grinning and tell me a story."

I told her a sea elephant story and she critiqued my telling of it: the inflections in my voice that didn't fully match the narrative emotion, the pledge that lacked energy, the monologue that needed a more reflective tone for its delivery.

The warden waved at me. He was on his way back from his morning constitutional.

"You got something in the mail," he hollered. "I left it on your bed this morning."

"Must be a letter from Ma," I said. "Thanks."

"It's something big, all the way from England."

When I got to my room, I saw on my bed a ripped-open packet and a statue of Hanuman.

"Thought there might be some chocolates in there," Rusty said.

He sat on his bed, a letter in his hand. Most of my classmates were still asleep.

"You don't need chocolates," he said. "God help us if *you* get fine chocolates."

"Rusty, give me my father's letter."

He looked at me for a prolonged moment.

"He mentions something about photos. Want to show me?"

He cupped his palms under his chest and swung them up and down. "Does he know? Poor thing. Wants his son to be a man."

"I'll tell the warden you opened my letter."

"Sure, be a baby. Give me an excuse to tell the boys how Daddy is all worried about his baby."

He flung the letter in the air. It crinkled and fell to the floor. I kneeled to pick it up. He got swiftly to his feet. Certain that he'd kick me in the gut, I stumbled against my bed frame with my hands wrapped around my body.

"Pissed your pants, did you?" he asked.

I fixed my gaze on the floor.

He said, "I'll get married one day, have kids. Our family name will survive. You? The day you die, you're gone." He snapped his fingers. "Like you didn't exist."

After he left the room, I scanned Pita-jee's letter for the mention of the photographs.

He wrote: "I know it's embarrassing, to be caught on camera like that. It wasn't easy for me. But real men don't choose the easy path. Show those photos to a friend. Ask his help. Pray to Hanuman. He will give you the strength to be a real man."

I went that evening to the phone room in the dorm's basement, a wood-paneled chamber that had four rotaries nailed to the walls. I placed a collect call for Ma. As I waited for her to call back the two scone lamps, on either end of the room, came on. They emitted a dim glow. One of the four rotaries rang. I picked one of them up and heard static. The ringing continued. I tried another handset. And heard Ma's voice.

"Listen, your husband wrote me a super-melodramatic letter," I said. "Can you tell him to calm down?"

"You're being quite melodramatic yourself," she said, chuckling. "Maybe you're growing up to be just like him, Shagun."

"Don't say that," I cried.

"What exactly did he say anyway?"

"The usual 'be-a-man' nonsense he pulls on me."

She started laughing.

"I'm glad I amuse you," I said, sulking.

"I still think of you as my little boy, but look at you, growing up in such a hurry, studying on the other side of the country, your papa telling you about the ways of a man."

Together we imitated my father. "No Daddy-Papa business. You will call me Pita-jee."

My laughter braided with hers, across all that distance, and my frustrations fell away. The scone lamps in the room abruptly brightened. I was startled. Later, the warden told me they were fitted metal halide bulbs. They take time to warm up.

DISAPPEAR, REAPPEAR

My cauldron friend's visits ended abruptly. Was it because I told him about Furniture? Or because he told me about his Furniture?

During sleepless nights and the morning hours when I found myself incapable of focusing on labs or classes, my anger was interspersed with gratitude to him for offering me an experience that resembled friendship, and consequently, I was overcome by remorse for getting mad at him at all.

I sat on my bed one night and listened keenly to the dorm room conversations, cocking my head if a particular lilt or consonant's pronunciation reminded me of his voice. The friendship was bound to end, I told myself. He was ashamed of our friendship. The indifference resulting from this clarity evaporated the next morning.

I stopped going to the cauldron.

Late one night, in the middle of March, shortly after I took my chest strap off and repaired to my bed—my dorm-mates were by then fast asleep—the room's door opened. In the wedge of light that formed on the floor, a tall shadow appeared. I shut my eyes.

Soft footsteps, punctuated by pauses, pottered about in the dark, then came to a halt at the foot of my bed. My blanket was pulled away. My knees trembled in the cold. A weight collapsed over me. He pulled the sheet over us.

"Hey, boy," Senior said and spat on my face.

Unbuttoning my nightshirt, he whispered, his chapped lips moving against my ear, "Stupid exchange program. In stupid hot Bombay. Good to be back."

His lips didn't slobber noisily as they slithered up my skin; he moved his muscle upon my thigh with a foot pressed firmly to the foot of the bed so it didn't creak; he didn't grunt, not when he reached his crescendo, nor before, when he dug his teeth in deep, there where, not an hour before, the strap of the belt had dug in. I pressed a palm to my pursed lips and gulped over and over as we shuddered; our bodies lay squished together and congested under the hood of the sheet like I was buried under him in the same coffin.

When he was done, he zipped his jeans and got up. His wet lips moved in the argent window light, but I couldn't hear what he said. He took my blank look for acknowledgment. He nodded and padded silently out. He left behind a deep throbbing on my left breast, on my thigh a patch of wetness. My throat was tight from all the swallowed screams.

I turned and found Rusty staring at me, one brown eye shadowed, the other lit by moonlight. His forehead was concealed under a mop of un-combed hair. Did anyone else see? I strained my ears and looked around the room but discerned no active movements in the dark, no audible signs of shock or curiosity. Above me, Viren's slow breath of sleep.

I looked back at Rusty, and he broke into a crooked smile.

I smiled back. And winked. I was not assaulted, my smile said.

His smile fell off his face. His visible brown eye flapped shut.

"Why you?" he asked. "It hurts my eyes to even look at you."

"That's what people will say about you," I said. "If you breathe a word."

"As if he can," he said. "Your lot are limp. Until you see little boys, of course."

I could tell, from his tone, how pleased he was with his comment.

I said, "So you're telling me you're not going to keep your mouth shut?"

"They're quite a menace in Bombay, your people, next only to rats. Dad's words."

"I'll let him know."

"And I the boys."

During the lunch recess that separated morning and afternoon classes I made my way to the college building. I roamed the corridors until I spotted Senior smoking and talking to some friends. I stood in the shadows of a wall. When he separated from the group and walked in my general direction, I stepped forward. He saw me and started. I stepped back into the shadows. He came and stood next to me at some distance.

"What are you doing here?" he asked, looking straight ahead.

"The boy who sleeps next to my bed, he saw us," I said.

He tilted his head toward me like a bird. "I'll come find you."

"I'll be in the sickroom," I said.

I entered the dining hall through the back door. To my right, servants furiously washed our meal plates and cooking utensils. To my left was the kitchen that I stole into. The ayah was right: it was empty. I found the pantry's green door and opened it. On the floor lay the sack of onions. I stuffed two into my pocket and stepped out and ran straight into a cook, a big man whose belly sagged over his crotch. I began to mumble an excuse.

"Out of my way," he grumbled, rubbing his sleepy eyes with the heel of his hand.

I placed an onion under each armpit, securing it between body and belt.

We had biology lab that afternoon. A hot afternoon breeze came in as we waited for our frogs. The pages of the lab calendar fluttered. The performances of Manna were a week away, I calculated. Rusty came up to me and pointed at a bottled fetus.

"Look, your baby," he said.

The boys around us burst out laughing.

"Will you name him after his father?" Rusty asked.

"Obviously," I said. "I'll call him Rusty. See, he even looks like you."

Rusty's smirk evaporated. He cut the boys who laughed a sharp look. The lab assistants walked in with frogs pinned belly-up to cutting boards.

As the teacher gave us instructions on dissection, I could feel the onions work their magic: my neck and shoulder started to pulse with an unnatural heat.

Rusty stood outside the lab, waiting for me. The other boys lingered not too far and watched on. He grabbed my arm the moment I walked out.

"Shoo," a lab assistant said, coming out. "Take your cockfight somewhere else."

"I'll sort you out at the dorm," Rusty said, and spat on the ground.

The burning took over my whole body. I discarded the onions and went to the clinic. The doctor took a thermometer out of a beaker full of Dettol and stuffed it in my mouth. He extracted it and examined it through the lower lenses of his bifocals. His eyebrows shot up. He gave me an antibiotic and a glass of water. I placed the pill under my tongue and gulped the water down. He led me to the sickroom, where one other boy slept close to the wall. After the doctor left, I took the pill out of my mouth. It left a bitter aftertaste. I covered myself and slept.

I was shaken awake. I opened my eyes and found Senior standing over me. I sat up and steadied myself with my feet on the ground. When the light-headedness gave way to clear sight, I followed Senior out of the sickroom.

Outside my dorm were three other college boys. One had a camera on him. Senior introduced me to them as his friend's baby brother.

"He told us about the boy who's making mischief," one of Senior's friends said.

"Him and his bootlickers," I said. "Monkey see, monkey do."

"You're funny," he said. "Well, you're friends with Dheeraj, we got you, kid."

Dheeraj. That was Senior's name. I turned it in my mouth, as if testing its taste. It felt foreign, unsuited to who he was to me. Senior, I silently said and felt familiarity return.

We went up the stairs and into my room. I pointed to Rusty. They squatted next to him, two on either side. Senior shook him awake. He looked sleepily from one face to the next, and his eyes widened and he opened his mouth. Senior clamped it shut.

"If you make any noises," Senior whispered, "we'll bury your face inside your ass."

"So small, his ass is," one of Senior's friends said. "It won't fit his face."

Senior released Rusty's mouth. They picked him up and planted him on his feet. He walked out with them. Senior's hand was placed on the small of his back. They opened the door, and in the wedge of light that filled the doorway, Senior looked at me. I shook my head. What I sought was more functional than vengeful: I wanted Rusty to let me be.

I lay down but couldn't sleep, not until the door opened and I heard Rusty walk back in and lie down. I wanted to ask him what Senior had done to him.

During lunch recess the next day I called my mother and told her about my upcoming trip. "I'm off for the weekend," I said. I couldn't tell her I planned on cutting school for a week. "You like street theater?"

"I've never seen a show."

"How come?" I asked. "They perform the stories you read to us."

"It just wasn't something we did in my family or your father's."

I recognized, for the first time perhaps, the insularity of our lives, our collective vision as a family myopic to the world beyond the one we inherited.

"Mud and Milk would've liked to see one," I said.

"I was thinking about them today," she said. "Remember, they would do their homework on the stairs and shout if they had any questions."

"And you would shout the answers out from your room, yes," I said.

When I returned to my dorm room, my head ringing with my sisters' loud questions, I found several of my classmates standing between Rusty's bed and mine. They were in uniform, some with schoolbags still strapped to their shoulders, some with notebooks in their hands. With a flick of his chin a boy pointed my way and they watched me approach my bed. They fanned past me, avoiding my gaze, their bodies giving off the heat of the day. They went to their respective beds and made a great show of busying their hands with shoes, bags, books.

Rusty and Viren stood leaning against Rusty's bunk bed. Viren cleared his throat.

"Not you," I said.

"I second what Viren's about to say," Rusty said.

"You'll say it. Let's hear your cricket captain voice."

"We'll quit messing with you, in word and in action," he barked. "Happy?"

His spit got sprayed on Viren's cheek. Viren winced.

I shrugged. "Happy for you, friend."

Rusty grimaced but didn't retort. Viren's face fell. As he rubbed his cheek against his sleeve, he appeared to be shaking his head.

"Stop fidgeting like a chick," Rusty hissed, but his eyes, ripe with hate, were fixed on me, and I knew he wasn't done with me. The full force of his reaction, not canceled, merely deferred, would be realized after Senior graduated and left.

Rusty left the room. Viren went up to his bed. The tension in the room eased and the boys seemed sapped of their energy, as though a bus had returned them to their homestead after an epic loss in a game of cricket. For a moment my eyes scanned the room and took note of their movements, their pace sluggish, their actions unfinished, a bottle of water reached for but never picked up, a tangled sheet, shoved at but half-heartedly.

I sat down on my bed and reminded myself that Senior would graduate and leave Magpies the week before our finals. A lump formed in my throat. Did I grieve because Senior was leaving or because I would lose his protection? I wanted no part of what Senior did to me. But his assault signaled his desire for my body. It made my body feel wanted. A body that, until then, was ridiculed or, worse, invisible.

I pushed the window open and gulped air by the mouthful. As if who I had become was nothing more than smoke in a room that could be remedied with fresh air.

BRIEF TUTORIAL ON HOW
THE ADULT MALE PISSES

I looked, as Senior pleasured himself, at Hanuman's statue sitting on the window ledge. Hanuman's face looked bloated. Senior's mouth filled with my flesh. Moonlight washed Hanuman's face. Senior drenched my thigh.

With his body still on top of mine, he raised his thighs, zipped up, and whispered, his wet lips grazing my ear, his breath musty upon my face, "Come out."

So I followed him, the soft tap-tapping of my bare feet amplified in that late, windless hour. My classmates were asleep. I envied them their nightly abandonment, their unflawed bodies. The ceiling fans whirred relentlessly; the moon, visible through the grilled window, was an up-turned crescent, smile-like.

I closed the door behind me. My skin was hot, my eyes raw. A lizard slithered slowly down the length of the tube light overheard, inching its way toward a fly that sat still and buzzed, drunk on the sick-white light.

Senior recovered a brown envelope from his trouser pocket and gave it to me. In it were five photographs. In each picture Rusty squatted on his haunches and had his face buried in a crotch, butt, or armpit not stripped of its clothing. His hands, wrapped around waists, thighs, ankles, or shoulders, performed desire. Whose body was he holding? Senior's? His friends'?

I said, "Was this necessary?"

"Bitch, I did you a favor," Senior snapped.

With my thumb I traced Rusty's squatting body.

"He knows," Senior said, calming down. "If he doesn't leave you alone, every boy in his grade gets personal copies—he knows." He pointed to Rusty's face squished against a crotch. "I threaten him. 'They will see you like squirrel digging for nuts. You want?'"

I laughed, and my eyes spilled over. My nostrils, clogged, let loose a snort.

"You have one more year with him after I leave," Senior said, ruffling my hair. "If he makes mischief again, call him squirrel, he will shut his mouth."

"There's something wrong, I think, with how I use bathrooms," I said.

"'Bathroom,' meaning? Bathing, shitting, pissing?"

"That. The last one."

"Why, how you do it?" he said. He didn't seem surprised by our absurd conversation.

I described my stance.

"You squat? How's that possible? Show me."

I took him to the bathroom, turned a switch, and four naked bulbs burned to life. I crossed the sink and started to make my way toward the stalls. He yanked me by the shoulders.

"Where you are going? Go left. There. Those bowls on the wall—urinals. That's what they're called. Didn't you notice other boys doing it?"

"I go straight for the stalls. I'm in a hurry."

He laughed. "I'm also in hurry when going to the toilet."

"Now I know why my father took pictures of me," I said.

"What pictures?"

I looked at the bowls nailed to the wall.

"Urinals," I said slowly. Like I was learning a foreign language.

He said, "Wait, he took peeing pictures of you?"

"He went away when I was two. He came last year for six months."

"And then he took your peeing pictures?"

Peeing pictures. Something to the phrase, or the way he said it, with a mixture of shock and surprise, made us seem like children figuring out a grown-up conversation. The knowledge that what took place between us was nothing childlike didn't diminish that impression.

He pressed a hand to the back of my head. He brought it to his chest. His heartbeat was rapid, his shirt warm, rough as if from too many washes. I raised my hands. The moment I pressed them to his back, he drew a sharp breath and stepped away. His eyelashes were wet.

"I'm going to Manna on Friday," I said. "I won't be here for some time. Sorry."

He touched me lightly on my cheek with two fingers. He lowered his head and reached for my lips but planted his kiss on my eyebrow instead.

I continued standing in the bathroom after he left. My eyebrow warm from his lips. My hair warm from his hand. My chest smarting from his teeth.

A boy walked in, sleepy-eyed, and went up to the bowls by the walls. In the bright bathroom light I watched him finish his business and return to his dream. Urinals. How many times did I see boys standing there? Why did I not wonder what they were used for? Why did I assume they stood facing a wall to talk? Why was I asking myself these questions, why was I not used to being blind to things placed right before my eyes?

Walking up to a bowl, for the first time, at the age of seventeen, eighteen almost, I stood erect and emptied myself the way a man is expected to.

THE DRAVIDIAN BOOK OF SEAS AND STARGAZING

The people of Manna poured out of their houses. Men in tunics, dhotis, and turbans and women in saris who had flowers tucked into their hair, stringed tuberose or jasmine that imbued the air with a densely sweet fragrance reminding me of Ma: the flowers she wore in her hair, the vendor she bought them from every Friday, a man who cycled to the cinema with a basket full of jasmine strapped to his back seat, stopping at our house en route.

In the gathering dusk the crowd pottered down the road and took a left, some holding lanterns, others clapping as they chanted the name of Rama. I joined their stream, and together we entered a temple in whose courtyard grew an ancient banyan, its bark, thick and gnarled, wrapped with threads: red for wishes made, green for wishes fulfilled. Wedged between tree and thread were sticks of sandalwood incense. A milky, fragrant cloud, suspended around the banyan, dulled the glimmering tips of the incense.

We sat down cross-legged before the stage that was built under the temple terrace and surrounded by torches stuck into pots full of mud, hissing, burning bright, their heat and the heat of the bodies around me a relief from the evening breeze, crisp and full of the mountains.

To the ululation of a conch shell and the clanging of cymbals, the play began: the first story in *The Dravidian Book of Seas and Stargazing, Volume 1*.

Between the Age of the Gods and the Age of Humans, the gods and the de-mons churn the ocean to bring to the surface the elixir of eternal life. Many unexpected treasures are released from the stirred-up sediments of the sea-bed. Pots of never-ending gold nuggets. Herbs that control minds. And the first ancestor of the sea elephants. Their Manu, their Adam. His beauty beguiles the gods, so they claim him by naming him. Iravat. Brilliant as lightning. His flesh is the white of pearls, his tusks are the blue of clear skies. He departs his home of the seas for the heavens, where he's greeted with trumpets and lotus showers and given a palace of his own. But his aquatic family grieves his absence, through their lives, on their deathbeds, in their song that no longer contains all seven notes of the octave. Because trauma, like a gene, is inherited by subsequent generations, the sea elephants never forget the original separation. When their grief maddens them, their patri-arch undrowns: he rises to the surface of the sea and enters the human world and commits a theft. He mesmerizes, captures, and brings home a child who drowns, dies, and awakens to another kind of life in the same body: its nose turns to gills and it loses its gender. It remembers its human family but in the manner of a story or dream. It becomes a part of its new family, who treated it like royalty: the walls of its room pearl-studded, its roof alive with bioluminescent starfish. When it's time for the child's soul to reincarnate, it vanishes like a flame extinguished. Its memory keeps the sea elephants content for a time. Then their grief makes its unfailing reappearance and their patriarch rises once more and humans pay for the greed of the gods.

For forty-five minutes the play mesmerized me. A four-handed God—painted blue, a pair of wooden hands strapped to his back—was lowered from the temple terrace with ropes tied around his waist; he hovered midair, his dialogue switched from prose to song to the staccato rhythm of verse. A slat of the stage opened like a trapdoor and out came a sea elephant in time to an elephant's trumpeted roar playing on the speaker. The rudimentary costumes and props—a paper elephant mask, a pinwheel, a sickle made of cardboard—allowed for intimacy because they didn't exact a beauty that held them above life. They allowed me to enter the extraordinary story of the gods.

After the performance ended, the audience stood up and clapped. As the villagers padded up a flight of stairs and entered the temple and the actors left the stage around which the torches burned dimly now, I thought of Mud and Milk: How would they have responded if they saw the stories of our treehouse skits turned into a production with props and professional actors? Would Mud's cynicism have endured, would she have said something in the vein of "they were good but they could've done better"? Would Milk have found specific details to praise, commended the hard work of the actors? Would they have switched traits? It was impossible for me to imagine Mud as sweet. But in truth I couldn't know how they would've changed. I couldn't even imagine the person I would be if they were alive: Would I have clung so steadfastly to the sea elephant stories, would I be in Magpies, in Manna, considering acting for a career?

I followed the sound of laughter to its source: a tent with an open flap. Inside, the actors, their faces lamplit, shed their makeup, beards, masks, strapped appendages. One of the performers opened his rag-stuffed blouse: I wouldn't have guessed, without this stolen glimpse, that a man played the mother of the drowned child. I ached to be inside, breathing in that tent, filled with the after-performance energy.

The actor who played the god, still in his costume, splashed his face with water from a basin and looked into the mirror that reflected the tent opening. He saw me, I feared, and I beat a hasty retreat.

Next to the stage, the torches had burned out and were smoking. The street beyond the temple gate was a stream of footfalls and bobbing light from lamps. In the dark courtyard stood a man holding aloft a kerosene lantern.

"Do you need a place to stay?" he asked, holding up my backpack.

My inner voice that urged me to not follow Senior on the first day of school at Magpies was quiet, so I decided to trust this stranger. I followed him out of the temple.

We returned to the street where I got off the bus and went into his house—a single room with a hard-dried mud floor. A charpoy leaned against one wall. A few upturned steel utensils sat on the floor next to a coal stove where he made some wheat gruel. He kept the embers alive by blowing at them through a hollow tube.

"You live here alone?" I asked, and when he seemed to hesitate, I apologized.

"No, it's just I've lived alone so long, I lose track of the years. Let's see. My wife died fifteen, no, sixteen years ago, and my son left to work in Bombay . . . eight years back, I believe?"

"And he hasn't visited since?"

All the villagers, he explained, who lived on this street and in almost all of those brick houses were middle-aged and aging parents whose sons and sons-in-law had migrated to Bombay or Delhi, shunning the familial farms in favor of employment in a metropolis.

"Nandi's our only son who comes back," he said.

"Nandi?"

"The theater chief. The god? This is his mother's hometown. Rama was her favorite deity. So he performs here every year for Rama's birthday. No matter how far his travels take him. And his travels take him far."

I pictured Nandi and his troupe traveling from village to county, town to district, city to city, Nandi buying train and bus tickets, one-way tickets, always, never return tickets.

"Where does he live?"

"Go to the end of the street, take a right, then walk down the hill. Not too far you'll find where they've set up camp."

"Set up camp? In his mother's hometown?"

"The performing artists must all live together, he says."

He put out two steel plates and poured us equal portions of the milky gruel.

He said, "You can meet him here tomorrow morning if that's why you're asking. He comes to see all of us and ask after our welfare when he's here."

My host said that the performances went on for ten days and I was welcome to stay on with him. He waved off my offer to do some chores for him in return. We ate the rest of the meal quietly. That night, in that window between wakefulness and dream, the farmer's hard floor became the floor of the treehouse. The play rose from the throats of Mud and Milk, and in that imagined theater I was a child again.

The farmer's cows stood under a thatched roof and watched as I squatted next to the well and emptied mug after mug of cold water on my head. The air was ripe with the sulfur smell of dung.

I dressed and joined my host, who, like the rest of the villagers, stood in front of his house. Their doors were pastel blues and greens, the road in front of each house a chalk powder patchwork of vines and paisleys.

Nandi appeared at the end of the street: a burly man, standing tall, dressed in a white dhoti and button-down, his mustache well groomed, his hair concealed in a white turban. He went from one house to the next as some villagers, women and men, took his hand and spoke to him with their shoulders hunched. Others were less sparing in their affection: they kissed his forehead, pinched his chin, held him hard against their bodies, and wept.

When he came to where we stood, the farmer spoke to Nandi for some time. Then he turned to me and said, "Nandi, this boy wants to talk to you."

Appraising me, Nandi said, "Come, let's hear what you have to say."

We walked down the road, Nandi and I, and before descending the switchback, I turned and saw the families still at their doors: the edges of the women's saris, drawn over their heads, shivered in the breeze; their expressions held, at once, hope and despair.

We passed four water carriers who tottered slowly down the road, carrying, on either end of a pole held across their shoulders, cloth-sealed earthen pots.

"Where are you from?" Nandi asked me.

"I study at Magpies."

My mouth was dry.

Nandi shook his head. "Everyone sends their boys to English medium schools."

I don't like Magpies, I wanted to say. But what if he thought I was a bad student?

"Why say Magpies? Why not name your hometown?"

So I told him. "By the sea," I added.

"No need to give a wanderer a geographic marker."

"You performed there?"

He nodded.

"I want to act in your troupe."

He said nothing.

I felt foolish about how abruptly I'd blurted out my desire. I wanted to tell him about what passed through me when I looked into the greenroom. But under the weight of his silence I felt incapable of translating that experience to expression.

After about ten minutes, as flowering mogra trees rustled all about us in their embankments, white tents came into view, bright and billowing against a rugged, rocky hillock.

Nandi stopped short, took a deep breath, and said, "The makeup room is our terminal ward. Our birthing room. The actor dies. A character is born."

"Beautiful."

He frowned. "Don't look at me like that, with dumb reverence. You don't know the first thing about what that kind of violence means. As for the rigors of performing itself? Forget it. Day after day in strange new places, traveling on nonexistent roads for weeks, sleeping on railway platforms, depending on the kindness of villagers for your meals, and in the face of these difficulties, living the myth for your audience—king, priest, god, demon, animal, whore—you don't become them, they become you."

"I grew up on these stories," I said. "I know the sea elephant myths by heart."

"You read, what, illustrated editions for children in English?"

"Ma read them to us in Hindi. We would perform them, my sisters and I."

We reached the tents. He took a few steps away from me, his hands crossed behind him.

He said, "We perform close to our audience. So close that we hear their breath in the pause between dialogues, and their response, not for us, mind you, but for the characters we play, becomes part of our performance. It's not a simple binary: we're performing, they're watching. No, we're *living* the myth together. That's why myth is always told in the present tense.

"Pah. Look at your blank face. Of course you don't understand."

He stepped dismissively into the tent. But I'd made my choice.

The next day, I went and stood some distance from the pitched tents where Nandi described scenes and called out the dialogues to actors who didn't have a script to read from. They listened only to Nandi. About an hour later, when the actors got up to practice the three scenes they'd heard, Nandi found me watching. He frowned.

"I'm only observing," I said.

He turned again to his group of actors and asked them to spread themselves out as they would on the stage.

For the next five days I watched them rehearse by day and perform by night. On the sixth morning, I helped the troupe erect their stage in front of the village houses, four doors from where my host lived. We piled five columns of bricks and tied wooden planks to them. To those planks we nailed three cotton sheets that were painted with bright images of goddesses and fanged demons. I'm not simply setting up a stage, I realized. Hereafter, the villagers' memory of the myth would contain these images staged on their street; conversely, the myth, its images, would become part of their memory of the street. Their lives, as individuals and as an audience, would constantly invoke and renew the other.

I found a middle-aged actor with gray hair and a pockmarked, goat-shaped face looking at me, and I thought of acknowledging him with a nod, but something about his stance had the air of a monk in meditation.

That evening, when the play ended, he signaled to me from the stage, asking me to stay where I was. Several minutes later, he walked up to me, his face washed, colored streaks running down his cheeks. He introduced himself as Rooh.

"So?" he said, gesturing to the stage.

"It was great," I said. "Better than great."

"Yeah? Fourteen years of doing this, but it still doesn't go away, the worry that we didn't give our audience a good time. Let's walk and talk."

"I really like the chemistry between you and the actor who played Sita."

"Saaya. We go back a long way. He can be a real pain, but I love him to death."

"He played the mother in the sea elephant performance?"

"Good eye," Rooh replied.

We strolled down a stone path drenched in moonlight, the mogra flowers—petals white, cores orange—washing the air with their fragrance of jasmine and pine.

"Have you ever seen Durga Puja in Calcutta?" Rooh asked. "They set up huge clay statues of the goddess on the road. So beautifully painted. People celebrate the goddess coming home to her mother. Her favorite sweets are made. Milk cake. Rice pudding. Rasgulla. Let her be pampered. She's taken care of the world. She needs a little rest. They wake her up with a conch shell. They sing lullabies, fan her to sleep. She isn't just the clay statue on the road. She is the goddess come home. Every devotee her mother. Brother. Sister. Her human family.

"Ten days later she returns to her heavenly home. Her statues are carried, in chariots, on shoulders, and immersed in the waters of the Ganga. People bawl their eyes out.

"My point is, people know the story. They know the ritual. Next year, her statues will line the road again: they know. And yet they weep when she's taken away. You see?"

"A certain kind of story never becomes old?"

Rooh nodded. "Emotion in myth never ages."

We stopped at the edge of a cliff. A village downhill, across the river, dotted with a hundred orange flames, fell under a slow spell of darkness, one flame, then some more put out, a hypnotic choreography, life dancing its way gently into sleep. In the moonlight we saw the hulls of two ships going downriver.

He asked me my name, where I studied. He said, "I saw you today. When you helped with the stage? I was there once. I felt what you felt.

I know what you want. Our time here is almost up. But come see me in the third week of June. We'll be in Bijpur. West of where you are. Come there and look for us. I'll train you. With Saaya's help. And when you're ready, we'll present you to Nandi. Then the decision is his to make."

I brought my palms together and bowed my head.

SHOULDER SEASON

In the fortnight that followed my return from Manna, before Senior graduated and left Magpies—through his finals and lab exams, before our finals and lab exams—Senior came to me thrice a week after midnight and left before daybreak. Something about his visits changed: he lingered after he was done, his teeth took on incrementally lower registers of aggression. It was a gradual accumulation of change whose cumulative effect I felt the night of his final visit.

He stopped moving over my thigh before he was done. His mouth stopped slobbering over my chest. He had not fallen asleep. He blinked and his eyelashes fluttered against my flesh. His heartbeat softened against my skin. Around daybreak he drew in a sharp breath and said, "Let's get out of here."

We put our shirts on and stepped out of the dorm room into a deep blue dawn. I followed him at first. But he had me walk by his side. I hunched my shoulders and clasped my hands.

We went out of the school building and approached a slowly brightening sky. He took me up a hillock where we sat with our legs drawn close to our chests and our hands around our knees. A stack of fluffy clouds was colored crimson by the still unseen sun.

"Those photos of Rusty," I said. "Did you actually do things with him?"

"What, you're jealous?" he asked.

"No," he said, but only after I shook my head.

A wave of relief washed over me.

"I disappeared for a time, remember?" he said.

"You went to Bombay."

"When I was there—it's where home is—my dad found out," he said.

"About?" I asked, but understood. "How?"

He shook his head. "Dads have a knack for this kind of a thing. Only this kind of thing. The rest they're blind to, don't care, but if their boys turn out odd, man, they can sniff it."

"What did you say?"

"You think we spoke about it?" Senior guffawed. "Wake up, boy. He brought a girl to my room and watched."

"And did you?"

"Did I have a choice? I pretended she was a boy I like."

Did he think of me?

"After she left, he came to my room. 'Yours is big, I'm proud of you,' he said."

I sidled closer to Senior and placed my palm upon his back. He accepted my touch.

"I can never pretend she's a boy I like," I said. "I can only be the 'girl.' You see?" For the first time, I named my pleasure.

"I know," he said. "Why you think I'm telling you, duffer?"

He gripped my shoulder, I wrapped my hand around his waist. He didn't flinch from my touch. With my eyes closed, I tilted my head. He took my upper lip in his mouth. My flesh stirred against my trousers. He pressed his hands to my neck. But—bafflingly, unexpectedly—I wanted nothing more than to release myself from his grip. Fear accompanied his nocturnal visitations. But what I felt now when I sought him and he sought me back was not fear. I was unbearably anxious.

A flock of finches flew right above our heads, wings flapping, loudly chirping, and we startled apart.

"I go first, then you," he said.

He lingered a moment. As if he wanted me to remember his face.

Sun-washed and beautiful in the manner of something intimately familiar.

He got to his feet. I closed my eyes and heard him walk away. When I looked back, assuming I'd see him walking rapidly downhill, I was faced with an empty road.

He was gone, and with time, so were the marks of his teeth on my chest. What made him real was the memory of pain, of weight, of protection. Of my body learning for the first time the taste of being desired.

HANUMAN MALE FIXING CENTER

We had extended study hours in the weeks leading up to our final exams. I was on my bed, my book open on my lap, pondering over those few seconds that passed with my lips inside Senior's wet mouth: Why did I respond to desire with anxiety? Why was my need to disengage more severe when contact became consensual? The warden came to our room and interrupted my reverie. I had a call.

"I told him to call back in ten," he said.

The sound of Rusty's slippered footfalls followed me out of the room, down the stairs, into the phone room. The glow released by the two lamps, fixed on either end of the long room, was still dim.

Neither Rusty nor I acknowledged the presence of the other. One of the four rotaries started to ring. I picked up a handset but encountered a low static, not a voice. The phone in question continued to ring. It was Rusty, of course, who picked the right receiver.

"Yes, he's here," he said. "I'm Rusty. Rohit-jee's son. We met, remember?"

Rusty used one hand to give me the receiver and with the other he gave my man breasts a squeeze. I opened my mouth to protest. He brought a finger to his lips and pointed with his eyebrows at the rotary. I turned to face the wall, the receiver pressed tight to my ear.

"I told you to stay away from him," Pita-jee said. It sounded like his teeth were clenched. "And you choose *him* to confess. Anyway. I'm happy to hear your change of heart. God finally put some sense into your head."

"What exactly did he say to you?"

"He told his father what you told him, and that man, after what he did to our family, he gets to pretend like he's on some moral high ground, telling me about my son, the bastard."

"After what *he* did? Like it wasn't your choice."

"We didn't start on the right note, you and I, but now things will get better, you'll see."

"And that will happen how?"

"I made some calls," he said. "A man who runs a center for people like you—"

"People like me?"

"He's on his way to see you."

"Yeah, not happening."

"Don't be stubborn, boy. I called in a favor because you told Rusty you wanted to become normal. I'll look terrible besides if I don't do anything about it."

"You don't want to look wrong, that's what this is about."

"Just talk to him, okay? If things go well, you will marry a girl and have a family. A son. God will reward you for mending your ways."

When I hung up and turned, Rusty was standing right behind. I tried to punch him in the stomach, but he dodged my fist, nabbed my shoulders, and turned me around. He struck the side of my head against the wall and held it there with his hand pressed to the back of my head. His other hand grabbed my wrists.

"If you have boobs," he said, "did your sisters have little dicks?"

I twisted my wrists, trying to release them from his grip.

"Oh hey, my brothers say thanks. They like using that pretty princess comb to fix their unruly hair down there."

"If your family was their future, I'm glad they're dead," I said, breathing hard.

"I bet you are," he said.

"The hell do you mean?" I asked, shoving my back against his chest.

"Did you know there's no word for 'sister killer' in Hindi?" he said.

I pictured Ma going to their house, armed with bad news and my misdeed. There was to be no marriage, the prospective brides died, and their blood is on their brother's hands. My wrists relaxed in Rusty's fist and I stopped struggling.

"There you go," he said. "Stay. Good boy."

The lights brightened to their full capacity of brightness, as I had expected them to. But Rusty was startled: he released my head from his grip abruptly. I raised my foot swiftly and kicked his crotch and heard him stumble away from me. I turned and found him doubled over, with a hand pressed to his mouth. I grabbed a receiver, wrapped its cord around his neck, and dragged him with it. I struck his head hard against the wall. Once, two times over. When he fell to the floor, I wrapped the cord around his neck two more times and tightened it until I heard him choke and cough. The upper-left corner of his forehead was bleeding and swollen.

"Come up with a story for why your head's busted," I said. "Your boys will ask and you're too thick to come up with something on the spot."

I left him on the floor and started to leave the room, my veins pulsing. It felt good, to not be violated, to violate instead.

"I called Dad soon as your manboy left," Rusty said. "He called your old man pronto."

"What did you tell him?"

"You smile like a five-rupee whore when men leave your bed. But you wanted to fix it."

I turned around. He was sitting.

He mimed a camera click. "Too late to use your boyfriend's blackmail swag. I made my move before you could stop me, but you know what the kicker is? I didn't have to spread my legs to fuck you over."

With his thumb he blotted the drop of blood on his forehead as he unwound the telephone cord off his neck. He sucked his thumb, dropped the receiver, and got to his feet.

•———•

It was the end of May. Classes had ended. Our exams were upon us. During what turned out to be one of the last meals that my classmates and I shared, as I scanned the faces of the boys around me to see if I might recognize my cauldron friend, if he might, on the verge of our collective departures, give something away that might allow me to recognize him, I was informed by the warden that I had a visitor.

I followed him into the visitor's lounge where I stood before a tall stranger who had a saffron shawl wrapped around his neck. His eyes, wide and amber, were pronounced by the bags under them and the sunlight in the room.

The warden left us. Rusty hadn't followed me. The man's mustache muffled his words. It was unnaturally black. A dark spot dotted his lower lip.

"Your father told you I'd be visiting," he said.

He placed a brochure on the table next to him. THE HANUMAN MALE FIXING CENTER it said on the cover; REAL MANHOOD IS 45 DAYS AWAY it said under.

"When are you done with school? I'll come pick you up."

"I don't think so," I said.

"Oh, you will go," he said. "I won't let a Brahmin boy go down this road."

"My father didn't say anything about force."

"When asylums come for mental patients, they resist. Taking them anyway, that's service, not force."

"So what I have is a mental illness?"

He said, "You are an illegal person, did you know? They put people like you away for a long time. And, let me tell you, prison is no place for boys who go to fancy schools."

I didn't know I was an illegal person. I tried to keep my face neutral. But I doubt I concealed my fear.

"What you have is a spiritual illness," he said. "When I come back for you it won't be just me."

So he was here to see how amenable I was to his plan, to understand how much force will be necessary.

"June seventeenth," I said. "That's when school closes."

I gave him the right date. I had decided to leave the week before. During finals. Rooh wanted me to meet him in Bijpur in the second week of June.

"Are you lying?" he asked. "We know where you study, we know where your home is, and, really, where else will a boy go?"

I said, "If you're going to take me, I'd rather it be from here. Ma doesn't know."

"And we will give her back a boy who loves girls. As nature intended it."

Abruptly, he came and hugged me tight.

He said, "Say 'Praise be to the masculine Hanuman, the faithful servant of Rama.'" I did, but he wasn't satisfied. "Don't they give you milk at school? Louder, boy. Louder."

He hollered, I hollered after him. Praise be to the masculine Hanuman, the faithful servant of Rama. Praise be to the masculine Hanuman, the faithful servant of Rama. Until my warden came and asked us to keep it down. The visitor released me from his grip. I stepped away, my throat raw and hurting.

My warden asked, "Aren't you supposed to be studying?"

"He's learning with me," the visitor said.

"There's a stain," I said, rubbing my lower lip.

He reddened and I followed the warden out of the room.

I browsed the brochure later that night. It had images of men in different stages of the "cure process": they wore saffron robes printed with the name and face of Hanuman and posed for a group picture on the day of their arrival; six men, appearing naked, were surrounded by clouds of ash; a final group picture of the men, now in their civilian clothing, their hands joined, their faces fixed with smiles; some pictures of "cured" men, posing with their wives and toddlers in their arms.

The day-to-day of the cure process wasn't detailed, but it said that after forty-five days the "patient" was brought together with a female volunteer, and if he succeeded in performing with her "the Shiva-Shakti Union under the priest's observation," he would be declared a cured male, a full male, a proper male, a free male. Those who failed to perform the Union repeated the forty-five-day process. Until they were cured. The last picture was of the man who came to see me. Vikrant. He ran the center.

I pictured joining with a batch of men, all of whom pass the test and get cured and leave—all except me. I imagined posing for one "before" group picture after another, the faces around me changing but I never make it to the "after" group picture, my body never returned to its civilian clothing. That was the fate of men like me. Men who liked to be fucked, not do the fucking.

I'd returned from Manna filled with desire to join Nandi's troupe. Now the desire turned to need: If I don't come back to Magpies, Vikrant can't apprehend me. If I was surrounded at all times by actors and an audience, if I kept moving, from one place to the next, if I spent my life becoming other characters, no one would be able to find and ungay me, even if they wanted to. I couldn't fail my theater training. My life depended on it.

PART III
1991–1996

WALK LIKE A LION, CRY LIKE A HORNBILL

I wrote Ma a letter, telling her I was staying back at Magpies for my summer between eleventh and twelfth grade to take classes for college entrance exams. I decided to tell her the truth if Nandi accepted me into his troupe.

Early on a June morning, I arrived in Bijpur, an agrarian hill town that was ripe with summer heat. Rooh had arranged for my stay with a farmer. The next day, Rooh took me into the greenroom, where I changed into a white pantaloon and a polo-necked T-shirt that had uncomfortably tight sleeves, flaring cuffs, and a pleated skirt sewn to its hem. What on earth am I wearing? I wondered as I stepped out into a dawn that burned with a deep crepuscular glow. Their bleached, wrinkled tents were set against a rocky hillock.

Rooh placed on my head a conical topee with a tassel sewn to it. He clutched both my wrists, raised one hand above my head, and set the other alongside my body. He stepped in front of me, cupped my face, and tilted it. "Eyes open, look skyward," he said.

He held my shoulder and turned me around slowly. "Feet fully on the ground, always," he said. "I shouldn't be able to slip even a leaf between your sole and the earth."

With Rooh's deceptively simple instruction in mind, I turned, and my feet, pressed to the ground, drew a circle in the sand; by my eighth revolution the other parts of my body claimed my attention—my stomach began to churn, I felt nauseated—and unwittingly, raising my heel off the ground, I turned a full circle on my toes. I become aware of my error only after it came to pass. The tents seemed to sway, and seconds later, I landed on my buttocks with a thud. I lay there, jaw dropped, my hands hanging limply at my side. Rooh squatted in front of me, pursed his lips, shook his head. He clutched my cuff and raised my hand.

"What are these," he said, pointing to one limp finger then another. "Tails of dead mice?"

I smiled despite myself.

"What kind of a dress is *this*?" I said, pointing to the skirt, the shirt, the cuff.

"It's a Sufi suit—what I'm trying to teach you is based on the Sufi whirling dance," Rooh said. "Nothing sacred about street theater, of course. Quite the opposite."

He let out a sigh and sat next to me. "Sahdëv, a veteran who worked with us until a few years ago—my, what a stalwart he was, the word 'stalwart' was made for men like him. If only you could have watched him play the gods or the kings of ancient lore—I'm talking Bharata, Pandu, Yudhisthira. Anyway. He always said: we may play the gods but we live our lives in the dirt."

"I'm off to a good start, then," I said, looking at my mud-streaked pantaloons.

He placed a hand on my shoulder. "Sahdëv would approve of your humble beginnings. Our duty, he'd say, is not to put the gods on a pedestal but to bring them closer to people. No fancy amphitheaters for us, he'd declare. The street, where life is lived, where accidents happen, that is where we'll put up our stage. Our meals come from the humble kitchens of those who watch us. Same reason why he never went to the big temples. He bowed his head at only roadside shrines where anyone could go, whatever their bank balance or caste. We use this dance as a means: to help your body shed its dead weight. To become fluid onstage."

After a pause, he added, "The secret to keeping nausea from invading your mind and gut, from causing your body to collapse, is not to draw your attention away from but channel it toward your body, specifically toward your feet on the ground."

"How'll I know when I've done it—shed my dead weight?"

"You will," he said. He held out one hand. "Let's try again."

I practiced every morning for the next six mornings while the other actors slept. Each day, I spun for a little longer. I did not sense the lightness that I imagined would follow the dispatch of "dead weight," as Rooh called it. What was it anyway and how had I acquired it—a little at a time, all at once?

Often, during those days, the life I had led thus far felt not so much hazy as impersonal: the countless meals we'd eaten in the kitchen as a family, the hours I spent in the cauldron at Magpies, it all came to me as expenditures of time with no attendant emotion. When I put on the Sufi suit, memories of my treehouse performances with my sisters came to me as fleeting, fractured recollections, tactile in nature— Milk pinning to my shirt the pleated folds of a chunni, Mud tucking a chunni between my shorts and my belly. My attention was claimed, when I wasn't learning or practicing, by a fear of the future. A future where I didn't make it to Nandi's troupe and Vikrant carted me off to Hanuman Male Fixing Center.

On the seventh morning, I went early for practice. It was still dark. Nandi wasn't around. In the greenroom I changed into the skirted top, pantaloon, and topee. Outside, I pressed my soles and toes flat to the ground, and emptying my head of all thoughts, I started to spin. Slowly, I picked up the pace and felt a rush of blood, of energy, rising from my feet, surging up my calves, my thighs, an electric charge that coursed through my spine as I whirled and whirled, returning my attention from the fact of my feet's momentum to the fact of their contact with the earth, which continued unhindered even once I slowed down and then, eventually, came to a halt like a train easing into its final destination.

My tongue tingled when I was done, as though I'd eaten a mint. The reality around me returned: the ochre of early morning washing the tents, Rooh standing before them, rubbing his jaw, the hills around us draped in glowing emerald tresses.

He came and embraced me. His heart beating against my chest, his palms pressed flat to my back, his chin on my shoulder. A hug free of lust. I wrapped my hands around his back. He pressed me to himself harder. The fabric of his shirt, which contained the heat and smell of him, gave me the permission to close my eyes, to let them brim over. He held me—he let me hold him.

When I stepped back, he wiped my cheeks with his thumb. I cleared my throat.

"Now what?" I said.

"Now," he said, "you learn how to pose."

The shedding of dead weight, I realized, was not a one-time event that I worked toward; it was the capacity to gather speed or slow down as unconsciously as we walk. The dance helped me cultivate an innate ease in acts of staged movement.

Rooh took me to a clearing in the woods the next morning and asked me to stand on my knees and fists like a four-legged creature. I folded my legs at my knees, pressed my feet to my buttocks. "Now walk like a lion," he said.

As soon as I raised a knee and a fist off the ground, I collapsed on myself like a house of cards, scraping my forearm. I assumed the posture and tried again, fixing my mind on the stagger of a lion, willing my body to replicate it. I could take two, then four steps without falling. I was not allowed to eat until evening during this phase of my training.

Three days later I could walk entire circles on all fours, my face burning with the hunger that I imagined was particular to a lion on the prowl.

Rooh turned me into other creatures over the course of that week: a grazing deer, the skin on my face twitching when I sensed a predator's eyes upon me, Rooh taking on the role of a predator, appearing from behind a tree, a thicket of bushes—never the same spot twice. I imagined the predator that Rooh performed to be Vikrant.

"If your body can carry the movements of the beasts, it can carry the life of any character," he said one evening as he ran Dettol-drenched cotton over a scraped knee.

Saaya undertook the third phase of my training. He led me one morning into the woods. He wore a brick-red sari over a white T-shirt, his long hair in a bun atop his head.

"The art of dialogue is not words, but how your voice forms the words," he said, arcing his long neck, running his hand along it. "Your voice must reveal the emotional state of your character. The audience should cringe, even if you cuss in the dark. Even when your voice is low, like that of a sad farmer, the person farthest from the stage must hear you."

"How can the audience hear me when my voice is low?"

"Hush," he said, and clutched my shoulder. He moved his face close to mine. "Listen."

I heard a low blubbering voice that sounded almost human. But there was an untrained quality to it, something that made it belong to the habitat of the wild, not to the human throat. He raised his hand and pointed. Several feet to our right, an orange beak peeped from between banyan leaves. He whispered, "If that bird were onstage, as its audience you're far away. But you hear." The orange beak disappeared. The sound of flapping wings rose from between shivering leaves. The bird glided past us, above the canopy.

He said, "Learn from the hornbill. How your voice goes far even when it's low."

I began imitating birdcalls that day: the happy whistle of a thrush, the guttural hoot of an owl, the angry screech of a bat, the hungry caw of a crow, the mating call of a myna, the longing coo of a nightingale. The hornbill's contemplative whimper.

"You're exercising your vocal cords with sounds of different kinds," Saaya said.

He made me drink a steaming hot juice of honey and beetroot to keep my voice from croaking.

"Like those street wrestlers exercising with different sorts of weight," I said.

"Yes," he said, bringing a hand to his chest. "Those oiled chests—"

I said, "Wiping the sweat off their stubbled upper lip with their fists. Slowly."

"Go away!" he said, laughing, playfully slapping my shoulder.

I went to bed each night with my fingers on my neck, feeling the tremors of the birdcalls in my throat.

Before leaving Magpies, I'd found, in the library's newspaper archive, four articles on missing adolescents forced into conversion therapy. I made copies and read them frequently over the course of my training. It kept my fear purposefully alive. One story in particular stood out to me. A boy who fled Hanuman Male Fixing Center. Never to be found again. His father forced him to go, his mother said. He went through six training cycles before he ran away. Forty-five days times six. Two hundred and seventy days. Nine months. He wasn't reborn. He continued to remain a boy like me. I said his name. Pritam Deogarh. He liked to be fucked, not do the fucking.

During one of those practice sessions with Saaya in the woods, as I mimicked after him his birdcalls, we heard heavy footsteps crunching the bed of dry leaves. We looked toward the sound to identify its source, and from between the thin branches of a creeper that had formed a curtain between two tree trunks, we saw the hazy form of Nandi as he made his way toward us.

"We're so dead if he sees us," Saaya exclaimed.

He pushed me behind a thicket of wild passionflowers.

"Just stay there," he whispered. "I'll come get you when the coast is clear."

When Nandi was almost upon us, Saaya took three big steps forward and crashed into Nandi, almost losing balance, finding his equilibrium with a hand to Nandi's shoulder.

"You scared me," Saaya said.

"What are you doing?" Nandi asked.

Saaya released a birdcall in response. Peacock.

"I heard that. Who were you doing it with?"

Saaya looked around, scanning the empty wilderness. Then he snapped his fingers. "Actually I was miming a peacock and his peahen. Listen."

He produced two shrill squawks of different registers.

"Enough with that now," Nandi said, covering his ears.

"I was so good you thought there were two of us?" Saaya said, clapping.

"Are you high or something?" Nandi said.

I pressed a hand to my mouth to hold back my laughter. They turned and left. The sounds of their departure were absorbed by the thicket of leaves that placed an increasing distance between us. The woods returned to a near primordial stillness.

Hours passed. The light of morning thickened into an afternoon heat that covered my flesh in perspiration, then ebbed into the melting-butter glow of twilight, then bled away, making way for night. I stayed where I was, listening: to the stillness, to its interruption—the chaos of birds returning to their nests—to the stillness that followed, deeper somehow, in the quiet after noise, in the dark after light.

My sisters, I remembered, collected dragonflies. They kept them under the domed grille in our treehouse. On the nights we playacted myths, the lantern light made them think it was morning. They buzzed out of their slumber. Their rainbow wings trembled. Their blue tails shivered. They hovered in fixed circles above a blue dish, and the water in it rippled.

What happened to the dragonflies the night the storm flooded our treehouse? Did they drown that night, did they escape and start families and flourish, or did they perish later, no longer able to survive in the open?

I heard the approach of thumping footsteps on the forest bed of dry leaves. A quick movement in the air before me, then the weight of Saaya falling next to me. Huffing, panting, breathless. I couldn't see him.

"Rooh was right," Saaya said. "You're still waiting here."

I shrugged.

After a pause, he asked, "What do you want?"

"What do you think I'm training for?"

"But why do you want it?"

"To be free," I said, then corrected myself. "To feel safe."

Safe from what, he didn't ask. I'm like you, I didn't say. Our bodies spoke in our stead. He wrapped his hands around me and cradled me against his chest. His heartbeat streamed through my flesh. I had a friend. A friend not separated by an iron wall's thickness.

Rooh commenced my training in swordfights. Lanterns winked off the edges of our painted cardboard swords as we leaped and turned in midair and landed with our torsos leaning forward, our swords positioned on the neck of our opponent. This practice, he told me, would teach me how to use my hands during performances and how to optimize use of the stage.

Then I learned the enactment of the nine principal theatrical emotions: stony face of fury, eyes brimming with compassion, cheeks swollen with laughter, lips trembling in horror, parted in wonder, shriveled in disgust, chin stiffened with pride, nose held high heroically, forehead creased with mercy, eyes twinkling with love. I approached them directly at first, mimicking an expression Rooh had, then at a slant, applying it to a character: Arjuna's sadness, Draupadi's disgust, Brihanalla's horror. Every morning, I woke up and wore these expressions like they were prized ornaments.

I started to enact characters in stories with arcs. Male-female, young-old, god-demon, human-animal: I swam across binaries like a fish moving from one river to another at the point of confluence.

Some nights Rooh massaged warm sesame seed oil into my weary

feet. The actors in the troupe did this for each other after every performance, he told me.

"You can return the favor once you join us," he said.

His words carried a sense of promise: my joining the troupe was
merely a matter of time.

Saaya and Rooh took me to the tent of the chieftain early in August.
Nandi, who sat cross-legged on a jute mat, reading from a palm leaf
manuscript, looked up and regarded us with an unblinking gaze, not a
trace of shock or anger on his face, as though it were perfectly normal for
the boy he had dismissed and his two seasoned actors to turn up together
in his tent.

"Give me any character, I'll perform for you," I said.

"You're here," Nandi said.

I apologized. I'd angered him, I thought, by following him to Bijpur
despite his rejection. He shook his head.

"But you're here," he said again, slowly this time. His tone, its texture,
was placid. "And I see these two," he said, pointing at Rooh and Saaya.
"My beloveds. My kids. My terrible, terrible parents. My Krishna, my
Bhima. My Sita, my Rama. Look, how they lean toward their protégé.
They want to hold you in their arms and carry you away to the stage this
second."

He piled the manuscript pages into an oilcloth and continued. "You
think an audition will tell me anything about your ability to travel with
us, share our beds, our makeup, our masks? Cry with us, laugh at us, fight
us, be reduced to your rawest animal self? There's no question of pretense
when we live together day in, day out *and* perform something so intense.
Will an audition measure an actor's desire to slog through the worst of
conditions, driven solely by our shared love for our myth?"

It was growing dark. Nandi lit a kerosene lantern and turned its knob.
A flame reared its head. In its light, I held his eyes and found a feeling
of kinship.

"What story do you want for your first performance?" he asked.

Saaya exclaimed, "Thank goodness. I broke my back training your stupid face!"

Rooh shrieked and clapped my back. He answered Nandi's question for me. "A sea elephant myth, of course."

Slowly, it sank in.

THE MOTHER OF
THE DROWNED CHILD

Nandi held my hand and led me into the greenroom at dusk. It was early August. The air was nippy. Monsoons would begin soon. Rooh, Saaya, and another actor, Adi, sat cross-legged before a mirror flanked by lanterns. The makeup man colored their faces, he gave them pencil mustaches.

Rooh would be my onstage husband, Prince Arjuna. The prince I became for the twins, the prince who, in myth, is cursed and becomes a woman for one year. Today I would be a woman for some hours. I would enter the greenroom as Shagun and leave it as Draupadi, the mother whose child is taken by a sea elephant. I sat down and gulped two glasses of water.

"It's your first time onstage today," Nandi said. "So I'll anoint you myself. Shagun?"

"What if I mess things up?" I asked.

"That's not possible," Nandi said.

"What do you mean *not* possible? Of course it's possible. I could forget a dance step, or my dialogue, or my position onstage—"

"You might forget a dance step *and* a dialogue *and* your position on stage," Rooh said.

"That's a distinct possibility," Saaya said.

"Thanks." I sulked and reached for the jug again.

Rooh said, "If you keep drinking, you'll want to piss so bad, you'll for sure forget your lines."

Saaya laughed. In the mirror Nandi's reflection smiled. He held my chin, tilted my head into his cupped palm.

"After Draupadi loses her child, will she *forget* what she wants to say?" Nandi said. "What to do when she and her child reunite: Isn't that her flesh knowledge?"

He gave me a copper bowl to hold. It was warm and contained a paste made of red beans and Kumkum powder. He dipped his thumb in it and ran it up my forehead, anointing me for my debut performance.

"You know what my father used to say?" Nandi said.

"How would he know what your father said," Rooh said. "Unless you're his uncle."

He laughed at his own joke, and Saaya joined him.

"How much did you two smoke?" Nandi said. Ignoring their raucous laughter, he continued, "My father was a farmer. When I was a boy, he'd take me out to the field at night. Some nights, when it was dark as a chunk of coal, we would look closely and find the shape of the new moon. A disc in black, a breath lighter than the rest of the sky.

"He would say that as the moon wanes from full to sickle to new moon it empties itself into the earth. So crops and plants may flourish and nourish every creature."

"No offense, Nandi," Rooh said, "but when you were a boy, what century was it?"

I smiled as I presaged my lovely loss: when I went up onto the stage, Shagun would be expelled from this body and Draupadi would possess it. I realized what it felt like to be the sky and watch the night fill your body.

The makeup man dipped his brush in a bowl of blue color and ran it over my skin.

"I will dress him myself," Nandi said after the color dried.

He held a maroon blouse stuffed with rags. I took my shirt off and stood with outstretched hands. His lowered eyes lingered for a second on the teeth marks that tattooed my breasts, faded but still there.

He slipped the blouse over my arms and onto my chest and then turned me around and hooked it. He held out a brick-red gown that I stepped into. He pulled it up. It sat snugly on my waist. He dressed me in a sari and held my shoulders.

"Remember," he said. "Myth is always told in the present tense."

In the violet hour of twilight, we gathered on the open-air stage where Nandi, in the unwavering light of an oil lamp, chanted verses in honor of the stage: triangular, bare, a white cloth serving as its backdrop. This single space would become many over the course of the performance: the left-hand side the sea where the elephants dwelled, the right-hand side the palace home of Draupadi and Arjuna; the back the heavenly abode of the gods, the front the beach where the three worlds would meet.

Nandi placed a pot filled with Ganga water next to a jute mat where our cardboard crowns, ornaments, and swords were spread out. He took the lamp and walked to the three corners of the stage and held the flame to each of the three torches. They crackled to life and, in the gathering darkness, spilled a vermilion brilliance across the clay-colored stage.

The performance began. I waited backstage.

Once upon a time, the gods took away the first sea elephant. His descendants cope with the trauma of this separation by taking human children away to their underwater abode. The practice continues, one generation after another. One day, a child the sea elephants kidnap is Avyukt, who is destined to serve as a key aide in the transition between the Age of the Gods and the Age of the Humans. So the gods conspire with Avyukt's mother, Draupadi, and come up with a plan to retrieve him: they launch upon the sea elephants an army of storm monsters and the elephants get busy fighting them.

"Look, the elephants are distracted," the gods say to Draupadi. "Bring back your son!"

That was my cue. I entered the stage and became Draupadi. The story's action became my present tense.

I plunge into the deep of the ocean. I swim for hours, going down, down, down, through a desert of liquid darkness. Then, in the far distance,

I see light: the ocean floor, glimmering like a bejeweled carpet. It is there that I find my son.

Starfish twinkle as they circle his forehead. He laughs and claps as an octopus taps eight corals, each producing a different note along the octave. A sea raga. A humpback and blue whale sing a duet in the sea language.

I move closer to my son. To steal him, to bring him to the surface, where the gods are waiting to give him back his mortal body. But the moment I touch his shoulder I sense that my boy is not a boy but a soul. And souls are beyond the confines of gender. So I refer to my child as "they," not "he."

I hear the trumpet of the sea elephants rising from their flesh. As though their shoulder is a shell, my hand an ear.

A hermit crab passing by notices my perplexed expression. He tells me in his grandfather voice that a longing has remained in the sea elephants ever since their first ancestor was taken by the gods. Only a drowned child's company can soothe them.

"The sound of their longing fills everyone who becomes part of the sea elephant family," the crab says, looking at my child. "It's as much a part of them as breath. As sight. As being. The throat of this child too is no longer capable of songs with more than five notes."

I pause a moment. But I have made my decision. I wrap both hands around my child.

"Are you happy here?" I ask, and they confirm that they are and press into my hands a shell.

"Did you know, Ma," they say, "every oyster goes to the surface of the sea, swallows a raindrop, and turns it, over time, into a pearl. As it sits quietly on the ocean bed."

I open the shell and find the pearl they describe. I can't tell if it is the ocean's salt I taste on my lips or my own. I swim back to the surface.

When the gods see me empty-handed, they're confused and angry.

"Where is our boy?" asks Arjuna, holding aloft the corpse of our son.

I caress the gaunt, lifeless cheek of my child, his small chin. How was it that only hours back I had seen him alive and happy, at home inside the sea?

"Our longing is of a lifetime," I say. I gesture to the sea. "Their longing is old as time itself."

"You've made the biggest sacrifice a mother can make," say the gods. "Are you selfless or coldhearted?"

"I'm a mother," I say.

They take my son's body from my husband's hands and leave. He embraces me, his hands still warm from my son's heat. I close my eyes and lean into that warmth.

We left the stage, then returned to take a bow. I observed our audience: the lanterns at their feet, the shadows on their faces, their brows lined with furrows as they joined their hands above their heads. As though we had, by virtue of enactment, become those gods and sacred characters.

As I stepped off the stage, I turned and found her amid the smoke and torchlight and we locked eyes: Draupadi and Shagun, occupants of the same body. I brought a hand to my wrist, to sense my pulse, to check which body was real.

I returned to the greenroom and took off my blouse, sari, gown, and wig of long hair. I cried and laughed all at once. Rooh and Saaya hoisted me on their shoulders and ran around the greenroom.

"Clean up now and join us for a meal," Rooh said. He left with Saaya.

As I put on the shirt and trousers in which I'd entered the greenroom earlier that day, the voices of Mud and Milk came to me: in quick succession they each declared a line from the play.

The elephants are distracted, bring back your son, said Mud.

The oyster turns a raindrop to a pearl, Milk said.

I started, looked around, closed my eyes, aching to cradle their voices.

The next time a performance ended I will be prepared to receive them, I decided.

The need to get away from the site of my sisters' death had influenced my decision to go to Magpies, just as the desire to turn our childhood game into a living had fueled my desire to be a performer. I recognized both truths. The stories from the myths were now our childhood geography: Mud's, Milk's, mine.

I heard footfalls and turned quickly to splash water on my face.

"Are you crying?" Nandi asked.

"The makeup must've gotten into my eyes," I said.

"I have something for you," Nandi said. He handed me a heavy red bundle. I opened it and saw a brass crown studded with blue and green stones.

"Five generations have worn this crown, Shagun. It holds the stories of a hundred heroes."

He leaned forward. His face shone with excitement. A bell chimed in the distance.

"Every hurdle you have faced, every persecution, they brought you to this exact moment," Nandi said. "For embracing the destiny you were not born into, this gift is yours."

I touched his feet in gratitude, for the ancient heirloom he gave me, for the story he let my body live.

CIRCUS SON

I wrote to Magpies, telling them I wasn't coming back for twelfth grade. I will let the school inform Ma, I decided. I felt a severe pang of guilt for not telling her myself. I pictured her letters to me arriving at Magpies, unanswered at first, eventually getting returned along with a letter: the news of my removal from the roster, rendered clinically on a school letterhead. She would call Magpies seeking my whereabouts. I felt her frantic fear when she learned of their ignorance on the matter. Still. My own fear selfishly kept me from alleviating hers. She would tell Pita-jee that I was dropping out of school, and I didn't want him to know until my severance with the school was official. It felt, at an instinctual level, inevitable to my safety: that sequence of events. So I carried her fear inside my chest next to mine.

After I dropped my letter to Magpies and turned away from the postbox, I remembered that my studies had for years been my one reliable source of validation. I snapped out of anonymity when my teachers quoted my skill—with chemical equations and trigonometry, for remembering with precision Assam's vegetation and the many battles at Panipat—as qualities my classmates should aspire to. As I headed back to the tents, I thought of my grade book and my friend, the ayah, the critiques, claps, and clove chai she shared with me, and I sat down on a roadside bench and allowed my loss to wash over me.

We left Bijpur the next day. Our time on the road began. Six of us—Rooh, Saaya, and I, the troupe's permanent actors; Adi, Deva, and Esha, our seasonal performers—sat in the open back of the truck, on top of folded tents, sleeping bags, and dhurries. We were performers who doubled as stagehands, technicians, and set builders and dismantlers.

Nandi drove. The passenger seat was stacked with two boxes that carried our props and makeup. As we drove uphill, the cold August winds gradually gave way to air thicker with moisture. Up in the Himalayas, the monsoons had already begun.

I hollered to be heard over the noise of the wheels on the bumpy road.

"I like this," I said. "Being on the move all the time."

"You'll get sick of it," Rooh said. "The wind in your hair is romantic only for so long."

"We're not 'always' on the move, darling," Saaya said. "We've been grounded."

Rooh slapped his forehead. "You love starting shit," he said. He turned to me. "Listen, I've been with the troupe—"

"For fourteen years," Saaya said. "You old."

"And it's happened twice—twice in fourteen years—that Nandi took a gig that needed us to stay put."

"Stay put for how long?" I asked.

"Some five-six months?" Rooh said.

"Why did it happen?" I asked.

"Recession once, once war with Pakistan. Made money tight, so people spend less for entertainment."

"Nandi found us sponsors who kept us going until things got better," Saaya said. "The second time I was there. It was this landlord who gave us shelter and fed us and we performed for his friends."

"For six months?" I asked.

"We took on gigs as farmhands," Adi said, pointing with his chin to Deva and Esha.

"So it was just Nandi, me, and this bully," Saaya said, wagging a finger at Rooh.

On the fourth night, we set up tents in a town where we were going to perform for three days. I went up to Saaya with my two bedsheets.

"Can I sleep next to you?" I asked.

"What do you have in mind, naughty boy?" Saaya teased.

I spread a sheet on the floor and lay down. The lanterns were put out. Six Tortoise Pesticide Coils were burned. The town was notorious for its mosquitoes. Our tent filled with a thick smoke, and we started to cough.

"Dad sent this man to meet me," I said. "He runs Hanuman Male Fixing Center."

The dark was punctuated with coughs, mine, my fellow actors'.

Saaya said, "They have a reputation. In cahoots with the cops, I heard. What did he say?"

"That he'll come find me wherever I go. Of course, if I'm always on the move—"

"That's your solution?"

"Until I cook up something better."

"Like putting the bastards out of business?"

I heard him sniff. My throat felt raw but I didn't cough.

"Tell Nandi," he said.

"He'll think it's the reason I'm here."

"He'll understand. If things get bad, he'll help."

In the dark, he took my hand.

"It stopped," I said. "The coughing."

"Our lungs get used to the smoke."

We performed in a cluster of six different hill towns in Uttar Pradesh during that summer. I played walk-on parts, minor roles, central characters. When we shed the skins of gods, I became an animal with a shape-shifter's ease. We threw stuff at each other, mugs if we bathed in the open, fistfuls of sand on our way to the tents. We stole from each other's plates. From my mouth flew the sort of vile vocabulary that I did not know existed within me. We knew each other's smell like our own. "Saaya, is that you stinking up the room? Go take a shower!" I once said, and I was right.

Physical proximity sharpened our craving for flesh. When we traveled by night, six of us sleeping in the back of the truck, we used the rumble of the rickety ride as a mask to pleasure ourselves in a way that we could not in the stillness of our tents. Imagining the men I'd desired—Rusty, Senior, Furniture—coupled with Bollywood actresses allowed me to climax. When I imagined mutual lovemaking—Senior/me, Furniture/me—the anxiety that had gripped me when Senior and I kissed filled me and I would wilt in the grip of my fist. After one unsuccessful attempt a memory came to me in my dream: Ma and Pita-jee, illuminated by the lighthouse. Thereafter, I excluded myself from my fantasies.

I woke up one morning to the smell of weed. My fellow actors, huddled under blankets, were fast asleep. Saaya's bed was empty. I got up, pushed aside the tent flap, and stepped into the foggy blue morning.

Saaya, squatting on his haunches, faced the woods. When I sat next to him, he offered me the joint without looking at me. I shook my head. His face was varnished with sweat, his neck red.

"Was it good?" I asked.

"It did the job," he said.

"How do you find them?" I asked.

"Easy," he said. "They look at me a moment too long when we go take a bow."

The tip of his joint brightened, the burn of paper and herb a crisp, clean sound. The smoke drained out his nostrils.

"The man I met today," he said, "he's my regular. Whenever we pass through this town. One time he dropped his wallet. I saw a photo of his woman and kid."

"That doesn't bother you?"

"Rooh does it too," Saaya said. "Nandi doesn't care. Just don't bring them over."

"Knowing my luck, it'll happen the one time I decide to fool around with someone," I said. "I'll get caught and they'll put me away."

"'They' being that Vikrant character and his goonies?"

I nodded. He stretched his hand and squeezed my shoulder, his gaze fixed forward.

"You can either be you or be your watchdog. It's going to have to be one or the other."

He offered me the joint. I shook my head. He returned it to his lips.

"Pick a town that's big enough. No one will notice."

On one occasion, a village chief hosted us. He invited us to his living room after dinner and took out an album of photographs. I was worried he'd subject us to an elaborate family story, and we had to wake up early the next day to practice our performance. The chief, however, opened the tome to a page in the middle and located, with the ease of a homing pigeon, a particular picture. In it, he stood with a man who looked like him but younger. Next to them was a light-skinned foreigner.

"He's our friend," the chief said. "From America he is."

The information will lead into an anecdote, I thought. But he had no more to say. He closed the album and bade us good night.

Rooh told me later that it was not uncommon: locals photograph themselves with unknown white men, claim they are friends, and take pride in that claim.

"It sickens me, fascination like this," Nandi said.

"We have only a thousand years of light-skinned monarchy to thank," Rooh said. "First the Mughals, then the British."

"Your heart wants what it wants," I said.

"It's not like they're in love with him," Saaya said.

"It's not romantic love, sure, but fascination is a kind of love," I said.

"Educated people say such fancy things," Saaya said.

"I'm a senior secondary dropout," I said.

"Nandi is a fifth-grade dropout," Saaya said. "Rooh and I never went to school. By our standards you're a scholar."

We arrived in the pilgrim town of Uttarkashi, nestled in the Himalayas, nearly four thousand feet from the sea where my sisters had drowned. It was September. Nandi bought us each a glass of chai, and I held it at my mouth but didn't drink it. It steamed my face with the scent of ginger as I shivered in a borrowed oversize sweater and watched the Ganga roar by.

School would've begun by now. Had I been removed from the roster? Did they inform Ma? My greater concern, I realized, was to tell Rusty.

I gulped down my chai, now cold, and got up to make the call.

"Don't be out too late," Nandi hollered as he watched me leave.

From the phone booth at the post office, I called Magpies and asked for Rusty. The metal of the earpiece was cold against my ear. I was told to call back in ten. I shivered and sat with my shoulders hunched. When I called back, Rusty picked up the phone on the second ring.

"What do you want?" he asked after I identified myself.

"I left Magpies."

"Did you?"

"Classes started and I'm not there, am I?"

After a prolonged pause, he said, "Call home, Bitch Bags."

A question surfaced to my mind and I posed it before I could censor myself.

"My sisters—how did you know?"

"About what you did to them? Call home," he repeated and hung up.

The next day, after the performance, after our audience left, after my troupe members retreated to their tents, I stepped into the waters of the Ganga and walked until I was completely underwater, the noises behind me replaced with the gulping noise made by water. As if I was swimming in the throat of the river goddess. With my eyes closed I imagined Mud and Milk in my place but without the option available to me: to bring their heads up for air when needed.

I held my breath and heard devotees taking a holy dip: stepping into the river, bending their knees, and immersing themselves fully in the water, then rising back to the surface with a splash to say a prayer, to make a wish.

I remained underwater even after I became breathless. My lungs started to burn. I counted to six and surfaced, but slowly. When I wiped the water out of my eyes and looked toward the shore, the water lodged in my ears belching against my eardrums, I found Nandi sitting cross-legged and working his prayer beads. His eyes were open, his gaze fixed on the horizon.

I sat next to him, hands wrapped around my knees, dripping, cold, shivering.

As the sun rose farther up and filled the air with warmth, with brightness, my clothes started to dry. I turned my head skyward. I unwound my limbs. The cold slowly left my flesh.

"Didn't you tell me you playacted these stories with your sisters?" asked Nandi. "In your hometown that's by the Bay of Bengal?"

"I did," I said. "The day we met."

"See, I do listen. Even when you're annoying. Which you were that day. Admit it."

I laughed and pressed my wrists to my eyes.

I said, "If, say, someone finds out where I am and comes for me, what happens?"

"If you want to stay, end of discussion."

"Even if I'm not like everyone else?"

He said, "You're the first upper-caste actor I accepted into my troupe."

"I don't care about caste," I said.

He smiled. "Isn't that nice, to not care about caste?"

I understood my blunder.

"I'm sorry," I said.

"I took you in," he said, "because I recognize that you are not like everyone else. You are as much an outcast as us in the eyes of your fellow upper-caste folk."

He moved closer and wrapped a hand around my shoulder.

"When I was young, I used to ask myself: Why do I love telling these stories of the gods when religion has done nothing but punish my people? As I got older, I realized that injustice in the name of religion— that's the work done by men of god. My love for the stories of gods has nothing to do with them.

"My performance is my personal religion, Shagun. I want us to tell the stories of our gods properly. That's all I ask of my family—all of you."

We shared a moment of silence.

I said, "There's a second volume, apparently, of the sea elephant stories."

"So I've heard. Never seen a copy myself."

Before we left Uttarkashi, I went back to the post office and placed a collect call for Ma. As I waited inside the booth for her to call back, I watched the activity outside: people posted letters, made money orders, employees branded stamps with the postal seal, mailmen left with letter-bloated satchels.

The phone exploded with a loud ring and I started and grabbed the handle. It slipped from my hands and swung on its spiral chord. The voice it emitted sounded like a little girl's. As if Ma was possessed by Mud or Milk.

I picked up the handle. "Hello? You can hear me?"

"No need to shout," Ma said.

The people outside were staring at me.

"Where are you?" she exclaimed. "We've been looking for you high and low."

"The school contacted you?"

"And this man came looking for you. Wait."

I heard her rifle through some papers.

"Who's this Vikrant?"

"You told him I dropped out of school?"

"Do we mean anything to you, son? You apply to Magpies, you don't tell us, you decide to drop out, nothing, now your vanishing act. Your father was ready to file a missing person's report. It took all my power to stop him. I knew you were okay. Call it a mother's instinct."

"Your *mother's instinct* didn't figure out why Vikrant is after me?"

"*After* you? What kind of mess did you get yourself into?"

"Ask Pita-jee. Tell him he's the reason I'm a dropout."

"And what do I tell him you're doing instead?"

I told her then that I had joined a street theater troupe on a permanent basis. My first role was Draupadi, I said.

"So that's what I should tell your father? That his boy joined the circus?"

"You wish it was me, don't you? Wish it was me instead of my sisters."

She'll refute my claim, I thought. Vehemently. Instead, she asked, "Where are you?"

"Why should I tell you," I said, stung by her response. "You'll go tell Pita-jee."

"You think he'll come drag you back to school? He has better things to do. It's your life. Ruin it as you please. Strut around wearing Banarasi saris all you like."

"Oh, I will. Send your wedding bangles. I'll wear them for a bridal night scene."

"Shagun!"

For another moment I heard her labored breathing. Then came the sound of dead air. I went to sign the slip that recorded the start and the end time of the call. The postmaster offered me a glass of water that I drank in slow, loud gulps, never separating my mouth from the lip of the glass. "More?" he asked when I was done. I thanked him, put the glass down, and left the post office. Wind brushed my cheeks, and they felt colder than the rest of my body. I touched my face and found it wet.

By the time I returned to the campsite, the last of our tents had been pulled down, rolled, and loaded into the bed of our truck. From the distance Rooh hollered, "You conveniently slipped away when it was time to do all the hard work, you bastard."

It was all said in jest. It was nearly time to leave.

SHAGUN, OR THE 1980S BOLLYWOOD (MELLOW)DRAMA QUEEN

Nandi's troupe, I discovered, had six seasonal actors, and during my first year with the troupe I worked with all of them. Adi, Deva, and Esha joined us during the Kharif cropping season, June through September; Swastik, Tomer, and Usha during the Rabi cropping season, October through May, a time during which we returned to Nandi's hometown, Manna.

It felt like a pilgrimage, that return, exactly a year later, in April 1991. I met the farmer who hosted me, I returned to the temple where I had witnessed my first performance. The sea elephant myth. That act of witnessing the performance had forged a connection between the treehouse that contained my sisters and me and the temple courtyard that contained the actors who became my fellow performers, and in the gentle wash of that connection, the gods, who had become the exacting overlords of Pita-jee's principles, became once more the heroes of the stories that my sisters and I shared. I could, through performance, invite them into my body, live their lives, and speak their language freely.

After one of our performances in Manna, Saaya told me I played the parts of women with particular effectiveness. We were washing off our makeup. I had played Rama's brother that day.

"Today I wasn't good, then?" I asked.

"You were good," he said. "But you seem more in your element in female roles."

I started to splash water on my face from a bucket to wash off the blue paint. Then, as I closed my eyes and began scrubbing a cake of soap against my skin, he said, "Nothing wrong in dressing like a woman if that's what you want. Offstage, I mean."

"I know. But—" I paused as I put the bar away and reached for the bucket again to wash the slime of soap mixed with makeup off my face.

"No shame in it," Saaya repeated.

I clutched the edges of the bucket, and with my eyes still closed, I said, "I can play women well onstage, like that, and wear T-shirts and trousers as I go about my day. Right?"

No sooner had I said it than I realized the severity of my tone. But I felt no guilt. I had not left one kind of bounded life to enter another where everything I did had to be nonconformist.

"Right." It was Rooh's voice. "You do you."

I washed my face with a few quick splashes of water and, with my hands still on the bucket, looked over my shoulder and sensed in the air a tension that I was not the source of; it belonged to a history Rooh and Saaya shared.

"Now," Rooh said. "If you two slowpokes are done cleaning up, should we go to the ghat? They're starting the show soon."

We changed and followed Rooh and joined the crowd gathered to witness the concluding event of the Rama Navami festival. A man, painted blue, shot an arrow, whose tip was on fire, at a ten-foot cardboard effigy of Ravan that was stuffed with fireworks. The arrow made contact and set fire to a spinning wheel in the demon's belly. Glorious explosions followed: rockets taking off from the demon's ears, erupting in the sky into glittering circles of red and green, flowerpots shooting sparkling fountains from his shoulders, sparklers spitting fire from his fingertips. He was surrounded by a cloud of smog as he quivered under the force of all that energy's release.

Saaya and I stood next to each other, but neither then nor later that night did we talk.

By the next morning, though, we fell back into an easy camaraderie again, he in his favorite brick-red sari, I in a T-shirt and old jeans. We didn't address the night gone by.

Early next year, we performed in the riverside town of Nasik. I was with Saaya at the farmers' market, shopping for hibiscus flowers for our second performance, and we were having a discussion about the color of the flower: Yellow or orange?

"Take the yellow," a man said, his eyes fixed on me, a full head taller. "And we can go eat after. There's a restaurant near my house that makes very good puri."

He didn't expend time with the formalities of introductions and courtship. What he sought was fleeting. A one-time rendezvous that would end before the day did.

"Actually, we'll take the orange," I said, turning to Saaya. "We're performing at dusk and the color stands out better in that light."

"Glad you got that figured out," Saaya said, placing a hand on the man's shoulder. "Because I'm starving and just about ready to stuff my face." He turned to the man and added, "With puri of course. Get your mind out of the gutter."

They laughed as they turned together and walked away.

When Saaya came back that evening, he found me running a thread around the stems of the flowers, stitching a hibiscus canopy for our show. He sat next to me and let out a contented sigh.

"*Puri* that good, huh? Glad you had fun while I carried two baskets full of flowers back through a crowded market."

He leaned back on his elbows and said, "You should've gone with him. No boogeymen came for me, see?"

I slapped a bundle of thread and a needle cushion onto his lap. We worked together quietly for some time.

"It's not that I don't have wants," I said. "I say I don't want to risk it, and it's true, but that's because a hookup isn't really what I want, so it doesn't feel worth the risk."

"What do you want, Brahmin boy? To be a temple bride, married off to the Lord Himself?"

"I want a man who comes home to me, day after day. I wake him up with bed breakfast and pack his lunch. I keep his house, wash his sneakers, do the dishes, and iron his clothes."

Saaya burst out laughing. "What you want is to be a housewife from a 1980s Bollywood melodrama. Or that lady who mopes and coos to a swan as she pines for her prince charming to come back from exile—what myth was that again?"

"Mellow Drama is more my speed," I said.

"The desire for roots, it's against our troupe's basic values, Mr. Smarty-pants," Saaya said. "On the move all the time, no attachments."

"Adi, Deva, and Esha work part-time," I noted. "So do Tomer, Swastik, and Usha."

"Nandi makes that exception for farmers. They till their lands and perform with street theater after their harvest. That's tradition. And Nandi honors tradition."

Our canopy was stitched. We stretched it across the four poles that Rooh had erected earlier. It was a perfect fit.

"Sit with me awhile," Saaya said, so we sat next to each other, under the canopy of hibiscus. Between the orange petals lay strips of a star-studded, violet sky.

"My body wouldn't just open itself to pleasure like that: meeting a stranger for a bit, getting down to business, then going our separate ways," I said. "If it's a man who loves me enough to wait and we live our lives together in the meanwhile, I'll start to trust him and eventually my body will too. Thing is, would I matter that much to anyone?"

Saaya grabbed the nape of my neck and kissed me on the temple. I made a show of feeling disgusted and wiping my face.

I wanted it all: to be safe, to be free, to perform, to belong to someone. Who do you think you are? I asked myself bitterly. Has your history taught you nothing? I remembered Rusty's hands on my man breast, my father's hands on my back, my sisters' hands trembling as they drowned. You're not lucky, I told myself.

"So you don't want to get caught, that's why you're on the run, won't hookup, et cetera," Saaya said. "But you'll set up a house that has an address and live there with your man? Is a wedding also a part of your plan, you know, complete with the evidence of a video recording and wedding cards? Very logical, Shagun. Makes so much sense."

He ran into the night, laughing, and I chased after him, willing myself to forget the truth whose blow his joke had softened.

THE SIXTH SUMMER

My sixth summer with the troupe, the summer of 1996, was unlike the five that came before. Our performances in the hill towns of Uttar Pradesh did not draw the crowds that they typically did and the mood of our troupe started to turn somber. Nandi left town, asking us to carry on with our performances, appointing Rooh as the troupe's interim head.

When Nandi returned, about three weeks later, he took Rooh, Saaya, and me for a walk along the Ganga. It was a humid morning. We were performing in the town of Uttarkashi. Nandi informed us that we would not, as planned, go to Banaras when August ended. We would go to Chamba instead, unaccompanied by our seasonal actors.

Nandi said, "Between September of this year and May next year, the four of us will collectively teach one class on street theater to the students of the National School of Drama. In return we will each receive private accommodation and a monthly renumeration."

The breeze smelled of silt and was sticky.

"We've had three prime ministers in this one year and the political mess has translated, naturally, to an economic mess," Nandi said. "Share market, city rents, the great middle class, their struggle with the prices of petrol and onions: that's all the newspapers write about. The rural sector's the worst hit, but who cares."

He unknotted his turban and wiped his neck with the cloth. He continued, "In U.P. there are farmers so deep in debt, they're hanging themselves. In Bihar, families are taking out loans on their unborn children. Can you imagine that, to become indentured before you are born?"

Given the reality of our audience, Nandi said, it seemed irresponsible to seek out their already-strained resources. In pursuit of an alternative, he had been corresponding with the school's principal since May, a man he was introduced to by a common friend and whom he had met in person in Chamba, the destination of his recent trip.

He said, "We lack the education to stand before a class, but we have experiences that the school's full-time faculty lack, and I will help you turn that into compelling classroom material."

"What happens after this nine-month stint?" Saaya asked.

"I don't know yet," Nandi said.

We found a spot and sat down. For six years, I had been on the run, from Pita-jee, from Vikrant; for nine months now I would be stationed in Chamba.

Over the years, I'd added to my collection of newspaper clippings about boys trapped by the Hanuman Male Fixing Center. It traveled with me along with the brochure. I didn't want to forget what I was fleeing. I didn't want to get lax. I now remembered that one of the stories was about a college-age boy who'd fled his hometown when he heard his father on the phone, informing someone about his son's proclivities, begging them to come take him and fix him. Two years later, they found him anyway. Two states away, where he worked in a garment factory. Who had given away his location? The article didn't reveal this information.

As if he'd read my mind, Nandi said, "Shagun. If anything strange happens—anything that feels even slightly out of line—"

"I'll come to you, yes," I said.

That was how, toward the end of August, we came to Chamba and mounted, on the first Sunday of September, a play called *First Desire*: a play that gave our students and the local audience an impression of our aesthetic, a play that introduced me to the love of my life.

PART IV
1996–1997

FIRST DESIRE

The performance began. The hour wore the dark skin of night. The lanterns of our audience, who sat in an open field, flickered in the mountain breeze. The deodar woods behind them flickered with a swarm of fireflies.

A gas lamp illuminated the giant egg—wooden frame, satin skin—that sat center stage. Six of us sat inside. Nandi's baritone narration began.

"At first, there was only the primordial egg. Filled with the unrealized seeds of Life."

The gas lamp was extinguished. We who were inside the egg passed around a lantern in time to a drum. Our audience saw a buttery light swish swiftly against taut, translucent satin.

The performance ended. The sun was out. The egg was loaded onto a truck. The stage's khadi-white backdrop, unknotted by men on ladders, slipped against a timber backbone and fell to the floor, liquid as waterfall.

I walked to the edge of the ground where, a few hours ago, our audience sat. I heard, as always, snatches of the myth in the voices of my sisters. Mud first, then Milk. And we shared a moment. A line of theater.

"The egg thought, I exist," Mud said.

Milk followed. "But I exist alone."

"That was one hell of a show": that line was not in the play. I heard it in neither Mud's voice nor Milk's.

I turned around and took note of the speaker: a man with ginger hair, curled at the tips; his nose a pointed marble ridge; his eyes a shade of blue I couldn't name.

It was a dance I had seen often: men approaching me, postperformance, conveying their interest directly, tangentially, or, at times, quietly, their body speaking in their stead. I tried a tactic that often succeeded in thwarting such advances: I crossed my arms and looked behind me, away from him. After a moment, I turned in his direction again, expecting to see his back as he walked away from me.

Instead, I saw him standing there, still facing me. He held his hand out and smiled guilelessly. As I shook it, he took a step toward me. He was long-limbed; even his simple movements exuded the practiced elegance of an acrobat. My palm felt sticky when I repaired from the handshake.

"Got you messy, did I?" he said.

He extracted an apple from his pocket. The red, unbitten side faced me. I took it, turned it, and saw the marks his teeth left on the cream-white flesh. He was eating it a few seconds before he met me, he said. His tongue wasn't navigating a language learned at school with physics and maths. He was born into English.

"What brings you to Chamba?" I asked. "You a tourist?"

He touched his pale cheek. "That, mister, is stereotyping."

I opened my mouth to protest, to mention his accent.

"Breathe," he said. "There you go. You promoted your play at the train station, remember? You obviously did a great job—I'm here! Something about it struck a chord. Weren't you wearing the same thing?" His inquiry had to it the ring of the genuine.

We arrived in Chamba the fortnight prior, I told him, and walked through the markets and streets, picking up gestures and lingo particular to the townspeople and then incorporating them in our promotional announcement last week. We wore for that occasion the costumes that we would eventually perform in.

"That combination—familiar mannerisms and words and unfamiliar costumes—it captures your attention," I said. "The announcement is its own kind of theater."

He looked impressed.

"It isn't my idea," I said. "Our theater chief, Nandi, he came up with it."

"The way you spoke about it," he said. "Clearly your work is a thing you love."

"So what were you doing at the train station that day?"

"Not buying tickets for my next tourist destination."

I smiled.

"I work for the railways," he said. "What's your name?"

How many men who came up to me with the intention I suspected this man of had asked my name?

"Shagun Mathur."

"Marc—Marc Singer."

Singer like Singer sewing machines, I wanted to say but my tongue thickened at the thought of joking with him.

"This is where you say 'Nice to meet you,'" he said, switching unexpectedly to an English accent. It was, as I would soon learn, one of his ticks.

I remembered, as I stared at him, running with my sisters to the port to see Englishmen. As if beauty was our tourist destination. I remembered Mud's pretense: her face powder-caked, her accent a poor but confident imitation. They would've liked Marc, I thought. I imagined all three of us courting him, vying for his attention.

Marc circled my face with a forefinger. "What am I to make of this look?"

He'd assumed his American accent again. Six workmen entered the grounds, three from either end. They picked up the durries where our audience had sat and whipped and folded them as whorls of dust surrounded them, solar-tinted. Their actions felt like theater, meticulously choreographed. Only Marc felt real: his red hair, the oud scent of him, the unnameable blue of his eyes. A vein throbbed on his forehead. The wings of his nose flexed when he drew a sharp breath. A bead of sweat slid down his upper lip. He wiped it with a fist and looked at me and I quickly averted my gaze.

I heard the truck honk and turned. Saaya stood on the bed of the truck, next to the egg.

"I have to go," I said.

"'Go' as in leave town?" Marc asked, rubbing his throat.

"Some of our actors leave tonight. Some of us are staying."

He smiled. "Staying where?"

"School guesthouse."

"I know the place. You're working with the school?"

"Nine months."

"That's brief!"

"It's actually long. We usually stay anywhere between three and ten days."

"When is it three, and when is it ten?"

What did he want? Now I was really curious.

"Three-four days is more standard. Two performances, with a day or two separating them. We stay longer if our performance coincides with a festival, like the Ganesha Puja or the Durga Puja—"

"Or Rama Navami?" he asked. "For Pete's sake, don't look so surprised that I know it."

Who is Pete? I wanted to ask.

"What are you doing on Friday at five?" he asked. "I'm having some friends over and there's going to be food and music. Want to join us? I can come get you."

His invitation gave me the clarity I sought. He struck a conversation because he was interested in me, not in executing a carnal transaction. The thought exhilarated and rattled me. What if I squandered what potential there was with my inadequacies and fears?

"Nandi—my boss—might have chores for me," I said.

"Listen, I'll show up, if you can make it, great, if not, I'll be on my merry way. Yeah?"

"I like how you Americans speak."

He smiled as he stepped closer. His hands, when he spread them out, grazed my arms and I flinched. When he continued to stand there, with his arms spread open, I decided to accept his invitation to hug him. But as I took a step toward him—my hands, partially raised, my fists clenched, my body language suggesting a wrestler's pose more than a reciprocal gesture of affection—he, perhaps having noted my initial hesitation, dropped one hand and held the other out, inviting me to a handshake. And just as he noticed my delayed reciprocation of his hug and reverted to spreading his arms like Shah Rukh Khan in *DDLJ,* I placed one hand behind my back and held the other out.

I broke into a laughter that occupied a vector between embarrassed and awkward. He cupped my hand with both of his and pulled me gently toward him, and when our bodies touched, he wrapped his arms around me.

The hug we finally fell into was one of compromised heights, he bending forward, I standing on my toes so we could each set our chin on the shoulder of the other. I held his apple in one hand and pressed the palm of my free hand to his spine. He shifted his head. His stubble scratched at my neck. His breath exploded on my nape. Warm. Smelling of apple. I closed my eyes. His body's heat swelled against my chest, my thighs. He moved his hand down my back, up my arm, leaving on my skin a trail of himself, finger-shaped bands of heat. I pressed my forehead to his neck. The wariness I felt toward him evaporated. I wanted to hold him for as long as I could without coming off as a creep.

Anxiety congested my chest. My heart palpitated, like it would break off the sinews that kept it anchored in place and slip and fall into my belly. Then I lost the smells: his breath's fruity zest, the underlying musk of his sweat. Then I lost my sense of touch: my hand no longer sensed the hardness of his back muscles, my body no longer felt his heat. For a moment I had the distinct impression that he, Marc, was no more than a fabrication of my love-starved mind.

My eyes flew open and I stumbled back. His hands fell to his side, and there he was, grinning like mischief itself, his hair teased by the wind, his body material as mine.

He said, "You look like you've seen a ghost."

I brought his apple to my nose. Its smell milder than it was in the air from his mouth. The anxiety I'd felt when Senior kissed me had returned.

Amplified. Its aftereffects lingered: I was short-breathed; the wind on my skin had a razor's edge.

The truck honked again. He pointed to the apple.

"Keep it—you're welcome," he said in a voice that felt like a wink.

Before I could tell him that I didn't want it, he walked away with a swagger that suggested comfort more than confidence—confidence that had become habit.

I hurried toward the roaring truck. Rooh hauled me up. I sat down between him and Saaya. The truck moved and we exaggeratedly tumbled onto each other. The game never got old. A few minutes later they each brought a head to my shoulder and closed their eyes.

I licked his teeth marks on the apple and remembered the play. The second scene.

Nandi had said: "The egg thought, I exist, but I exist alone. If only there was someone else. Incubated in the heat of this longing, the seeds inside the egg ripened. Then they spilled out, became manifest expressions of Life."

We moved our fingers on the satin surface. Rooh ran a penknife along the center and we leaped onto the stage: a human, a serpent, a lion, a fish, a flower.

Nandi said: "With life came the need to keep an account of creaturely hours, to create, where there was a beginning, an end. Time was born from the first desire."

BACK-TO-SCHOOL DAY

Our classes at the drama school commenced the day after our performance. We each taught the same group of students one day a week. Nandi taught his class on Monday. On Tuesday, my first day of teaching, I went to my class with a flask and six paper cups. I asked my students to follow me. We went back to the site of our performance. It was the second week of September and the air was nippy—Chamba was surrounded by mid-range Himalayan hills—but not cold enough, not yet, to warrant sweaters.

I had my students sit on the stage cross-legged and gave them each a cup that I filled with ginger chai from the flask as I learned their names. Ronit. Gupta. Sahil. Ankit. Mohit. Dev.

"High, firm, tilted," I began. "These are the requirements of a stage. High, so the gods may descend and possess the bodies of the actors. We don't play Krishna, Draupadi, Chitrangada. We become them."

"Who's Chitrangada?" asked Mohit.

"The hero of the show in which you will be the stars," I told him. "Have you heard of her?"

They shook their heads, as I'd expected. So I gave them a succinct version. With enough detail to hook their interest.

Once upon a time, the god Indra bestowed a boon on the king of Magadha: his children will all be boys, they will grow up to be fierce warriors, fine princes, and expand his kingdom far and wide. The king's fourth child, however, is born a girl. The king, nevertheless, raises her as a boy, he equips her with every skill intended for a prince: sword fighting, horse riding, hunting. One day she encounters a prince from another kingdom: she's chasing a wild boar and her chase brings her to him. He watches her make her kill and commends her for hunting like a prince. "I am a prince," she says, her head held high. "You are a princess," he says, his smile wry. They disrobe, and in the dim light of the crescent moon, the act of comparing anatomies brings the truth to light but also leads to an attraction that they give in to. Upon her return to the palace, she confronts her father. "You are a boy because the gods say so," he says. "No, I will be who I want to be— boy, girl, both—because I say so," she declares and abandons his palace.

"That's her story—in brief," I said. "Her full story's in here."

From my shoulder bag I extracted a tome that I'd borrowed from Nandi.

"The *Mahabharata*, the Sanskrit original," I said. "She's been censored out of the more widely read Hindi translation."

"And out of the TV show," Ronit observed.

Ankit said, "Conservative bastards."

"Conservative bastards is right," I said, and Dev cheered.

I returned to describing the attributes of the stage as prescribed by the *Natya Shastra*. The ancient Hindu treatise of theater and dance.

"Firm, so it's a solid foundation for the story performed."

I got to my feet and charged between two students and made my way to the stage's southern end.

"Slightly raised in the south," I said, squatting on my knees, caressing the stage floor, "to pay respect to our ancestors. South is the home of ancestral energy."

"South *India* is the home of curd rice lovers like me," Gupta said.

They broke into chants of "curd rice." I went and sat in their midst.

"I'm from the south too," I said. "Where's everyone else from?"

Saaya washed his long hair every Friday morning; it was a ritual that he stuck to, year after year, irrespective of where we were. Whatever may be the local weather, he found a bucket of well water, a stream, a river, and, after soaking his hair, he applied to it the paste of fleshy shikakai fruits and let it cake dry. Our Chamba accommodations with their attached bathrooms made the process easier. On our first Friday morning at the school, I took one flight of stairs to Saaya's room, which was on the third floor. I heard him hum as he showered. Rooh and Nandi had their rooms on the fourth floor.

When I heard Saaya turn off the faucet, I heated a nugget of coal on the stove until it sizzled and glowed. It released a short, rapid flutter of sparkles when I dropped it in a censer.

Saaya came out, towel-dried his hair, and sat down on the floor, cross-legged. The air burned with the earth-citrus afterscent of shikakai until I sprinkled a spoonful of myrrh onto the embers. Smoke billowed out of the censer's mouth and infused the room with the perfume of myrrh's resinous essence. In one hand, I gathered the tip of his hair and raised it until it was parallel to the ground.

I gripped the wooden base of the censer and ran it slowly under the length of Saaya's hair. Pale smoke curled through and condensed on the thick, damp strands.

When the smoke thinned, I set the censer down, moved closer to him. As I started to braid his hair into a plait, my knuckles grazing against the cool skin of his back at regular intervals, Saaya asked, "So. What makes Marc feel like a man worth pursuing?"

I slid a rubber band up the tail of Saaya's braid until it met the last knot, and said, "Because he invited me to come hang out with his friends," I said.

"Which implies that he wants more—and that makes him attractive."

"I found him attractive right away," I said. "The promise I sense, that he wants something more, makes that attraction worth pursuing. He didn't stand there staring at me when we took a bow. He met me after the show instead *and* introduced himself. Like a gentleman."

"It helps that we're here for nine months," Saaya said, getting up. "When you meet him remember to do one thing that shows you tried—clothes, cologne, hairstyle, you pick. And if he notices, you know he really likes you."

I was tempted to tell him how my senses reacted violently to our hug. I asked, instead, "What if he thinks I'm a painful bore and we never meet again?"

"I'll have to nurse your heartbroken ass when you're back. Lucky me."

My confidence found its expression exclusively in the context of theater: I didn't dismiss the praise I received for my performances; when Nandi wanted me to perform wildly different roles in the same week, sometimes on the same day, I didn't doubt my ability to deliver. That's why, I thought, as I threw away the burnt-out embers, I was confident when I spoke to Marc: his questions were primarily about my performance, and I was still in costume when we met. When he hugged me, my body took precedence over the costume that concealed it.

I said, "When I go to meet Marc, can I go in costume?"

He didn't respond. I turned and faced him.

With a blank face, he said, "Darling, that isn't what I had in mind when I said 'do one thing that shows you tried.'"

FIRST DATE

I was ready by five that evening, rose oil massaged onto my wrists and underarms. When I heard a knock on my door, I combed my hair once more, drew in a deep breath, exhaled as I opened the door, and said with an air of casual surprise, "Marc."

"Your sup told me where to find you," he said.

"I was reading something and lost track of time," I said.

He squeezed his ear and smiled.

Rooh and Saaya ran into us on the landing of my floor.

"Dinner—" Rooh began.

"Dinner plans are canceled," Saaya interrupted, looking from me to Marc.

"What?" Rooh said, looking perplexed.

"Are you going to introduce us to this handsome devil?" Saaya said.

Marc crimsoned. Rooh's expression resolved into an understanding. I introduced Saaya and Rooh as my teachers, fellow actors, and friends, in that order. Rooh squeezed my shoulder.

"Stop with your fatherly fawning," Saaya grumbled. "We have to go do not-dinner things, remember? Sorry, Shagun, we don't have time for you."

He bounded down the steps, two at a time, dragging Rooh behind him.

We went down the stairs laughing and got into Marc's jeep, a red Mahindra with an open top.

"Quiz time," Marc said. "What happens to Jewish boys when we turn thirteen?"

I couldn't have conjured up the fact of his ethnicity from his surname. Did he glean my caste from mine?

I said, as we took off, "You're pledged in marriage to a girl?"

"What?" He guffawed.

"When Hindu boys come of age they're promised to 'decent girls.' Dad's words."

"Marriage definitely isn't top of agenda at a bar mitzvah."

"You're playing bar mitzvah songs tonight?"

Marc laughed. "You have no idea what a 'bar mitzvah' is, do you?"

"No, but in my defense, you said there'd be music tonight and brought up this . . . *stuff*."

"I wanted to impress you by telling you that I didn't just have a coming-of-age ceremony—I will tell you all about it one day I promise—I truly came of age at thirteen by moving countries and picking up a new skill and a hard language. But you totally threw off my script."

"Script?" I said, smiling.

"Naturally," he said. "My nerves don't show? That's something."

"Go on, then," I said, thumbing my palm. "Impress me."

When he was thirteen, Marc said, his family moved from New York to Jew Town, an old settlement near Cochin. I wanted to ask him the reason for his move but I wanted to hear his script uninterrupted, so I made a mental note to ask him later. In the weeks that followed their arrival, he continued, as the walls of their rental lay bare and the familiar wall hangings—his sisters' drawings, his parents' framed degrees—were making their slow, ship-bound journey toward the Malabar Coast along with the rest of their belongings, his sisters, one seven years old and the other six, took easily to the new country. They made friends with the girl who lived downstairs. In the evenings, as Marc stood on his balcony and nursed a mug of Milo, he saw his sisters and their friend in the park across the street. They taught their friend Knock-Knock and

Pretend and their friend taught them Thief while their mothers, sitting on a bench at some distance, laughed and chatted as they kept an eye on the children.

"It was like they'd simply moved neighborhoods," Marc said.

"It was harder for you—why?" I asked.

His fear, Marc said, had condensed into a particular visual: a match of cricket he could, at best, watch from the periphery, not because he grew up on baseball instead but because the nature of his desire—which, Marc was convinced, would be plain as day to boys his age—made him ineligible for membership on a team constituting, exclusively, of boys turning into men.

"You knew?" I asked. "At thirteen?"

"I knew at nine."

The signal turned red. A man appeared at my window, his shoulders draped with puppets. "Only twenty for a pair," he said in an appeasing voice, holding out a bearded man with a cello, a woman with a billowing gown. A singer, a dancer. Each was the length of my arm. His face had a black painted mustache, hers a nose ring with a faux pearl. I bought them on a whim. The signal turned. Marc resumed driving.

"A month into that summer," Marc said, "I came down with the flu. When it started to lift Dad wanted me to join him on his evening walk to, you know, get some fresh air but also so I would open up to the place that was now my home. Whether I liked it or not."

"Did you go?"

"I didn't want to," Marc said. "But he knew exactly how to coax me out of bed."

"Which was how?"

"He has this camera—did I mention my parents were both journalists in New York? It's a Canon F1 from the 1970s, a real beauty. I'd been eyeing it for as long as I can remember, using any excuse I could to ask to use it—school project, friend's birthday; I once invented a funeral for a teacher who, let's put it like this: I wasn't her favorite."

I laughed, and if it was the wrong reaction, he didn't show it.

He continued, "Dad, of course, wouldn't let me borrow it: it was an expensive piece of equipment—he had something like six lenses that went with it—and he needed it for work, besides. But I, of course, didn't quit trying."

"Very persistent."

"When you see it you'll understand why. So he comes to get me out of the house, right? He sits next to me on my bed and places the camera between us and I sit promptly up and, man, I *felt* my eyes light up—they turned hot, like when you're about to cry, but there were no tears."

His father, having quit his journalism job in New York, didn't intend on returning to the profession. So Marc could have the camera—if he still wanted it. After waiting a moment, Marc picked the camera up and thumbed its curved matte body and its constellation of buttons. His father pressed one. The shutter slid open with a click.

Marc went with his father to the river Kaveri where six elephants bathed, standing neck-deep in water, drawing water up their trunks, and dousing their bodies and the mahouts who sat on their backs.

Marc said, "I'd never seen an elephant outside a zoo and never so many of them."

I knew then that I had to tell him about the sea elephants.

His father told him, as they observed the vista, that the first thing to know about a camera is that the lens offers him a choice: zoom in on the specifics or zoom out onto a relative whole.

Marc said, "With one eye to the viewfinder, the other screwed shut, I turned the zoom ring, to the right, to the left, and it sounds exactly like your typical teenage fantasy now but that day I did feel like a scientist with my eye to a microscope, finding out things about the world that my naked eye couldn't see.

"Dad told me, 'You're dealing with limited real estate, remember: thirty-six shots per reel. So choose first, then click.'"

Marc zoomed in with patience he didn't know he possessed. He isolated a mahout whose pleasure was made visible to him only by a close-up: on his wrinkled, soaked face was a smile small and shy. When he zoomed in a little farther the detail lost the contrast that allowed its delicateness to stand out: the energy surrounding him, the chaos of splashing water, that drama of bathing elephants. So he zoomed out until the mahout and his elephant's head were centered, framed on either side by the gray wall of an elephant body, the space between one animal and the next a blur of water topped by a thorny crown of droplets. Marc pressed the shutter button. He took his first picture.

He didn't lower the camera. The mahout he had photographed turned in his direction, and the meeting of their gaze was interrupted and negotiated by the lens.

"He beckoned me over," Marc said. "So I handed the camera to Dad and, there I was, shrieking and charging into the waters, a child again, forgetting the adolescence my body was growing into."

The elephant curled his trunk around Marc's waist and lifted him, and Marc saw himself rising higher and higher, the sound of water dripping from his feet and into the river growing quickly distant.

"Afterward," Marc said, "the mahouts stood on the riverbank single file and sang a song together, in sync, note by note. I recognized some words—they were Hebrew—but not the rest."

The elephants responded to the song: they stepped out of the river and, as dusk lilaced the sky, they stood before their mahouts until the song ended.

"'Tender' isn't what you think when I say elephants and men with all that muscle. But there's no better word for what I saw, I swear."

"Did you photograph the moment?"

He nodded. The mahout told Marc, in fluent Hebrew, where to find the elephant again. He belonged to the mahout's employer. He invited Marc to come by the next evening.

That night, as Marc's father tucked him into bed, he told Marc about early émigrés to Jew Town: back in the day, they forged a new language, Judeo-Malayalam, a blend of Hebrew and the local tongue, Malayalam. It was the language Marc heard when the mahouts sang to the elephants.

"I asked Dad, 'Why does that man have an elephant as a pet? Aren't dogs and cats the only pets? Can we have a pet elephant?' 'Absolutely not,' Mom said from the next room. Dad laughed and patted my chest. 'So many questions,' he said. 'All in good time.'"

"You have a good relationship with your father," I said, thumbing the male puppet's wooden sandals.

That night, Marc said, as he drifted into sleep, he remembered how the act of taking a photograph had allowed him to forge his first local connection. He woke up the next morning feeling clearheaded, his body warm but not hot, his fear resolving itself into a belief: if he photographed the local geography and learned the language his predecessors had forged in this country, this new place would become his home.

"Together, Mom, Dad, and I made a decision that day: my education in Judeo-Malayalam and photography would begin the day I had my bar mitzvah," Marc said.

In the light of his story—his vulnerabilities, his triumphs—his beauty transformed: from a beauty that kept me at arm's length to a beauty I wanted to be held by.

Cute, Saaya once told me, gets tired quickly—it even becomes the source of your annoyance sometimes. A cute smile, he said, by way of example, would be annoying if you come home tired one evening seeking a silent hour free of people, voices, and activity, an emptiness you could pour yourself into or that you pour into yourself to put out the fires in your head. If your boyfriend senses your need and assigns himself an errand and steps out, then upon his return, your appreciation of the cuteness of his smile deepens because it now encompasses something more than that smile.

"As if you would know," I mocked Saaya.

"Darling," Saaya said. "Singles understand relationships best—or they have the potential to, if they're not idiots too absorbed by poor-me feelings."

"Hey," I protested.

"He has a point," Rooh said. "If you're not in the thick of a relationship, you have the space to make meaning of it."

Rooh rarely took Saaya seriously, and even when he did, he did not acknowledge it. He didn't want Saaya to have the satisfaction. So Saaya's point must have struck a deep chord with him. As it did with me, now, years later, as I sat next to Marc and watched him back his jeep into a tight parking spot. He turned his head and looked back and rotated the steering wheel with his big hands. I wanted his profile on a coin so I could dip my hand in my pocket and thumb it whenever I thought of him. He killed the engine and turned to me.

I ran a hand down his forearm. The hair soft, nearly downy. I brought my hand to his jaw. His scruff, less tender. I committed the two textures to memory. He sat there patiently. Patience that only affection allows.

"I'm impressed," I said and removed my hand from his body and got out of the car.

Marc lived in a residential neighborhood with brick houses that were rented out by the government to senior railway employees who in turn sublet parts of their home to junior employees like Marc. A flight of stairs took us to a cement-floored terrace and Marc's studio. Under a lamp outside his door was a blackboard chalked with his full name: Marc Singer. Hill jasmine grew out of three pots and snaked onto wooden armatures nailed to the parapet. We stood there and scanned the street.

A man walked a boy down the road. The boy—in uniform, a school-bag saddled to his shoulders—walked a pace behind and held the hand of the man who had a file secured under one arm. Three girls in the same uniform, cream shirts under brown frocks, ran past them, laughing. The boy stopped short and pulled at the man's hand. He followed the boy's gaze and watched the girls who ran with their heads thrown back, their water bottles slapping against their bodies. They turned a corner and were gone. The boy and man stood there, faces unmasked of routine.

I belatedly posed the question I wanted to ask Marc when he started telling me his story.

"Why did your parents decide to migrate from New York to Jew Town?"

"So many questions," Marc said. "All in good time."

"You can't do that!" I protested, both flustered and pleased by the untold story that held the promise of future meetings.

He took out of his pocket a key, which he wagged in the air. And I followed him, filled with the excitement of entering his house for the first time.

MARC, MEET MUD AND MILK

"Smells good," I said, standing in his living room.

He said, "Oud. Incense, spray, candle. Different forms, keeps the scent consistent. Mom's trick to amplify fragrance."

His desk sat snug against the window that overlooked the back alley. On the narrow sill, a stoneware dog, cow, and crow sat precariously close to the edge. Marc's bedroom, separated from the hall with a curtain, contained a different smell. It smelled of his body.

"What are you thinking?" he asked, stepping in front of me.

"Is that a story?" I pointed to the image on his bedsheet: a bear and a girl, dancing.

"*Beauty and the Beast*. It's a fairy tale—a love story."

"That's our story, then," I said. "Except here the man's fair and beautiful and the girl's the savage."

Marc lowered his head as he smiled and covered half his face with his big hand. The other half of his face turned red. His skin wore his feeling like a dress.

"Indulge me," he said.

He draped my hand over his shoulder, held my waist, and pressed his body against mine. We danced in his room to the tune he whistled.

"It's a song from the Disney version of *Beauty and the Beast*," he said.

"You know what the kicker is?" I shook my head. "The beast is actually a handsome prince who's cursed to be, well, a beast."

He resumed whistling. What's with cursed princes, I wondered, that they endure across time and geography?

"You smell good too," he said.

"Rose," I said.

He didn't resume his whistling after this interruption but we continued our dance. My thighs burned. Was it his heat or ours? My forehead grazed the tip of his nose. I timed our breaths: breathing in when he breathed out. I made myself pliable as he led me through the room, to one end, then around the bed. His foot, on occasion, trampled mine. I liked that.

I thumbed the pale scab on his chin. I pressed my mouth to his. He parted his lips and his tongue spread his warm spit on my upper lip. As if marking me as his. A moment of bliss.

Then my senses lost their sensation. The visual and the aural replaced by a black so thick it would never know the taste of color, a quiet so deep, it would drown every memory of sound.

I gasped and disengaged myself.

The darkness turned slowly back to light. A black haze lingered on the peripheries. Sounds returned, compounded in volume and detail: birds calling, shirt rustling, Marc breathing. I pressed my hands to the sides of my lowered head.

"Hey, are you okay?" Marc asked, bringing his hands to my shoulder.

I stepped away from him. "Sorry."

He turned away and his shoulders tensed.

"Come here," he said.

I went up to him. His back radiated his heat. He turned to face me. I leaned toward him, as if stooped under the weight of my desire. His hand found my crotch, a touch light and brief.

"Good," he said, withdrawing his hand. "You do want this. I had to make sure."

I followed Marc to his kitchenette. I wanted to ask him to show me his photographs, but in that moment I feared the request would come across as compensation for the intimacy I had aborted. He took a saucepan from the dish rack and pointed to a cupboard and then to a tin box in it. I took tie biscuits out of the box and set them on a plate.

"I gave you a mini autobiography," he said as he poured, without measuring, milk, tea leaves, and water into the pan. "At least tell me who's in your family."

He ignited the stove with a match. A flame hissed to life. The smell of gas lingered in the air briefly. He mounted the saucepan atop the burner and turned to me.

"I had two sisters like you," I said. "Also younger."

I spoke about them in the past tense and he noticed: his expression visibly shifted.

"What are their names?" he asked me.

"I called them Mud and Milk. They were identical twins."

He smiled. "How come?"

"Milk liked the taste of milk. Mud liked to eat wet earth."

He took a step closer. He gauged my reaction. I felt his breath on my skin. All the attention in his eyes was for me. In that moment, the rest of the world ceased to exist for Marc.

"They drowned in the sea," I said. "I just stood there and watched it happen."

The mention of the fact brought the moment to life vividly and I was once again a sixteen-year-old standing on the shore, my body drenched in rainwater and seawater as I watched the Bay of Bengal devour them.

I was quiet for a while. Marc filled a glass with water and offered it to me. I drank it in small sips. Behind him the tea vessel hissed as the liquid, which by now had turned russet-brown, rose dangerously close to the surface, ready to spill over. Marc lowered the heat and let it simmer on a low flame.

"It was a childhood game," I said. "It wasn't meant to end that way."

He turned to me again. His eyes found mine and he held my gaze. A spate of words came spilling out of my mouth and I told him what had happened with more detail than I had included in my previous accounts: to Ma, to Nandi, to Saaya. I did, however, exclude the fact of my culpability.

"We liked to climb up parked fishing boats because they gave my sisters an elevation to watch these Englishmen who got off the ships and came to our town sometimes, except that day the boat they got onto wasn't parked and was kind of in the water but they got onto it anyway and the sea took them and I should've stopped them but I didn't and by the time I noticed their boat had sailed away and I did what I could to save them and you know how that ended but did I mention it was raining hard—because it was."

I brought the glass to my lips. It was empty. He refilled it. I guzzled it and put it down on the counter.

"They never found my sisters," I said, stating aloud the fact for the first time. "Maybe they would've—if I told someone sooner?"

"I'd like to hug you, Shagun," Marc said. "Is that okay?"

I nodded. He held me to himself. He brought a hand to my head. I pressed my forehead to his shoulder and cried in great hiccups. It was a long-deferred cry, one that I hadn't had since my sisters died. Marc's presence had allowed its release, its expression.

When I stepped away from him, wiping my cheeks, I asked, "How long was I crying?"

"I didn't turn my timer on. Because it's not an exam?"

My nostrils were clogged so my laughter came out sounding like a grunt.

"Your friends will be here. I should go freshen up."

He led me to the bathroom built behind his studio. I closed the door, stood next to it, and heard his footsteps fade. A single switch turned on two naked bulbs. One dangled over the shower, the other over the toilet, whose tank was stacked with magazines. There was no mirror.

As I splashed my face with water, I remembered that Marc had held me through my wailing and my senses had remained intact. They vanished violently only when his touch was sensual.

A thought came to me as I patted my face dry with Marc's towel. Did my body remember Senior's abuse and recoil from intimacy? Abuse that I had pretended to like, that had made my body feel desirable. I lowered the toilet cover and sat down. Sat for a moment with the choices I had made. Wondering if I'd lost a chance to turn the tentative unit that Marc and I were into something more concrete. I allowed myself to stew for a while.

Then I looked up and saw on the sink a glass that held a toothbrush. I pictured placing my toothbrush against his, the bristles touching. And the chaos in my head stilled.

When I rejoined Marc in the kitchen, he said, "If you're not up to socializing today, we can do this next week."

"No, it will do me good," I said.

"It was nice to meet Mud and Milk. I'd like to know them better."

He poured the chai into five cups and I mixed sugar in them, spoon clinking against ceramic as we stood quietly in his kitchenette. We placed the tray of tea and biscuits in between four cushions that formed a rect-angle on the living room floor. Their pastel-blue covers had come undone at the edges. I tucked them back in and smoothed out the wrinkles.

His friends arrived before the cups stopped steaming. The engine of a car was killed, three doors were opened and shut.

"There's still time," Marc said. "I can go down, tell them to turn around. They'll get it."

I shook my head. "I want this."

He leaned forward and gave my lips a quick peck as they came thumping up the stairs.

LIKE *SWAMI AND FRIENDS*

Marc hugged his friends and made introductions: a couple, Su and Sagar, who looked younger than Marc, and Karan, who looked older and kept a dowdy mustache and an unruly mop of hair. He wore a black leather jacket and carried a guitar.

Su pulled out of her canvas boat bag a packet of samosas wrapped in newspaper. She took a cup off its saucer and emptied into it a packet of mint chutney. Sagar went into the kitchenette and got himself a straw for his tea. They inhabited Marc's home with a sense of ease. They lived away from their families and met often at Marc's.

"Why did you have your show so early in the morning?" Su asked me.

"Su wakes up at eleven and looks like she's crawling out of a cave," Marc said.

"Don't exaggerate," Su said.

"We timed it to end with sunrise," I said.

"You're Konark sun temple or what?" she said, and the room filled with our laughter.

"Tell us nice theater things," she said.

"Have you heard of the sea elephant myth?" I asked, looking at Marc.

I part-performed and part-told the origin story. Karan strummed his guitar as I spoke, and the notes pooled around my words.

"Isn't he amazing?" Marc said.

"Wait until the honeymoon phase is over," Sagar said.

"This is how Su will be after her honeymoon," Karan said, pushing a cushion under his shirt.

"Shut up, Karan," Su said. "Not every woman has to be like this"—she drew a belly bump with her hands—"at the end of a honeymoon."

"Then why bother with honeymoon? Waste of money for Sagar," Karan said.

"Sagar and I will share our honeymoon expenses, jackass," Su said and threw a cushion at him. He dodged.

Marc went to get us Indo-Chinese takeaway. His friends, Su in particular, made me feel included: directing comments at me, asking me questions.

When Marc came back, he asked, "What did I miss?"

"Next Friday's movie night," Su said. "*GoldenEye.*"

"That's the one where—" Marc began.

"Don't even think about it," Sagar warned.

"—Janus fakes his death," Marc said.

They made loud noises of protest. Sagar particularly hated spoilers.

As we ate dinner, Su made a great show of being miffed with Karan. When we were done eating, he kneeled before her and held his ears, apologizing in a playfully self-deprecating way. She laughed. He got to his feet, and she hugged him.

It turned out that not Marc but his friends provided the music he had promised. Karan was good with the guitar. In a voice that melded the husk of a folk singer's voice with the sweetness of Bollywood playback, Su sang:

I wait for you
Like the sunflower
waits for daylight
with its face to the Sky

When you do arrive,
You simply pass by like a train

And like the tracks underneath,
I quietly tremble
as I watch you leave.

The lyrics, playful and wistful at once, were from a poem composed by the Hindi poet Dushyant Kumar. Sagar had set it to music.

"Will you show us some of your photos?" I asked.

Karan said, "He's painfully shy about it."

"Today he won't be, given who's asking," Su said.

Marc said, his expression giving nothing away, "Yeah, okay. I can do that."

He went to his room and, in the anticipatory silence that followed, we heard the opening and closing of a drawer.

"So you've never seen his photos?" I asked.

"We have, a couple times," Su said.

"And we had to literally force him," Sagar said.

"At a certain point we stopped trying," Karan said.

Marc reentered the room with a manila envelope. He sat next to me. He took out a stack of photos and perused them. Then he set three aside and returned the rest to the envelope. He presented them for my consideration. In the first, a singer sat before a harmonium with his head tipped, his mouth wide open. A vein on his sweaty throat bulged prominently. Marc had, in a still image, captured the sensation of the singer's fingers moving feverishly on the keys of the harmonium; it was the odd knuckle-bends, the room between the thumb and the pinkie, details that were foregrounded. I passed the picture to Su and looked at the second one: a close-up of an elephant trunk and tusk, in the background a river that, I assumed, was the Kaveri, its banks dotted with palm fronds. Here too the image seemed to have captured the animate: the breeze whipping the palm leaves. The third was the first picture he took: the mahout with the shy smile, around him a rise of water that, it seemed, would any minute now splash out of the photographs and onto our skin.

When Karan, the last to look at the photos, was about to return them to Marc, I took them from him, and driven purely by instinct, turned them around and found labels behind each: a caption in English separated, with a thin vertical line, from words in a language I didn't recognize.

"That's Judeo-Malayalam," Marc said, pointing to the words next to "Ehud Banai Performs in Jew Town, October 1991."

"Huh, I didn't notice that before," Su said, leaning over the words.

Marc took the photographs from me. I clapped and his friends followed suit.

"Our friend group feels complete with you in it," Su said, ruffling my hair. "We're like *Swami and Friends*."

"Marc's home is our Malgudi," I said.

"Finally someone gets your references, Su," Sagar said.

Later, well past midnight, Su, Sagar, and Karan lay sprawled across the floor and shared the warmth that people generate when their lives rub together. I stood on the balcony, surrounded by the fiercely fragrant hill jasmine. The flowers glimmered in the moonlight. Marc switched the lights off, left the window and the door open, and came and stood next to me. I told him what I had seen in his photographs. He smiled.

"It is what I spend the most time trying to capture. Movement."

"Why are you shy about showing them?"

"It isn't because I don't like how they turned out," he said. "It's because I do nothing with them."

"What's stopping you?" I asked.

"Fear," he said. "I want a job that's safe: predictable routine, a salary like clockwork."

"And hence your job with the railways."

"When I started working here, Dad came over. I thought it was to see me. But he came to take the camera away."

"The Canon?"

"He said, 'When you decide to do something with your talent, come back and claim it.'"

"He's hoping your favorite camera is once again the incentive that does the trick. You have a good father."

"It's the second time you said that."

"I wouldn't have thought fear plays any part in your decision-making. You were so confident when we first spoke."

"And you were shy when we spoke, but what an incredibly confident performer. You took a risk on something you love, and I admire that about you."

"Thank you."

"It's something I cannot do, I don't think," he said.

There are fears that cripple me as well, I wanted to say. I couldn't bring myself, in that moment, to tell Marc about my fear of Vikrant. That defied logic and hounded me, despite the six years since my last encounter with him.

"Things might change," I said.

Marc shrugged. "Now you have my story," he said. "More or less."

"You left out the most important detail."

Marc smiled. He'd never had a boyfriend, he said, but he did have his share of flings after he got into college. He and his fellow faggots practiced a particular breed of whoring: as the night thickened, the carnal led to the romantic. They held hands after they were done, they spoke quietly of futures they had no hopes of realizing: buying homes, clocking their lives with anniversaries, paper to diamond, two men appearing as parents at the convocations and graduations of their children. When morning bleached the night, they went their separate ways, returning to their cages of daylight, and on the buses that took them back home, on the trains that returned them to their hometowns—yes, they traveled to meet their one-night lovers like pilgrims—they were pinched by grief, the heft of it at odds with the duration of their contact. They never met each other again. They tasted in breaths and snatches a lifetime that, in another version of reality, might have been theirs.

"Were you ever with girls?" I asked.

"Once," he said. "I wanted to see if maybe I swung both ways. I hoped I would."

"Did you?"

He smiled, and I got my answer. I pressed my cheek to his chest, closed my eyes, and for a few moments allowed myself all the luxury at

my disposal: the bony hardness of his rib cage, his hair's ginger smooth-
ness between my fingers, his chin on my head, firm as punctuation. I
eased out of his arms before I lost control. I stepped back, ran my hands
down his arms and into his hands, laced my fingers with his. I brought
his hand to my crotch.

"See, I want this," I said. "I just need some time. This is new to me."

He removed his hand. I looked into his clear, hopeful eyes. I felt
ashamed for not revealing to him the truth of my suffering. How would
I describe it? It was a failure of language, courage, and imagination.

"I'm happy I stand a chance," he said.

"I'm picturing our wedding invites," I said. "Gora Dada-jee weds
Curry Kid."

"Did you just call me a white granddad?" Marc said. "First off, I'm a
Jew; second, I'm twenty-seven, you little shit."

"At twenty-four," I said, "twenty-seven seems old as the hills."

He shook his head, turned, and looked down at the two puppets in
his jeep, identifiable by their bright fabric, their features—big painted
eyes, aquiline noses, bright red mouths—indistinct at this distance.

"Those are for you," I said. "My gift."

He didn't ask me why I had chosen them as my first gift to him, and
if he had, I wouldn't have had an answer for him.

RHYTHMS

Now that I was stationed in one place for a little while, I wanted to fall into the rhythm of a more frequent contact with Ma. Over the last six years, I had called Ma three times every year: her birthday, my birthday, and the death anniversary of Mud and Milk, when we spoke not about my sisters, but about the house—the repairs that surfaced, the domestic help she now hired. I ended each call with the customary question about her health. She kept up her end of the bargain, not asking where I was performing, and I kept mine, staying in contact, letting her know I was alive. She'd say, on my birthday calls, "Your father sends you his regards." He never asked me to call him, and he didn't come back home. She hadn't heard from Vikrant again; he was reforming more readily available gay men, perhaps. Even so, I had exquisitely vivid nightmares about encountering him. In one, I did a masked dance for a performance in which our audience surrounded me. When I finished with a flourish of my hand and the audience applauded, a man stepped forward and removed the mask I was wearing. That man was Vikrant. Our eyes met and the audience broke into a chant. *Praise be to the masculine god Hanuman.* I kept a log: date and summary of the nightmare. I kept the log with the brochure and collection of news clippings.

I called Ma and told her about my nine-month-long stint as a teacher. I gave her the guesthouse phone number on the condition that she wouldn't share the number or the news with Pita-jee. Ma called me every Monday morning, and I received her call in the guesthouse's reception room. Her conversations picked up where the letters she sent me when I was at Magpies left off. She needed the rhythm of regular contact, it seemed, to open up about the past. She spoke about meeting my father at their roka ceremony. She spoke about their first home, a rented one-bedroom in Delhi. She spoke about the ancestral home of Pita-jee. They moved into it after my grandfather's death. They wanted to save on rent and the expenses of a city. They were saving to start a family. It was the home where my sisters and I were born and raised. My childhood home.

She offered no more than a small nugget during each call. I knew I would eventually learn the history I sought. I knew I wouldn't be prepared for how that knowledge would alter me.

Marc gave me a copy of his house key. Every evening, I let myself into his home and waited by the phone. When he called, I picked up on the second ring. I didn't say hello.

"I'm leaving," he said, words that made me feel full, as if the heart is a second belly.

I hung up and set to work: milk and tea leaves, brought to a boil on low heat, the concoction infused with cardamom, peppercorns, ginger, and saffron. When Marc got home and sat on the one chair he owned, a wingback saddled with old cushions, I brought him chai with four tie biscuits, lined along the saucer, their pale bodies dotted with cashews and raisins. He dipped each biscuit in his chai and ate it. Slowly, the weariness of the day lifted from his face and the beauty of its geography was restored. I reveled in this routine, the bliss peculiar to the domestic.

He was quiet one evening. When I asked him why, he told me that mid-October, dedicated to audits, was the worst week at work. It entailed hours of standing around as senior government officials checked the records kept by entry-level employees like Marc.

I warmed a cup of sesame oil, sat down before him, and relieved one foot of its boot and its sock and placed it on my thigh. I dampened my knuckles with the warm sesame oil and ran them up and down his sole, the pressure even against his flesh. When he set aside the empty cup and slouched, the heel of his foot slid up my thigh. The friction of his dry skin against my trouser made a sound like fabric ripped open, like a zipper lowered. He closed his eyes and his breath fell effortlessly into the rhythm of sleep. When I took his other foot in my lap and unsheathed it of boot and sock, a strand of his ginger hair came undone. I paused, worried he would awake. But he did not. My hand moved between the cup of oil and the curve of his foot, my thumb making oiled circles on each toe, the pressure I applied alternating between mild and hard. The musk of dampness between his toes was replaced with the scent of sesame and clean skin. I sat there, even after I was done, present to the beautiful burden of his feet in my lap.

Then, I recognized something: there was no anxiety, my senses were intact. So my body allowed physical contact when it was not reciprocated. I was slowly gaining an understanding of my affliction.

I had started imagining myself with Marc when I pleasured myself. He brings his face so close to mine that the sweat licking his forehead marks my skin; he sniffs hard and I kiss the crease that forms on the bridge of his perfect nose: that was how it always started. For the first time I featured myself in the imagination that excited me. Marc had birthed me into existence in my fantasies.

Marc's shoulders stirred. He arced his body forward, opened his mouth, and let out a groggy sigh. In that mouthful of breath was a residual scent of ginger and milk that lingered in the air between us. He rubbed both his eyes with the knuckles and the heels of his big hands. He moved his feet. Perhaps the fabric and flesh against his heels surprised him; his eyes flew open.

"I was out like a light," he said. "How long has it been?"

I picked one foot up and kissed the curve of it. He sat next to me on the floor, pressed me to himself, and cradled me. I tucked the truant strand of hair behind his ear.

"You gave Marc boy a wicked good massage," he said, his smirk deliciously lopsided, his accent English.

"Thank you, sir," I said, giddy with delight as I released myself from his grip.

This reversal—who *should* express gratitude, who *actually* did it—filled me with pleasure.

"That's it for today—no more, okay?" Marc said, his original accent restored. That was the rule: English accent for role-play, American accent for being.

"Can I make dinner?" he asked.

"I already did."

"I'll do the dishes, then."

Unable to refuse him, I shot him a look of such absolute dejection that he made a gesture of retreat: shoulders pulled back, hands raised.

"See how this works?" he said. "I only *perform* being the one with power."

"Don't ruin the illusion," I said, half joking.

He unlidded the pots in the kitchen and breathed deep. "Smells amazing. And there's enough to feed a crowd."

"I made extra for you to take to work," I said. I brought my backpack and took out of it a new lunch box. "I don't want you eating outside every day. It's not good for you."

"So no more giving business to the dhaba?" he asked, feigning disappointment. He turned and said, "Now you can't leave, you know that, right? My body will reject dhaba food after eating home-cooked meals for nine months."

Later, we wound up, as we always did, on his terrace. My parents threw fleeting shadows on our nocturnal conversations, but my sisters had become a familiar presence. That night I told him that my sisters and I wrote in each other's notebooks to see if our teachers could point out the difference. We liked to mix up proverbs, I said. "The pen is mightier than blood" was our favorite.

Every Friday, Marc and I met his friends, who were becoming my friends too. We were content with hanging out in Marc's living room, talking, entertaining ourselves with Su's songs, Karan's music, and my performances.

On some evenings Su and I met, just the two of us, and spoke as we sipped on sodas at a hillside bakery. She was Marc's only friend whom I told about what had happened to Mud and Milk. She, like Marc, got the incomplete version, and her response, empathetic like his, left me feeling ashamed. If they knew what I'd actually done, I was certain, they'd respond not with love but with the decision to weed me out of their lives.

She liked my rendition of the mythic feminine, she once told me.

"Your Sita and Draupadi are so different from the Sita and Draupadi of Doordarshan and Amar Chitra Katha," she said.

"No matter where you're from, you've grown up watching Doordarshan and reading Amar Chitra Katha comics," I said.

"True," Su said. "Talking about them makes me feel nostalgic. I used to think those were simpler times, but it seems that simplicity came at an expense."

I told Su that women and lower-caste characters were simplified to the point that they no longer were people but tropes defined exclusively by their duty toward the story's leads, Brahmin men, men of the ruling class. Queer characters were, of course, axed.

I shared the story of Chitrangada. Her removal from the epic, her continued presence in folk songs and fables of the lower castes, where she breathes in the shadows alongside a fleet of gay deities and transgender demigods who had been erased out of translations.

Su nodded thoughtfully.

"Hey," I said. "Want to sit in on my class someday?"

"My work schedule clears up mid-November, so I can take a day off. I'll be there."

As we sat down to lunch one day toward the end of October, Nandi said, "We've been teaching for a month and a half, can you believe it? How's it going?"

"Horrible, thank you very much," Saaya said.

Rooh said, "Storming out when one of them disagreed with you—that must've helped?"

"You aren't doing that great either," Saaya retorted. "I saw Ankit asking you to *calm down, Grandpa*."

"Let's hear your bad news, Shagun, and get done with this," Nandi said.

"I'm actually liking it—a lot," I said.

"Figures why they hate us after attending your class," Saaya said. "Thanks, man."

"You sound happy," Nandi said to me.

"Is that wrong?" I asked, laughing.

"Did I say that?" Nandi asked.

"Well, you sure look it."

"We hate it, it's a crime, Shagun likes it, also bad," Saaya said. "What's the correct answer?"

"How about you?" I asked Nandi. "Are you liking it?"

"I'm doing a duty," he said. "What's there to like or not like? My students are getting the education I promised them in exchange for a salary and housing. A better question is: Am I doing my job? And the answer is yes."

"I do miss performing," Rooh said, and that was something we all agreed on.

"Less than eight months left before we're back on the road," Nandi said. "Now *that's* something that makes me happy."

Rooh and Saaya agreed with Nandi. I remained quiet.

It was on his terrace that Marc told me about his family's migrations. It was a slightly chilly October night.

In 1933, he said, the year the first concentration camp was opened, his mother's and father's parents emigrated from Austria to the United States.

"The two families knew each other?" I asked, unable to decipher Austria's size or designation—town, city, country, village.

"No. But they both moved to New York."

It wasn't so much the right decision as the inevitable one, Marc continued: leaving behind their belongings, their homes, their histories.

"Over time, escape routes for my people became fewer and harder to find," Marc said.

In the days to come I'd recall the way he said "my people," his voice soaring, as if stepping forward to greet them—lives that had not intersected with his, even as their stories, passed down to Marc's parents and to Marc, cast a shadow on his face.

His father, Marc continued, studied journalism and found his place in America by immersing himself in the Beat movement. He loved jazz and Kerouac and spoke about traveling and bumming joints from friends he hung out with in Greenwich Village. I couldn't anchor those words in their histories. Beat. Jazz. Kerouac. Greenwich Village. I remembered my cauldron friend. He wanted to put some clothes in a bag and go somewhere.

"He went to Israel on a college trip," Marc said. "That's where he heard about Jew Town. He decided to write about it, so he spread the word about his project: made his pitch, if you will. A man in the shipping business offered Dad a place on his cargo vessel."

I asked, "And did he? Write?"

"Another journalist got there at the same time—to tell the same story."

"Who won?"

"Dad fell in love with her and she with him, and they wrote the story together. They returned to the US, got married, and started a family: one beautiful boy, two smart girls."

"Your parents' story is the stuff of movies," I said. "Your mom? Tell me her story."

"Ask her yourself," he said.

"I'd like that," I said, smiling.

"You never say much about your family's history," he said.

"We knew little about our past, my sisters and I. Maybe that's why we loved ancient myths, now that I think about it: those characters became our adopted family, and their histories, when we were performing them, became our own."

I told him about the time Ma found, in a secondhand bookshop, a tattered copy of the *Matsya Purana,* a book of fables, each fable narrated by a fish swimming in a celestial ocean. From it she read to us a fable about distant future people with big heads and small bodies. Mud decided that what the movies called aliens were really these future generations traveling back in time to take the resources they'd run out of. She had conjured up connections that had occurred to no scientist or fabulist. Aliens are future humans traveling back in time. For an evening she was convinced she had a bright future.

"Milk agreed with her assessment?" he asked.

I told him that Milk, in those days, was obsessed with the story of Dhanvantri, who bestowed on humans the gift of Ayurveda. On Creation day, when darkness is tamed by sunlight, he slipped out of a pearl's pink-white belly and rose from the bed of the sea, bringing aloft an overflowing pot of creamy elixir that, when poured into the land, birthed the three hundred herbs that are at the heart of all Ayurvedic potions. She was fascinated by the idea of a celestial liquid altering our geography.

He smiled, immersed in the story. How did Mud and Milk look in his head? Paint and show me, I wanted to say.

"It's pretty late. Crash here?"

It was the first time he was asking me to stay over. His hands had gripped my waist, he spoke with his mouth close to mine. After a few seconds he released me. He took my hand in his, patted it, and let go before anxiety darkened my senses. He figured out there was a window between initiation of touch and the loss of my senses. A short window in which my body allowed us the intimacy we craved. He now spoke the language of my body with a near-native fluency. Had he sensed the presence of my man breasts, his hand brushing against them or their softness pressed to his chest when we briefly hugged? If he had, he didn't mention them.

"Stay," he said. "Nothing needs to happen."

His patience made a knot in my gullet.

"If I stay," I said, "I get to warm your food tomorrow and pack your lunch box."

"Done and done," he said.

With his hands to my shoulders, he steered me into his room and took out of his cupboard an extra pillow and an extra blanket. He quietly made a bed on the floor.

"You take the bed," he said, standing up.

"No!" I cried and made a scramble for the floor.

He clapped in time to the laughter that left his throat. He tucked me in, kissed my chin, and turned the light off.

"You still didn't say why your parents decided to move," I said. No reply. "Marc?"

How did he fall asleep so quickly? I stayed awake for hours, listening to his breath.

REVELATIONS

Rooh came to my room in the morning at six. He gave me three man-uscripts: *Mahabharata, Devi Bhagwatam, Yoga Vasishta*. Uncensored, in Sanskrit.

"Nandi said you wanted them," he said. "He came to give them to you himself yesterday evening."

"I was at Marc's," I said.

"It's every day now?"

"Saaya does his thing, so do you, but I'm not allowed?"

"It's obvious Marc's more," Rooh said. "Nandi wants to keep our troupe together."

I closed the book and smoothed its cover.

"Just talk to Nandi," Rooh said. "Get to it before it gets out of hand."

Marc took me to a crafts fair one Saturday in November. I kept a keen track of time during those days. My time with the school and in Chamba was finite, as was, therefore, my time with Marc.

Strangers paused midstride, they turned away from a bargain—a sari, a marble elephant, a chest—to stare at Marc, the light-skinned man, with a mixture of awe and affection. A man and an older woman walked up to us.

She said, "Can we have a picture with him, son?"

With what seemed like a practiced move, Marc stood between them, an arm looped around each of their shoulders, as I brought the camera to one eye and closed the other.

I imagined, as I returned the camera, the family album Marc would make his way into, the stories in which he would be named a friend.

The gaze of strangers who put Marc up on a pedestal deepened my need to desire him in a particular way. In the futures I imagined for us, I willingly relinquished all power to him in those routines couples fall into: evening walks (Marc choosing our path, our destination), matinees (Marc selecting the cinema, the film), dinners (Marc surprising me with the venue, then ordering for both of us).

We bought ice-cream cones. Mine vanilla, Marc's mocha. We walked until we came to an amphitheater, its stage a terra-cotta circle at ground level, encircled by tiered seating. We sat down and licked at our cones.

"How does that feel?" I asked. "Flattering?"

"Flattering? I just fit a stock role: they would've done the same if they had seen an Englishman or an Australian." He was a replaceable bit actor, valuable only insofar as his appearance could be accessed, documented, archived. "The irony of it, though: I've suffered for the way I look, back in America. In high school, I was called Period Head. They called my cap, when I was foolish enough to wear one, a tampon. And you, whom I love, love the color of my hair."

"What else did they call you?"

"Carrot Pubes."

After we went back home, to his place, behind the safety of the shut door, I closed his lids and kissed his ginger lashes. And I wondered if it bothered him, my adulation directed toward those aspects of his appearance that once were the object of derision and that now made him a replaceable subject of strangers' attention.

He kept his eyes closed until I asked him to open them.

Su came to class, as promised, mid-November. I split my students into two groups, three students each. I gave them three characters. They spent twenty minutes fleshing out scenes for each character. Then, the performances commenced. The actors of the first group spread themselves across the room, left to right. The one on the left-hand side of the room delivered a line of dialogue in the voice of Bhima, a conventionally masculine hero from the *Mahabharata*. The actors to his right performed, one after another, Nachiket, a male character who's described as "sensitive like his mother," and Sita, described in the *Ramayana* as demure, feminine.

We sat on the floor cross-legged, forming a close circle, our knees nearly touching.

"Why is the 'sensitive male character' exaggeratedly feminine?" I asked, looking at Su, encouraging her to chime in.

"You think that's how women behave?" she said. "Have you ever *seen* women?"

Some students nodded. Some visibly reddened. We discussed how performing male characters with feminine gestures becomes a problem when the tics are exaggerated, reducing the complex characters to those tics. To stereotypes.

I said, "On the second of December, there's a performance by an all-women troupe at the Chinmasta Temple. We'll observe them. In the class after that, Team Two gets to perform and Team One gets to revise their performance."

"One more thing," Su said. "Why did you use the room space like that? Like, why arrange yourself from 'most masculine' to 'most feminine'?"

They looked at each other. The bell rang.

"Just be aware of why you chose *your* method," I suggested.

After they left the classroom, Su asked, "Did I overstep?"

"You told them what they needed to hear, and it needed to come from you."

"How are you so good at it, you in a troupe of all guys?"

"I had two good teachers. Saaya once took me to this riverbank. It was summer, but still early, so the air was pleasant. A group of women came to fill water. Saaya wanted me to observe them. How tense their movements were before they filled their pots, even when they knew there was enough water for all of them. They watched with satisfaction as the water gurgled into their pots. I remember that sound distinctly. And then they sat by the banks for some time, talking, content. Now that they had *their* family's water secured."

Su's eyes had welled up. It was rare, she said, to hear a man describe a woman and speak of anything but her body.

"Joining us for lunch?" Nandi asked me from the door.

"A friend of Marc, I take it?" Nandi said after Su left the room.

His tone was even-keeled, but I knew Nandi and knew this wasn't idle talk to keep us occupied as we walked to the dining hall.

Upon seeing Rooh and Saaya waiting for us by the buffet service, I stepped swiftly forward, left Nandi behind, and clapped Saaya on the back. I laughed as Saaya hissed exaggeratedly and nursed his back. Nandi and Rooh braided their laughter with mine.

"Don't know if you two are faring any better since we last spoke," Nandi said, looking at Rooh and Saaya, "but Shagun is thriving as a teacher. He's come up with his own lesson plans, did you know? Today he had a guest speaker to boot."

"What guest speaker?" Rooh asked.

"Su," I said. "I met her through Marc, but now she's one of my best friends."

"One of your best friends," Saaya said. "Am I being replaced?"

Around us, students and teachers dropped their lunch trays in dish bins and left the café, walking in groups of two or three.

"When we go back on the road"—Nandi looked pointedly at me until I looked away—"it will be in the spirit of service. The school is paying us well, we have no expenses, and we will pass it forward. We will not take a penny or a morsel from the people we perform for. We will soothe them in their times of need, by telling the stories of their gods. To do anything else would be an act of selfishness, and I will not stand for that."

Over one of her calls, Ma sounded hesitant. It was the Monday after Su came to my class.

"What is it?" I asked impatiently.

"Your father wants to visit you," she said. "I tried to dissuade him by telling him you're hard to track down because you're making merry with your circus."

We laughed, the phrase, so full of bitterness when first used, now a shared term of endearment.

"He said he'll come to you—wherever you might be performing."

"Why's he dying to meet me?"

"He wants to talk to you about your marriage."

"Not again." I groaned. "I thought he let that go."

"He did," Ma said. "Then he heard the news. Rohit-jee's youngest, he's getting married."

Was Rusty the proverbial sword that would dangle permanently over my head?

"Rohit-jee didn't even invite us," Ma said.

"Good."

Ma said, "Rusty has a bachelor's in finance, did you know? Now he's a banker in Bombay."

I said, "Whereas I'm a circus boy and dropout rolled into one. But if I get married, I'll put the Mathur family back in the game."

"You know your father so well," she exclaimed.

"Ma. Here's where you say, 'No, son. I'm proud of you just the way you are.'"

"Listen, I have a plan," Ma said, laughing. "I want you to meet this girl."

"Just tell Pita-jee I met her already."

"Won't work. He knows the family."

"When is Rusty getting married anyway?"

"How does that matter! Just meet her and we'll tell your father you're both talking things through and need some time."

"What happens after 'some time'?"

"You have a better solution in mind, then?"

"Yes," I said. "Let's crash Rusty's wedding and ruin it. Instead of salvaging our name, we'll spoil theirs."

"Not funny, Shagun."

"Oh, I know it's not funny. I don't treat people wrong, not like Rusty—"

"What did he do?"

"He's Mr. Perfect with a degree and a job and a marriage in the offing, so it doesn't really matter what he did to me, does it?"

"We just started talking properly and look, already I upset you," Ma said.

"It's not you," I said, calming down.

"So you won't cut contact with me, then?"

I wouldn't, I promised. We soothed each other with a moment of shared silence.

When someone died at school, I remembered, we were told to stand up and "observe a minute's silence, please." We followed the ritual in honor of Mud and Milk as well. The whole school stood up, students and teachers in classrooms and staff rooms, janitors in bathrooms, sweepers in corridors and the playground, "Girls that young don't deserve to die," our principal announced on the intercom.

Pita-jee still thought that Ma spoke to me three times a year. So according to his understanding, we would speak next on her birthday and she would report his conversation to me. So I had about a month to decide: meet a prospective bride or meet Pita-jee. I hung up.

I wanted my father to die. So long as he was alive, he wouldn't stop trying to straighten me out, to append me to the long canon of family frames in which a biological man, coupled to a biological woman, produced a brood of children to be raised, prepped, and, if necessary, whittled into shape so they appear in the next family frame, appropriately gendered, appropriately partnered. I didn't want to destroy that system; I wanted to make a place for myself in it. Shagun coupled with Marc. A family frame that earned its rightful place in the Mathur and Singer histories. Why not?

If anything happens, come to me, Nandi had said. Die, die, die, I chanted as I pictured Pita-jee and climbed three flights of stairs. I stood before Nandi's door. Heard a low buzz of voices. Smelled a pungent grassy odor. The door opened before I knocked.

"Were you spying?" Nandi joked.

A smoke infused with a stronger version of the grassy odor hit me now; it hovered over Rooh and Saaya, who sat on the floor with their backs to the wall.

"We saw your shadow," Nandi said, running his toe along the length of the threshold.

I had been separated from the "we." I still hadn't said a word.

"We thought you were at Marc's," he continued. "Join us if you want. Just don't tell your chuddy buddy the school principal."

He mimed smoking a joint.

I stared at him to see if he might say something to give the conversation an amicable turn: make a joke, say "I'm just joking," even if he didn't mean it, or laugh and invite me to join them with an indulgent pat on the back.

Then I turned and started to walk away. Behind me Nandi made no sound of protest. Just one "come back" and I would, I decided. Instead, I heard the door close. That thud passed through my flesh and stopped me in my tracks.

I returned to the reception room and called Marc up at his office. I did not speak when he picked up. He knew it was me anyway.

"You," he said. "You never call. Am I in trouble?"

Inserting a finger into the slot for the number nine, I turned the dial all the way round and held it there. My eyes welled up.

Marc tapped his receiver. "Earth calling Shagun?"

The line bubbled as the dial turned back and stopped with a clink. I broke down.

"Come shopping with me?" Marc asked. "I'll get out early."

"Yes, thank you, Marc," I said in between my sobs. He did not hang up. The sound of his breathing gradually calmed me down.

KEN AND ME AND THE WORLD
IN BETWEEN

We tried on green shorts in the fitting room. I kneeled in front of Marc, and he planted both his hands on my shoulders. I unbuttoned and un-zipped his trousers and pushed them down. They sat bunched at his feet. I held the shorts out and, with his hands now planted on my head, he slipped in one foot then the other. I pulled them up and zipped and buttoned them.

He did not ask me why I had cried. I didn't ask him why we were buying matching shorts.

He helped me into my pair of shorts. When I raised a foot, Marc tickled my sole and I giggled, lost balance, and fell down.

"Sir, you okay?" asked someone from the other side of the door.

"Yes!" Marc and I said together. We heard him walk away quickly, and laughed. As I lay on the floor, Marc leaned over me and pulled my shorts up and zipped them, his upper lip, dotted with stubble, inches away from my lips, my body allowing me to be present to his almost-contact. I stood up, and he cackled.

He said, "You pitched a tent. Who lives there? Brigadier Coxswain?"

"No need to be so vulgar, Marc."

"What do you want to do? Sit here and wait it out?"

I opened the fitting room door and pushed him out. He fell against a man who stumbled against the wall. "Idiot!" the man growled, slamming the door of the fitting room next to mine. I took a wooden hanger and threw it over the divider wall. The man squealed. Marc and I ran out of the store, laughing, not stopping until we mingled with the market crowd. We sat at a roadside bakery and ate biscuits dipped in tea. We were wearing stolen shorts. We'd forgotten our trousers in the fitting room.

We walked to Connaught Place, Chamba's colonial-era strip mall. Pointing to a shop that sold British memorabilia, I said, "Let's go."

Marc sighed. He said, in his English accent, "Go on, then. Be an anglophile."

The countertop was stacked with trays full of Victorian trading cards, black-and-white photographs of British officers and their wives, pamphlets from the East India Company, hardbound editions of Dickens. The showcase behind carried ceramic dolls in ball gowns, perfumes in labeled glass vials, Yardley soaps, silk gloves and satin gowns for girls five to seven. One doll drew my attention: he wore black shoes, a black frockcoat, and a black bow tie on a white silk shirt. His ginger hair looked real and his eyes were deep blue.

"I want him," I said.

The woman minding the shop lowered the newspaper she was reading and wrapped her hair into a bun. She stepped out from behind the counter. I turned to Marc to elicit his endorsement, or a joke at my expense, or a comment of some kind.

He merely stuffed his hands into his pockets and hunched his shoulders, as if bracing himself against a cold morning. I was perplexed.

The shop woman leaned a ladder against the showcase, and climbed up. She took the doll off his perch and handed him over to me. I dusted his coat and looked up.

"That's Barbie's lover, Ken," she said.

"What say you, Marc?" I said. "Let's bring Ken home?"

Marc said nothing. He looked away, toward the shop's glass window and the porcelain sculptures that were on display. Victorian harp players, pianists, and flautists.

"You want him, he's yours," the shop woman said.

She started to wrap Ken in tissue paper. "Wait," I said, and she paused in her swaddling. My desire to possess Ken, clear when I laid eyes on him, was now clouded by Marc's reaction. But just as I was about to tell her I'd changed my mind, he fished his wallet out.

"I got this," he said.

"Are you sure?" I asked.

"You like him," Marc said, the smile on his face restored.

"Because he kind of looks like you," I said.

The woman laughed indulgently as she finished mummifying Ken and dropped him in a bag. Next to me, Marc, I could sense, had stepped back into himself.

We walked quietly down the stairs, out of the mall, and into the sunny parking lot. What had just happened? I wanted to ask. But a wall to our left caught all my attention. It was plastered with posters of soon-to-be-released Bollywood films, and amid their bright reds, blues, and greens was a flyer in black-and-white. HANUMAN MALE FIXING CENTER it said in thick letters. Underneath was a phone number, underneath Vikrant's name and his designation. Head of Center. I had seen the name only in the brochure that I still had. This was my first sighting of it in public.

"See something you like?" Marc asked.

I pointed to a movie poster in which a god with the face of a lion holds on his thigh a burly, red-lipped demon. The god tears the demon's belly open with his claws.

"We make family men of men gone astray," the flyer promised. "Our patients married women and had children. 100% success rate." "Women" and "children" were underlined. The methodology they practiced to achieve a 100 percent success rate was absent from the poster.

"Is that horror?" Marc asked.

"Parents and wives," it demanded. "Send us your men-gone-astray."

"It's a myth," I said. "About a boy who falls in love with a god."

"That's our story, then," Marc said, accent English.

The glare of that flyer dimmed from my consciousness and I said, my tone obsequious, "It most certainly is."

"Then you will listen to your god," he continued in his performance accent. "This will be our little secret, this Ken doll business. And not another word about our so-called resemblance."

I was surprised: he rarely allowed our game to go beyond a single beat.

"Your wish is my command, Sir Singer. Thank you for the opportunity to obey you."

"Happy?" he asked, reverting to his regular speech, and I nodded.

"Hey, listen," he said after a moment. "You know this isn't real, right, this kink talk?"

"But I like it!"

"And I play along because I see it makes you happy, but if it does get to be too much, if it actually stings, you'll tell me, right?"

In the light of his concern, my deception—concealing why I kept us physically apart—felt particularly wrong.

Two women walked toward a car with bloated plastic bags. A blue Contessa coasted in search of a parking spot.

I said, "I want this—us—but I can't seem to do a thing about it."

I wanted him to comfort me, to draw my head to his chest, to rub my ear, to say, "It's okay." And when he did not—when, instead, he stood with his hands crossed, his gaze, fixed on me, giving nothing away, I violated a rule I had set for us: of avoiding physical contact in public spaces, not even the kind that straight men slip into without a second thought. I wrapped my hand around his back, worried that his coffers of empathy had run dry. At first, he didn't hug me back, as I hoped he would. He didn't push me away, as I expected he would. I curled my fingers, gathering his shirt into my fists, I pressed my forehead to his shoulder. And then he did hug me back: one hand warm on the back of my head, the thumb of the other tracing my ear. "It's okay," he said.

When I opened my eyes, reassured, I saw a cop standing behind Marc. When he met my gaze, he brought a whistle to his mouth and blew it hard, producing a shrill, discordant note.

Marc turned around in time to see the cop raising his baton and stepped away. The baton landed on the ground, instead of on Marc's leg. Marc stood between me and the cop.

"Ay, hero, what are you, prince of Chittor protecting his whore?" said the cop. His khaki shirtsleeves were rolled up to the elbow. AJAY BISWAS, his name tag read.

"Sala," he said. "As if this is Amrika for you to do randipanti in public."

"I'm an Indian citizen," Marc said in Hindi.

Ajay Biswas bore his baton into Marc's chin. His breath smelled of milk and cigarette.

"Chup," he said. "Or I'll ruin your pretty face."

I looked around to see if anyone was watching. Those in the parking lot hurried from their cars to the mall, or the other way around, their necks kept stiffly away from us.

Ajay led us to his jeep, parked on the rim of the lot, and made us sit in the back. As he was about to shut the door, Marc said to him, "What will you get by arresting us?"

"Proper example I'll set. If you bring vilayat culture to our country, you will pay price."

"Maybe there are other ways to pay a price?" Marc said.

"What, bribing and all?" He yanked Marc's ear and twisted it.

I wanted Marc to fight back.

"Not a bribe," Marc said, his teeth clenched, breathing hard. "A thank-you gift. For teaching us a lesson."

I clenched my teeth. Momentarily, Marc was less attractive.

The policeman let go of Marc's ear. "I'm listening," he said.

Marc and I emptied our wallets. Between us we had eighty rupees.

"I can throw you in prison for the dirty things you do," he growled. "That's all your freedom is worth? Eighty rupees?"

The reminder that homosexuality, illegal in India, was punishable by a ten-year prison sentence felt particularly foreboding coming from a police officer.

"Even my wife's stingy brother brings five kadak hundred-rupee notes when he visits," Ajay said. "From gora toh, I won't take less than thousand."

"We don't have so much," Marc said. "We can go get it from the bank."

"Not *we*. You go," Ajay said. "Leave him here."

He took the eighty and let Marc out. Tucked under the seat in front of me, the seat where Marc had been sitting, was a stack of posters for the Hanuman Male Fixing Center. Same one I'd seen on the bulletin board. Next to it were a box of nails and a can of wall glue. Where else in Chamba had he put them up? Did he know Vikrant? Or was he an errand boy, spreading their word in exchange for a small fee collected from an employee low on the chain of command? He didn't, after all, threaten to send Marc and me packing to the Center.

I looked up and out of the jeep, not wanting Ajay to catch me staring at the posters. The fear I'd nursed for years, that Vikrant would find me, no matter how far I traveled or how much time passed, had made me feel delusional. Now, as I sat in a police jeep across from the advertisement of his services, I felt vindicated.

"What's in that bag?" Ajay asked me.

"Nothing," I said.

He struck it with his baton. The tissue paper crinkled. Ken thumped against the stick.

"Don't sound like nothing to me," he said.

He reached into the bag and took Ken out. He thumbed Ken's red hair and looked at me and grinned. I wanted to break his perfect teeth.

"What do you do?" he asked.

"What's it to you?"

"Gandu, I don't have to accept your sahib's money," he said. "You know there are other payments I can demand?"

He rubbed Ken's face against his crotch.

"Stop," I cried, and leaned forward to take Ken back.

"Shh," he said, stepping back, out of my reach. "First answer question."

I sat back down. "I'm a teacher."

"In charge of our children? I better not hear complaints."

"Children? I teach at the drama school."

"Then I don't care. Those boys are weird and useless."

He flung Ken into the bag.

When Marc returned, fifteen minutes later, the scenario to him looked unchanged: the cop outside, I in the jeep's back, Ken in his bag.

After securing Marc's money in his pocket, he let me out. He took both our names down.

He warned, "If you do dirty things in public again, I won't spare your bottoms."

He brandished his baton in our faces. We started to walk away. He stood in our way.

"You're forgetting something," he said.

"Thank you," Marc said.

He placed his baton on Marc's shoulder.

"Thank you, sir," I said, not wanting Marc to say those words.

"You trained him well, gora," Ajay said. "Now you say."

And Marc did.

Ajay spat on the ground and smoothed his mustache with his thumb. "Get lost before I change my mind."

When we got to Marc's jeep, he said, "He pull any shit on you when I was away?"

"Like you would've done something about it."

I got inside, slammed the door shut, and sat with my arms crossed.

"I was trying to help," Marc said, getting in.

I wanted Marc to snub me, to strike me even, to twist my wrist. He quietly started his jeep.

Gray clouds gathered as Marc took a whole a new route. He was taking me on a long drive. We left the town behind. The winding hill roads and the cool breeze, perfumed by the trees, eucalyptus and pine, calmed me down. As Marc drove farther up the hill, slowing down at the bends, sidling to a side and coming to a halt to let bigger vehicles pass—school buses, trucks—I thought about my contradictions: avoiding public displays of affection, then initiating one; on the run from an authoritarian, then wanting Marc to confront a cop. I had blurred my fantasy of him with who he was and needed to be in our reality.

"Sorry," I said.

Marc squeezed my shoulder. At length, I told him about my first encounter with Vikrant.

"Slow down," Marc said. "Who's this man again? As in what gives him that kind of authority?"

"He runs a center for conversion therapy, it's—"

"I know what it is," he interrupted me. I was surprised to detect in his voice a tremor.

"Sorry, continue," he said, so I did, telling him that my encounter with Vikrant spurred my foray into Nandi's troupe; in the years that followed he was a constant presence in my mind.

The words came tumbling out of me like water that's broken a floodgate. My voice cracked as I spoke, but I didn't care.

"I haven't seen him in years and I wish logic dimmed my fear, but it hasn't," I concluded.

He pulled over at a scenic viewpoint. He leaned over the steering wheel, looking straight ahead. Sweat formed on his upper lip. He was breathing hard.

I touched his shoulder. He flinched slightly. He turned to me. He was fully present again.

He said, "So you believe he might still be after you, this Vikrant character?"

"That's why Dad doesn't know I'm here. Or he might give Vikrant my whereabouts."

"Your mom will tell you if your dad tries anything, right?"

"If he tells her. He's done stuff she doesn't know about."

"Like what?"

"He photographed me peeing because I did it like a girl."

I unbuckled and stepped out of the car. Marc came and stood next to me. I leaned my face into his chest. He bracketed me in his arms and held me in a steadfast grip. A moment later, fearing my body's inevitable violence, I disengaged my body from his hold.

I said, "When I travel with Nandi, locals we stay with ask us about our families. I invent stories where my father has a new name, a new profession. He's kind."

"Were you thinking of him—is that why you, earlier today . . . ?" he asked. He mimed a phone with his hand, thumb to his ear, little finger to his pink lips. I nodded.

"I've been thinking about it," he said. "This problem we're having, with going all the way, you think it has to do with your sisters? Like you're denying yourself happiness because you didn't save them like you wanted? Maybe it sounds wild, but give it some thought."

He didn't know exactly how complicit I was in causing their death. Yet, it felt like his words had a ring of truth to them. I made a mental note to dwell on his suggestion.

"Let's get away for a bit," Marc said. "Come to my home?"

He meant his hometown, which was surprisingly hot even now, when the rest of the country had started to simmer down. This was the reason he wanted us to get the shorts.

"Your parents, they know?" I asked. "About us."

"No, but they're easy to be around."

"Family, easy—two separate entities."

He chuckled. I told him that early December my students would travel to the Chinmasta Temple to watch a play. I could arrange for an escort to take them in my stead.

"I promise you," Marc said. "If anyone comes for you, they'll have to deal with me first."

We stood and watched the sunset as if we were lovers who'd found their happy ending.

JEW TOWN, COCHIN

Marc's family lived in a quiet housing colony where, in that postdusk hour, the houses released dim murmurs of television and radio programs and the turmeric, ginger, and garlic smells of dinners being prepared.

Marc pushed open the gate to his house, and I followed him past a fenced garden of peppers, carrots, and cauliflowers, past a wisteria tree. The door opened before Marc pressed the bell. The house exhaled a breath of oud. Marc's mother cupped his face with a hand. Her wrist was adorned with a single silver bracelet. "How thin you've become!" she fretted.

I bent forward and touched her feet with an outstretched hand. I belatedly realized I had unwittingly brought a Hindu custom to a Jewish doorstep. As I was about to step away to correct my mistake, she pressed her palm to my head and blessed me. When I stood up and met her gaze, searching for some indication that I had done something out of place, I found, instead, her happiness.

"Welcome to our home," she said.

Inside, I met Marc's father, his eyes the same blue as Marc's. I held my hand out to him. He slapped it away, wrapped his arms around Marc and me, and pressed us to himself.

Marc's sisters, Mira and Delia, were twenty and twenty-one. Undergraduates in Chadigarh, here to meet me. They pulled faces at a comment Marc made. Identical expressions of disgust on different faces.

I, of course, knew that Marc had younger sisters, but the fact of it and the stories he told me—how readily they adapted to their lives in Cochin, how they affectionally sparred, a universally necessary condition, it seemed, for siblings to coexist and thrive—hadn't prepared me for the physical expression of affection between Marc and them, the back-and-forth of speech and reaction. I looked away, not knowing how to name the feeling I was overcome with: Did I resent Marc for having what I no longer could? Had the sight of him with his sisters refreshed the anger I'd felt at myself for letting mine die? The image resurfaced: my sisters on a boat, seesawing away from the shore, their eyes wild with terror.

I repeated his sisters' names in my head. Mira, Delia. I turned my attention away from their familial role as Marc's sisters and turned it toward them as individuals: their responses to the questions I asked them, about their hobbies, their friends, their dream travel destinations.

We gathered around a teapoy, set with cups of milk tea and slices of plum cake. I observed them: Marc's raised eyebrows, his father's hand cupping his cheek, his mother's rich laughter. A breeze swept in. The thin curtains billowed. Outside, a nocturnal flower opened its mouth to the sky, exhaling one note of jasmine, then another, then another. The air was drenched in its breath.

Marc and I shared a room that night. He placed two pillows between us, one below the other. He turned the double bed into two twins.

"The Great Wall of Singer," I said, patting one pillow, then the other.

"It's for show," he said. "My parents don't care. But still."

Being level with him made me attuned to his body in a new way: the heat and night smell of him, his breath one volume in his nose, another in his throat.

I picked my sock up from the floor, shrouded my erection with it, like it was the head of a man headed for the gallows, and started to stroke myself. I froze when he moved. With his back to me, he put away the pillows between our bodies and inched toward me until the shell of his butt met my hardness. His breathing was steady, like he was asleep. I never wanted to penetrate him, only to be penetrated by him. Our present mode of contact had one degree of separation from what I did not want. So I held his calf, pressed my organ to his foot, and remembered Senior's movement against my flesh as I moved against Marc. My thrusts heightened in velocity, in pressure. He tensed his calf muscle to hold his body in place for me. I came seconds later and immediately turned away, worried that I'd stain him. Shame thickened my throat. There was a new odor in the room: something pungently sour. I swatted the air like it was smoke. I closed my eyes. Miraculously, I fell asleep.

A newspaper landed with a whack on the porch and woke me up. The milkman hollered for Singer Madam. The air was sweetened with the fragrance of oud. The Great Wall of Singer had been restored.

The room had an attached bathroom. I showered and changed into a fresh pair of clothes. Marc was still asleep. I came out and closed the door behind me. Marc's mother, who sat on a chair, combing Delia's long black hair, pointed to the kitchen.

On a low flame sat a lidded pot. She came in, washed her hands at the sink tap, and poured me a cup of tea. She spoke to me as she stood at the countertop, chopping green chilies. Marc's father joined us moments later. He had on a vest and striped pajamas. He wished me good morning and started washing the dishes. I'd never heard of a man helping in the kitchen.

"Marc told me you were a journalist, Mr. Singer," I said.

He burst out laughing and a spoon slipped from his wet fingers and clattered to the floor, splattering foamy droplets of soap.

"Mr. Singer! Fancy," he said. "More people should call me that. You were saying?"

"You wrote about Jew Town, that's how you two met?"

"She still writes!" he said, picking up the spoon, pointing to his wife. "I'm a jolly old tour guide now. So, drop the Mr. Singer. Call me David."

"And me Giti," Marc's mother said.

David set each freshly washed utensil on the countertop. I got up, reached for a dry towel, and started wiping them dry. Mira piled the dried plates and bowls in the cupboard, hung ladles and pans on hooks above the window, and plopped the spoons into a mug.

David said, "So, street theater. Does it get disorienting, performing without a stage?"

"Disorienting?" I asked, genuinely perplexed.

"Yeah, it's not a fixed place where you've practiced, know where the boundaries are, so, you know, you won't topple off the stage."

Delia, Mira, and I laughed. Giti shook her head, as if disapproving of his humor. David giggled as he ran his wet hands down his trousers.

Giti clicked her tongue. "Would it hurt you to use a towel for once?"

Delia said, "You've been saying that since I was six, Mom."

"I've been saying that since you were a baby."

"Sometimes we perform onstage, but to be honest, I like not having one," I said. "My troupe gets to incorporate the landscape in our performance."

"How so?" Giti asked.

I said, "We sometimes move as we perform, from the fields that farmers till, to shops where merchants sell rations, to their wells, and end at the village square. People respond to plays that include their land."

Giti said, "What a beautiful phrase. 'Their land.'"

I said, "I once asked Marc if he'd go back to New York. He said he can go to New York, but not go back. Because things change. It wouldn't be the same."

"Why does he never speak to us like that?" David said.

"At least he has a friend to talk to," Giti said, looking at me. "That's nice."

"What's nice?" Marc asked, walking into the kitchen. He met my gaze, smiled, and rubbed his eyes with two fingers, using the length between knuckle and first joint. It was a gesture he reserved for moments of pleasure.

"Nice that you were asleep so we could shit-talk you," Mira said.

"Language!" David said.

"How many times do I have to tell you to not come into the kitchen with your slippers on, Marc?" Giti said.

"Like father, like son. He'll never learn either," said David, waving his dried hands.

"What?" said Marc, looking confused.

They passed around an easy laughter. I lowered my eyes, hot with tears as I watched their life hum with the ordinary.

After breakfast, Marc, David, and I left the house. Jew Town was flanked by the Arabian Sea on the one side, the Kaveri river on the other. A short taxi ride got us to the old town. We walked up a narrow lane flanked by shops that sold antiques and batik clothing. I asked David if he would give me the spiel he gave tourists.

The earliest Jews in India, David told me, were sailors from King Solomon's times. After the fall of the First Temple in the Siege of Jerusalem, exiles traveled on treacherous seas until a mostly wrecked ship brought them, quite by accident, to the Malabar coast of Cochin. No one knows what their original destination was, but as time went by, they didn't attempt to leave.

"There's, of course, no proof to back this legend," David said, pointing to four masks displayed on a brick wall: two demons, two gods, all blue-hued. "The first written records of Jewish settlers in Cochin date to much later. After the destruction of the Second Temple."

Local rulers protected these settlers during the attacks, which targeted the wealth that Indian Jews had over the years accumulated through the spice trade. The cemetery, where we went next, still held their gravestones, mostly intact.

"The legendary Jewish traveler Benjamin of Tudela wrote about them," David said. He pointed to the epitaphs. "They even developed their own language."

"Judeo-Malayalam," I said.

On our way out, David told me that a second wave of Jewish migrants came to Cochin in the sixteenth century. They were fleeing forced conversion in Iberia and religious persecution in Spain and Portugal. They built the Paradesi Synagogue, our next destination.

Inside, chandeliers and glass lamps in bright reds and greens washed the tiled blue floor in rich butter-yellow. One lamp, not electric, a flame—steady, still—the one that David called the ner tamid, the eternal light, burned above the podium where, David told me, the torah was read. The back wall was flanked by menorahs.

We sat there awhile. Marc unconsciously leaned into his father.

"There were tensions between the early and later settlers," David said as we stepped out. "The British called the earlier settlers 'Black Jews' and the later ones 'White Jews.' They were given prominent positions in the Empire. Nowhere else was there a caste system within a Jewish community. There was a time when Black Jews sat at the back of this synagogue."

Things changed, he said, after Abraham Barak Salem, a Zionist lawyer, led a peaceful protest outside the synagogue, demanding equal rights—which were granted. He was called the Jewish Gandhi by the locals. Soon after, a Black Jew became the synagogue's rabbi, and over time, the social divide between the groups decreased.

He said, "The Cochin Jews didn't face anti-Semitism here. Which is more than what can be said for their contemporaries elsewhere in the world."

We arrived at the banks of the Kaveri. We breathed a new kind of heat, the sort that sets your nostrils throbbing and leaves you with a strange longing for salted peanuts. I sat between Marc and his father on the stone steps leading up to the water.

"In the thick of summer, when temperatures are boiling-level hot and there are hardly any tourists, my sisters would come here for a swim," Marc told me. I learned from his father that the Kaveri did not flow into the Arabian Sea on the west coast of India; instead, it traveled through the breadth of my country and entered the Bay of Bengal, the sea on the east coast, the sea of my hometown, the sea that had swallowed my sisters.

"Marc told us about your sisters," David said. As if he'd read my mind. "I cannot imagine what it must've felt like, facing loss of that magnitude at such a young age."

"Shagun called them Mud and Milk," Marc said. "They were identical twins."

I said, "People thought they were the same person but they weren't anything like each other."

"How were they different?" David asked.

"They liked different foods, different subjects—different stories, even."

"His sisters and he would perform stories—that's what they did for playtime," Marc said.

I said, "Milk was a very go-with-the-flow girl and Mud needed to know why before she committed to things. Milk became angry on the inside, but Mud, if she was angry, you'd know."

"What did they think about it—their perceived similarity?" David asked.

"Milk was indifferent. Mud didn't want people to have opinions on her, period."

David smiled. "You know them well."

"The understanding came later," I said. "And honestly, back then, only one thing mattered: whether we had fun or fought like dogs, we got to do it together."

Father and son each simultaneously squeezed my shoulder, the one nearest to them. It was a long time back, I wanted to say to David, but I checked myself. What the statement implied, that it had stopped hurting, was incorrect, and its intent, of relieving people who feel obligated to offer comfort, was incongruous with the present circumstances, for there was nothing awkward about David's gesture of comfort, his willingness to sit next to me, giving me the gift of his patient silence, his listening. I also realized I was now more comfortable talking about them in specifics rather than in the vague generalizations that we sometimes reserve for the dead—she was kind, she was a good person—because such speech, with its separation from the life that had been lived, hurts less.

"Is there a bathroom close by?" I asked.

"I have to go too," David said.

People waved to him as we walked up a winding cobble pavement: drivers of taxis and rickshaws in white and khaki uniforms, street vendors of earthenware and fruits. They regarded him, this light-skinned man in their midst, with an everyday intimacy, not with the remove of reverence with which guests once regarded my upper-caste, foreign-returned father.

"They treat you like you're one of them," I observed.

"I'm hardly the first foreigner here," he said. "Jew Town has always been a migrant community."

He paid for both of us at the pay-and-use toilet. One rupee each. He walked toward a urinal. I locked myself in a stall. Even after Senior's lessons in adult male pissing, I couldn't relieve myself around other men: I froze until the others zipped up and left.

"One rupee each," I said, joining him outside. "That's an expensive pee, David."

"Tourist towns, tourist prices," he said. He placed a hand on my shoulder as we walked. "So. Is there a myth in particular you like performing?"

I told him then about the myth of the sea elephants.

"An ancient myth, a thousand years old, maybe more, talks about intergenerational trauma," he said. "Amazing."

"Is that something you experience?" I asked, then bit my tongue. "Sorry, that was blunt."

"Don't apologize," he said. "Giti was the first to notice. In the face of conflict, whatever its scale, trivial to critical, I'm talking the whole spectrum here, my instinct is to withdraw, to bring things back to a state of peace or at least an appearance of peace."

We spotted Marc sitting where we'd left him, by the banks of the Kaveri, his torso upright, his shoulders slightly folded.

"There are aftereffects to such behavior, of course," David continued. "Over time, this second nature bottles things up, and one day . . ." He formed a fist with one hand and struck with it the palm of the other. The sound startled Marc, who was now no more than a few feet away.

"What'd you do that for?" He sulked, facing the river again, idly casting into it a pebble.

"For this," David said, circling Marc's face with a forefinger as he sat next to his son.

"Look," Giti said, pointing to her family napping together on one big bed, Marc and David at the center, turned toward each other, Mira and Delia flanking them, their legs thrown over the men's waists. Giti led me back to the living room, where we shared a pot of tea.

"Marc told me how you met," I said. "David and you. You must've loved it here the first time if you decided to come back for good."

She asked, "Did Marc ever mention my family?"

"He never speaks of his life in the US."

"My family is very religious. And I'm not."

"I relate. Dad is. I'm not."

"Things came to a head when Marc's uncle, my brother, went to Israel."

"A pilgrimage?"

"No. To have himself fixed."

"Fixed?"

"He was like Marc. Like you."

I sat up.

"Let's share a secret. Just you and I? When we first moved, Marc had a hard time with the food here. He came home from school with an empty lunch box, but I knew he hadn't had a morsel. So I started making him things he liked. Toast, eggs, cereal. Peanut butter and jam sandwiches with chips in between—don't ask. That's his favorite."

"I'll remember that."

Giti leaned forward. "Then he tried to fool me with an empty lunch box. Now he tries to fool me with a pillow wall."

My heartbeats rained rapid as hail against my chest. She squeezed my hand reassuringly.

"We can't choose who we love," she said.

Relieved, I sat back.

"You didn't stop him, your brother?" I asked.

"I didn't try. I was worried about my son."

"Oh?"

"I'll never forget that day. New Year's, 1982. My brother came home for dinner. I'd made his favorite dessert. Pomegranate custard. Then I saw the way he was looking at Marc. His nephew."

"Marc was thirteen?"

"Had just turned thirteen. He's a December baby, my boy."

"A Sagittarius through and through."

"At first, I didn't know if I was reading him right, my brother. Then he caught me looking. Instantly he reddened. And I knew. Come, let's sit outside? I need some air."

She picked up the pot and both our cups. Four easy chairs sat snugly on the small balcony that overlooked the street and offered a view of the Kaveri in the distance. We sat down, leaving between us a seat on which I set down the pot and her cup.

"The next week my brother comes home and declares he'll go to Israel and fix himself."

"Marc was there?"

"All of us were. David, me, the children. David and the girls have blank looks. But Marc, his face is ashen."

Marc hadn't mentioned this when I brought up Vikrant. He never mentioned his uncle either. What did the man do to him?

She said, "David breaks the silence. 'What do you mean "fix" yourself?' he asks. My brother starts to reply. I stop him. 'God be with you,' I say. After a moment, he leaves."

I said, "If he left, Marc was safe, no? So why did you leave?"

"Because I know my brother. I know he'd come back and promptly go knocking on the doors of our most conservative relatives. He'd tell them about my boy. He'd use that soothing voice of his, 'I was just like Marc but I chose God and so should our Marc.' I can hear that 'our' in his voice, and it disgusts me. He'd plead his case with those so-called relatives, so they would put pressure on us, use force, if necessary, to get Marc 'fixed'—I hate that word."

"So he knew about Marc," I said. "And until Marc is with a girl, he's a source of temptation—a threat."

"That would be his twisted reasoning," she said. "As if there aren't married men who do their thing on the side."

I remembered the married man Saaya spent a night with whenever we passed through his city.

"I've seen that pressure in action. I have. With girls who didn't want to get married, couples who didn't want to start families. I've seen their suffering. But, hey, the boy is now married to the girl, the girl is married into a respectable family, the couple have a baby."

I squeezed her wrist. She patted the back of my hand and refilled her cup. She took a sip and puckered her lips. It had gone tinny or cold. She was about to get up.

"Sit," I said, a hand to her arm. "I'll do it."

In the kitchen, as I washed the pot and refilled it—two tablespoons of Assam, milk, slivered ginger, some cardamom pods—and as I waited for the water to boil, I recalled how easily it had come to me: my hand to her wrist, her arm. I always left a cautious inch between my body and the next as I moved through life. Only during performances did I breach this distance. My body didn't deserve human contact, I felt. Marc's warm, sure, tender touch, to the extent my body permitted it—his hand to my cheek, shoulder, back—had shifted, over time, my relationship to my body. He was the light in which I started to see myself as worthy of human contact.

I returned with tea and sugar. I poured us each a cup and mixed in some sugar.

"Smells nice," she said. "It's hard to talk about these things. You listen."

I told her about the Hanuman Male Fixing Center. How Pita-jee wanted to send me.

"Those places have no business existing," she said.

"They're impossible to shut down, I think. Higher-ups, political money."

"It's possible. The one in Israel was shut down just recently. A journalist checked himself in undercover and went through the whole process."

"And then he wrote about it?"

"He did. It caused a media frenzy and enough public pressure to shut the place down."

She fell quiet when she heard some movement in the bedroom. I changed the topic of our conversation. By the time Marc emerged from the bedroom, we were discussing street theater.

A SONG IN JUDEO-MALAYALAM

Marc and I took a bus to Ernakulum, twenty minutes from Cochin. At a tea shop on the intersection of MG Road and Temple Street, we sat under a thatched roof and ate banana fritters. Around four in the evening, I heard the thuds and the trumpets of elephants that slowly came into view as they strode up Temple Street, flapping their big ears, their trunks now curled, now straight, each body the gray of an overcast sky. The mahouts mounted on the elephants chatted amicably, their words inaudible at this distance, their bodies swaying in rhythm to the elephants' stride.

Gates creaked open and the elephants entered their homes. The street's silence—its stillness—felt amplified in the wake of the commotion.

I followed Marc to House No. 6. The road was drenched, as was the courtyard, where an elephant stood dripping. The air was thick with the smell of petrichor. A watchman opened the gate, greeted Marc in Malayalam, and invited us in. Marc returned the greeting in Malayalam, a language I had never heard him speak, and entered the house, its external walls ochre, its slanting roof made of terra-cotta tiles.

He came out with rice, steaming, heaped on a copper plate. Next to him was an older man, shirtless, his potbelly swaying over a spotless white dhoti. He was bald but for a small, oiled plait that sprouted from the back of his head.

Standing before the elephant, Marc opened his mouth and from his throat rose a rich, melodious song in a language unknown to me. When he finished singing, he held out the offering. The elephant uncurled his trunk, scooped up most of the rice, and tucked it into his mouth. In the next round he swept the plate clean and sat heavily down.

Marc kissed him between his eyes. The elephant's expression was the visual counterpart to a cat's purr.

Marc made introductions. The man, chief priest at a Krishna temple, put his hand on Marc's shoulder and, as he spoke, he affectionately pinched Marc's cheek.

"What did he say?" I asked.

"His elephant is getting married next summer. He's invited us."

"What language are you talking in?"

The priest pointed to the elephant and to Marc and said, in English, "I speak to both my boys in the same tongue. Judeo-Malayalam. I taught Marc the language."

The elephant before me, I realized, was the one who put Marc on his back when he was sixteen.

"May I?" I asked.

The priest nodded. I caressed the elephant's head. His skin was a paradox: rough and smooth, tough and soft. I imitated Marc, pressing my forehead to the elephant's. I wrapped my arm around his head and hugged him, tentatively at first, then hard.

We left shortly after. As we turned a corner on the street, I pinched Marc's cheek and said, "Wasn't *that* sweet, my *boy*."

"Behave yourself," Marc scolded. "He's my teacher."

"He's a priest in a Krishna temple. You know what Krishna says?" I made my voice sultry. "The soul has no gender. How does it matter what the gender of his soul mate is?"

He swiped my head and laughed as he rubbed his eyes with a thumb.

We ate sweet rice from paper plates as we sat by the Kaveri's banks. A wind rose from the river and bathed us in its wet breath. Its waters reflected the moon, full and bright, thus amplifying its light.

"Traditional Jewish stories change in Judeo-Malayalam folklore," Marc said. In the climactic battle of David and Goliath, for instance, a mosquito enters the helmet of Goliath, and when he removes his helmet, David flings a coconut at his head. It explodes on his temple and drenches his face with its water and kills him.

"The stories aren't told as is," he said. "They have become indigenous to Cochin."

Marc's fingers were turning sticky from the rice. I eyed them longingly.

"Judeo-Malayalam is a dying language," Marc said. "Less than ninety speakers left worldwide. I'd like to help change that."

"What do you have in mind?"

"Once I have a collection of photographs of Jew Town, I'll take them to New York, work with the Center for Jewish History to organize an exhibit," he said, his gaze distant. "Tell my people there about the language to raise awareness and, hopefully, some money."

He rubbed his jaw with his clean hand. I was scared by the thought of Marc going to New York. What if his path crossed his uncle's? Sharing my fear would mean betraying knowledge of his past that he hadn't shared with me, so I decided, for now, to bite my tongue.

"The money can fund people to come to Cochin and learn Judeo-Malayalam and translate the stories into other languages. Too idealistic?"

"Maybe," I said. "But so what? What's art if not idealistic?" He nodded. "The language was formed by a people who fled their land to survive," I continued. "It feels like a celebration, no? It's like the migrants are saying 'You wanted us gone, but we're still here.' And if you pull this off, more people will know about it."

Marc was about to lick his fingers clean. I grabbed his wrist.

"Use the Shagun Towel," I said.

He shook his head but dipped his hands into the river, rubbed them together, then wiped them clean and dry on the sleeve of my shirt. I felt content as I observed my damp, dirtied sleeve: Marc marked me as his; I belonged to him.

He sidled closer. Our bodies were huddled together on the stone steps, which glistened with river water, illuminated by moonlight. I placed my head on his shoulder; he leaned his head onto mine and buried his nose in my hair. His breath smelled of fennel. He moved away after a moment. He knew he couldn't reciprocate for long even the most basic gestures of intimacy. He spoke the aberrant grammar of my need with a native's fluency.

"I like what you said earlier," he said. "Honestly, how does it matter what the gender of your soul mate is." Then, he fell quiet.

"I will say this once," he continued. "Let's just do it one day. Let's go all the way. You understand?" I nodded. "It may be hard for you, but only at first, and by the time we're done, it'll be behind you: your guilt, or whatever's holding you back. Sometimes you have to allow yourself happiness to see you deserve it."

Freedom by orgasm: it sounded too fantastic to be true.

THE MEETING

Soon after returning from Cochin, I called Ma and agreed to meet the girl she had mentioned. We came up with a script to keep Pita-jee from knowing that I was in Chamba until May: we'd tell the girl and her family that the itinerant troupe I was a part of was stationed in Chamba for a few weeks. The intimacies of the Singer family swirled about my head as I spoke to Ma.

"We were never close," I said. "Physically, I mean. Why?"

"You all slept in my room until you were ten."

At once, a memory stirred to life: awakening to the folds of a sheet, warmed by our bodies, Milk huddled against Ma's body, Mud against mine. I felt a phantom limb against my flesh. How had I so thoroughly lost access to this memory? How did it return so viscerally now?

"Why did things change?" I asked.

"Your father wanted them to," she said.

"Of course he did."

"He felt a growing boy shouldn't be too physically close to his mother."

"And if he is, poufff! He turns into a woman."

She ignored my comment. "So to be fair to you, I sent your sisters down as well."

"My masculinity isn't at risk if I sleep in the same room as my sisters?"

"You can be real pain sometimes," Ma said.

Over dinner, I said to Marc, "I didn't cook extra today, so no home-cooked lunch for you tomorrow. Good news is, you get to eat at your favorite dhaba."

"Won't lie, I missed it," he said.

"Go get that grease."

He stood up and made a little show of dancing, a fork in one hand, a spoon in the other.

"Marc," I said, leaning forward. "I'll be there too. Dad wants me to meet a girl."

He sat back down and placed his cutlery on the table.

"If I don't, he'll show up," I explained. "So I'm going to meet her. Ma's bringing her over."

He picked his chair up and set it next to mine. I'd never seen him drag a chair.

The food I'd made smelled better when it wafted from his mouth, warmed in the heat of his breath. The mild November night filled with the chorus of cicadas.

"I got to meet Giti, now I want Ma to meet you," I said.

"So I should just 'happen' to be there at the same time? Got it. I'm no actor like you-know-who, but I'll try to make it look natural."

I could tell I'd made him happy by saying I wanted him to meet my mother.

"You'll tell her about us?" he asked.

"I won't have to, she'll know when she sees you," I said. "Giti did too. Moms know."

"They do," Marc conceded, leaning his head until it met mine. I smiled, relishing the contact, the softness of his hair underneath the hard shell of his scalp. He stood up and grabbed both our plates.

"Got you," he said. "I'm doing the dishes tonight."

I stood next to him in his kitchenette, admiring his slow industry, his hand working the dish soap on a plate to a lather with a sponge. On the stove before me was a pot of milk, and when it came to a boil, I lowered its heat, added turmeric, black pepper, cinnamon, and honey, and watched the concoction simmer. I'd felt no resistance to him doing the dishes, and though to most that was an utterly ordinary state of affairs, to me it was a milestone I'd floated up to, buoyed by Marc's reciprocation, his patience, his respect. I had begun to consider the possibility that Marc and I could be equals.

The next afternoon, I met Ma and the girl at a dhaba on the outskirts of Chamba. It was a Monday in the second week of December. Ma cupped my cheek and kissed my forehead. She watched my face as she ran a thumb down my eyebrow, smoothing it down. She wiped my tears, and I hers, and I noticed then the bags that had appeared under her eyes. Her face, other than that, remained just as it was in my memory.

Ma introduced me to Radha.

"He was a boy when he left home," she said, to explain to Radha the emotion that informed our reunion, I guessed. "We haven't seen each other in seven years."

"I cannot even imagine what that must feel like," Radha said.

We sat down.

"So what do you do, Radha?" I asked.

"Finishing my bachelor's," she said. "Chemical engineering."

"You're far more educated than I'll ever be," I said.

"Street theater," Radha said, thumbing her glass bangles. "Papa used to take me."

When the waiter brought us bottles of Campa Cola with straws in them, Radha and I ordered gobi manchuria simultaneously.

"You have similar taste." Ma beamed.

I rolled my eyes and Radha laughed as she folded the edge of her sari over her shoulder.

"I have some letters to write," Ma said. "So why don't I leave you to it?" She went and sat a few tables away.

"I'll say this directly," I said. "I don't actually want to get married."

"That's good news," Radha said. "There's someone else I like. Parents don't know."

"Caste issues?"

She nodded and said she planned on keeping it a secret until she and the boy, who was her classmate, had jobs. Then they would get married and inform their families.

"What's his name?" I asked.

"Rupin," she said.

"*Rupin*? What does a man called *Rupin* study?"

"Accounting, but he has a thing for Hindustani classical music."

"As pretentious as his name."

"Stop!" she said, laughing. "You have someone in your life?"

"I do," I said. "It's complicated."

"More complicated than caste issues?"

I shrugged. Our food came and we ate quietly for some time.

"How long before you finish college?" I asked.

"One more year."

"Let's tell our parents that we'd like to talk some more before we decide?"

"That'll buy us time," she agreed. "Let's actually make those calls, though. Keep up appearances."

"Once you marry Rupin and move someplace safe—pick a big city so you're hard to track—well, they'll know. Deal?"

"Will you be okay?"

Her concern moved me. "Tracking a street performer in this country? Finding a needle in a haystack is easier."

"Then deal," she said.

A little while later, when we were halfway through our meals, Marc entered the dhaba, three men in tow. His colleagues, I guessed. They all wore formal attire: button-downs tucked into trousers. His eyes scanned the dhaba until he found me. He met my gaze and held it. We smiled at each other, not a smile of collusion, but a simpler one, the pleasure of seeing someone you love in a public space.

Radha looked from me to him. He joined his group who, by then, had found a table. Ma, I saw, from the corner of my eyes, was staring at me.

"It is complicated," Radha asked. "What's his name?"

"Marc."

"Rupin's way better than Marc, haan! At least it's unique."

I smiled, warmed by her response. Marc came up to our table. Almost immediately, Ma came swooping down. I introduced them.

"How do you two know each other?" Ma asked.

"Marc's a photographer," I said. "It's a small town. Artists run into each other."

"We're good friends now," Marc said. "Your son's a great guy."

"Have you met Radha?" Ma asked Marc. "We're trying to get the 'great guy' to say yes. Help me convince him."

Marc laughed. "Shagun's an adult, he should be making his own decisions."

"A very Western way of thinking," Ma said. "Anyway. If this works out, Shagun will bring you a wedding card."

"Do send my parents one. They love Shagun. He came home one weekend. Such a lovely time we had. *Anyway.* My colleagues are waiting, I must go."

After Marc left, Ma turned to Radha and asked, "So. You two hit it off?"

"We'd like to keep talking," Radha said. "Can we have some time?"

Radha excused herself to use the restroom. She wanted Ma and me to have a moment, I guessed. Ma gave me a piece of paper with two numbers: Radha's and, under that, Pita-jee's.

"He wants you to have his number," she said. "You don't want it, I know. I'm just finishing a chore so I can tell him when he asks."

I folded the paper and put it in my wallet. The gesture seemed to please her.

"I have to get Radha home," she said. "Or we could've done something together."

"Maybe I'll come home soon."

"You should," she said. "Especially if you can make the time to go to Marc's."

"Do you remember Krishna's birthday—the year I left for Magpies?" I asked. "You'd forgotten the oil and I fetched it for you. It just came to my mind for some reason."

We shared, in that moment, a look of acknowledgment: Marc's presence in the dhaba was no accident, and I'd learned the tactic from her. Well played, the look on her face seemed to say.

"You know why your father went to London?" she asked.

I shook my head, willing her to speak.

"He wanted things," she said. "Things his Indian salary couldn't buy."

"What things?"

"English education for his children, dowry money for your sisters so they could get married into decent families, for you, a London degree. That's why he went."

"I bet he's taking a big fat dowry from Radha's family," I said.

"He never would," she said. "He knew what it felt like, as the father of two daughters. He didn't want to put someone else through that experience. He told me so in as many words."

"Why didn't he come home as soon as he heard about my sisters? Waiting six whole months to pass before he makes his appearance doesn't exactly scream 'paternal love' to me."

She chewed her lower lip and frowned. "He ever mentioned Rohit-jee to you?" she asked.

"That he'd fixed my sisters' marriage to Rohit-jee's much-older sons?" I said. "He didn't. But Rusty did."

"When?" she gasped. "That's just wrong."

"And the fact that you didn't tell me isn't wrong?" I said.

"I was waiting for the right moment," she explained.

"That's your standard excuse for keeping things from me," I retorted. "Listen. For a change, could you use your secret-keeping skills for me, instead of against me?"

She frowned, confused.

"Don't tell Pita-jee about Marc."

"I'm not an idiot, Shagun."

"Well, you told him what I did to my sisters—after you promised not to tell anyone."

Her expression softened. "He's your father—and theirs too. He can know about it."

"I see. And Rohit-jee? What's your reason for telling him?"

Her lips parted in surprise. Radha came up to us. Ma composed her face and smiled. I turned and saw Marc chatting amicably with his colleagues.

I skipped my evening visit to Marc's place that evening. I had a meeting with Nandi. I'd informed him about my meeting with Radha and he wanted to know how it went. So I went and told him. My retelling excluded the detail of Marc's presence.

My interactions with Nandi had become cautiously polite. With comments and questions that seemed casual, Nandi frequently checked on my intention to leave Chamba with him. "What should we perform in Banaras, Shagun?" he would ask. Or, to Rooh he would say, in my presence: "Our next performance should be the sea elephant myth. To humor Shagun, who will no doubt be homesick for Chamba." His gaze would linger on me to read my reaction.

Now Nandi said, "You got yourself some time, and before that time ends, we'll be back on the road and your father can't get a hold of you." Nandi brought a hand to my shoulder. "Best not to develop attachments. Makes departures difficult."

I asked Saaya to walk with me that night. I gave him the detail I'd kept from Nandi.

"I wasn't expecting Ma to accept Marc," I said. "I just wanted her to meet him. That happened, and I'm happy."

"I can tell," Saaya said. "Time to stop running, maybe."

"Are you suggesting I don't travel with you after Chamba?"

"Yeah, because it seems to me you want to be with Marc. No? If Marc's going to become available, tell me. I'll quit Nandi for him, I don't care."

"Shameless."

"Are you the jealous sort? 'If I can't have him, no one else can'?"

"I don't want to have him," I said. "I want to belong to him."

"Oh really," he said, with mock surprise. "I would've never guessed."

"I want to marry him and I want us to have a child—his biological child. I even have a name. Marc Singer II. Or Marc Singer Junior. What's the difference between the two?"

Saaya said, "Here's a better question: What if you have a girl?"

"We'll call her Marc Singer II or Junior anyway. I'm Shagun Singer, naturally."

"The heart wants what it wants—you dropped that shit on me, you five-rupee philosopher," he said. "Just don't keep all of the husband-wife shit that you've clearly lapped up from Bollywood films and our myths. Weed the toxic stuff out, keep what excites you."

"Like fasting for his long life on Karwa Chauth," I said.

Saaya slapped his forehead. "Boy, you want him more than you want to travel with us."

A SHAM

The principal of the drama school called me into his office the next day before my class and showed me the midterm evaluations.

"These are better than what some regular teachers get," he said. "Ever thought of switching professions?"

"I'm not sure I'm qualified," I said.

He smiled. "We're a private institution. We can relax rules for good teachers. You have a full-time position here starting next semester—if you want it. I know street theater can be exhilarating, god knows I was a rebel too when I was your age, but this school, it's the best of both worlds, you get to make art and have a stable job. Helps if, say, someday you want to settle down, start a family, that kind of a thing?"

He held his hand out and I shook it.

"Think about it," he said.

In class that day, I brought up the play from the Chinmasta Temple.

"You missed a good one," Mohit said.

"I know, I had to go to Cochin for a family thing," I said. "So what was the premise?"

"Woman invokes goddess to nuke stupid husband," Ankit said.

I joined their laughter and said, "This, as you may know, is a spin on the original myth where the goddess possesses and kills the husband. What changes in this adaptation?"

"The goddess wants the wife to have her agency," Gupta said.

Ronit said, "Right. So she has the wife do the honors."

"And the goddess and the wife, now a widow, get together," Ankit said. "I dig that transgression. But why not do more—why not show them kiss?"

Everyone laughed. I raised my hand. They fell silent.

"I get it," Ankit said. "We all put on a face in public, we laugh on cue if a classmate says 'two women kiss.' But that play? It had us in its grip. We didn't find it funny when a woman fell for a goddess who decides to stay with her. They could've used that chance to normalize two women kissing. Not saying the play's bad. I just wish it went all the way."

"That's what he said," Mohit said.

My students laughed again. I reddened, as if Marc were here to attest to my impotence.

"That's an excellent point you make, Ankit," I said. "But also remember the context: the performers were in a temple."

"Can we be real with our play: tell it as it is, censor nothing?" Ankit asked. "We're not performing in a temple, are we?"

There were murmurs of agreement. The spirit of the conversation inspired me to tell them about another act of censorship: the second volume of *The Dravidian Book of Seas and Stargazing*.

"A whole book?" Ankit said, leaning forward. "What, destroyed?"

"Removed from circulation more like. Legend has it there are a few surviving copies. How I would like to get my hand on one. Volume one is my favorite book."

"You tried looking for it?" Mohit asked.

"Our troupe travels all over the country, and over the years I scoured every secondhand and antique bookshop and scrap market, which, pro tip, are great places to discover banned books. But no luck."

"How did you hear about it?" he asked.

Over the course of my search for the book, I hadn't given thought to the source of my information, my father, and I couldn't tell if the omission was deliberate, but now I did make the choice of lying when I responded to Mohit's question. "Nandi told me," I said, not wanting to bring my father up, not wanting talk to my students about him in case they asked follow-up questions.

After class was over and my classroom emptied, I picked my bag up and turned to leave. I found Marc standing in the doorway. I hadn't seen him since our formal meeting at the dhaba last afternoon, and it felt like an inordinately long interval. How would I leave him and go on performing, town to village to city, pretending like my life hadn't intersected with his?

"Lunch?" he asked.

"Where are we going?"

He smiled. "To Chamba's oldest bakery."

"I'm sorry," I said. "Ma was hard on you."

He waved his hand. "I sassed right back, so we're good."

"What does one even eat in a bakery?" I asked, smiling.

As he made his way up to me, he announced a litany of baked goods. Pastries, bagels, garlic bread. Vegetable puffs. Pancakes. I looked at him blank-faced.

"I might as well be reciting a Greek comedy," he said.

"My travels took me through mostly rural places." I said. "Your fancy bakeries don't exist there."

"You have a favorite Indian dish, then?"

I thought about it a moment, but couldn't come up with one.

"Oh, Sham. You know more about gods and demons than you do about yourself."

"Did you just call me a sham?"

"I didn't call you a sham. I called you Sham. *Sha* from 'Shagun,' *m* from 'Mathur.' Sham."

Marc drove us out of College Street and onto Main Street. He turned onto a dirt road laid out between wheat fields. Workmen in khaki overalls cycled toward us single file. Behind them a factory chimney smoked against a lilac sky. Clinking their horns, they broke into two lines and peddled to our left, to our right, chanting the name of Krishna in low, gruff voices. A breeze swept through the fields, and the stalks lowered their mustard-yellow heads. The workmen fell into a single file behind us. The sounds of rolling cycle chains and crunching dirt turned faint.

"I'll pack us some food and we'll have it at this scenic viewpoint," said Marc. "You'll have a favorite bakery dish before you have a favorite Indian dish."

I bobbed my head in time with his words, said nothing. He stopped across from the bakery, a gray stone building with tinted windows and a slanting wooden roof.

"Come here," I said.

"It speaks!" he exclaimed like a high-pitched Englishman.

He got out of the jeep, walked over to my side, opened my door. Gripped my seat's backrest. Framed my head between his arms.

"Sham," I said. "My first pet name. Mud, Milk, and Sham. That would've been nice."

Marc stepped aside; I got out. A passing truck whipped our hair. He kissed my cheek.

We sat in his car and ate. I went to church after my sisters died, I told him, as we bit into warm bagels with cream cheese. I told Jesus our Hindu stories, I said. Marc lowered the bagel from his mouth and looked out the window. When he spoke it sounded as if he were continuing rather than beginning a story.

"I went to the staff room before we left for India," he said, "to thank all my teachers. Ms. Cavendish, my sixth-grade English teacher, was there. She'd taught us Russian short stories.

"When I thanked her, she said, 'Don't thank me, we have to be nice to everyone these days.' She said my last name, under her breath, but she moved her lips slow enough that I could read them. She soured her whole face theatrically before smiling again.

"I left the staff room feeling like a fool," he said. "How had I not known before? There were signs. She never called on me when I raised my hand. My friend Liam once copied my assignment; he got an A, I a B."

"Marc, you were a child," I said.

"That night I criticized the food Mom made, snapped at Dad when he asked how my day went. Asked them why we had to move to India. As if being Jewish was their fault." After a pause, he said, "If I went to church, those Russian stories are what I would tell the son of God."

He turned to me. "Share a soda with me, to wash down the grease?"

Off he went, back into the bakery, skipping to some internal tune, hands stuffed into pockets. He resembled a silent film hero.

I met Saaya after classes the next day and we walked together to the café. "You said you missed our performances. How about we do something together, just Rooh, you, and me?"

"Hmm," he said suspiciously. "Since you didn't mention Nandi, would this performance perchance involve Marc?"

I giggled as I said, "You know me really well."

"Stop flattering me," he said. "You came to me first because you know I'm the weakest link, you bastard."

"Language," I said, gesturing to the students around us. "You're the teacher."

"Unfortunately. So. What's the occasion?"

"The occasion," I replied, "is Marc's birthday."

HAPPY BIRTHDAY, MARC

On the eighteenth of December, at 11:45 P.M., I asked Marc if he would like to go for a walk. A twinkle entered his eyes, as though he suspected that I planned to usher in his birthday with a surprise. But he didn't press me for details, and together we left his apartment.

Ten minutes later, we were at the park, the spot Karan had booked for our celebration. It was dark, but as soon as we opened the gate and went in, a chain of string lights came brightly to life: wrapped around the tree trunks, crisscrossing from the branches of one tree to the next.

All of my friends, the ones I shared with Marc and my friends from the troupe, got together and clapped. Sparklers were lit and passed around. And at the stroke of midnight, we sang a loud happy birthday song. Marc was hugged and showered with all the love that I knew he so richly deserved. Su sat him down on a park bench and sat next to him along with Sagar and Karan. I joined Saaya and Rooh. We slipped on our paper masks and began our performance.

On one occasion, a child stolen by the sea elephant patriarch is a mute. She speaks with her hands to her elephant family: the fish she wants to eat, the bright purple seaweed she likes. Her expressions reveal if she's sad, happy, angry, but the elephants can't tell why she feels a certain way. The empress devises a solution: she teaches the child how to form letters and then entire words with pebbles on the sea floor. Then a whole world of stories spills out of the child:

about her time with her human family, the friends she didn't have, her father's resentment of her silence. The elephants press their trunks to her head, her back, hugging her in their elephant way. With time, she has new stories to tell: the pranks she plays on her elephant family, their food she likes, the dreams she now has. She finally has the childhood she never did, and when she leaves her underwater family, her soul is light.

When the performance drew to an end, our audience gave us a standing ovation. I took my mask off, went up to Marc, panting, and said, "Happy birthday, Marc."

He said as he hugged me, his throat wet with happiness, "Thank you."

"Hello! Where's our thank-you?" Saaya asked.

Afterward, we sipped on sodas and ate the samosas that Sagar had bought from our favorite local eatery, Kali Mithai Shop.

"How did you manage to move around like that and give the voice-over without becoming breathless?" Su said, linking her hand to mine.

"Are you the guest who came to Shagun's classes?" Saaya asked, walking up to us.

"Guilty as charged," Su said, and introduced herself. Saaya returned the introduction.

"We've been friends for six years," he said, squeezing my arm. "Shagun's done that many times, voiceover with acting, for much longer. What he did today? Easy as walking."

"What he did today was what I saw," Su said. "I liked it."

"Special guest, and so easily impressed?"

"Saaya!" I exclaimed.

Su smiled. "This isn't a competition. And you'll know him in a way I never can, I get it."

That placated Saaya somewhat.

"Maybe I'll know something about him that will surprise you," she continued. "We express different facets of ourselves to different friends, no? That's why I find the idea of one best friend so ridiculous."

"Not a chance," Saaya said. "Nothing you say about him will surprise me."

A Bollywood song started to play on a stereo. Marc and Rooh came up to us.

"We had a nice long chat," Rooh said, patting Marc's back. "A man with a stable job and a kind heart? I approve."

"Dance with me?" Marc asked, blushing.

Su said to Saaya, "You win. You are his best friend."

"It sounds like you're giving it to me."

"Stop it," she said, slapping his elbow. "Come dance with me."

"I don't know about that," he said, crossing his hands.

She grabbed his wrist and dragged him. He yelped but laughed and went with her to where the rest were dancing. Rooh joined them.

"This is the best birthday I've had," Marc said, bringing a hand to my head.

"The first of many," I said and kissed his chest.

"And maybe for one of them," Marc said, his voice filled to the brink with hope, "it will be just the two of us, and we'll be more than what we are now—what we're now, I won't trade for anything. Want to add to it, is all. Someday, when you're ready. No need to say anything."

I wanted, with all of my being, to fulfill his birthday wish.

We joined our friends, and together we danced into the wee hours.

THE ARGUMENT

A new rhythm began starting the third Monday of December: before Ma called, I called Radha. We spoke for twenty minutes. If her parents were around, she spoke about college, the classes she was taking, the books she was reading. If they weren't around, she shared her dreams: the kind of home she desired with Rupin, the holidays she planned to take before they started a family, the money she wanted to sock away for her children's education. It was a comfort to hear her speak. I found in her domestic dreams an echo of the dreams that I nurtured. The kind of home I wanted with Marc, the meals I wanted to cook for him. Sometimes she gave me simple recipes that I wrote down and made for Marc, sometimes I sought Marc's advice on men's clothing and passed them on to Radha. Our elders had us believe the sexes were different like day and night. But I hadn't found another who was as much like me as she was.

She once whispered, "Maybe we were sisters in a past life."

"Oh, we're sisters now, Sis," I said, and she burst out laughing.

The power was out, so Marc lit a lantern, and we gathered around it. As he told us about retro night at the new disco on New Year's Eve, Karan opened his guitar case and took out a pipe and a drawstring bag.

"We need to dress up, of course," Marc said. "Shagun scoured the market and got me a killer outfit. You guys better up your game."

Su said, "Take a leaf out of his book, Sagar love?"

Karan held the glass dome of a lantern with a tea towel and un-screwed it.

Sagar didn't respond to Su's question. "Go on, ignore me," she said.

"I'm available," Karan said as he turned the knob of the lantern. The flame leaped and filled the room with kerosene's pungent odor. He picked a coal block from the drawstring bag, dropped it in the bulb of the pipe as he held the base of the bulb over the flame.

"You charge by the hour or by the day?" Su asked.

"Brutal," Marc exclaimed.

The coal crackled and released a flurry of flares. Karan took out a folded tissue from his guitar bag, and from it he pinched a finely ground white substance. He sprinkled it on the coal blocks, releasing a sickly sweet aroma. He wrapped his lips around the pipe's mouth and took in a deep drag. He frowned and drained the smoke through his nostrils.

"Want to try some?" Karan asked me.

"Don't," Marc warned.

"Why not?" I said and took the pipe. I drew a drag, held it in my lungs, and released it slowly through my nostrils. Just as I felt smug about han-dling it like an old-timer, I was struck by a coughing bout, and when it ended, I felt light-headed. An aftertaste, something leafy, lingered at the back of my throat. I took another hit and didn't cough this time.

"Nice!" Karan said as he took the pipe back.

I said, "You guys, Marc bought me a Ken doll."

I was giddy but conscious enough to know that I was using the drug's influence as an excuse to speak freely, to disclose the information that Marc forbade me to.

"Sham!" Marc exclaimed.

"Marc thinks that Ken looks like him," I said.

"Why'd you tell on him?" Su said, kicking my knee playfully. "You're so dead tonight."

"Is he though?" Marc said. He laughed, but his eyes had hardened.

Karan wrinkled his nose. "I don't want to know about your bed business."

"A senior secondary classmate used to call it 'bumping uglies,'" Sagar said.

"Same," I said.

"I can't imagine how an all-boys boarding school can be anything but a nightmare," Su said.

"Bed business?" Marc said. "I know nothing about bed business. Do you, Sham?"

"Stop it," Su said. "You're making him self-conscious."

"Shagun does get very self-conscious," Marc said. After a pause, he added, "Unlike Saaya."

The rim of Marc's ears and the bridge of his nose had reddened. He wanted to hurt me. And it worked.

I said, "Can I have some more, Karan?"

At once, Marc said, "Absolutely not," and Karan said, "Absolutely."

I took one more hit. My drowsiness evaporated. An unnamable agitation took its place. A moth wove closer and closer to the flame. I leaned forward and cupped the flame with my palms. My fingers shivered, as if in tandem with the moth's flapping wings.

"Karan," Marc said, rubbing my back. "Keep that away from my boy."

His body language had softened, as had his expression. On his face I found concern but no regret for the words he'd spoken. When the power came back, the room exploded abruptly with the white flare of a tube light. I shuddered as though waking up from a dream. Air from the whirring fan snuffed the flame out. The moth flew up, higher, higher still, in search of the tube light. It found instead the blade of the fan.

The next morning, I woke up and found Marc nursing a cup of tea. I accepted the kiss he planted on my lips and stood next to him. He pointed to a cup covered with a saucer.

"That Saaya comment," I said. "Can we talk about it?"

"Funny," Marc said. "That's where you want to begin?"

"Instead of?"

"We're chaste as dolls in a child's wedding game: How about that?"

He did not raise his voice. His speech had the texture and pace of a normal conversation, even as his whole face turned crimson. He took a towel and went to take a shower, leaving his cup of tea, half drunk, on the edge of the sink. He did not slam the bathroom door.

Later, as he took off for work, I asked, "I don't teach today. Can I spend the day here?"

He shrugged, bounded down the stairs, got into his jeep, and left. I picked up his teacup and sought the side that had a pale-brown band lining the inside wall. I held the edge between my lips until I felt his saliva dissolve with mine. I tilted the cup and swallowed stone-cold tea in slow gulps. I lay down on his bed and fell asleep to his smells. I woke up to a hand on my forehead.

"Marc asked you to come check on me?"

"Why would he do that?" Su asked, looking from me to the unmade bed on the floor.

I shrugged. "Things are not all fairy tale in the Singer household."

"They aren't in any household ya," Su said.

I said, "Stay with me?"

"I'm not leaving, even if you ask me to," Su said.

We went to the balcony when the sun started to set.

"My mother loves these," I said, pointing to a bloomed jasmine. I told Su about the flower man who cycled down our street and to the back of our bungalow on Saturday at three. When he sounded his cycle horn, Ma placed a one-rupee coin in a wicker basket and lowered it from the window of her room with a rope tied to its handle. He took the coin and slipped it into his shirt pocket. A basket on his back seat was piled with all his flowers. He measured two cubits of stringed jasmine, tip of forefinger to elbow.

"Two cubits," Su said, "is how much Mom takes. What's it with moms and two cubits?"

"Ma always says, 'Add some more.'"

"Same!" Su exclaimed.

I said, "He'd cut the two cubits and 'some more' with his blade and place it in Ma's basket. She'd pull the basket up and lean her nose into the flowers. Strange thing is I don't feel any particular longing to go home, but this smell still makes me nostalgic."

"I relate," Su said. "I'm more excited by the *idea* of going home than actually going."

"What happens when you do go?"

"Same nonsense every girl from a middle-class home faces. See this boy, see that boy, chi, you're twenty-five already, no one will marry you if you become an aunty."

"They don't know about Sagar?"

"If they know I'm living with a boy without being married to him, they'll lose it. Mom thinks I'm single and moping. Guess what she thinks is the solution?"

"Oh god, do I want to know?"

"Fair and Lovely fairness creams."

"Those are still around?"

"It comes with a Fairness Meter now," Su said. "A paper strip printed with eight shades, dark brown to pale brown. Each tube promises to take your skin down by two shades."

"Oh, I know. My sisters started using them when they turned fourteen."

"Fourteen?" Su said, shaking her head.

"Ma insisted," I said. "They kept the pink tube in our bathroom next to the tube of toothpaste. Also to be used twice a day. White teeth, white skin. They imagined using four tubes to travel from one end of the Fairness Meter to the other. They wanted to become as fair as Madhubala or as fair as Goldie Hawn, depending on whether they were in a Bollywood or Hollywood mood."

"Hollywood," like all things American, brought our minds to the only American we knew.

"You know he really loves you, right?" Su said. "Whatever this is, it will pass."

Will it, though? I wondered. I found myself telling her, then, about the trouble between us, my body's violent reaction. It was the first time I spoke about it out loud.

"Slow down," Su said. "Start over."

I paused, took a breath. Spoke again. Detailed my disease step-by-step. A brief window of intimacy followed by erasures. Sound touch sight.

"You told Marc?"

I shook my head. "Now I feel like I need to give him more when I do speak up."

"Like what?"

"Something to justify the delay, I guess? If I can figure out why it happens, I can say I wanted to understand it first."

She linked her arm with mine. We stood silently next to each other. Marc came home. He raised an eyebrow at us.

Su said, "I'm talking to my friend. You got a problem?"

"If Shagun's *talking* to you, you have it better than me."

How did he carry this anger within him, intact, unaltered, all day long?

"Why didn't you call? I would've made chai."

"I did, you were too busy *talking* to hear the ring," Marc snapped.

Su looked at her wristwatch and announced that she had to go. As she slipped her sandals on, I asked her if she could give me a ride, and at that Marc started and his anger swiftly dissolved into concern.

"Why are you going?" he asked.

"I have school tomorrow."

"I'll drop you," he said.

He came and held my wrist as he fixed his gaze on the floor.

"Looks like Romeo and Romeo want to kiss and make up, so I'll leave you to it," Su said.

After we heard her car leave, Marc pressed my body to his, buried his head in the hollow of my neck. "I'm sorry," he said.

"I deserve it," I said, combing through his hair.

"Nobody deserves to be treated poorly, Sham."

"I prefer that to you bottling things up."

He stepped back. His eyes glowed with a film of water. I unbuckled his belt and slid it off.

"So you can say anything you want to me," I said. "You can even hit me."

I lowered my head and offered him his belt, coiled across both my palms. He pressed one hand to my jaw as he kissed my forehead, with the other he pushed his belt to the floor.

"Don't say that. You promise?" I nodded. "Good. Spend the night here? Wear my clothes tomorrow, I'll drop you off at school?"

We spoke that night about our upcoming outing to the disco. New Year's Eve was just a few days away. We were in the dark of his bedroom. Marc on the bed. Me on the floor.

"Will they play Rasputin?" I asked.

"ABBA's the rage now. How do you know pop music but not cartoons? No *Beauty and the Beast,* no Chip and Dale—"

"—no James Bond."

"Don't say James Bond in the same breath as Chip and Dale."

"I organized a birthday party for my sisters the year they turned twelve."

"Mother General agreed?"

"She's not that bad, okay! I borrowed a bunch of LPs and played them through the evening. Elvis Presley, Bee Gees, Boney M."

"You danced too?"

"Yeah! Mud said, 'If you dance like that, no one will marry you.' And I said, 'I'll never get married. I don't care for girls.' She went, 'That's what all the boys say.'"

Marc said, "I'm sorry I said we're like dolls in a child's game."

"Come here," I said, and in the dark, I sensed his body, its heat, settle next to me. I groped for and found his hand. I placed it on my man breast.

"If you want to, you can," I said. "When I'm asleep."

He took his hand off my breast, placed his palm on my chest, then removed it.

"I came looking for you," he said. "On the dhaba night. You weren't there. I ran into Saaya on my way out, and he was flirty and touchy-feely."

I replayed that evening in my head, reorganizing its contents to accommodate this information: when I was with Nandi, telling him about

Radha, Marc came to meet me and ran into Saaya instead; I took a walk with Saaya later that evening and Marc was the exclusive topic of our conversation, but he failed to recount his exchange with Marc or even share the fact that Marc had come to meet me.

I asked, "Where did he touch you?"

He brought my hand to his chest.

"Punch here."

He placed my hand on his shoulder.

"Slap here."

"You remember," I said.

"That's not fair."

I heard those sounds in my head. Punch. Slap. Friend's hand, lover's body.

"Nothing happened," he said. "So relax, will you?"

He playfully grabbed my neck under his elbow and made me sit up. We burst out laughing, and it was lovely, being suspended in that pleasure for a moment, untethered from our discontent. To forget, however temporarily, the source of our pain.

LUCKY

On New Year's Eve, I was outside, waiting for Marc, when I noticed Rooh and Saaya walking home from dinner. Upon seeing Saaya, anger quickened my heartbeat.

"All decked out for your party," Rooh said.

"Marc's coming to get me," I said, without looking at Saaya.

"Such a pretty boy," Saaya said, pinching my collar.

"Tell him yourself," I said. "He'll be here any minute."

"I meant you, dummy," Saaya said.

"Plans?" I asked.

"This thirsty bastard does," Rooh said. "Someone's picking *him* up soon."

Marc's red jeep appeared at the end of the street, its headlights bright in the poorly lit street. He pulled up in front of me and I got in.

"Dudes," Marc said, doffing his imaginary hat, at Saaya first, then Rooh.

"How fancy that sounds," Saaya said. "I'll use it on my man. Get me a drink, dude."

"You would," Marc said, and Saaya laughed.

If there was an undertow of sexual tension between them, I didn't sense it. Rooh slapped the car, and we took off.

Su, Sagar, and Karan joined us at the venue. The manager of the disco-theque greeted us with a pair of scissors.

"Our first guests must inaugurate the place," he said, a fake gold tooth shining in the canopy's spotlights as he handed the scissors over to Marc, who in turn handed them to me.

I hesitated a moment, self-conscious. Marc curled a hand around my shoulders. I smiled and the jaws of the scissors closed in on the red rib-bon. We went in clapping, and the manager photographed us against a tangerine wall, rough-textured and illuminated with accent lights.

Inside, crushed electric-green sofas stood against blue walls. Beneath the smell of the lavender room freshener was the smell of fresh paint. The deejay's long hair was draped over his shining white shirt, two buttons of which were open, revealing a thick steel chain. He waved at us an LP record and played ABBA's "Dancing Queen."

I felt overdressed in my neon-purple shirt and leather bell-bottoms and looked with admiration at Marc, who was at ease in a sparkling red shirt, tight black trousers, and a belt with a big Harley Davidson decal for a buckle. He'd slicked his hair with brilliantine into a pompadour. Affecting a cocksure swagger—a slight frown, shoulders swaying, thumbs tucked into trouser pockets, elbows poking out—Marc walked onto the mirrored dance floor. He raised his hands above his head. The orbs of pink, orange, yellow lights that swept over him seemed to be courting him as he turned this way and that. How, I wondered, did he inhabit his body *and* his mind so fully?

When the guests started to trickle in, Marc got off the floor and sat next to me, legs spread out, one hand resting on his crotch, the other placed on my shoulder.

"Why'd you stop dancing?"

"Now that everyone's here the music will start and I need silence to dance. See, I don't want dancing to get all the attention while music cheers from the sidelines."

"You want to dance at a disco only when there's no music playing? Nice plan."

Marc started sniffing my face.

"Marc, what are you doing?"

"That *is* the smell of sarcasm. Sort of weak. But still."

"Darling, sarcasm's too subtle to smell."

We laughed as he punched my arm. Meanwhile, Karan eyed the young crowd. I saw some familiar faces, students from the drama school.

When Eddie Rabbitt crooned "I Love a Rainy Night," everyone sprang off their couches and to the dance floor, where they remained for several songs, taking breaks between numbers to tilt stemmed glasses over their lips, vodka or gin cocktailed with orange juice or lime and vinegar.

Side tables were stacked with square papers and ballpoint pens. Guests wrote down their song requests and placed them on satin-covered trays that the waiters carried away.

Karan's eyes settled on a girl sitting by herself on a green armchair. Her hair fell to her shoulders in a wavy tumble. Crescent-moon earrings bobbed against her neck as she rocked her head to "Stayin' Alive." She wore a chunky turquoise necklace and a canary-yellow dress. Karan walked up to her. She saw him, turned away, then turned her eyes back on him. He spoke to her with a lopsided smile. She thumbed her necklace and watched him with a tilted head. A few minutes later, they went to the dance floor.

Elvis Presley's "Jailhouse Rock" played. They went to opposite ends of the floor, leaned forward, and trotted toward each other, arms swaying back and forth in front of them. They stood side by side, each with one hand to their waist, the forefinger of their other hand pointing to the floor, then to the ceiling.

"What kind of a dance is that supposed to be?" I said.

"Bhangra that got shitfaced and thought it was disco," Marc said.

Toward the end of the song, they moved back and forth, foreheads touching, holding hands. On the final beat they were back-to-back, her high-heeled foot pressed against his calf.

A roar of applause surrounded them.

Marc said, "The rest don't seem to share our sentiment."

With a hand on her shoulder, Karan looked at the deejay and hollered, "Something romantic for us young couples here, chief!"

"*Chief?* Seriously?" I said.

Marc said, "What horseshit. Karan's so not young."

I said, "Standing with that college kid sure doesn't help him."

"Guys, stop," Su said. "You're such divas, I say."

"Sassy divas," Marc said.

I said, "Sassy divas is better than Shitfaced Bhangra."

Marc nodded gravely before we laughed. Karan raised his hand, and as the lights dimmed, I saw his erect thumb against blue lights. Billy Joel's "She's Always a Woman to Me" played. Mist wreathed the stage. An overhead machine scattered tinsel onto the bobbing heads. A dim light cut across the floor, revealing flashes of flesh: rouge-cheek beard-cheek touching, lipstick and mustache kisses. Onlookers sat up and emptied shots of vodka or whiskey in quick gulps and asked for more, please, some more.

Red light slashed the floor. Karan pressed his nose to the girl's ear. She laced her fingers around his neck. Darkness, then blue light. She slipped her hand into his shirt. The people around them were blurs.

"She steals like a thief, but she's always a woman to me," Joel sang.

"He's lucky," Marc said.

Warm fingers squeezed my shoulder, slipped down my arm. Unable to tell him to stop—how could I, when I'd kept our life sexless for four months and, miraculously, he still wanted me?—I waited resignedly for the disco lights to be silenced, for the music to darken, for smells to be deafened.

But nothing happened: my body didn't react. I panicked at the anomaly.

Pink light. Karan grabbed her waist and pulled her closer still. Their thighs packed tightly together. Darkness. Joel warned, "The most she will do is throw shadows at you." Red light. Hot-red. Her red mouth on his. Darkness.

"I want to be lucky too. We can be lucky." Marc's lips moved against my ear.

The deejay played an instrumental version of the song. No lights swept the stage. The tinsel floated around, caught in the spotlights above the bar table. Marc inched closer. My thigh burned against his. My arm throbbed in his grip. His lips swallowed the rim of my ear, gave it the moist touch of his tongue. His hand moved down my neck, dangerously close to my breasts. Still my senses didn't protest. I said nothing. I didn't move away.

"Good boy," Marc said. "Marc Boy wants to be lucky, you must see to it," he said. Voice hoarse. Accent English.

Knock-knock. Who's there? Lucky.

The lights came slowly back to life. Marc shuffled away. His fingers released my arm. Someone began clapping. The rest followed, some standing on the sofa, some applauding with hands raised above their heads.

"Why you looking at me like that, Sham?" Marc asked. His eyebrows shot up. Inching away from me, as though I reeked of some foul bodily fluid, he said, "Stay. I'll get you something to drink. Sparkling water? Okay."

When Marc was at the counter, his back to me, I got up and made my way to the door. Su and Sagar were on the dance floor. I pictured Marc returning to the sofa, his swagger stalling when he saw that the spot where I sat was empty. It was 11:45 P.M.

UNDER ARREST

A half-empty bottle of vodka sat in the parking lot, its cap missing. I guzzled it all neat. Chemical, acidic, sharp. I screwed my eyes shut, puckered my lips, and ran a hand down the length of my body, as if coaxing the heat that coursed down my gullet, my chest.

I walked away from the disco, entered a two-way street lined with streetlights. Stray dogs slept on the road divider, sluggishly wagging their tails when flies landed on their shaggy coats.

The gate to my guesthouse was padlocked. I clambered up the side of it, and as I started to clamber down, fireworks exploded in the sky. I slipped and fell into the garden, crushing two hydrangeas. The year 1997 was here.

I remembered, as I stood up, welcoming the new year from the cauldron in the backyard at Magpies. Without dusting myself, I entered the building. The watchman's seat was vacant.

In my room, I peeled off my clothes. A nerve above my right eyebrow started to throb, so I punched out three aspirins from the packet and downed them with a bottle of water. I slid under the sheets. The moon was framed by the grilled window like a convict under arrest.

The pills knocked me out and I fell into a vivid dream of mixed memories: Rusty and Viren drowned as Mud and Milk sat on the beach and talked about a ship bringing Englishmen; the scene turned to a watercolor in a storybook that Ma read out loud in the voice of Nandi; the wall behind her shivered, became a curtain that rose, revealing Marc and me as stage animals with painted whiskers; Bitch Bags! a voiceover said, and like it was his cue, Marc broke into a run that turned him into a moving mass of light until soft grass sprouted under his feet; when he stopped he had my face; I stood before a bed; I removed the sheet and Pita-jee's body, lying underneath, broke into a thousand pieces, turned to the shards of Hanuman's broken idol; light rose from between the shards, it blinded both the dreamed-up me and me the dreamer. A word poked at my edges, became louder, insistent: Sham, Sham, Sham.

I opened my eyes, shut them, opened them again and frowned as I blinked, my vision slowly adjusting to aureoles of daylight that surrounded a pale smudge. I rubbed my eyes.

"Hangover or nightmare?" asked Marc.

"Both," I said, rubbing my forehead.

"Have some coffee," he said and held out a steel glass. Whorls of steam released an inviting chicory scent. He was still in his party clothing.

Realizing that I was naked under my sheets, I said, "Marc, I need a minute."

He went out and closed the door behind him. I put on my clothes from last night, the shirt reeking of sweat, mud caked to the knee-cuffs. I opened the door and let Marc in. We stood on my balcony in our worn retro shirts and trousers.

Marc said, "When I went to get you water—"

"*Sparkling* water. Which you somehow decided I wanted."

"I could've gotten you booze."

"Why's everyone holding umbrellas?"

"What?"

I pointed at the street.

"It was raining literally seconds ago."

"But it isn't right now."

"How long do you intend to keep at this senseless conversation?"

"Next time take Saaya with you to the disco. Maybe you'll get lucky."

"Are you out of your mind?"

With a rumble the clouds launched into a drizzle that turned swiftly to a downpour.

"Still curious about umbrellas, wise guy?" Marc asked.

"Sure, you're the one who gets to be mad."

"Instead of, what, you being mad at me?"

"You know I don't like getting cozy in public places."

"Why didn't you say something?"

"Because I felt I owed you after not giving it up all these months."

"You think hurting me will make your problem go away?"

"It won't. I know. I live with it every day."

"And what are you doing about it? A big fat nothing. What drives me nuts is not your problem, it's your goddamned inertia about it."

A silence fell between us with the abruptness of a curtain drawn mid-scene. He came and held me against himself tightly.

After a few minutes, both our heartbeats softened. I planted tentative fingers on his back. "I'm sorry," he said. His words, wet and full of suffering, mingled with the thunder and rain that surrounded us.

"There's a game I play when this happens," Marc said.

It was close to midnight and we were at his place. He held his hand out. I took it and together we walked out to his waterlogged terrace. The sky had cleared by now, and ripples ran through the reflected starry sky under our feet.

Marc said, "I pretend I'm walking in the sky. The trick is to not look at things around you: buildings, street, traffic. Nuh-uh. Only look at the sky below. After some time, it starts to feel real, like I'm really up there."

We reached the parapet wall and turned and stood there with our eyes to the water until it stilled. A few jasmine flowers floated near Marc's ankles. I caught my reflection and quickly looked away. Only when transformed by makeup into another did I give my double my undivided attention.

After finding me gone from the disco, Marc told me, he went and sat in the car, isolating himself with his frustration so he wouldn't ruin the night for the rest. A cop saw him and thought he wanted to drive drunk and arrested him. He spent the night in jail. I brought his hand to my mouth and was about to kiss it.

"Don't," Marc said. "I had suggested a solution, which you chose not to act upon—and that's okay. Figure things out your own way, but until you do, we'll keep our distance."

"How's that going to work?"

"Because this halfway intimacy is convenient. You have zero incentive to fix things." He kissed my mouth. "But you like this enough that not having it at all will put some urgency under your butt. No pun intended."

I laughed despite feeling miserable.

From now on we would be fully chaste. I pictured our relationship stripped even of its brief expressions of intimacy.

"So this will have to wait," Marc said and kissed me again, "until we can do more."

At once, I said, "Happy New Year," and he said, "Happy '97."

PART V

1997

VISITORS

Su came over to meet me a few days after New Year's Eve. I wanted to tell her about what transpired on Marc's terrace, but I noticed that her eyes were a little swollen and her cheeks had salty traces of dried-up water.

I brought her in and made her a cup of chai.

"Sagar's parents are visiting him tomorrow," she said. "They called today and told him."

And I understood: they couldn't know that she and Sagar lived together.

"How long are they here?"

"Six days."

"Then we get to be roommates for six days—the year's off to a good start," I said. "When should we go get your things?"

Relief eased the muscles of her faces. She took a sip of chai.

"We have to clean the place up too. Removing all traces of me like a thief from a crime scene."

"Leave that to me. I'm good with cleaning. I clean Marc's place all the time—I insist."

"Of course you do," she said. "Listen, I have a book for you. Remember you told me about the problem you're having? It might help."

Not only had she remembered, but she had also given the matter thought, and in the middle of her own domestic issues, she'd gone out seeking material that would help me. I was moved.

"Thank you, Su. Tell me. Did Sagar and you talk about his parents visiting? Are you two okay?"

She had shown up for me so often. Now it was my turn to not take up room but to, instead, give her my attention.

She nodded and said, "Sagar told his parents about me—as in they know I'm his colleague and he likes me. Now they want to meet me."

"That's good, right?"

"Either they'll like me and want to get us married and I'll have to tell my parents, which will be fun, especially Dad—oh, the joy of it. Or they'll hate me, and as of tomorrow I won't have a boyfriend."

"Hating you is humanly impossible."

"I want to make a good first impression: get a new dress, put on some makeup. But the feminist in me is shouting in protest: pandering to the man's parents, tsk, tsk."

"How about this," I said. "We'll go shopping together and I'll do your makeup. You get what you want and feminist-you won't object to you having some fun with your gay best friend."

She turned and hugged me.

Her boxes, surprisingly few, were stacked in my living room. From it she took out the book she'd mentioned and set it aside. She wore the outfit we had gotten her last evening: a white sari with a red border, a white blouse with red peacocks printed on its edges. She stood before the only mirror I had, nailed to a wall in my tiny bathroom. I had just finished her makeup. She studied her face, touching, with satisfaction, her nose ring, her bindi, her eyebrows, her bangles.

I folded in half the brocade shawl I had borrowed from Saaya. I draped it over her right shoulder and knelt and smoothed the folds. We went down the stairs and to the phone room. I called Radha. Her mother picked up.

"Second call this week." Her mother beamed before handing it over to Radha.

I presented Radha with my request: my best friend was about to meet her potential in-laws, are there things you can tell her about how to navigate the conversation? The chat, I knew, would help Su, irrespective of its contents. Radha agreed. I thanked her and handed the receiver to Su. As she held it to her ear, said "hello," and leaned over the table, I left the room, closing the door behind me, and sat on the steps outside.

When I dressed Su up, the fabric of the sari between my fingers was a touch that felt like home. It felt comforting when I pictured myself housed in its cotton folds. Saaya had once recommended that I expand my personal wardrobe to include churidars and saris. I had rejected his suggestion, claiming that my love for playing women characters did not signify who I was offstage. Now I wondered if what he really was trying to tell me was that acknowledging my femininity might help me step more fully into my flesh.

A car pulled into the driveway. Sagar stepped out and asked, "Will she be long?"

"As long as she needs," I replied.

He sat next to me. We shared a companionable silence.

The next week, Su returned to the apartment she shared with Sagar. Sagar's parents, particularly his mother, loved Su. I read the book that she got me, a medical book stripped of jargon, meant for rudimentary self-diagnosis by a layman. I concluded that I had a psychosomatic disorder: my anxiety triggered physical symptoms even in the absence of a physical disease, like a temporary blindness even when my eyesight was fine. Specific nerves convey perceptions from our five senses to our brain, and our brain gives them an identity: the sea is blue, the ice cube is cold, this sound is a drum. My brain transmitted my anxiety through the same nerves to my senses and turned them off. Isolating the root cause of my anxiety and eradicating it was my only possible solution.

I questioned and rejected my previous theory: that Senior's abuse caused my condition. The pain and fear I'd felt during his nocturnal visits didn't escalate to a state of anxiety; but I did feel deeply anxious when I kissed Senior consensually on the day of his departure. I started to consider Marc's suggestion: the deaths of my sisters as the origin of my undesired abstinence.

Before I could mull on the subject further, I heard a knock on the door.

The policeman Ajay Biswas stood outside my door, picking his teeth with his little finger. I was reduced to the boy who stood at the mouth of a staircase, watching my father walking briskly toward me, his eyes crazed by anger, his hands stretched out.

"You waiting for him? Sorry to disappoint." The policeman laughed a throaty laughter.

I felt ashamed, not of what he said—as if Marc was my crime—but because fear had been my instinctual response to his presence. Even when I had done nothing wrong.

"How'd you know where I live?" I asked.

"We have two options. You let me in, I talk. Or I take you with me, I talk."

I stepped aside and he came in and sat on the bed. He patted the spot next to him and I sat. From his pocket he took out a newspaper clip, unfolded it, and gave it to me. A picture of Marc, me, and our friends dressed in retro outfits and posing outside the club.

"Just out with some friends," I said. "No crime."

With his forefinger he circled the figures of Marc and me, standing next to each other.

"Only both your heads are touching," he said, returning the paper to his pocket. "I told you to keep it low," he said. "But, vilayat culture, it likes flaunting."

He planted his baton on the floor with a thump. He wrapped his palms around it and leaned forward.

"I'm not rich," I said.

"If I put you and gora in prison, think about how much more you'll lose."

He grinned. His teeth were smeared with the red of betel nut. Something snapped in me. If they came for me—Pita-jee, Vikrant—then he'd protect me, Marc had promised. So I made a decision.

I said, "How much?"

"No manners. You need to be delicate about these things."

"Delicate? Hmm. What kind of bribe do you have in mind?"

I reached for his knee. He got swiftly to his feet and cussed in Bengali.

I stroked his baton. "But you sat on my bed. You put my Ken doll down there. And hey, it's Valentine's Day soon."

"Out. In the jeep. Now."

I took the slip of paper that Ma gave me out of my wallet. I tore it in half, kept Radha's number, and gave him Pita-jee's.

"Here's Dad's number," I said. "Call him. He'll give you what you want."

"He better," he said. "You're in so much trouble if he does not."

He pocketed the slip, grabbed my collar, and pulled me to my feet.

I drew a deep breath and said, "Your breath smells so good, officer."

He pushed me away. I fell on the bed. With my wrists at the small of my back, I said, "Will you handcuff me, please?"

"Your father should be ashamed of what he made," he said.

He looked in the mirror and ran his hands down his shirt, his trousers. He set his topee straight and left.

MAY I BE A CROW?

In the days following Su's stay at my house, to the beginning of January, Marc's conflict with me about our Little Chat on his terrace had escalated in frequency and scale. "Have you done something about our Little Chat?" he'd ask. "Have you given it any thought?" I offered him nothing tangible or conclusive. In the stilted conversations that followed these exchanges I paid close attention—to the point of exhaustion—to his gestures, his tone, attempting to anticipate in his speech that particular moment where it took a turn for the worse, hoping to alter its course when it appeared, always failing at it—failing to prevent our descent into bitterness. Sometimes, he'd storm out and disappear for one day or several. Once, when he came back after nearly a week of no contact and we stepped into a hug, I noticed, with a start, a mark on his neck: a circle of faded brown, almost gone, still there. I pressed a thumb to it. I wanted to trace the teeth that left them there. Marc held my wrist and put my hand away.

At school the next day, Saaya neither avoided me nor expressed excess affection. Would a seasoned performer slip into such dead giveaways? When we left the table after lunch, Rooh walked next to Nandi, I next to Saaya. I covertly examined his neck for a bruise. His skin was clean.

On the first full moon of '97, Marc did join me when I floated oil lamps in the river to honor the memory of my sisters. For Valentine's

Day, Marc took me out for dinner to Kali Mithai Shop. He bought us pistachio ice cream that we ate together on his terrace, passing the pint back and forth as we talked. We also found comfort in each other when the routine downers came—bodies succumbing to seasonal fevers, leaking roofs, burned fuses, late paychecks. When I told him about Ajay's visit, he and Saaya took turns to sleep in my room at least for a few weeks: in case Ajay came back. But it was only a matter of time before the problem of us reared its head again.

Whenever our friends came visiting, the air carried, as before, a lightness—humor, warmth, easy conversation—so that I turned their visits into occasions: I cooked using quirky recipes (cabbage marinated in vinegar and sage was everyone's favorite), I made four-course meals that, Karan once remarked, "called for special lighting." So on my birthday, March 9, Su brought candles of different fragrances and lit them all at once, the air saturated with one too many smells that left us sneezing and laughing. I came to prefer sharing him with our friends over his exclusive company.

The week after my birthday, we started planning the play our students would act in as a culmination to our classes.

"Chitrangada must be a puppet to begin with," Nandi said.

"I see your point," Rooh said. "She has no say in her gender until she meets Arjuna. So she's controlled by her father like a puppet."

"Yes," exclaimed Saaya. "After she's in control of her life we could have two actors play her: one when she's Arjuna's husband, one when she's his wife."

"A third actor plays her when she romances Arjuna's wife, Draupadi," I said.

"Shagun," Nandi said, "you know we can't show that scene."

I had no intention of redacting the Chitrangada-Draupadi kiss. But, instead of disagreeing with Nandi, I changed the subject. If we didn't dwell on it, he was unlikely to remember it, and I could call upon this lapse of memory if the staged, forbidden kiss became a point of conflict. I told myself I was doing this for my students. Wasn't it what they said they wanted? So I started our discussion of logistics. Nandi, Rooh, Saaya, and I would direct specific sections of the play, and two students would assist us with makeup and set design. We decided to stage the play on May 7.

"Then we're home free—out of Chamba, back on the road," Nandi announced.

The light in the kitchen still wasn't working, so with the fridge door open, I made tea for Marc and me. Then I sat on the moonlit floor next to him. I shared what transpired with Nandi with an air of near celebration. I was pleased with how we were enacting the story. So what if I had to resort to manipulation?

"Su once asked me if performing Hindu stories bothered me, given what men of god—priests, preachers, and such—say about the gay community."

"Sure," Marc said. He sounded remote, his attention absent, nothing but the shell of his body present for our conversation, for us.

"You okay?" I asked.

Still no response. So I spoke at length, as if compensating for his absence.

"What I didn't tell Su, because I just figured it out, is this. Performing these stories is also an act of resistance for me. Why should I only love Hindu stories or only love men? That's why I breathe the originals back to life. They have characters who're both."

"You don't want to censor the stories, but censoring us, no problem, yeah?"

And he was back. His expression darkened and he pursed his lips. He set his cup down heavily and stood up. I thought he might strike me. I shielded my face.

The fridge started to buzz. I lowered my hand slowly. Marc stood before me. He pressed a thumb to his chin, ran four fingers up and down his jaw and regarded me.

"Who, I wonder," Marc said, "do you take me to be?"

A jingle entered the silence. His car key winked in the moonlight.

"Why are you so angry?" I said, in a voice so low that he leaned toward me, a hand cupped around his ear. I said, "Sorry for making you angry."

"Don't expect me to say it's okay. What have you done about it?"

"Not tonight. I'm exhausted."

"Then when? Give me a deadline."

I shook my head, meaning to convey "I don't know" but realized it looked more like a refusal to answer his question. I opened my mouth to clarify. But he walked out of my lightless kitchen, into the tube-lit bedroom. Why couldn't I allow Marc and me to be lovers in every sense of the word? Why couldn't I be a crow that sat on the electric wire of my body and not feel a thing?

When he opened the main door, we found my building superintendent standing outside.

I had a call, he informed me, looking over Marc's shoulder.

We went down the stairs, the sup first, me in between, Marc behind me. I entered the anteroom. Marc walked past me, toward his jeep. I picked up the phone.

Before I said hello, I heard his heavy breath. A breath saturated with water. A breath clogged by anger, by snot. And I knew who it was. His crazed look came to mind, clear despite the years that had passed.

"How did you get my number?" I asked Pita-jee but realized, after a moment, that I had made no sound. I posed my question again. I heard Marc start his jeep. I fought the instinct to drop the receiver and flee.

"What have you done?" he said. "Do you know the danger you have gotten yourself into, exposing yourself to a cop like that?"

It took about a fortnight, I calculated, for numbers to trade hands: I giving Ajay my father's number, he giving my father my number.

"You won't pay him so he'll teach me a lesson—is that it?" I asked.

"I'm worried sick for you."

"Just like you were when you sent Vikrant."

"He's different. He's not the law."

"He said he'd use force if I didn't cooperate."

"I didn't know that."

"For all I know you gave Vikrant my number and he's on his way to me."

"Shagun, listen to me."

"I have a boyfriend. But you know that already. The cop told you."

"So those phone calls to Radha, that was just a smoke screen?"

"You're never going to fix me."

He made a sound that was a mixture of a sob and a grunt.

"I'll make sure I don't have a child of my own. You know what they say, traits skip a generation. And we can't let that happen, another you in this world."

"Children are a decision made by god, son. If you're meant to have one, you will."

"I won't. I'll go under the blade."

I hung up and willed the phone to ring again. He didn't call back. I got up, left the room, and walked out of the building, down the street, off the campus. The lights of cars and scooters felt like the eyes of the sleep-deprived. The air smelled of petrol and blared with vehicle horns.

After what felt like several hours, I arrived at Marc's door. Marc opened. My fury, exhausted neither by telephone aggression nor aggressive walking, was spent at the sight of him. My knees buckled and I dropped my head to his shoulder.

"My father called," I said. "It happened, finally. He cares. Even after all these years."

Marc cupped the back of my head. That night he slept next to me on the floor.

The next morning he came with me to my guesthouse. He pulled my bag out from under the cupboard and filled it with some of my clothes.

"You're going to stay at my place for a few days," he said. "Your dad doesn't know where I live."

What if he paid Ajay not to back off but to find Marc's whereabouts? Had I put Marc's life in danger as well? Was leaving Chamba without Marc and traveling with my troupe the safest option?

"What's this?" Marc asked. He sat next to me. He started to flip through the conversion therapy brochure, quickly at first, then more slowly. Until he paused on a page, read it, then turned the page and read it as well. He placed his thumb on a photo and looked up. "Why did you keep it?" he asked. Then, he cleared his throat and repeated the question. As if I hadn't heard him on the first instance.

"In case I get complacent," I said. "In case I forget."

I turned to the page that detailed the test.

"You've been with a girl," I said. "You'd pass the test. But I lack your talent."

He kissed my shoulder. I wrapped my hands around his waist and closed my eyes. He gave me the nonreciprocation I needed.

COWS TAKE YOU TO HEAVEN

The practice for our upcoming performance commenced at the end of March: four days a week I practiced, with the cast, the scene I was directing. Over lunch, I worked with Nandi, Rooh, and Saaya on stage design and music. The routine, I thought, would shape the next four weeks, until the night of the performance. Then I received a telegram.

You lost your father, come home.

With my eyes closed, I examined myself, as if to sense, under the surface, some kind of an undercurrent—of shock, of relief—but all I found within was a great stillness and its refusal to be stirred. Hearing Ma grieve, I thought, might provoke some primal, dormant emotion into expression. As if grief were a contagious disease. So I called home, but Ma didn't pick up.

Nandi took over the responsibility of directing my scene. I told my students not to talk about or practice the Chitrangada-Draupadi kiss before Nandi. It's a surprise, I said. A mixture of shock and disbelief passed over their faces but they didn't press the matter. I'd just lost my father, so they cut me more than a little slack.

Marc said, as he drove me to the railway station, "If you need me, just say the word and I'll be there on the next train."

I got home after midnight and let myself in. The house lay curled like a bat with its wings folded over its face. In the dark I reached for every switch as I made my way through the foyer, up the stairs, into her room, leaving little explosions of harsh white light everywhere.

She lay in bed, her face beaded with sweat, her eyeballs swishing against paper-thin eyelids. She drew in a wheezing breath but I didn't know what pained her: her hands didn't strain against her stomach or her chest, they didn't point to a source. I pressed a handkerchief to her damp forehead. She opened her eyes and frowned, blinded by the light. When she saw me, when she was able, a childlike resentment registered on her face: she tightened her mouth into a pout, turned away, and pulled the blanket over her face. A patch of it darkened, glued to her cheek.

Slowly, I backed away. When her breath fell back into the rhythm of sleep, I spread a blanket on the floor, at some distance from her bed, then switched the room lights off and lay down.

A scratching noise woke me up. Through the fog of interrupted sleep, I saw Ma's silhouette turning the brass elephant on the side table. The sweeping arm of the lighthouse glazed her eyes. They were fixed on me. The path of our gaze was now obstructed by, now cleared of, the thick legs of the spinning elephant.

I turned away. The room fell quiet. I turned to face her again. I saw her in the lighthouse's white spells, cast in nine-second intervals: her smile was full of teeth; she lay sideways. Her face was pressed to her folded hand, causing her cheek to bulge.

"Jaanu," she said. "Why are you sleeping on the floor? Are you still mad at me?"

My heart seemed to slip down my chest.

"Come sit with me awhile, soon you'll be leaving." She patted the bed. "London is my soutan, I tell you."

"Ma," I said. "Go back to sleep."

For a moment she glared at me wide-eyed. Then a jolt passed through her flesh. Her silhouette wrinkled and she turned away. The room was imbued as if with a foreign scent.

I left the room. The rest of the house had all its lights on still, and all that glare tugged at the muscles of my eyes as I stumbled down the stairs and made my way to the Wall of the Dead, where I stood before Pita-jee's framed portrait. I thought I'd inherited nothing but his hazel eyes. But I was all of him: big jug ears, the particular slant of his jaw, his broad forehead.

Perhaps I knew how similar we looked: that's why I'd avoided my reflection.

My face was embossed over his photograph. Same cleft chin.

"Now I stand to pee," I said. "Isn't that nice?"

I stumbled away.

A doctor arrived in the morning to check on her. It was he who'd dispatched the telegram. He gave me her medication and dosage instructions. The grieving sick are treated with medicine meant for viral fever, he said. The prescription had her name, Mrs. Meena Mathur. I couldn't recall the last time I'd heard—let alone seen—her full name.

"My father," I said. "Do you know what happened to him?"

Gleaning the information from him, I hoped, would save my mother the difficult task of recounting the incident.

"She only said it was an accident," he said. "I'm sorry for your loss."

When I brought her lunch to her room, I found her squatting on all fours. She rubbed the scratched surface of the side table with the edge of her sari. The elephant sat on her pillow. She looked at my blanket on the floor, wrinkled and unmade.

"You're a big boy now," she said. "You shouldn't be sleeping in your mother's room."

I felt stung. I quietly picked the blanket up and folded it.

"I will call you if I need you," she said. "Get me the bell."

I went to the prayer room, where Krishna looked fresh: his marble flesh clean, the sandalwood paste on his forehead still fragrant. I picked up the prayer bell and, holding the clapper down with my thumb, silencing its call, I went back up the stairs and stood outside her room, as if standing guard. I heard her munch and gulp down balls of rice, a roasted cauliflower at the core of each. When her fingers swished through the water bowl, I stood in the doorframe.

"You think it's my fault," I said.

"That's what you thought when your sisters died."

"He never did treat me right—you saw for yourself."

"Show some respect. It's not even been a week."

"What happened to him?"

"This food's good. You cook for your *friend*?"

I looked away, ashamed by her implication, angered by my shame.

"Knowing about his accident means nothing," Ma said. "Not if you don't know what came before."

The doorbell rang. I placed the handbell by the bedside elephant, opened the door, and stood before a cow. She shared the height and build of her keeper, a portly, bald priest.

Ma and I stood in our backyard. The priest commenced conducting the first of two funeral rites that are particular, he said, to those whose bodies are unavailable for cremation. Unavailable. An odd descriptor, I thought, for people consumed by fires, swallowed by seas, decimated in war. It seemed better suited to describe things that might be available at some point in the future. Sorry, madam, barley is unavailable. Come back next Friday, it will be in stock.

"She's too old for the first ritual." He pointed at Ma. "It's down to you."

Following his instructions, I bowed before the cow, walked to her side, and ducked and stepped under her body, careful not to touch her udder, then stepped out and walked back to face her. In the drizzle that pocked the courtyard with raindrops, I did this 108 times. The priest tapped my head with the cow's tail when I was done. He then had Ma and me commit to three days of silence. In our solitude, we were to count the name of Krishna on basil beads. The ritual and the silence were necessary, he said, to bring peace to the souls of those who didn't get a proper funeral.

"Why didn't we do this for Mud and Milk?" I asked Ma.

The priest hissed, "I said no talking."

On the final night of our seclusion I woke up thirsty. I came out of my room and looked up and saw, in what light there was, Ma slowly pacing the upstairs corridor. I went and drank a glass of water and stood for some time in the kitchen without turning on any light. On my way back I looked up again. Ma had stopped walking. I couldn't see her face or her shoulders. But her feet were visible between two posts. As were her hands, which she'd placed on the banister. I sensed that she was watching me.

We met the priest in our courtyard on the fourth morning. He came without his cow and made us sip on Ganga water as it rained on and around us.

"Now good fortune will visit your father," he said, rubbing ghee over his chapped lips. "He will be born again as a Brahmin man. Hari bol, God's grace is infinite."

I closed the gate after he left and turned and saw Ma still standing in the rain. When she found me staring at her, she clenched her eyes shut, tear-size raindrops turning to a line of water between her lashes.

JANAK REFORMATORY AND
JAILHOUSE, MADHUBAN

Ma came into my room a short while after the priest left. She looked out the window. She had changed into a cotton sari. It had stopped raining. The afternoon was brilliant with postshower brightness.

"Do you want to go?" she said, without looking at me, gesturing toward the treehouse.

We climbed up the ladder, which leaned over the bark. We went past branches thick with leaves, past chirping bulbuls that flapped their wings but didn't take flight. A blue feather landed on my lips.

Ma pushed the door open. Sunlight flooded the space. The glass of the lantern was stone-cold. We shared silence for a time.

"Your father," she began, then paused. She brought a fist to her mouth, as if she was about to clear her throat. Her next few words came out muffled.

"A matchmaker came to the house the year your sisters turned ten," Ma said.

"Did they know they had husbands chosen for them?"

She shook her head. "Your father, when I told him, he was ecstatic," she said.

"Ecstatic?" I said. "To pack his daughters off with men twice their age?"

"We were following the rules laid out for us," she snapped.

"Who's us?"

"Middle-class folk, parents of daughters."

"My sisters grew up in a world different from yours."

Ma said, "Oh really? You think your sisters could do what you're doing? Strapping around the country as they please?"

There was an all-women troupe, I wanted to say, but to do so would be to ignore the truth at the kernel of her question: our social ecosystem was designed to ease my movement, not my sisters'.

She shook her head. "The world may change for men, but for us, change is slow to come, slower still to take hold. A single woman runs into one kind of trouble when she's young, another when she's old."

"You did your bit to keep the old ways going," I said. "Cooking lessons, fairness creams."

"Not with pleasure," she said. "I did what I felt was needed to get them married into good homes. Where they'd be treated well. Have something close to dignity at least."

"If the brothers are anything like Rusty, I doubt they would've gotten dignity," I said.

"Rohit-jee asked your father for dowry: fifty thousand rupees for each boy, to be paid in full at once. Your father took a loan from his employer," Ma said. "His passport was collateral."

"Why? I'm sure he could've found another so-called reputable family for my sisters?"

"Because with Rohit-jee's sons, they'd get to live together," Ma said. "And the family's right here, in our town, they could come to us if they needed anything."

Ma paused, as if wanting me to appreciate my father's intent. It was hard for me to accept that good of any kind could culminate in a decision that struck me as entirely monstrous. Whatever good there was got misplaced in the messiness of the outcome: my fourteen-year-old sisters pledged in marriage to men twice their age.

When it became clear that I had nothing to contribute, Ma continued. "Once Rohit-jee received the money, the matchmaker fixed a marriage date: it was to take place the year your sisters turned eighteen."

I asked, "And the dowry money was a loan that left him stranded in London?"

She nodded.

"After what happened to your sisters, after that, I went to his house," Ma said. "I asked, requested, begged that he return the dowry. I thought he was an honorable man, thought Pita-jee could repay his loan and come home for their funeral."

It was a damp morning in the thick of monsoon. Rohit-jee smiled when Ma presented her request. As he slurped on tea that wasn't offered to Ma, forbidden as it was to offer refreshments to the recently bereaved, he likened dowry to a spiritual offering. He asked Ma: Will you go to the temple and ask for your money back if Krishna doesn't fulfill your wishes?

"He claimed that your sisters committed suicide," Ma said. "He asked if they did anything shameful, were they pregnant? Since when do little girls drown in the sea by *accident*?"

My jaw started to hurt, and I realized my teeth were clenched.

Ma said, "That's why I told him, Shagun. I had to. I emphasized it was an accident."

I went to the kitchen and made her a glass of glucose water. She accepted it.

"Your father, he pleaded with his boss: permit me to attend the funeral of my daughters, please. No debt clear, no go, his boss said. So he took extra shifts, worked side jobs, earned money under the table. It took him another six months to clear his loan. And he did come home."

She turned and looked at me for the first time since we stepped into the treehouse, her gaze searching, her cheeks red, greasy.

"Last week his employer called," she said, looking away.

Six slabs of concrete had collapsed at the construction site. It was Pita-jee's job to supervise the quality, particularly the dryness, of every slab before he gave the go-ahead to add another layer on top, and he did a sloppy job, permitting new slabs to be layered before the old ones were bone-dry: that was the diagnosis of the insurance company that surveyed the site of the accident.

"He'd been distracted for days, said his boss. But your Pita-jee doesn't do distracted. You remember his construction stories. You know he loves his work."

He was standing below the layers of slabs when they gave way, caving him in. Under thirty tons of concrete, steel scaffolding on top.

Airlines are only allowed to fly bodies that are embalmed, and Pita-jee's body, by the time it was recovered, was too mangled for the journey, so they sent his ashes instead.

Ma said, "That was how he spoke the whole time, that boss of his. He used the word 'mangled' without a thought. He referred to your father as 'the body.'"

She drained the glucose water. I freed her hand of the empty glass. She joined her palms and bowed her head. As if she wanted to pray. After an inconsolable pause, she said, "Every time your father called, he asked, 'Does Shagun ask about me?'"

"How am I expected to 'ask' about him after what happened between us?"

"He's your father."

"Is that enough?"

Ma got up and started climbing down the creaky ladder of the tree-house. She paused on one rung and her voice came to me amid the rustle of leaves.

"I can't stop thinking of his expression when he knew this was the end."

"The man who came looking for me—Vikrant? Pita-jee sent him. Did you know?"

"What are you trying to say?"

"He wanted to fix me."

I heard the wooden rungs creak again and assumed she was leaving. Then I saw her face, washed in afternoon's light.

"He came back for you and when he failed to earn your affection, he left again," she said.

"Whose fault is that?" I asked.

"So he left," she said. "You really believe such a man would bring you harm?"

"What if in his mind he wasn't harming but helping me?"

"Is that why you never wanted him to know where you live?"

I nodded.

"It's never too late to give someone a place in your life," she said. "Now. Are you coming down? How long will you make your old woman stand on a ladder?"

When Ma lay down to take a nap, a stack of photos stuck out from under her pillow. I took them with me to my room. My father was present in only one of them, a date printed in orange on the bottom right. It was taken about three months ago. Behind him, a crane loomed over a four-story skeletal frame that teemed with workmen. I touched the wrinkles that had appeared since I last saw him. As he stood facing the camera in gray coveralls, thumbs tacked to the pockets of his jeans, his visor-glasses smudged with fingerprints, did he think that someday I would look at his picture with the hazel eyes that I'd inherited from him?

I felt my throat go heavy. You're being a sentimental fool, I told myself, you didn't even know him. But a thought rose: he's the reason you were clothed and fed and went to school and had a roof over your head. What I'm experiencing is nothing new, I told myself: once someone passes away, we exaggerate—or focus exclusively on—their good deeds. But the knowledge that I would never see him again, even if I never felt the desire to see him, defied all logic and overwhelmed me. His contradictions arose before me: taking my pictures, anxious that I learn the ways of men before I learned it the hard way, regretting it after; hitting me, then leaving for London; coming home for me, leaving for me. He suffered between being the father he thought he should be and the father he wanted to be. Under the shadow of that thought, just looking at his image made me physically sick.

I turned to the other pictures. Black-and-white photos of the sites he'd constructed: a fenced house with a woman in a skirt at the gate; a church on a hillock, a kite soaring above its weathervane; clouds pressed against a glass-domed greenhouse; a dam, a man crawling out from a pipe to its left, the flashlight on his helmet shooting forth a beam of light; a power plant; four factories with neat geometric shapes that produced practical things in England. I turned each picture to check if they had notes identifying the buildings. Only one of them did. It showed a fortlike building with an iron gate and two floors lined with grilled windows. JANAK REFORMATORY AND JAILHOUSE, MADHUBAN, it said on the back.

I closed my eyes and remembered seeing my father for the first time, sitting with fifteen relatives, partaking of my sisters' funeral dinner. A man with the build of a banyan, dwarfing Ma, tucking two strands of hair behind her ear.

I started when I heard the bell ringing. I ran up the stairs, where the window framed the setting sun and Ma's hand rattling the bell. I switched on a light.

"Were you crying?" she asked.

I pointed to the Madhuban photo. "Why's there only a description on one photo?"

She turned it around. She touched the words as she said, "There's a diary too. It came with the rest of his belongings."

She raised the edge of the bedcover and showed me Pita-jee's trunk under the bed. Its lid was open. On top was the coverall he'd worn in the photograph, its fabric wrinkled, weathered, faded. It sat on his skin for days, absorbing his sweat, his smells. It was closer to him than anyone else had been in recent years. It brushed against my wrist as I sifted through the trunk, and I cringed. I took out a spiral notebook. I leafed through it and for the first time saw his handwriting. A bright-yellow can caught my attention. I plucked it out of the trunk and planted it on the floor. On it were the words DABUR DALDA in red.

"He took ghee with him?" I asked.

"Careful," she said. "Your father's in there."

It took me a moment to understand what she meant. His ashes.

"I made a decision," she said. "There's a widow ashram in Banaras."

"My friend, Marc," I said. "If he were a girl, you wouldn't do that."

She said, "I want to say I'm doing it for me. But I won't hide things from you anymore."

"I can't choose who I am," I said.

"Nor can I."

"Will they let you write to me or is that a sin?"

"They ask for three months of separation. To cultivate detachment."

I found the phrase odd. Cultivate detachment. It wasn't a part of her language. The way she said it, with a certain tightness, made it sound like she had spoken in a tongue she had just learned. Had the widow ashram supplied it to her, did they say, *If your children tell you to call or write to them, say you cannot because you must cultivate detachment?*

"But after that, yes, I'll write. You can come visit."

"So can you. This is your home."

"I can't live in my home once I start living there. That's one of their rules."

"I'll come visit you alone, don't worry, I won't embarrass you."

"Don't be like that," she said. "Let's have a good time together before I go?"

Her face had the look of someone whose prolonged fever had passed. I carried the Dabur Dalda tin, filled with my father's ashes, downstairs and set it on a table under the Wall of the Dead.

IF MIRACLES HAPPEN
IN THIS WORLD

The next day I helped Ma clear her room. We arranged her jewelry and most of her clothes in cardboard boxes that we donated. The few belongings that were left she packed into a duffel bag that she lived out of until she left. She started to wear khadi saris in pale cream and gray. She was cultivating detachment. I pictured Ma removing her bangles at the widow ashram's entrance. I imagined her wearing white saris week upon week, year upon year. I thumbed the edges of her long hair. A barber would bring his scissors to the base of her neck, allowing what was above to stay, shearing the rest away.

We went out one day to buy spices. She wanted to prepare a feast for us before she left, at the end of April. The shop was at the end of a sloping serpentine street where turbaned vendors squatted on their haunches and ministered over baskets of shiny vegetables and fruits. When Ma started to prepare my fourteen-year-old sisters for their upcoming lives as housewives, she brought them with her to this market. She taught them how to pick vegetables and how to bargain. All the beggars sitting on the street had similar-looking begging bowls, Milk once said.

Ma and I took long walks in the leftover light of evenings. On one of those walks, we went to the beach.

"Your sisters would come to you when they couldn't sleep, remember?" Ma said. "You would take them to the treehouse and play with them."

"Then they became brats who no longer needed comforting."

"Story of every parent. You'll know when you have children."

An uncomfortable silence spread. The subject of children inevitably brought to mind the fact that Marc and I were a couple. Was my child, barely birthed in Ma's sentence, rejected before that sentence found its period? A raucous flock of seagulls passed overhead. Together we turned to look at the port.

"He didn't feel a thing," I said. "Was it because he'd never met them?"

"If you saw him grieve, you'd relive the whole thing, and he didn't want that," she said. "So he limited his grieving to his morning walks."

"Is that why he always went, come rain, come heat wave?"

Grief with a timer is what my father practiced. Grief under the guise of a constitutional. On his way back from one of his walks, I remembered, he saw me with Furniture. And I thought his face was wet with rainwater.

"He loved the sea," Ma said. "When he was a child, he'd run off to play on the beach. His mother would joke, 'When you're big and start getting post, we'll have it delivered in the sea.'"

When we got home, she looked at his ashes and said, "Take him home someday?"

"I will," I promised.

The night before she left, she asked me to wash her hair. She stood in the bathroom and leaned over the sink. I dipped a mug into a steaming steel bucket: it sucked in water with a squelch, it clinked as it struck the bucket's metallic edge. I poured water over her hair and scrubbed a hibiscus-gooseberry paste onto her scalp. Afterward, as I ran a comb through her fragrant hair, the strands thicker, still damp, she hummed: *Fair moon/come cradle my boy/soothe him with a puddle/of your milky light.*

"I sang this song after your mundan ceremony," she said. "You were a year old. You wouldn't let the barber touch your hair! The priest was getting impatient. So I took you from the barber. You melted, at home in your mother's hands. And the barber shaved your hair away. The moment you realized what happened while you trusted me . . . how you scowled at me." Ma laughed. I joined my laughter to hers. "I sang this song to placate you that night."

I sat on the floor next to her. She brushed my hair away from my forehead.

"I never expressed the love I felt for you properly, not often enough," she said. "But know that it's as real as the pain I felt at childbirth."

"Can you ever love all of me?" I asked.

"If miracles happen in this world," she said.

She left the next day. She insisted that I not see her off at the station. As she walked up our alley, and I watched her from the gate, her things, I noticed, started falling out of her bag. "Ma," I hollered, and she turned, frowning in the sun. I gestured to her belongings on the road. She slapped her forehead, leaned forward, and started to collect them. I walked toward her, picking up Pita-jee's pictures, her blouse, an oil lamp. As we put them back in and zipped up her bag, I became certain it was no accident: she had meant it to be, this error, so we could have another moment together. She rubbed the back of my head as I held her to myself.

"You'll be okay," she said, her heartbeat calm, her breath steady, her palm warm against my scalp.

SCENT SAVIOR

I hadn't shared my return date with Marc. April 27. My train got to Chamba at nearly midnight. When I reached my lodgings, I went up the stairs and was about to turn into my corridor when, from the floor above, I heard low murmurs. I left my bag and took another flight of stairs.

Marc stood leaning against the wall. He wore a sweater that stretched tight over his body as he stood with his back to the wall. Saaya stood facing him, his hands crossed. The elbow of his left arm touched Marc's belly. They spoke softly. They were in front of Saaya's room. The streetlight's dim glow filtered in from the grilled window that was on one end of the corridor. It washed their sweaty faces in a dull amber.

Marc turned and saw me. He brought a hand to Saaya's chest and pushed him aside. Saaya followed his gaze as he wrapped his hair into a bun. They came up to me and hugged me.

"I would've picked you up," Marc said.

"He was waiting for you all alone, poor thing," Saaya said. "I told him to come up."

"Thanks," I said curtly. "Marc, let's go."

"He was just being kind," Marc said as I unlocked my door.

"My dad died and he's who you're feeling sorry for?"

I went to the balcony. The cool breeze calmed me some. I heard Marc pour water from a bottle into a glass.

I drank it, sat down, and asked, "Were you checking on me every day?"

"For the first five or six days," he said, sitting next to me.

Only the first week then. I had been gone for three weeks.

If I did not come back, would he have stopped checking altogether, his work, friends, and music erasing his memory of us, one patch at a time, like rust? How long can absence and remembering travel together? How far can you carry grief before it starts to lose its weight, a little at a time, then quicker, until, eventually, it slips away from your consciousness? And then one day, your grief makes a reappearance: when some or a lot of time has passed, when the guard of conscious thought isn't up—as you wake up but aren't fully awake, for instance. You feel your throat tighten. The passing of time is a weight you feel on your bones. Then the day starts to claim your attention: its appointments, meetings, errands. By the time you leave your bed, your grief ceases to be the subject of your attention. And in that first sobering moment of wakefulness, you find yourself in the mirror as you brush, and in the middle of an act so mundane, you're faced with your own brutal capacity for forgetfulness.

Marc squeezed my hand. "Your watchman, he said he'd call when you got back, guess he didn't want me hanging around. That's why I stopped coming by every day, but you, you were in my thoughts every day, don't think it was otherwise."

Because he understood, with precision, the hurt I was nursing silently, I hugged him and I cried for the first time since Pita-jee died, since Ma left home. I shared with him an episode that I hadn't recollected since it happened because whenever I thought back to that day it was only the death of my sisters that I remembered. After my sisters' fingers sank out of view and a wave socked my face, I realized I'd have to tell Ma that her daughters had drowned. I ran, through the port, out into the fish basti, past fishermen's wives who sat on their haunches under black awnings, the wet edges of their saris clinging to their ankles. A pain shot up my leg. I ignored it, continued to run, but it returned, biting deeper this time, and I screamed and stopped and inspected my right foot and found a nail pinning my slipper to my sole, releasing a red stream that trickled quickly into the rainwater flowing down the street. I tried to keep going: dragging my injured foot, hopping on my healthy one, counting my steps. Eight steps later I gave in and sat down, a sense of weary acceptance replacing the panic. The relief was of course temporary; pain rushed back up my nerves, brought me to my knees, forced me to act. I hailed a rickshaw to drive me home.

"I showed up at home with a bleeding foot and asked for five rupees," I said to Marc, withdrawing from his arms. "Ma asked me, 'Where are your sisters?'"

He pushed me into the shower. Water washed over me, like rain.

"How is your mother holding up?" Marc asked from outside.

"She's living in a widow ashram now," I said, poking my head out of the water. "I can't see her or write to her for three months. She's cultivating detachment."

"How about you?" he asked. "How do you feel about it? Your father?"

I turned the shower off.

What I felt when I saw his photograph, him in his workman's clothes, wasn't sadness. It was more primal. An uncivilized grief I could neither name nor approach through metaphor.

"I felt something," I said. "Don't know what."

I didn't mention the photo in response to Marc's question not because I wanted to conceal, but because saying it out loud would give it a weight, a permanence, one that I wasn't prepared for. I was about to mention his diary.

"Sham?" He was closer now to the bathroom door. "You feel safe now?"

I recalled my reflection on Pita-jee's photograph.

"I should," I said as I wiped my face with my hand.

There's no greater haunting than resemblance, I thought, no ghost more immune to exorcism than genes. Condensation had turned the bathroom's mirror to a haze.

I turned the faucet off. The sound of Marc's breath braided with the trickle of leftover water dripping from the showerhead.

I dried myself and left the damp towel on the sink and put on my pajamas and nightshirt and stepped out.

"Su sent you a gift," Marc said. "But first eat."

He fetched his backpack from his jeep, unzipped it, took out a lunch box, and opened it. He held it as I stood there and scarfed it down, tearing at butter naan with my teeth, shoving the cauliflower curry into my mouth by the handful. After I washed my hands, he took Su's gift out of his backpack and gave it to me.

It was a blue notebook, and pressed on each of its pages were jasmine blossoms, three or four of them, gone pale, but not brown, retaining their fragrance. Marc leaned forward and pressed his nose to the book, which lay open in my hands. On my breath the two scents met: the flowers from Marc's terrace, entombed in a book, the flowers that Ma brought to her nose. I heard both their breaths: Marc's, Ma's. Su gave the scent new meanings. Ma's hand, collecting Pita-jee's letters, touching our head to bless us on our birthdays, stitching our sweaters, picking up a cubit of stringed jasmine, turning the knob of her radio and listening to Geeta Dutt sing, Marc plucking the flowers absentmindedly when we spoke on his balcony, his beautiful fingers now touching the petals on the page—all of it assimilated in the fragrance of jasmine.

Marc lay down on the bed and switched off the table lamp. I lay down next to him, a few inches separating our bodies. The night ticked away, second by delicate second.

The next day, I resumed directing my section of the play. Two days prior to the show, Nandi wanted us to do a run-through: perform together all four acts, which were separately directed. He wanted to check the transitions and smooth out any wrinkles. I spoke in private to Ankit and Mohit, the actors who would enact the kiss.

"You wanted more from the Chinmasta Temple play," I said. "*We* should do more—but for that we must skip it out of the rehearsal. If Nandi sees it, he will censor it."

"Will we get in trouble?" Mohit asked.

"I don't care," Ankit said. "Let's do it."

"I will take the hit if there's trouble," I assured Mohit.

CHITRANGADA

On May 7, the day of the show, our performance began at 7:00 P.M. I borrowed from Marc the female puppet I'd given him. She became, in the opening act that Rooh directed, Chitrangada onstage. My student Dev, who played her father, doubled as her puppeteer. He was not concealed by a screen, so he was seen not as an artist who brought a doll to life with a deft tug of strings but as the man who controlled Chitrangada during her upbringing.

Saaya directed the next act. When she's sixteen, Chitrangada, chasing a boar, goes deep into the woods, and there she stumbles upon Arjuna, the Pandava prince, now in exile. For the first time in her life she experiences attraction as she studies his body: his taut back muscles rippling as he bends to pluck an herb, his bare chest glistening with sweat, his dhoti clinging wetly to his thighs.

Arjuna commends her for riding the horse with the finesse of a prince. She says that she is indeed a prince, whereupon he smiles and tells her she's a princess. The two disrobe to compare anatomies, and on that full moon night, intoxicated by the smell and sight of each other's bodies, they lie on a bed of jasmine vines and make love.

To the throaty whine of the trumpet, my students entered the stage: Ronit from one end, the first human Chitrangada, Gupta from the other, as Arjuna, and together they performed the mating dance: kneeling, their bodies pressed as they moved in a circle on their knees, his arms wrapped around her, her fingers locked at the back of his head. Arjuna mouths a love ballad, set to drumbeats. Chitrangada sings a hymn to the tambura's drone.

Nandi directed the next act: when Chitrangada returns to the palace she has the mark of a woman who's lost her virginity, and her father, the king, played by Sahil, shames her. She challenges his decision to raise her as a boy. It's God's will, he says. No, she retorts, I decide whether I'll be a woman or a man, my gender is in my hands. She abandons his kingdom and goes back to Arjuna.

Shortly thereafter, Arjuna is cursed to be a woman for a year. And Chitrangada, embracing her identity as a man, marries Arjuna in a forest ceremony—she wears a rose crown, he bracelets of marigolds. She becomes the husband, he the wife. These versions of Arjuna and Chitrangada were played by Ronit and Gupta as well, their genders and their clothing switched, their characters the same.

Marc entered the candlelit greenroom, a tent set up behind the stage. Mohit was being transformed into Chitrangada for the fourth and final act that I directed. He had on a green gown. A wig was pinned to his hair with sixteen clips. His palms were red with henna paisleys. The makeup man painted a white swallow on his forehead.

Marc brought a bottle of whiskey to his mouth and said, "The sex dance was hot."

"Saaya directed it," I said.

Marc licked his lips. "'Course he did."

"If Nandi finds you drinking in the greenroom I'm done for," I said.

"Poor Nandi is done for anyways. This is where Chitrangada and Draupadi kiss?"

The makeup man's hand jerked, and the black dot he was now painting on Ashwin's chin became a wave flowing down the cleft. He fixed it quietly. I looked at Marc in the mirror. With his head tilted back, his lips wrapped around the green bottle's mouth, he gulped and gulped.

Saaya walked in as the makeup man, who was studiously avoiding my eyes, rubbed red over Ankit's lips with a brush.

"You should've played one of the girls, Sham," Marc said. "You'd make a pretty one."

"That's what I say but he never listens," Saaya said, bringing a hand to Marc's shoulder.

"Oh, he will," Marc slurred. He placed his hand on top of Saaya's and squeezed.

After a year in disguise, Arjuna turns into a man again and Chitrangada becomes his wife, as does Draupadi. On cue, six cymbals clanging, Mohit entered the stage, wearing the brass crown Nandi had given me. Ashwin followed him, his face and forearms painted blue, his sari brick-red.

Chitrangada and Draupadi, wives of the same man, are confined to their room as their husband holds court, goes to war, acquires more kingdoms. From a latticed window they watch the street and its vendors of carpets and trinkets and sugar treats. They turn to each other and share their vulnerabilities. One languid afternoon, in the room's lonely heat, their husband gone by then for six months, they're drawn to each other. The lips of the two queens meet.

The kiss forbidden by Nandi lasted two seconds. The gasp of the audience came afterward, a delayed reaction, as I'd expected, a gap between surprise and its expression, and by then Arjuna reentered the stage to the heightened tempo of the drum.

Then Chitrangada breaks into a three-minute tandav, her body a river in spate, rushing to the left, to the right, her quick-moving feet ready to take wing and lift her into the dark belly of the sky. She moves across sexual and gender identities, fluid as wet sandalwood on a statue's limb, as she declares, "I can be anything I want to be."

Su and Sagar met me in the greenroom after the performance.

"We have to talk about that kiss," Su said, bumping her shoulder into mine.

"This was fun," Sagar said. "We have to go. Got to wake up early and get to our boring desk jobs, but at least we came, unlike stupid Karan."

After he and Su left, I said hurried goodbyes to my students. I wanted to leave before I had to face Nandi.

Marc held my waist as we walked toward his jeep. I suggested we call a taxi.

"A few drinks don't make a bloody drunk." Marc climbed into the driver's seat. Puppet in hand, I got in reluctantly next to him.

With a steadiness that belied his inebriation, he drove us home. When he parked outside my lodgings, I stepped out of the car, breathless, into the cold womb of the night. He sang aloud as we bumbled up the stairs. He grabbed the puppet from my hands.

"Hush," I said, "you'll wake people up."

"Hush," he said, his lips grazing my ear. I stepped away from him and bounded up the stairs. When we got to my room he went to the balcony, peeled his shirt off, and lay sweating on the wooden floor.

"You!" Marc barked, pointing a finger up at me. "Come here, it's nice outside."

I sat next to him.

"Where's your lipstick?" he asked, running a thumb over my lips. I swatted his hand.

"I didn't act today," I reminded him.

He grabbed my jaw. "When will you do something about your love for me?"

"Please don't get started about our *Little Chat* again."

"Are you calling me a nag?"

"I'm tired and hurting all over."

"My sweet procrastinating princess."

He set the puppet leaning against the railing. "Chitrangada," he said. He blew a puff of air onto my face. I gagged on his whiskey breath.

"We should sleep," I said.

"Here, we'll sleep here," he said.

"I'll go get blankets," I said.

"I will," he said and tottered into the room, his hands clasped behind his head. He came back out and spread the blankets. We lay down, Marc between me and the handrail, his body touching mine, a column of heat trapped between our thighs. I closed my eyes but opened them again when he tapped my shoulder. The puppet nodded in my face.

"Chitrangada," he said. He got to his knees, leaned over the handrail, and held the puppet out. He looked at me. Then he let go.

Between the rusting iron rails, I saw the puppet's skirt flare as she went diving down.

"What are you doing!" I cried, getting up.

He pressed the heel of his foot to my shoulder and pushed me back to a sleeping position.

"I need privacy," he said, curling a leg across my waist. My stomach burned from his heat. Through the crumpled sheet underneath, the cold floorboards pinched my back.

Marc brought his face close to mine. I looked away. He held my chin and swung my head back to face him. "Why would you turn away from me like that? Am I ugly?"

I shook my head and brought a hand to his cheek.

Exhaling heavily, he climbed on top of me.

"I can't," I said. "Please."

"Can't or won't?"

"I want you, Marc. But not like this."

"If you won't give me what I want, I'll have to find it elsewhere."

He started to lift his body off mine. I placed a tentative hand on his sweat-slick shoulder.

"I won't have to go far," he said. His eyebrows pointed to the floor upstairs.

I tightened my grip on Marc's shoulder.

"Atta girl," he said.

He opened my shirt buttons. His fingers moved with heartbreaking tenderness down my neck and to my chest.

"Slow your engine, boy," Marc said, accent English. "You'll have a cardiac arrest."

He slipped his hand to the left. Under the flap of my shirt his fingers paused. He pushed my shirt away to confirm what his touch revealed.

It was his first sighting of them. My anticipation of his reaction was haunted by memory: Senior's teeth, "Bitch Bags."

"They're wee but cute, princess," he said.

His eye didn't widen. He didn't smirk. He planted a kiss on one nipple and started to fumble with his belt. He was drunk and on an agenda, or he didn't care for man breasts: they neither bothered nor interested him. A fleeting relief coursed through my flesh, and consequently, I felt for him a little tenderness.

The unbuckling took a moment but finally happened. He unzipped his fly and pushed his pants down. The buckle of his belt landed on the floor with a clink.

"We'll keep it basic today," Marc said. He wagged a finger at me. "Only for you."

He sat down on my chest. He stuffed his hand into his red boxers and fished out his erection. He wrapped my hands around it, his soft hands around mine, and moved them up, then down, up, then down: a sharp jolt of an ascent, the descent hard, deliberate, his organ hot, throbbing, wet in my fist. He sniffed hard and sucked his lips in. His eyes were closed. Moonlight colored his eyelashes white.

"You can do this for Marc Boy, yeah?" he said, his English voice a low hum. "You'll land on your feet at the end of it, you'll see."

I waited. What would go first: my sight, my hearing? What would happen when Marc, unaware, continued? I'd never crossed that frontier.

But nothing happened. My senses were fully present.

I decided to hurt him to make him stop. I saw his pubes swaying in the rush of my breath.

"They were right," I said. "Carrot pubes."

He froze. I grinned. He unclenched one hand, leaned back, and groped my belly, my gut. His other hand never ceased moving, not until he found what his other hand sought. My crotch. I was limp.

Shock drained the color from his face. I felt ashamed. He unclenched his hand but I continued to hold him. I sensed him slacken inside my sweaty palm. He yanked himself free of my grip, got up, and pulled the trousers up and squatted near the handrail with his back to me.

I made my way toward him on all fours.

"Let's talk about it," I said.

"What's left to talk about," he said. "After what I did?"

"I wanted it too," I said.

"But how can I trust that?"

Each word tight with disbelief, each word cracking with hope.

"Do you want to hug it out?" I asked, clumsily gripping his head.

"Are you nuts?" he said, pushing me away.

"But you said you'd protect me," I said.

"Yeah, you got the monster's name wrong, man," he said. "I'm the one you need protection from."

He got to his feet and put on his shirt. I pressed my forehead to the railing and found the puppet sprawled on the ground next to Marc's jeep. I closed my eyes.

If Senior's abuse had caused my sensory losses, then wouldn't my anxiety mute my senses in nonconsensual situations? But my body had remained fully present when I was with Marc on my balcony—and at the New Year's party.

I jerked my eyes open. The room was still. Marc was gone. So was the puppet.

REMOVAL

The school had arranged a formal farewell gathering for us in a seminar room a week after the play. Our students sipped on sodas and ate the snacks provided: paper plates set out on a cloth-covered table, each plate holding one samosa, one ladoo, and some chips. They didn't know what to say after they thanked us, told us how much they would miss us, and asked the usual questions: Where to next? When are you coming back? They gathered in a few small circles and spoke to each other.

I flitted around the room, from one group to another, avoiding Nandi, not prepared yet for our inevitable conversation. I went and thanked the principal for the invitation to teach full-time at his institution.

"But you aren't going to do it," he said. "Call me if you change your mind."

"I have a love letter for you," Saaya said, waving a folded note as he walked up to me.

"From Marc? You sure it's for me?"

His face pinched.

"It's from Nandi," he said.

I snatched it from him, aware that Nandi, smiling pleasantly and chatting with a student to our left, had watched me, from the corner of his eye, receiving the letter. I pocketed it without opening it.

As the evening was winding down, and I was talking to Rooh, my students, led by Mohit, walked up to me. They had gotten me a present wrapped in a ribbon and velvet.

"Have some shame," Rooh joked. "You had four teachers and only one gets a gift?"

I undid the knot of the ribbon and extracted from the folds of the fabric a book.

The Dravidian Book of Seas and Stargazing, Volume 2.

"How?" was all I managed to say. Emotion coursed through me as I flipped through the pages, lost in memories that, in this moment, felt like they were life's major turning points: Ma picking up the edge of a sari on display at a crafts fair and thumbing it, Milk making a paper boat with a receipt forgotten at the bottom of a plastic bag, Su pausing mid-stride during one of our evening walks to pick from the sidewalk a fallen gulmohar. Life can feel long sometimes, she said once.

"Thank you," I said, without clearing my throat, letting the heaviness in my voice show.

"My father told me about the book, not Nandi," I added, feeling the urge, in the wake of his death, to credit him.

A pause followed, not awkward. They were waiting to see if I wanted to say more about the man whose recent death was fresh in my consciousness and theirs. I closed the book and smiled to signal that I had no more to say.

"There's a story in there you'll like," Mohit said. "Why Chitrangada was born a girl—why the God's boon failed. It might be the story that got the book pulled off the racks."

"He *read* the book before giving it, can you believe it?" Ankit said.

"Of course I believe it, it's Mohit," Ashwin said.

Good comic timing, Nandi once told us, means offering relief at precisely the moment when the burden of the myth's emotion, through a steady accumulation, act upon act, has become nearly impossible to bear.

I entered the greenroom and caught my appearance in the dresser's side mirrors. The centerpiece reflected Nandi as he leaned over a steaming pot to relieve his blocked nose. He looked up, red-eyed, pointed to the bag in my hands, and said, "Is that what I told you to bring?"

I said, "I forgot what you said about the kiss, I did. I'll apologize to the troupe."

"Not the point," he said. "What you did, it stripped us bare before the audience."

"It lasted two seconds."

"Two seconds in which a goddess, Draupadi herself, kisses a woman."

He closed one side mirror, reducing me to a single reflection.

"It's a pity, but I cannot perform in Chamba again," he said.

He closed the other side mirror, erasing my remaining reflection. I'd looked into it a hundred times, brushstrokes transforming me into Draupadi, Kunti, Chitrangada.

He came up to me. He smelled of menthol. Water droplets beaded his cheeks.

I handed over the bag that had the crown in it, the crown that he'd gifted me the day I concluded my first performance with his troupe. My body, that evening, had thrummed with fulfillment.

"I wish you well," he said. "I'm sure the school would like to have you for another year?"

"Are you throwing me out?" I asked, dumbstruck more by the delivery of the decision than by the decision itself.

"I'm asking you to take a break for a year," he said. "I can't face my troupe if I let this pass."

He gave me a piece of paper that detailed the troupe's itinerary over the next year: places where they'd perform, phone numbers of local post offices I could call to reach him.

"Don't be a stranger," he said. "Keep in touch."

His pleasantry was accompanied by matching gestures—a smile, a hand to my shoulder. His theater sharpened the sting of my severance. I wanted no part of that charade.

"Chitrangada was raised as a man," I said. "Wouldn't she be drawn to another woman?"

"Your perspective doesn't change mine," he said, smile intact, hand removed. "A year from now you are welcome to join us—if you wish."

"That scene is in the *Mahabharata*—the original Sanskrit text," I said. "A book that, let me remind you, I borrowed from you to show my students on the first day of class."

"But not in the version our audience knows," he said, smile gone.

"You say you want to tell the stories of the gods properly," I said. "So 'proper' means appeasing the audience because clearly your loyalties lie with them, not with the stories."

"Stop shouting. You can't apologize for your action *and* defend it."

He left the greenroom. I came out a few minutes later. Rooh and Saaya had gathered around Nandi. They were listening to him with rapt attention.

I found a note Marc had pasted to my room door.

Meet me at Kali Mithai Shop, 8:30 p.m. tomorrow. Don't be late. I leave Chamba at 11:30 p.m., Bokaro Express.

I sat leaning against the door, as though I'd lost the key to my home. I acknowledged, in that moment, that I *knew* Nandi would fire me if I performed the kiss he forbade. That's why I included it. Not because I wanted to honor the request of my students. I didn't have the gumption to leave, so I forced him to make the decision for me. Back then, I wanted to go to Marc. But now it was clear that was not an option. At least he'd left the note on my door and not with Saaya, I thought.

I checked into Ganesh Hotel. I didn't want to meet Rooh, my first teacher, and tell him I'd been fired. I didn't want to see Saaya and ask him why he'd slept with Marc.

The room was small, without adornment or furniture. The ceiling fan creaked when I turned it on and the brown sheet of the mattress, directly underneath, shivered in its current. I stripped, lay down, closed my eyes.

OTHER USES OF EARTHEN LAMPS

I found Marc waiting for me outside Kali Mithai Shop. We stood before each other in an awkward silence before we, without greeting each other, walked away from the shop and into a narrow lane. It was flanked by tents that were selling firecrackers. Dark Dussehra, the festival that celebrated the ten shadow forms of the goddess, had begun, and the first night belonged to Matangi, the outcast goddess worshipped with soiled clothes and leftovers. Devotees burned flowerpots and sparklers to honor her.

Suspended from Marc's wrist was a plastic bag that, weighed down by objects that pressed darkly against its translucent white surface, swayed in rhythm to his step.

I'd made a decision: I would offer Marc consummation by pretending that our union was nonconsensual, so my body could be present to his body.

From a stall to our left a boy hollered, startling me, "Ten for twenty, ten for twenty, grab 'em before they're gone." He held out a box of flowerpots, and I remembered how my sisters and I, to Ma's count of "one-two-three-go!," brought our sparklers to flowerpots, placed one beside the other, stepped back, and watched them hiss and rise into columns of fire, watched to see whose flowerpot soared the tallest, a matter we never agreed on, each of us protesting "No, not yours, mine,

mine, mine!" The repetition of "mine," which annoyed Ma, made me smile as I followed in Marc's footsteps.

At the end of the road we found a bench that overlooked a pond and sat down. Marc placed the plastic bag between us. The objects it held clattered. I stuffed my hand into my pocket and pinched the slippery condom I had brought to our meeting, wanting to fish it out and offer it to him.

"They're earthen lamps," Marc said pointing to the bag. "Fourteen each for Mud and Milk."

"You remember."

"I won't be able to join you in the ceremony, naturally, because I leave tonight, and, even if I were around, it wouldn't be right, not after what I've done."

"You didn't do anything."

"But I will think of them on the full moon. Is that okay?"

I extracted one earthen lamp: it was mud-colored and small; I could easily hold four of them in my palm. I peeked into the bag. Marc had already placed wicks in all of them. All I had to do was pour oil, light them, and set them afloat.

"This isn't me compensating for what I've done," Marc said. "I'm sorry, Shagun."

The lamp slipped from my fingers and fell to the ground. Marc kneeled down, picked it up, and held it out. It was still intact. Grass had broken its fall.

"Please don't say sorry, Marc," I said, taking it from him.

He remained kneeling. He pressed his big hands to his eyes. "I ruined things."

"You're ruining things now," I said.

He unveiled his face. His cheeks were damp. "I don't want you to forgive me. Just show me I'm a monster. Any way you want. How about this?"

He pointed to the lamp in my hand and to his forehead, drenched in sweat. It took me a moment to understand. He wanted me to hit him.

"This isn't you," I said, my voice shaky from sorrow or anger.

"But it is you," he said. "Maybe you could use my belt?"

He looked at me hopefully. With deception, with evasion, with silence, I had reduced the Marc who introduced himself with the air of a spring breeze after *First Desire* to the Marc I witnessed now: broken, twisted, deadened.

I brought the lamp smashing against my jaw. It broke into a hundred shards and left my flesh throbbing.

"What are you doing?" he said, his voice a few decibels above a whisper.

I took one more out of the packet, smashed it against my forehead. Clay dust entered my eyes and they started to sting.

"Please stop," he said, taking his voice a notch higher.

I reached into the packet once more. He stumbled to his feet and steadied himself with a hand on my shoulder. He stood there a moment, shaking like a child in the cold, his face gone white. Then he ran. I watched him blur with the crowd.

I sat by the pond until midnight. He was gone. Marc was gone. No longer would I sit next to him in his red Mahindra jeep. His room with its oud scent and photographs locked me out. His voice wouldn't balloon my pet name. The flavors of the meals we shared would desert the memory of taste. My spirit lost its time. I understood what it meant to be a ghost.

Behind me the bazaar buzzed. Matangi's night was over. Firecrackers sold at throwaway prices.

PART VI

1997

IT

I checked out of Ganesh Hotel on the third night of Dark Dussehra, which belonged to Chinmasta, the goddess who severs her own head. The act is symbolic, Nandi once told me, of the conscious mind losing control to allow for the repressed to surface. In clothes that I hadn't changed in three days, I stood in the Chinmasta Temple. It was here where my students saw the play, I remembered, when I went home with Marc. The priest sprinkled myrrh over embers, and a fragrant white smoke hissed and shot to life, concealing the face of the goddess. To the beat of double-headed drums, four women in white saris fell to their knees and whirled their heads. Their unpinned white hair whipped the air.

After the ceremony ended, I left Temple Street and entered a narrow alleyway, my gaze fixed on the lone streetlamp flickering at its other end.

I got to my lodgings. How long before I faced Rooh—and Saaya? I took the first flight of stairs. Heard a ragged breath. Turned at the landing, dazed. Heard a whoosh, then saw the shadow of the stick before it made forceful contact with my forehead.

The warm wash of blood preceded the pain. Bone-deep. I lay sprawled on the landing with a hand pressed to my forehead. A man, reduced to a blurred silhouette, walked toward me slowly. I didn't hear his movement.

He kicked me in the crotch. Twice, in quick succession. The air was whipped from my lungs. Consciousness flew from my head.

A cold air that felt like panic revived my senses. I felt a soreness in my groin, my limbs heavy. My vision swam. Above me was a pale blue sky, not the darkness of my corridor that I'd expected. A man's face appeared over my head. I struggled to focus on it. When he spoke, recognition clicked in place.

"Your kutta dad promised me money," Ajay said. "But he stopped after one payment and now he's not taking my calls."

I blinked at him.

"You don't understand?" he said. "I will open the wrapper and put the toffee in your mouth. I called your father after you gave me his number. I called him and we had an agreement."

I tried to sit up. He pressed a boot to my shoulder and pinned me down. I noticed I was not in my clothes. I had on a blue hospital gown, worn thin. I lay on a gravel road.

"Your father asked me to leave you alone," Ajay said. "In return, five thousand rupees were going to show up in my account every month for six months starting March."

I tried to speak but my tongue was as thick as the tail of a dead fish.

"The March installment came through," he said. "But nothing in April, nothing in May."

I tried again. "What did you say to my father?"

"Your boy doesn't want bitch in his life, no sir, he wants to be bitch of another man."

I said, "Is that how you think of your mother? Her place in your dad's life?"

He unzipped his trousers. I closed my eyes. His warm, putrid jet of urine drenched my shirt, my neck. I covered the wound he'd given me with my palm.

"Where all do you put your tongue—you speak about my father with same tongue?" His words syncopated the pouring sound his piss made.

"What are you? Not he, not she. He-she? It. Correct. You're 'it.' Less than nothing. If I put bullet in your head, who will question my gun?"

When he was done, he zipped up and touched my temple with the toe of his boot. My head lolled away then toward him. I opened my eyes.

He reminded me that in 1984, when Indira Gandhi was our prime minister, her son had orchestrated the forced vasectomies of men to keep the population in check: particularly the poor, particularly Muslims. Policemen all over were given targets. He, Ajay Biswas, was in Delhi then. He had exceeded his target.

"The whole thing was called off eventually and I was transferred here, but I developed an addiction for it," he said. "So I made connections with the local doctors. Now whenever I feel like it, I have you dirty fellows sterilized. So you don't reproduce. Mother India will say thanks."

Instinctively, I brought my hands over my groin.

"Yes, that's right. You tell Daddy. That I had his boy sterilized like a street dog."

His guttural laughter was full of hate.

"Tell him the vasectomy is first warning. If I don't get my payment in two weeks, I'll cut it off fully."

He thought my father was alive. He mimed a scissors with his fingers. He stepped over me and started to leave. Then he stopped and added, "Oh, don't try to run. You have a satellite. There, see that friendly boy?" He pointed to a man who stood at some distance. He was dressed in a constable's uniform and smoked a cigarette. "He will be outside your school when you teach, outside your guesthouse when you sleep. Twenty-four seven he's with you."

I looked around for my clothes but couldn't find them. I walked back home in my blue hospital gown. It was still early. The only attention I drew was from milkmen and boys on bicycles doing newspaper deliveries. I went and knocked on the door to Saaya's room. I stepped back until my back touched the wall.

Rooh, who opened the door, promptly exclaimed, "We were looking for you."

"I don't have my key," I said. "I need to shower."

"Why are you—" Rooh began, looking now at my hospital gown. "Are you hurt?"

Saaya came promptly out and took a step or two toward me but stopped short. The stench hit him, I guessed. I held my hands across my chest. He came closer, looked down, and recognition flooded his face.

"Is he okay?" Rooh asked.

"Get out," Saaya said. "Leave. Now."

Rooh did as he was told. Saaya took my hand, led me in, and closed the door.

He took me to the bathroom and filled a bucket with hot water. He un-knotted and opened my hospital gown. With his hands to my shoulders, he made me kneel down. He squatted before me and poured mug after mug of steaming water over my head. The soap between his hand and my body thinned as he scrubbed me with vigor. When he made his way down to my crotch, however, his fingers on my penis were as gentle as the soap's lather and foam. In the wake of his gentle touch, I was struck by the full weight of the knowledge that my body had been altered—altered without my consent. I shuddered. Saaya removed his fingers from my flesh. He waited, squatting on the floor, his breath shallow, his gaze lowered. My eyes turned hot and the water on the rest of my body felt cold, even as it steamed on my skin.

When I was ready, he somehow understood. He looked up. I nodded. He resumed.

He toweled me dry and wrapped the towel around my waist. I dripped at the bathroom's threshold and watched him fetch me a T-shirt and a pair of trousers from his cupboard.

"Open it," he said, gesturing to the towel.

I made no move to fulfill his command. He looked up and found my anger.

"I'm sorry," he said, his eyes welling up.

I pummeled him, my fury gathering momentum as my fists met his shoulder, his arm, his thigh. He didn't fight back. He didn't shield his face with his hands. I turned him around and struck him on either side of his spine with the sides of my fists. I didn't know how to hit him. Eventually I tired and stepped away. He stood there, waiting for more.

I collapsed on the mattress. He came and lay down next to me.

"It was only once," he said, his voice thick with tears. "And we didn't go all the way."

"That makes it okay?"

"No, it doesn't," he sobbed. "I'm sorry."

Who started it? I wanted to know but didn't ask. I wanted to know that answer from Marc. The decision gave me hope: it was only a matter of time before I met Marc again.

"At least you shouldn't have done that," I said, touching my neck. "Animal."

We laughed. I sidled closer to him. We lay quietly for a moment. Next to each other. Our hands touching. He said, "I missed this. Us. Maybe that's why I did it."

My heart ached for all the time in the last nine months that I did not spend with him, the hours in his day that I'd emptied of my friendship. I looped my little finger with his and squeezed. He squeezed back. Our breath slowly steadied.

When Saaya opened the door, we found Rooh standing there.

"Eavesdropper," Saaya hissed.

He kept his gaze studiously away from me and said, "Shagun's door is open."

We followed him downstairs. The door was ajar, my room's contents ransacked: the mattress on the floor along with my clothes, scattered all over. Saaya tested the door handle. It was broken.

They helped me restore my room's order. We folded clothes, picked the mattress off the floor. Bagged a broken cup, swept the floor. We did not talk. It was quiet labor.

When we were done, I took Pita-jee's diary out, pressed it to my chest, and sat down. The connection between Ajay's call to Pita-jee and the consequent distraction that led to Pita-jee's accident became clear as daylight.

I realized, with a start, that I hadn't seen the brochure for the Hanuman Male Fixing Center. I got up and looked again in my cupboard, where I always kept it. Drawers pulled open, contents rummaged. Cupboard opened yet again. Stacked shirts and trousers pushed down so I could see clearly.

"I just folded," Saaya complained.

"What's going on?" Rooh demanded.

It was gone. The brochure was gone. Ajay Biswas took it, I was certain. If I didn't pay him the money, he'd hand me over. He would take the money and hand me over anyway.

"I have to leave," I said. "And soon."

"Shagun, what's happening?" Rooh asked.

The frustration and anger in his voice had given way to fear.

I told them. About the nonconsensual vasectomy. Ajay Biswas. His satellite. Together we went gingerly onto the balcony and peeped out. There he was, standing across the street, leaning against a wall, a cigarette in his mouth. He scanned the street. He looked up. We withdrew.

Rooh sat to my left, Saaya to my right. The weight of their bodies, pressed against mine. Their chins in my neck, Rooh's stubble, Saaya's clean-shaven skin. Rooh's curly oily hair and Saaya's long, smooth hair smelling of jasmine, all over my face. The kinetic energy of performance and their bodies, the heat, smell, and weight of them: I would miss it all.

"How did I get so lucky with you two?" I said and sniffled.

"Just 'lucky' won't do, Mr. Philosopher," Saaya said. "Lucky how? Blow our minds with your learned words."

I said, "Like when the power goes out but it's a full-moon night."

To Rooh, Saaya said, "Hear that, old man? Best case, we're a night with a power cut."

"Where will you go?" Rooh asked. "Home?"

I was filled with the need to acknowledge my father's personhood. I wanted to turn him not into a hero but into his human self.

Only one picture of his was annotated. Janak Reformatory and Jailhouse, Madhuban. Because it was special to him, I assumed.

It is never too late to make space for a person in your life, Ma had said.

I decided to go to Madhuban, sit in front of the prison he constructed, and, with his building bearing witness, read his journal and revise my memory of him: from a sex-starved repressive patriarch to a husband and parent who sacrificed his years for his family.

"No," I said. "But I know where I'll go."

Saaya kissed my bruise. "Let's talk to Nandi," he said. "This he'll help with."

He won't, I was about to say, but the words didn't ring true even in my head. He didn't want me in the troupe after violating his principles, but he would help.

Saaya and Nandi came up with a plan. Rooh fleshed out the details. We would all leave Chamba on the same day.

Over the last few months, I'd acquired a Ken doll, a retro outfit, and *The Dravidian Book of Seas and Stargazing, Volume 2.* I packed them with my clothes in the attaché I'd arrived with.

The bed was stripped, the room empty, ready for the next occupant. When Su came over, we took my attaché to the balcony and sat on it. She pressed my head to her shoulder and let me cry. When she sensed that the storm of my grief had subsided for now, she let me go.

"What do you want?" she asked. "Like, from life?"

Saaya had once asked me the same question.

"I want a celebration," I said. "I want to perform something beautiful and intimate, with Rooh, with Saaya. I want you to come see Marc and me running off into our bridal night, and oh, Ma too. I mean, why not. If wishes were horses and all that."

"'Run off into our bridal night,'" Su mocked. "You're such a drama queen." We laughed. "You want a celebration? You'll get one."

Su walked with me. Up one floor. My students, all six of them, were in Nandi's room. So were the other members of my troupe. We commenced preparations to stage my escape from Chamba, from Ajay Biswas's satellite. We traded our clothes for costumes. The room, like our greenroom, was lamplit, and in the light of those flames the bowls of makeup resembled precious stones: green like emerald, red like ruby, blue like lapis lazuli. The only movement was the hand of our makeup man, whose brush traced the contours of our faces, leaving in its wake trails of color, bright, viscous. Nandi started to sing a song and Rooh joined him and Saaya and me. The makeup man's mouth twitched into a smile even as his gaze was fixed on the faces our faces were becoming. Su and my students listened to us, and every time we repeated the chorus they hummed along. It was a song from the Hindu Romantic era, the Bhakti period, when art blurred the border between devotion and love, when a lover's home became your sacred address, and he, your lover, in all his fragile mortality, was no less a miracle than a god.

Even after we stopped singing, we continued to hum, falling quiet one after another, so that the silence that followed felt like a continuation of, rather than a punctuation to, the song.

We waited, sitting upright, on the bed, on the floor, our hands in our laps.

We heard our cue, a trumpet, a drum, an ululation, a human throat producing a sound that was on the register of birdsong. We filed down the stairs and exploded out of the gate, a messy flesh conglomerate, the slow rhythm of our movement escalating into something rowdier, explosive almost, I at the epicenter, dressed in regular clothing, my face painted white, on my head a wig made of jute strings, surrounded by a wall of dancing bodies. Su had my attaché. From the corner of my eye I saw my satellite, a quick, blurred glimpse. Seven musicians surrounded us and drowned us in their music. In tandem they blew their trumpets and struck the goatskin heads of their drums. We started to move like one body teeming with multiple heads and limbs.

We left the alleyway and entered the school's main street. Then out we went, leaving the campus behind, onto Market Street. Along the way, people joined us, college students, shoppers with bags of produce, couples out on evening walks. The junta surrounded the musicians who surrounded us as we moved along. Rooh and Saaya threw fistfuls of Holi colors in the air, drawing the powder from pouches worn around their waist. They blurred the air with reds and blues.

Three winding streets later we saw a parked minivan at one corner. The goodbyes began as we continued to move, as the musicians sustained their music at its crescendo, as strangers danced all around us. As I left the town where I met and lost the man I loved, I twirled in a circle from Nandi to Rooh to Saaya to Su. I gave them each a hug, pressed their bodies to mine, pressed my head to their necks, their shoulders. Three rounds, three hugs for each of those humans whom I loved, who had loved me in return. The shoulder of my costume was smudged with their makeup.

We slowed but didn't stop as our bodies surrounded the minivan, pushed against it, causing it to jolt back and forth. The driver slid open the back door, leaned his upper body out, and waved his fist at us. Su slid the attaché into the van. I crouched amid a press of bodies and entered the van through the same open door. I took my wig off and handed it to Saaya. Nandi and Rooh towered over the rest as they pretended to argue with the driver. Lying flat, my stomach pressed to my attaché, I watched the face of Su, painted blue, and of Saaya, painted green, the red of their eyes made redder against the surrounding palettes of color. Nandi struck the minivan with his fist and the driver slipped his body in and slid the door shut. Rooh and Nandi pressed their hands to the van's window and our eyes met. They were surrounded now by the people of Chamba. They were falling behind. They thumped the car once more with their palms and then they were gone.

I closed my eyes and listened to the music and their cries, relishing that aural contact. Until I heard a rap on the window. Wood on glass. The driver lowered his window.

"This is no place to park," a stern voice said.

"Sorry, sir. I stopped for a cigarette and was about to go when they almost wiped me out."

My eyes were closed. He started the engine and just like that, we drove away.

The procession was headed for the railway station, where my troupe members would board the train and the others would depart. When the satellite checked them, as I knew he would, he wouldn't find me.

The driver pulled to the side of the road. With two bottles of water I washed my makeup off. The driver took me to the Uttarkashi railway station. I had a ticket from there to Madhuban. On my ticket I was S. Singer.

As I stood on the platform with my attaché and watched my train pull in, I stuffed a hand into my trouser pocket and found a piece of paper. I fished it out. Written on it, in Hindi: *This isn't goodbye. —Nandi, Rooh, Saaya.*

Marc had said those words to me in a different language. On the night we had our Little Chat. The resonance was comforting. His promise, traveling through time, finding its place in Nandi's ink. I cried for all the tentative departures from my life, for the love that tentativeness contained.

TWO UNEXPECTED ENCOUNTERS

I got off the train at Madhuban. At one end of its single platform, bright with the glare of the late-May sun, I saw three women, each dressed in a faded cotton sari, standing before a handcart where a shirtless man sold freshly pressed sugarcane juice. Watching the women drinking the frothy chartreuse liquid made me thirsty. I walked up to the cart and asked for a glass. He ran three sugarcane stalks through the hand-cranked grinder, collected their juice in two glasses, and offered me one. I drank it quickly. The women spoke to each other in Bihari.

"What brings you here?" he asked.

From my attaché, I fished out Pita-jee's photograph of the jailhouse and showed it to him. His expression darkened.

"How do I get here?" I asked.

"You *want* to go there?" he asked.

His question piqued the interest of the women, who looked at the photograph. Their jaws hardened. Did they think I was here to get myself voluntarily arrested? I'm not a criminal, I wanted to clarify.

"Six rupees," the vendor said. I tucked the photo back in Pita-jee's diary and paid him.

"Go meet the village chief," he said.

"Why?" I asked, perplexed, but instead of responding to my question, he gave me the directions, a house two streets away from the station.

I rattled the latch on the gate and waited. On the wall to the right was a sun with a yellow face: ginger lashes, red whiskers. A blue-eyed moon decorated the wall on the left.

A woman came out. The edge of her sari, drawn over her head, covered her eyes and forehead. I introduced myself as the architect's son. She went back in and returned with a man. They stepped out of the shaded portico and into daylight.

His mustache was dyed jet black, his face ageless as a demon's. His turban was pink, his dhoti and kurta white. We meet our destiny on the road we take to avoid it.

Vikrant smoothed his kurta and said, "From the look on your face, it's clear you weren't expecting to see me here."

Two burly, mustachioed men emerged from the house and stood behind him at a respectful distance. They planted their lathis on the ground. The black of their dhotis and vests heightened the sense of menace they evoked. Vikrant opened the gate. It creaked on its hinges and my legs buckled.

I had fled from him once and if I tried now, his men would, I knew, apprehend me. So I came up with a plan as I stood before him, watching him sweep his hand in the direction of his house. I would tell him my father had died. If he was the man of god he claimed to be, the dead would be sacred to him and, if I was lucky, some of that respect might rub off on me and I would be allowed to leave unscathed.

I followed him in. We walked past the sweat-soaked, big-chested bodyguards. Vikrant pointed to a stool on his porch. After I sat down his wife offered me sugarcane juice that I emptied without separating the glass from my lips. He asked how my father was. I told him about the accident. He nodded slowly.

"Leave your bag here," he said, pointing to my attaché. "We're going for a walk."

He took me to a Hanuman temple a couple of furlongs away. His henchmen followed us. We went up a flight of stairs and through a sunny colonnaded corridor that ran by the sanctum sanctorum and led to a small back room.

"This is our Hall of Fame," he said. "Here we honor those who left a mark on Madhuban. There, see. Your father. The day he completed work on the prison."

Pita-jee stood with workmen dressed in dhotis and vests. He wore a shirt, tucked in, and stood with his hands crossed behind him. I stepped closer to the picture. He became a grainy blur of pixels.

"He saved our heritage," Vikrant said. "The fort of our kings. His company won the contract for the state-funded prison project. He came here to check out lands. They were going to build something ground up. But then he learned about the plight of our fort: The Archeological Survey of India had run out of funds to care for it, it became a breeding ground for rats and a health hazard for the village. It was about to be torn down. So he proposed renovating the fort into a prison. 'You'll be seen as a government that respects the local heritage, aren't elections coming up?' he argued. And he had a deal."

He turned to me.

"Of course, the prison isn't actually a prison," he said. "It's the Hanuman Male Fixing Center."

We stood on the edge of the hill. Vikrant pointed to the brick-red building drenched in sunlight. Built around its dome was a corridor lined with tall potted plants.

"Why are you here?" he asked.

"I wanted to read my father's diary in front of the building he made."

"You hope he's written that he's fine with who you are, something to that effect? So you can carry on with your way of life? Tell me. Even among you there is a man and a woman of the relationship, yes? Shouldn't that tell you something?"

Wanting to divert his attention away from his ideology and toward my absent parent, I said, "My father's diary has the usual: the day-to-day of his life dated and cataloged. I want to read it so I know him a little better. I miss him."

"He was away, wasn't he, for most of your life?" he asked.

"Pretty much."

"He told me when he first called me. Said you won't have turned out the way you did if he was around. I agree with him. It takes a father to make a man of a son."

A breeze whipped the branches of the crotons that lined the prison's rooftop corridor. A flock of pigeons exploded into the sky.

I asked, "When he made the building, did he know that it wasn't going to be a prison?"

"Not at first," Vikrant replied. "He and I met one day, and I told him."

Is that why Pita-jee identified the photograph: to mark the anomaly, a conversion facility masquerading as a prison?

"I can't let you leave," he said. "There's a reason God brought you to my door."

I'd had many nightmares about getting caught. I imagined the scenario when awake. All of those dreamed and dreamed-up scenarios felt erroneously heightened compared to the ordinariness of my present in which my worst fear had come to pass: me standing next to my captor like a free man, his henchmen behind me, before us my prison that I'd walk inevitably into, with no exit plan. My fear and imagination failed to conjure up the quotidian nature of brutality.

"Pita-jee promised you'd use no force," I said, my voice distant, without conviction, a drowning man's last, feeble attempt at survival.

"I'm doing this to honor your father. He worked with greater diligence when I told him what this place was. Because you're his son, I'll give you a special privilege. The others are allowed to bring in only one outside item: a statue or a photo of their family deity. I'll allow you to bring in his diary."

My knees did give way then. I collapsed like a child's paper boat in rain and leaned over the edge of the hill and retched. The sugarcane juice I drank and bile burned my throat on its way out and left in my mouth the stench of rotten guavas. When I stood back up heavily and turned, the pink of Vikrant's turban, amid the earth tones and whites, pricked my eyes, and I started to helplessly cry.

The yellow glare of the streetlight exposed water stains on the high prison walls. Vikrant introduced me to an inspector who was drinking a cup of chai at a snack stall that played Bollywood songs from the 1980s. He seemed to be my age. He was broad-shouldered and tall, a full head taller than me, like Marc. SAWANT KUMAR, his name badge said.

He looked at me closely. Then, unexpectedly, the hint of a smile appeared in his eyes, though it didn't shape his lips.

At the gate, Kumar blew a whistle. A short man emerged, bent low, and offered a salaam as he opened the gate. We entered Pita-jee's prison. The Hanuman Male Fixing Center.

In the red-floored dining hall we joined a line of men. We were given rice gruel in yellow caddies that had DABUR DALDA printed on them in red. Vikrant shared our plan with Kumar. I took Pita-jee's diary out of my bag and put it on the table.

I fed myself a spoonful of the gruel. It tasted starchy. My eyes scanned the inmates, six rows of them. They were all in uniform—orange dhotis, saffron shawls—so it took my eyes a moment to register his presence, despite his distinctive appearance: pale skin, long-limbed elegance even in the simple act of bringing a spoonful of drippy gruel to his lips; ginger hair; taller than the men who flanked him, who made eager conversation with him as he leaned over his caddy.

What on earth are you doing here, Marc?

The strength it took to hold myself back, to not hurl my question into the air, to not run up to him and hold him and feel the heat of him against my flesh for as long as my body permitted it, left me addled and light-headed. I felt the rapid thump of my heart between my man breasts. My lips, I sensed, were moving mutely, as if I was chanting on rosary beads the name "Marc."

How many surprises did Madhuban have in store for me?

"What do you think you're looking at?" Vikrant asked.

His voice snuffed out the dining hall chatter. The heads at all six tables turned to look at us. Including Marc's. Our eyes met.

"I know him," I said, my tone even as I looked away from Marc to Vikrant.

"Know how?" he asked, getting up. I opened my mouth. He raised his hand. "Whisper it in Kumar's ear."

I turned to Kumar, leaned forward, and whispered, "We were classmates at Magpies."

Surprise passed through Kumar's eyes.

Vikrant pointed to Marc. "You. Over here. Fast. We're not under the Raj."

"I'm not British," Marc said, making his way toward us.

"What was that?" Vikrant said.

"Nothing," Marc said.

"Better be nothing," he said. "Now. How do you know him?"

"Our fathers were friends," Marc said. "His dad built our home in Kerala."

"Does it tally?" Vikrant asked, looking at Kumar.

"Yes," Kumar said.

I felt my pulse quicken.

"Are you sure?" Vikrant asked, his arms crossed.

Kumar stood up and cleared his throat. "'Marc's like a brother to me.' He also said that."

Vikrant looked at me, long and hard, to see if my expression would give anything away. I struggled to keep my face from betraying not the lie itself but the mixture of confusion, fear, and doubt that Kumar's words had evoked in me: Why had he lied to his boss, the notorious Vikrant no less, on my behalf? Would he, later that night, show up in my cell and fuck me—or worse, demand that I fuck him?

Vikrant turned around and started to leave the room, his guards in tow. An inmate started to run toward Vikrant. His chubby face was pinched. His hands were stretched out in front of him, his fingers clawed. The sound of his bare feet slapping the floor reverberated through the hall.

The guards flashed past Vikrant. They got to the inmate before his hands were anywhere in the vicinity of Vikrant's neck. They grabbed his shoulder and dropped him to the floor. One guard pinned his hands to the small of his back, the other pinned his head to the floor. His strenuous, wheezing breath contorted his face. That could have been me in a different version of my history—had I not gotten into Nandi's troupe. I stole a glance at Marc's face and found fear.

Vikrant said, "Attacking me won't cure you, boy. Only you can cure yourself. Ask Hanuman for strength."

I followed Kumar down a long corridor. The dim lights from the brick walls barely illuminated the stone floor. At the corridor's end, Kumar turned left, fished a bunch of keys out of his trouser pocket, and separated one from the rest. With it he opened the door to a cell. He stepped in, switched on a light. My uniform, folded, was on my bed.

He stood outside. I put down my bag with Pita-jee's diary. As I took my shirt off and wrapped the saffron shawl around my body—it was rough against my skin—I was hit by the realization that I'd fled from Ajay into Vikrant's facility.

When I came out and joined him, the saffron shawl wrapped around my body, my ankles bared by the orange dhoti, he pointed to the cell adjacent to mine and said, "Your 'brother' lives there."

Kumar had given me the cell next to Marc's. It was his second act of kindness. I opened my mouth to thank him.

"We'll be late," he said.

The cells were all empty. We went back up the stairs, turned right, and walked down another long corridor to the cavernous temple room, where all the men had gathered.

"Oldest batch stands up front, freshers to the back," Kumar said. He took me to three men who stood at the back of the gathering. One of them was the man who'd attacked Vikrant. His chin was bruised. "Join them, they started earlier this week."

Kumar left. From where I stood, I could only see the statue's face: Hanuman, his orange monkey face illuminated by columns of oil lamps that flanked him.

"I'm Praneet," said the bruised man. "Marc's like a *brother*—really?"

"That was smart, attacking him when his guards were right there," I said.

"Cycle through the program three times, forty-five days each. Then we'll see about your smartness."

He raised his hand, and in the low light I saw three scars running vertically down his wrist. Would that be my fate? I thumbed my veins, as if checking my pulse.

"How'd you survive that?" I asked.

"The Servants of God," he said, pointing to volunteers who stood near the walls, keeping an eye on us. They wore saffron shirts and trousers. They'd found Praneet bleeding in his cell. "Suicide is a sin worse than murder," they'd said. They'd made him wash all the toilets. Doing the chore of a lower caste saved him from being reincarnated as a lower caste; that's what happens to a highborn who tries to end his lives, they'd added.

"How did you get the blade?" I asked.

"First you answer my question."

"Not brother-like, no."

He turned to me with a look of great pity. "Then you will fail the test too."

My nose turned hot. "You don't know that," I said.

"If you're with him, you're like me. You're not the man of your romance."

The ululation of a conch shell filled the room. Vikrant performed the ritual that Pita-jee performed before his Hanuman statue that I'd broken: he recited the forty verses written in praise of the deity, in tandem with the clanging of the bells and cymbals.

When it started to wind down, the instruments going quiet, Praneet said to me, "Marc spoke to me. He knows how I got the blade. Ask him. He recorded my story."

"Recorded?"

"I'm in the cell to his right."

"I'm to his left. Wait. You spoke through those thick walls—how?"

We formed five rows to exit the temple. Praneet stood in front of me.

"Marc knows how," he said.

As we filed out, the priest pressed prasad into our hands. The cere-monial offering. An apple slice. The Servants of God observed us: in the corridor leading out of the temple, on the stairs, and in the corridor of our cells, standing under dim lamps, backs to the walls.

Once I was in my cell, a Servant locked the door from the outside. I touched the wall that separated me from Marc. The Great Wall of Singer. I thrummed with fondness and worry.

I sat on the bed. A cement arm extending from the wall, carved with a slight depression so a thin mattress could fit snugly in. Had Pita-jee designed it?

The lights in the corridor outside and in our cells were extinguished. A Servant paced the corridor with a lantern. I lit a candle, fixed it on the floor, and in its unwavering light, read my father's diary.

In the years before he left the country, when Pita-jee came home from work and opened the gate, the front door would fly open and Ma would come out and take from him his office bag and lunch box. The towel on his bed was still warm from the sun when he pressed it to his face. They would eat together in the kitchen. Every night Ma would rub warm jasmine oil into Pita-jee's hair, brush-dry from the hours spent working on a construc-tion site. Roughness turned to a slick softness under her patient fingers.

That factory on the outskirts of my hometown that Pita-jee had con-structed was now an abandoned building that overlooked rail tracks.

Then Pita-jee left for London. On the first Saturday of each month, when we received Pita-jee's money order and letter, Pita-jee spent a few hours of his payday weekend at a pub. He went with coworkers, young men who, during the day, roared over the noise of cranes, cement mixers, and loaders, and who, when Pita-jee first joined the workforce, welcomed him into their bachelor homes and showed him around the city.

There was mail that went the other way too, I was surprised to dis-cover, from our home to London. Ma sent him little packets of sacred sugar cubes from the temple, the ones I sometimes found in small bowls in the kitchen and ate fistfuls of as dessert.

I put the candle out, slipped the diary under my pillow, and slept. A noise woke me up. I looked around the room, disoriented. I'd momentarily forgotten where I was.

In the light of the watchtower beacon that swept across my room I saw, on the floor next to the Great Wall of Singer, a brick. I squatted to the floor and picked it up.

"Are you awake?" Marc asked.

A match was struck. In the light of a stub candle I saw the hole in the wall. In the gap, Marc placed his pale palm. I took it, squeezed it, kissed it. My fingers felt sticky when he withdrew his hand.

"Got you messy, did I?" he asked.

He gave me his apple slice. The ceremonial offering. He'd taken only a bite. I thumbed the teeth marks and smiled.

"What are you doing here?" he asked.

"What are *you* doing here?" I asked.

"There's no time for this dance. We have ten minutes."

From 2:00 to 2:10, when the guards change shifts, we're left unmonitored, he told me. I told him why I came to Madhuban without knowing it was the location that for years I'd evaded.

"How could you not know?" Marc asked. "The address is on the brochure."

"I didn't notice," I said.

"You know, I actually believe that with you," he said.

I smiled, the pleasure of being seen in the eyes of my beloved, of finding him here, in the most unexpected of places, in the most terrifying of circumstances, holding at bay, for now, the bitter volatility with which we'd parted.

"Stop grinning," Marc scolded. "What an idiot."

There were two rituals we underwent every day, Marc told me. In the mornings, he said, the Servants flung three fistfuls of ash in quick succession at each of our genitals. So Hanuman possesses us and turns us into real men. In the afternoons we watched porn and masturbated while imagining ourselves to be the man on-screen. Then there was the business of the final test.

"We'll have to come up with a plan for you—an exit route," Marc said.

I said, "Your turn. What are you doing here?"

"You're not taking this seriously. You know what happens if you fail the test?"

"I know." I didn't want him to know exactly how afraid I was. I picked the brick up. "How did you do this?"

The cement joining the bricks at the wall's base had, over the years, been weakened by pressure and persistent dampness. With a coin he had scraped away enough to loosen a brick on either side of his cell.

"Praneet told me you were here," Marc said.

"Tomorrow you'll tell me what you're doing here?"

"I will," he promised.

"I want to see you," he said.

He lay down and brought his face to the hole and so did I. In the light of the candle, the short, straight strands of his ginger stubble glowed orange, the blue of his irises flickered with flecks of turquoise. Even so measly a light heightened his beauty. I pinched his chin, committing to my palm the twinned texture of flesh and scruff so I could carry that texture with me to bed.

"Thief," I said. "You stole my brochure, didn't you? That's how you got here."

He smiled as he closed his eyes. The fear that I felt so keenly, when I knew that Vikrant would bring me into the facility, weakened its grip on me in the presence of Marc.

"It's time," he said. His voice dulcet as birdsong, waterfall, poetry.

I gave him the brick and he put it back in place. I heard the whoosh of his breath. The candlelight lining the edges of the brick was gone.

We were woken up at three in the morning with the smoke of benzoin and the loud chanting of a Ganesha hymn, the one with which Nandi began all of our performances. The fragrance mingled with the mustiness of the stone walls, reminding me the place was once a fortress.

We filed out of our cells, up the stairs, and to the showering cubicles, which had no doors, each unit barely as wide as our shoulders. I stood hunched as I faced the wall and disrobed. I draped my dhoti and shawl on the short cement wall that separated my cubicle from the one to my right, where I saw, from the corner of my eye, Marc standing. His clothes were next to mine. There was no tap, no shower. Only a steel bucket full of ice-cold water that I retrieved with a mug and poured over my head till the bucket was empty. The shock and sting of first contact was replaced with numbness and then wakefulness. Six Servants of God watched us.

My skin was still wet when I put on my clothes. My man breasts stood pronounced against the shawl. I crossed my hands across my chest. We formed a line and took our dripping, shivering bodies to the temple, where we stood in front of Hanuman, sticking to our ranks: I stood with Praneet, all the way to the back.

A Servant, taller than the rest, walked past all the rows to make sure we were standing with our hands folded and our heads bowed. He went up front and stood next to Vikrant, before the statue.

Vikrant chanted the forty Hanuman verses. Then, he declared, "When the ash hits your organ, surrender to Lord Hanuman. Allow him to possess you. Beg him to. He alone can turn you into the instruments of masculinity that you were meant to be."

The air filled with a thin veil of smoke and the sounds of men wincing and groaning, and loud cries of, "Praise be to the Masculine God Hanuman."

Our bodies surged forward like an unruly wave. More groans, more cries soared through the air, clearer, louder. We moved forward again, then again, and when we reached the front row, as I watched a Servant raise his hand, his fist full of ash, I shut my eyes and plunged my mind into a performance in which I replaced the Servant in front of me with Marc—just as Saaya and Rooh had, a million times over, become, on-stage, characters from the myths. And the ritual became a punishment Marc subjected me to.

You don't know how to obey your man, Marc says. Accent English. What are you going to do about it? I challenge him. Your clothes, get rid of them, he orders. I remove my dhoti and wrap it around my neck. I am terrified of Marc's punishment and seek it as well. My terror heightens my seeking. You will be quiet as I do what I want with you, he says. Not a peep, Bitch Bags, he says. When the first fistful of ash leaves Marc's fist and makes rough, forceful contact with my penis, an electric current of pleasure runs up my spine and I harden. When the second fistful of gritty powder explodes on my hardness and my muscle starts to throb with a deeper pain, Marc sniffs hard and the skin on the bridge of his nose wrinkles beautifully. After delivering the third fistful, he wipes his mouth with his fist, turns, and leaves. He's done with me.

I opened my eyes. Reality was restored. A cloud of ash surrounded me. The Servants, mouths and noses covered in masks, stepped back. I put on my dhoti. My flesh was caked in ash.

In the afternoon we went to the movie room. With our bare bodies wrapped in sacred shawls, we sat down and watched a porn film: a boy and a girl on a beach, he on top of her, the scene shot from above. We saw the face of the girl contorted in pleasure. We heard her moan. He shifted his body and grabbed her breast.

Around me, men leaned forward and picked up a sock from under their seat. In the blue light of the film, I saw the hand of the man next to me forming a fist under his dhoti. A fist with a head that moved. His eyes, fixed on the screen, were glazed, his face expressionless.

A Servant proclaimed, "You must imagine you are the man. No sin in it because you're doing it to make yourself the man that God intends you to be."

Next to me, the man's hand moved like clockwork. Up. Down. Up. Down.

"No closing your eyes," another Servant shouted, rapping his baton on the armrest of a seat. A baton was struck against my armrest as well.

"What are you waiting for, faggot?" growled a Servant.

I ducked, picked up the sock from under my seat, and shrouded with it my organ, which was sore from the morning ceremony. I fixed my eyes on the screen. The girl became me. Her breast became my man breast. And her man became, naturally, my man.

We lined up before a table in the movie room. Each inmate deposited his sock into a tray. A Servant examined it with gloved hands. The inmate stood against the left wall if it was dry, against the right wall if it was wet. After all the socks were examined, those of us at the right wall exited the room. Behind us, the door was pulled shut. We heard music: a Bollywood remix, the tune retained, the lyrics replaced with lyrics in praise of Hanuman.

The brick in the Great Wall of Singer was removed. His candle came to life. I was ready, next to the wall.

"You survive the day okay?" Marc asked.

"Tell me what you're doing here," I said. "You promised."

He came to the Hanuman Male Fixing Center after he left Chamba, he said. He'd claimed that his father, a Hindu man, had married an American; his gayness was the price he was paying for his father's sin. Bring me to the path of god, make me a Hindu, he begged. They gladly obliged.

He recorded on a tape recorder the story of Praneet. He recorded the story of Varun, who had been in the cell that I was now in. Varun had passed the test and left. Marc had photographed Praneet failing.

Using the loose folds inside his dhoti, he had fashioned two secret pockets: one for the tape recorder, one for a camera.

"The Canon?" I asked.

"This one's smaller. Look."

He slid a camera through the hole the brick had left behind. I picked it up. Featherlight.

"Marc," I said as I returned it to him. "What if they catch you?"

"I'm their most willing student, they wouldn't suspect it," Marc said.

"But why did you do it?"

"I pictured a future in which you were free," he said. "In that world, this place was history."

He was here for me.

"Ma said it had to be an inside job, remember, shutting a place like this down?" Marc said.

"How many people know what you're up to?" I asked.

"People at our table, some of them, but that's it."

They cover him with their bodies, Marc said, when he bends and crouches and photographs public ceremonies.

"What if there are people who want to be here? Won't they snitch?"

"There are crazies everywhere. But spotting them is easy, which is good, so I know to keep the heck away. Now. How was your day?"

"I'll tell you tomorrow. I want to look at you."

During dinner the next day, Marc pointed to the table where the men he called "the crazies"—the men who came here voluntarily, wanting to be cured of their homosexuality—congregated. They began their meals with prayers: a thank-you to Goddess Annapurna with their heads bowed, a thank-you to Hanuman with their heads tilted skyward.

I read an entry in Pita-jee's diary. He went to one concert in London, a performance by Ravi Shankar that he had saved for: no pub for him for three weeks. Once in the music hall, Pita-jee listened to Raga Bhimpalasi on the sitar and wept, the melody bringing alive a memory of our backyard where, as a boy, he played gilli-danda with his friends. When we were children, I remembered, my sisters and I played hopscotch in that backyard when it rained.

Setting the book aside, I went to use the squat toilet on the other end of my cell. Its foot stand was ridged for a steady hold. As I stood on it and undid the folds of my dhoti, Vikrant unlocked my cell and came in.

"Good performance second night too," he said. "That's when most people fail. Too sore."

"I'm fine."

"Are you sure? You seem to be having trouble getting started."

I tried to relax. But my muscle wouldn't give up its waste. I turned on the creaky tap before me and let water trickle into the rusted caddy chained to the wall, hoping the sound would soothe my body.

"There are men who fool us during the daily ceremonies," he said. "How can we see what's going on in your head? Still no luck with your pee-pee? Real men don't care if people watch. And we will watch—your final test. If you do the daily ceremonies sincerely, you'll screw like a champ."

I cringed at the word that left his mouth as fluidly as the Hanuman chants. I rewrapped my dhoti and started for my bed. Vikrant stood in my way.

"Finish what you started," he said.

Reluctantly I went back to the squat toilet and took my position. Nothing.

"Take your time, I'm in no rush," he said.

I tried imagining I was in a performance. I struggled, I tried, I failed.

A Servant began his rounds. The light of his lantern washed my cell. The knot in my groin tightened. I was sweat-soaked.

"Your whole body is peeing," Vikrant observed. The Servant and he laughed.

The light in the corridor and cell went off. The Servant walked away. Only then did my body—plunged in darkness, eclipsed out of visibility—permit the weight of my bladder to exceed the weight of my shame: it let go, but reluctantly, for it knew it was still being watched by Vikrant: a trickle built into a slow stream but never gathering the momentum that it should've, the sound dull against the ceramic toilet.

If Marc had heard what transpired between Vikrant and me, he didn't bring it up. I told him, when we spoke that night, how I had passed the two daily ceremonies.

Marc said, "Use the same strategy for the final test."

"How? I don't know how it's done."

He laughed. "You make it sound like a physics experiment. Just watch when I take my test—everyone watches anyway. Commit what I'm doing to memory. Then, on the day of your test, tell yourself you're performing me. The temple is the stage, the inmates your audience."

"I don't know, Marc."

"A thousand times you've become a god. How difficult is it to be-come me?"

"Harder than it is to become a god."

"Don't say that. Not after what I've done."

Before I slept, I read my father's diary, I held it near my mouth and spoke to it, as if its cover was an ear to the beyond where my father was. I described the stories my sisters and I performed in the treehouse, confessed the secret I kept from Marc, I admitted my mistake, about wanting to befriend Rusty.

THE PUNISHMENT

I sat at Marc's table during dinner but not next to him. I didn't want to arouse Vikrant's suspicion. I was content listening to the men telling him about their life before a parent or a partner turned them in: a civil engineer like Pita-jee, an accountant who did the taxes for Air India, an assistant director in the Telugu film industry, a pilgrimage driver in Uttarkashi. With his tape recorder tucked between his waist and dhoti, Marc recorded their stories.

Each tape, Marc told me one night, recorded 120 minutes each on side A and side B. He had ten tapes in all, so he could record forty hours over the course of his stay at the facility. To use his limited resources effectively, he scripted the lunchtime conversations: the first ten minutes were spent in idle talk, the last ten minutes in silence, the twenty-five minutes in between reserved for real confessions that the men practiced in advance.

"How did you smuggle it all in here?" I asked one night. "The tapes, the camera?"

When he got himself admitted and requested to bring his shoulder bag with him, a Servant, present in the room, asked Marc what was in it. Marc opened it and showed him: framed photographs of Hanuman, of Rama. They're from my father's altar, he told them, looking somber. They reached to pick a frame up to see what was under. Please, with

clean hands only, Marc pleaded. It was at this point that Kumar had in-
tervened. What can he be hiding under portraits of the gods, for heaven's
sake? he scolded. So the Servants let him go. The contraband, I guessed,
was hidden under the portraits.

That night, the patter of rain began unexpectedly; all day it had been
clear. A tail of departing light, bouncing up and down in the distance,
signaled the Servant's retreat. But just as Marc removed the brick, a new
set of footfalls steadily rose, almost in rhythm to the rain that had now
started in earnest, filling my cell with its fragrance. We waited to see if
that intruder upon our nighttime meeting was going elsewhere. A tail of
light bounced down the stairs. Marc and I returned to our beds. I closed
my eyes. I felt something warm caress my lids and I sat up. On the other
side of the bars was a silhouette, sharpened by the glow of a lantern, held
in one hand. I got up and walked to the door. The lantern was lowered,
and in its flickering aura I saw the face of Kumar.

I walked up to the bars. The rain turned into a downpour. The thick
stone walls absorbed the sound of thunder and turned the cell, it seemed,
into an echo chamber: our words felt louder, our movements—a topi
fixed, a neck scratched—had the aural quality of bigger actions.

"Thank you," I said. "For helping Marc. The day he came here."

He smiled. "For helping Marc, not for helping you."

"That too. Marc's a dear friend."

"Like a brother, yes. What about your other friends from Magpies?
Tell me about them."

Where, I wondered, was this going?

"I never had any friends in those days."

He looked disappointed. Lightning colored his face purple.

"I should go," he said. "If Servants see me fraternizing with you,
they'll have another reason to complain."

"What do they say?"

"I always side with the inmates. I'm lenient. Et cetera."

Does that get you in trouble with Vikrant, I was about to ask, when a
thunderclap startled us both.

He said, "Whenever we have unseasonal rain, Ma says it's the ghost of a Darbhanga singer, belting out Raga Malhar."

He wished me a restful sleep, got up, and left. By the time I got to the wall, Marc was present, and the brick absent. He hadn't replaced it. It was, we both agreed, the oddest meeting.

Devan and Rahul were found kissing in the recreation room. After the morning ceremony the next day, they were made to kneel before the Hanuman statue. Their cocks, ash-covered, squished against their thighs.

"Which of you is the man?" Vikrant asked. "Rise."

Rahul stood up. One of the Servants pressed a whip into his hands.

"Whip him twenty-seven times," Vikrant said, pointing at Devan. "He will chant out loud for each lash."

Devan lay flat on his stomach, palms and forehead pressed to the ground. His buttocks, small and round, felt exposed as a wound.

Rahul raised his hand. The whip whined, on its way up, on its way down. The sound it made when it met Devan's flesh was like a sitar's string snapping.

"Praise be to the masculine god Hanuman," Devan cried.

"Loud and clear," Vikrant barked.

Lash met flesh. The sound followed. Praise be to the masculine god Hanuman. A Servant kept count on basil beads. On the last five lashes, flecks of blood stuck to the whip's tail, sprinkled Rahul's cheeks, his chest, his forehead.

Pressing his forearms firmly down, Devan peeled his body off the floor. He wobbled when he got to his feet. Vikrant took Devan's hand and placed it on his own shoulder.

After a moment passed, Vikrant asked, "Are you okay?"

Devan nodded, his head lolling slow as a tower bell. A Servant took the whip from Rahul and gave it to him.

"Now you will give him six lashes," Vikrant said.

The diminished number felt odd. Was it because Rahul, as "the man," behaved more in accordance to his "natural" role? Rahul started to lie down on his stomach.

"No," Vikrant said. "On your back."

Rahul frowned, confused, as he corrected his pose.

It took me a moment to comprehend: Rahul would be whipped on his penis. A collective gasp spread through the congregation.

"Please," Devan said.

"Don't beg like a girl," Vikrant said. "Man up. It's why you're here."

Devan hesitated.

"For each minute you waste, the lash count will increase by one," Vikrant said.

"What's wrong with you?" Marc said. He stepped forward and stood next to Devan, his reddened ears washed in the orange glimmer of the oil lamps, his profile, as he faced Vikrant, washed in shadows. "You call yourself a man of god?"

A Servant gripped his shoulder. Marc shook himself free. Vikrant raised his hand. The Servant retreated.

"I thought you, of all people, would like it," Vikrant said.

"The hell does that mean?" Marc said.

"Goras like such things—everyone knows," Vikrant said. "Don't tell me you haven't found pleasure in hurting the boys you've kept."

Marc looked up and met my gaze for a second before looking away. But Vikrant's gaze unfailingly found my face. A knowing smile ruined his mouth.

"Three lashes for Rahul," he said, turning to Devan. "Don't forget the chant, boy."

His anticlimactic decision terrified me. Devan swung his hand swiftly. The tip of the whip licked Rahul's penis and he howled: Praise be the masculine god Hanuman. Before the slogan left his lips, the whip found his flesh again. Then again. The second howl of a slogan bled into third without pause or break.

My heart felt like a wild animal, throwing itself against the cage of my chest.

Vikrant helped Rahul to his feet. A Servant led him and Devan back to the congregation. I kept my eyes away from Rahul's penis.

"Thank you, Vikrant," Marc said. "For showing Rahul some mercy."

"No, thank *you*," Vikrant said. "For sharing Rahul's burden."

Marc's face paled.

"There will be six lashes. It's God's way. And so it will be. Lie down." He raised his voice. "Shagun. Step forward."

My body moved like it was no more than a puppet whose strings Vikrant controlled.

"Be quick," he said, handing me the whip. "So we can go back to our day."

"Is there an alternative penance?" I pleaded. "I'll do anything."

"There was," Vikrant said. "We placed an ember, once on the man's organ, once on his sack. But Hanuman came to me in a dream. He said it was affecting the men's reproductive capabilities. You see, this all seems like witchcraft. But our religion is a supreme science. Our gods are scientists.

"I see how you cover your chest in the morning," Vikrant said. "Modern culture asks you to be ashamed of your man breasts."

A few inmates snickered. It was the only release for their tension.

He turned to the congregation. "Laugh again, you'll take Marc's place. Any takers?" He turned to me again. "Hindu science says man breasts are a sign of a saint. Every great savant has them. Paramahamsa, Vivekananda, Ramana Maharshi. So be proud, boy."

I wanted to wrap the whip around his neck and watch life slowly leave him. I never prayed. But I did that day. I faced Hanuman and joined my hands. I'm sorry I broke your statue, I said. The stories say you're strong, give Marc your strength, please, I begged. A strategy came to mind, then.

I turned, raised my whip high, and brought it down. Only in the first instance did the tail find purchase on his dick's tender flesh. I saw him gulp before his lips moved slowly.

"Praise be the masculine god Hanuman," he said.

Using the wrist flicks that Rooh taught me when he trained me to wield the sword onstage—so it appears the weapon has met your opponent's body—I let the second and third lash find a different part of his flesh: once above his penis, once the side of his thigh. Vikrant and the two Servants who kept a close watch voiced no objection. The first accurate lashing won their trust and made room for the deceit, which was sustained by the proximity of the point of contact and the swiftness of the movement.

I leaned next to Marc. Are you okay? I wanted to ask but found myself incapable of speech. Marc smiled, his eyes red.

"I'm okay, brother," he said, a crackle passing through his words.

Marc, Rahul, Devan, and I were confined to our cells without access to food, light, or water. I spent the evening near the Great Wall of Singer, and at two in the morning, I pushed the brick aside. He was already there. I held his hand and cried.

"You got stuck in this mess because of me," I said, my words making me sob harder.

"Shut up, Sham."

"I missed that name—you haven't called me that in a while."

"Clever boy," Marc said. "I know what you did. Only one lash to Little Brother."

I laughed despite myself.

Marc said, "Hey, seasoned masturbators must have it easy with the ash ceremony. You know, a toned-up muscle has greater endurance and all that. That's the real reason you never complained, Sham, you runt! You came in with plenty of practice."

I clapped my hand over my mouth, worried my laughter would wake someone up.

"Who did you think of when you did it—in the years before you met me?"

"The men I was attracted to were with Bollywood actresses. Until I met you."

"And then?"

"You were with me. I belonged to you. You owned me. Every ounce of my flesh."

"Yet your fear kept you from being with me—in real life."

"It wasn't fear," I said.

At last, I told him the truth. I described, using specific instances, the loss of my senses when our intimacy, however much I wanted it, lasted more than a minute: sight and smell went when we first hugged; the second time, in his room, it was touch and sound.

"Why didn't you tell me before?"

"I wanted to figure out why it's happening first. I still haven't. But here we are. Having this conversation. Might as well have told you way back when it all started. Would've saved us so much suffering."

"I thought I was helping you get over your inhibitions," Marc said. "I was enjoying myself while you were having an anxiety attack."

"I wasn't though, not that night."

"You don't have to protect me."

"Marc. It's the truth. And what happened on my balcony—I wanted that. Now you know I wasn't afraid of you—it was my body I was afraid of."

"I didn't know that, not that night. It makes all the difference."

The violence of separation had finally caught up to us, no longer held at bay by the joy of our reunion. The silence that followed Marc's observation felt saturated with irresolvable discontent, so I hastened to speak, to replace it with words of assurance.

"But now I've punished you—just as you wanted."

"Because you had no choice."

"Whips are worse than oil lamps."

He didn't respond. I couldn't, I realized, sever his guilt from him with pleas or blunt logic.

For the ash ceremony the next morning, I didn't enter my imagination. I was present fully to the subjugation: a Servant in charge, whipping my penis with gritty ash, the pain of it, not coupled with pleasure, reverberating through my flesh and attaching itself to my bones where it would remain for the rest of the morning.

Rahul sat at the same table as Marc and me during dinner. Devan walked past our table and up to the table of the voluntary inmates. The table's buzz lightened. Devan's lips moved but I didn't hear what he said.

"He won't snitch," Rahul said.

"Are you stupid?" I snapped. "Marc's collecting evidence—Devan knows things and he'll tell them what's what to show his loyalty. He desperately wants in, can't you see? This is your fault. Who does that—in a conversion facility of all places? What, were you just horny?"

"I spent thirty-six years of my life not desiring anyone," Rahul said, his teeth clenched. "Thinking I was unlovable. You know what that feels like?" He looked from me to Marc. "I didn't think so. So excuse me if I threw caution to the wind when I finally found myself desiring someone and by some god-fucking miracle, he actually desired me back."

"What will you do?" Marc asked.

"What to do," Rahul said. "He will go back to his daughter and wife. Whatever we could've had would've been in this facility. But I blew it."

Rahul told us how they got caught. "We always had a watchdog. Praneet, Sandy, Anup. If they saw a Servant coming, they tipped us off. No one was available that day, but I wanted to kiss him so bad."

We were quiet for some time. Later, we came up with a plan to keep Marc from getting caught in case Devan snitched.

Nothing happened the next day until dinnertime. Vikrant walked up to our table and held up Marc's shoulder bag by its strap like a dead rat.

"What was in here?" he asked.

"Icons from my father's altar," Marc said. "A statue of Hanuman and a few pictures of Lord Rama. They're all up in my room. In the little alcove behind my bed."

"He told us about it," Kumar said, and a Servant confirmed it.

"He's lying, search his room," Devan exclaimed.

"Where do you think we found this?" a Servant said, pointing to the backpack.

"Why are you doing this, Devan?" Rahul said.

"Not talking to you, fag," Devan said.

"Search me if you want," Marc said, raising his hands.

Devan turned to me.

"Him, search his room."

"We did," Vikrant said.

I said, "Without asking me?"

"This isn't a hotel," Vikrant said.

"They're lying to you," Devan cried.

"Shout at me again, boy, and we won't hesitate to use the whip, front and back."

The night before, Marc had, per our plan, passed the equipment and reels and the tapes to Praneet. I would have been too obvious as Marc's backup.

On the morning of Marc's test, after all our genitals were doused with ash, all but Marc's, we formed a wide circle around the Hanuman statue. Through a back door, Marc and a girl came out. God's Handmaiden, they called her. She, like us, had a saffron shawl wrapped around her upper body and wore an orange dhoti. I was sad and angry for her. What had Vikrant done to her—or her family—to make her engage in this public spectacle, have congress with a man who couldn't desire her?

Marc shed his clothes, and for the first time, I saw him fully naked: in a temple, alongside a room full of spectators. His penis was sheathed in a condom.

The Handmaiden lay down. Marc undid the knots of her dhoti and leaned over her. I watched him enter her.

He thrust his hips forward, over and over. He stiffened the muscle of his upper lip. His final three thrusts, slow, forceful.

When I was leaving the hall, Vikrant stopped me. He wiped my cheeks dry with his palm.

"Your brother cleared the test and you are shedding tears of joy. Or are you sad he's leaving? You can tell me, boy."

I said, "Have you ever loved anyone more than yourself?"

"God," he said. "I love God more than myself."

"Are you sure about that?"

"You have quite the mouth on you."

"Hinduism tells us to respect women, and yet look at what you force them to do."

"You mean the Handmaidens?"

"If you were the man of God you claim to be, you would let her go."

"Here, why don't you express your solidarity to her directly."

He beckoned to a Servant who was close by. "Go bring Katha," he said.

The Servant went to the anteroom behind the temple and returned a moment later with the Handmaiden. She wore a sari now. Her eyes had a slight squint to them and that feature somehow made her attractive.

"You," she said to Vikrant. "You promised dinner two months back."

I was taken aback by the casual tone she employed with him.

"Tomorrow evening?" he said. "If you're still around, that is."

She guffawed. "What?"

He placed a hand on my shoulder. "Boy here believes I'm oppressing you and I should set you free."

She looked at me and shook her head. "Not even a proper man but he sure has a man's savior complex. I do this because I want to. I hounded Brother Vikrant for six months before he allowed me in."

"But why would you want this?" I asked, dumbfounded.

"It's how I serve God," she said, holding her head high. "By helping bring strays back onto his path. We're all playing our part. You should too."

There was a celebration that evening. Vikrant was not in attendance, neither were the Servants. It was just the inmates and Kumar in the dining hall, its doors closed.

Marc and four others who had successfully graduated that week were hoisted on shoulders and carried into the dining hall. They were in their civilian clothing and garlanded. The door was shut. Loud music followed. Not Bollywood songs remixed, their lyrics replaced with hymns in praise of Hanuman, but Bollywood songs where hero and heroine express their undying love, dutiful sons express their devotion to family, friends celebrate friendship. Several inmates danced around the graduates as I sat at a short distance and watched. Kumar came and sat next to me.

"Not joining in the merriment?" he asked.

"I'm not much of a dancer," I said. "How did you pull it off?"

"I told the boss it really was a celebration of god's victory, the fixing of a deviant."

I laughed. "Of course he was sold. And how do you keep the Servants out?"

"That, I didn't have to do anything about. They didn't want in. Too materialistic for their religious stoicism. God forbid, something fun on their plates."

I told him about my conversation with Katha. There were eight Handmaidens, Kumar said, and they were all highborn: they came from upper rungs of caste and class. Their families knew Vikrant and idolized him. They chose to be a part of his "movement."

"Why do you do it?" I asked. "This job?"

"My father was a cop—the DSP of this state," he replied. "It's what the men in our families do. I didn't have a choice."

"You always have a choice."

"That's what a friend once told me. Growing up, I realized I don't have it in me to stand up to my father. So I decided to use my choice by taking this job." He turned to me. "So I can help men like me."

I wanted to squeeze his hand, but his uniform and the hierarchy it implied prevented me.

Kumar broke eye contact and looked to the dancers.

"My father was pleased that I wanted to pursue the family profession and serve our religion," Kumar said. "So he contacted the chief minister of Bihar. And that was how the police officer who worked here was transferred elsewhere and I landed here. My father's position and his connection to CM sahib are, I suspect, why Vikrant tolerates me. Even when the Servants complain."

Marc broke into a fast dance, his garland swaying from one side to the next. He held his hands above his head. His face lit up with a smile as the title song of the movie *Baazigar* waltzed into its final stanza. When the song ended, amid applause and protest, he left the dancers and came and sat in front of me. Kumar patted my shoulder and left.

"I will wait for you—at the train station," Marc said. "The day after you graduate."

"The only thing I'll ever be a graduate of is Hanuman Male Fixing Center. That's sad."

"You feel certain you'll graduate. That makes me happy. Be there by two. Bokaro Express leaves at two thirty."

"Where's Bokaro Express taking us?"

"Your place. No one lives there. We'll need that to have a chance at this—at us."

Kumar returned to our table. "Stop gossiping like old men."

He grabbed Marc's garland and my elbow and led us to the bevy of dancers. He rifled through the tapes, selected one, and inserted it into the stereo and hit Play. A song from the film *Hum Aapke Hain Kaun* filled the room.

A crow lands on the parapet of Mother's home
"Your daughter's an ascetic now," he caws, "she has given her heart
away to a god."

Marc held me close and danced slowly in rhythm not to the song but to our desire for this moment to lose its place in the sequence of time: no thought allocated to what came before, the reason that got us here, or to what would come after, only now existing without context.

"Are you okay—is this okay?" Marc asked.

I nodded. I don't want this, I convinced myself as we danced. What if the Servants sneak in, what if they're looking right now? My pretense of not wanting what I desired permitted that desire's fulfillment.

Marc pressed my head to his shoulder. I closed my eyes and breathed in his scent. His chest tattooed the sound of him onto my flesh, his breath sang into my neck his private song.

At length the song came to an end. Marc placed a hand on the back of my head. Around us the men clapped and hooted. Loud knocking on the door interrupted our happiness. It was time to go.

BHAKTI POEMS

One month after he came home, I remembered, Pita-jee took me to a country fair. I did not want to go with him and walked in stubborn silence by his side. I stopped in front of the Ferris wheel. He took his wallet out and gave me one rupee. As I went up to the ticket window, he hollered, "Wait, I want a ticket too." I pretended I didn't hear him. I got on the ride. Each time the wheel went plummeting down, with my ribs pressed to the steel bar, I watched him from the corner of my eye. He stood a little away from the crowd and looked at me. He said nothing when we walked back home.

On the flight to India he wrote about what he hoped to do once he came home: to mourn for daughters born six months after he left for London; to take walks with his one surviving child; to listen to stories from his son's boyhood; to tell stories from his own. There were no entries from the years after he'd returned to London.

When I spoke to the diary that night, I said sorry for the single ticket stub.

That night I constructed the script I would perform to clear my final test. I visualized the temple room and the faceless bodies gathered before Hanuman: my audience. In the gap between deity and spectator, I located Marc and the Handmaiden. I swooped down and entered Marc. I became him.

During my dinners with Praneet, we had become friends. The week of our test, he, I, and two other men went to the barber who came to the prison grounds on Monday morning. We waited in line.

"Where will you go after you're released?" I asked.

"Good joke, tell another one," Praneet said.

"You must have an exit plan?"

"I smell Marc-speak."

"Who did this to you?"

"My father."

"You hate him?"

"I hate what he did to me. But him? He left the country when we were little, my brother and me. Worked on construction projects in Abu Dhabi. Sent home almost all his income and lived in dirt-cheap conditions. We wouldn't have had an education, or a life, otherwise."

I found myself telling Praneet about Pita-jee: he worked in London so my sisters and I could have an education, so he could save for their dowry. His letters came once a month from London, I said. When the postman came home, Ma ran down the stairs, decked out for the occasion: crisp cotton sari, jasmine pinned to her hair.

"She held each letter close to her face," I said, raising a palm to my mouth. "She closed her eyes when she finished reading. We loved watching her, my sisters and I."

We wondered: Did she seek, under the smell of the foreign stationery, some lingering fragrance from his room? Did she locate his touch on that paper, his fist moving as he penned one line then another, his fingers tapping the paper's edge when he paused between thoughts?

"But he's also the architect who made this place," I said, looking around. "This is the legacy he left me with."

My turn with the barber came last. I sat on a stool. Underneath me the ground was littered with the hair of other men. He gave me a mirror and asked me to hold it before my face. As he rubbed a damp soap on my jaw, a rich lather clung to my beard's unruly tufts. I abhorred my reflection because of its resemblance to the parent I hated. But why precisely did I hate him, what was the seed?

Night after night I'd watch him paddle up the stairs, enter her room, and close the door, the sight of door-meeting-jamb bringing to my mind the image of a hand clapped over a mouth. One night I saw him sleeping on the cane sofa in the drawing hall, his arms crossed over his chest, his legs sticking out over the sofa's edge. "At least you're not here only to copulate," I said to his sleeping face. Some five nights later he went back to her room, her bed. After a month or so I found him sleeping in the drawing hall again. Then I understood. Whenever Ma had her periods, he kept his distance. I resented him for making me think of Ma's periods.

I judged him for not being chaste, for not grieving *in place* of sex. So how could I, who caused their death in the first place, be permitted pleasure? So my senses failed when Marc and I got intimate. My body imposed on me the censorship I'd wanted for him. In nonconsensual situations, however, there was no pleasure to be had, so my senses remained intact.

The straight blade scratched down my throat, it scaled my jaw. With a pair of tongs, the barber extracted a towel from a pot of water that bubbled over coal embers. He wrung it out and rubbed it, still steaming, against my face, removing all traces of lather and residual hair. The rough hot cloth soothed and stung my freshly shaved skin.

"All good?" the barber asked.

I locked eyes with my reflection. I looked at myself looking at myself. No makeup. No character. Just me. My face. I was present.

"All good," I said.

As I walked back to my cell, I put it all together: I had caused the death of my sisters so I had to endure the absence of physical love. I had to release this limiting belief. But how?

Marc had, with medical precision, even without the full story, diagnosed the origin of my malady.

I stopped outside Marc's cell. Now empty. A couplet from the Bhakti period, Hinduism's Romantic era, came to mind.

How many miles behind did I leave daylight?
For years now I carried with me the night.

A Servant tapped my shoulder. "Keep walking," he ordered. I entered my cell, and he locked me in. I buried my head in my hands. I remembered Marc: his voice his hair his big gentle hands his smell. Another Bhakti poem came to mind.

when you were by my side
there existed between us an unshakable distance
now that you are gone
the last inch has been breached
and I belong to you
as completely as darkness does to flesh of the night

I lay down, the diary under my head. I closed my eyes and tiptoed from one chamber to another, careful not to disturb the dreams they contained: moonlight on a bachelor's balcony; coins placed on a weathered palm; puppets leaning against parallel rail tracks; a turbaned man, a bearded man, the two bound in a child's wedding game; in the last room, a couple sitting across a table, a radio between them playing a Bhakti hymn: *summer scalds both body and earth/one gets drenched, the other turns dry/but aren't the two cast from the same dust?* Their faces are shaded. She wants him to carry her away. To a silent room on a farm. Oh, a room with a radiator, she says. She never heard a radiator hum. She'd like that. Her thumb and forefinger meet and she moves them up and down in rhythm to a song on the radio. As if she's stitching a sweater of musical notes. Pita-jee leans into the light of lilac lanterns and meets my eye. I don't wear the scorn he expects. His body undulates with relief. Ma and he kiss.

The day of the test, I waited in the anteroom behind the temple alongside Katha, our bodies dripping, shivering, covered in wet saffron clothing. This was the backstage, I told myself.

The door opened, and Vikrant led us out and into the temple room. The stage of my performance.

No sooner had I set a foot onstage than I became Marc Singer; the Handmaiden became me. Shagun drops his shawl, so do I. He bows to

Hanuman and lies on the floor. I lie on top of him. Conch shells, with their ululation, celebrate our union. In the dim light, I search for his hole, and when I find it, I breach the borders of his body.

I slipped out of Katha's body and stood up. My organ was tender. The whiteness inside the condom was streaked red.

"Look, I popped his cherry," Katha said, covering herself. "The way he went at me, who would've believed he was a virgin?"

The inmates laughed, as did Vikrant. He wrapped the shawl around my body.

For now, I felt only relief, for I had just earned my exit ticket from the Hanuman Male Fixing Center. I knew that one day, in the near future, what I had done to earn that exit ticket would hit me: the consummation I failed to bring to my relationship with Marc had come to pass between a stranger and me. With a slap to my back, Vikrant shook me out of my state of shock.

"Bleeding is common for a first time," he said. "It's proof that you haven't sinned. And now you're cured. Congratulations."

I expected him to shout "Praise be to the masculine god Hanuman." He conveyed a dull, logistical piece of information instead.

"You left your bag at my place," he said. "Don't forget to take it when you leave."

For my celebration, I wanted to dance with Praneet. He had failed his test. He would join the new batch of inmates. His fourth cycle of training would commence. At the end of it, he will have been here for 108 days. Six months. Half a year.

I walked up to his table and held out my hand. He shook his head. I didn't want to pressure him. I started to walk away, dejected. Rahul, who was sitting next to him, got up, joined me, and whispered, "Two tracks from now, his favorite song is coming up. That'll do the trick."

Kumar caught my eye and beckoned me over. I sat next to him.

He said, "Your first day here, you whispered 'I met Marc at Magpies.'"

I thought you recognized me then, and I wondered how. But then you said you didn't have many friends at school and I realized I wrong."

There was a twinkle in his eyes. The song had ended, another about to begin. The air buzzed with the chatter of the inmates.

"Close your eyes," Kumar said, and I did.

I heard three knocks. Without giving it a thought, or consciously making a decision to, I knocked three times on the table with my knuckles, as if, like walking, I had drawn it from muscle memory. The next song started. My eyes flew open. Kumar was grinning widely now.

"It can't be," I said.

My cauldron friend.

"I gave you so many hints," Kumar said. "I ditched you back then—for that I am deeply sorry. But know that I'm so happy our paths crossed. So you can see me, and I can say thank you. You're the reason I'm here, helping however I can, not hating my life."

I searched Kumar's face, to pull the boy that he was from the face of the man that he had become. I remembered the constellation of chalk faces on the black surface of the cauldron, each corresponding to an expression, an emotion. I looked at him now and wondered: Did I get Happy right?

The song ended. Rahul led me back to Praneet's table. The hall filled with a new song. "Chane Ke Khet Mein." His face lit up with childlike excitement that dissolved, however temporarily, his grief. He got to his feet. People around us clapped as we danced with our hands clasped, swaying our hips without a care for rhythm or music.

"You will give Madhuri Baby a run for her money," Rahul barked.

When the song ended, I hugged Praneet and he sobbed and sobbed. "There will not be another like you," he said. "Get me out of here," he asked. On the door began the pounding of a Servant. It was time to go.

PART VII

1997

HOMECOMING

When we opened the door, a draft whipped up from the floor a sheet of dust that then, in watered-down shafts of light, slowly settled down, as if executing the final move of a dance.

"Welcome home," I said to Marc.

I took a damp dishrag to the living room and wiped the photographs on the Wall of the Dead. Ma started teaching my sisters how to cook when they were twelve. Milk took to the task. Mud couldn't care less. If Ma wasn't monitoring her, she got distracted: she plucked the cauliflower into uneven florets, she burned the ginger-garlic paste. One night she picked up the turmeric jar with damp fingers and it went crashing down. The kitchen's floor was streaked with a splash of russet-orange that, over time, faded to a cream yellow but never went away, not fully, no matter how many times we scrubbed it with bleach.

At dinnertime that day, Ma said to Mud, "You're so reckless. Stay hungry for a night and think about what you did."

But Mud sat down at her usual spot on the floor. "I'm not skipping dinner," she said. "I'm starving."

"In that case I won't eat," Ma said.

"Your wish. I'm properly stuffing myself."

Ma glared at Mud, who mixed steaming rice with roasted eggplant curry.

"Delicious," Mud said, after a mouthful.

"Your sister helped make it," Ma said. "She knows her way around the kitchen."

Mud clapped Milk on the back and said in a deep man's voice, "Marry me, Moonface? Me the husband, you my wife, both daughters married off in one shot, saves Ma trouble and plenty of money. I won't take dowry, not a single paisa."

I burst out laughing.

"Shagun," Ma admonished. "Don't laugh at such vulgar jokes."

Mud said, "You're still here! Might as well eat something, no?"

I now looked at Mud's face, next to Milk's on the Wall of the Dead. Outside, there rose a roar of approaching laughter. I pictured children returning home from our school. I pressed the cloth to my eyes. Damp. Warm. Dirty.

Marc had, I turned and saw, wiped the photographs of Ma and me, on the Wall of the Living, surrounded by square stains.

"Introduce me," he said.

I named my elders as we walked from one end of the Wall of the Dead to another, not by their proper names but by my relationship to them. They each had to make the choices that they did for me to exist, find Marc, and stand with him before their black-and-white faces. "I" felt like a miracle to myself in the light of this thought.

Marc stood before Pita-jee. "I know I shouldn't be surprised, children resemble their parents, but, man," he said. I touched the can full of his ashes, the metal cold against my fingers.

We ended on the pictures of Mud and Milk. He tried but failed to tell them apart.

The power was out by the time we got home from grocery shopping and dinner. I lit a candle and we padded up the stairs. Marc took his shirt off in Ma's room. His arm was two bands of color: a patch of his upper arm, where his shirtsleeve ended, was the pale of my palm, the rest of his hand had tanned. I kissed the line where the two colors met. Marc stepped away from my lips and slipped on a nightshirt.

"Leave it on?" Marc asked, his gaze fixed on the candle as he swapped his trousers for shorts.

We lay down on the four-poster, one next to the other. And I understood: I had to cure my body of its aversion to intimacy, he had to reconcile himself with what had happened on my balcony. Two more steps before I belonged to him.

"We can sleep in my room—it has a bunk bed," I said. I tapped the pillow. "The Great Wall of Singer is also an option."

In the candle's soft light, Marc smiled and closed his reassured eyes. Anyone can paint the gods, Rooh once said. Give him a halo, color his skin blue, and "Remember," you tell viewers. "Remember you were told as a child that this is what your god looks like." But certain images achieve more. The haloed blue-eyed god is a child bringing his foot to his mouth, knee bent at an impossible angle; the goddess holds her own severed head in her hand. Not simply otherworldly, but something impossibly human enacted by human bodies. Blurring the distinction between miracle and possibility, divine and human, time-bound and timeless. These are things viewers see even if they don't notice. No need to say, "Look, remember, listen!" He sees, he closes his eyes, he surrenders. *That*'s a holy icon for you. We could be holy icons, Marc and I. We could evoke in each other complete surrender.

ACTS OF DISCLOSURE

I woke up to the cries of gulls, to the thought that I lay next to Marc in the bed where I was conceived, where I was born. The candle was a pulp of cold wax. Breathing heavily, Marc turned and opened his eyes, their blue turned to slate by morning's light. He started talking about his uncle.

"He had me over to his place," Marc said. "For a belated birthday celebration. Uncle-nephew bonding, he told my parents."

"How old were you?"

"I'd just turned thirteen. So practically twelve.

"He sat me in his lap, which I hated. He wrapped his hands around my waist and held me in place. He had me watch this Italian film about a fourteen-year-old who's seduced by two older women.

"I kept telling him I didn't like it, but he wouldn't stop the movie, he wouldn't bring me back to my parents. There was this one scene between the boy and a woman."

He fell quiet. I didn't stir or say anything.

"He moved me," Marc said. "He moved my body against him."

The man had used the buttocks of a child to masturbate: I had to say it to myself in all its brutality for it to hurt me in the way it should.

"When he was doing it, he kept calling me his Ken doll," Marc said. "When he was done, this stench filled the room. My shorts felt wet, so I ran to the bathroom and looked in the mirror. Nothing."

I understood now why my comment about Ken had upset him. It was an act of radical empathy, his buying me Ken in the first place.

"I thought he'd ask me not to tell Mom. But on the drive back home he spoke about some new soda I should try, some video game. I didn't understand what exactly had happened. Just knew it felt wrong. His behavior confused me. So I never told anyone about it—until now."

"When did you realize what he'd done?" I asked.

"The next time I saw him was when he visited us a few weeks later," Marc said. "New Year's Day, 1982. I remember that clearly. He told us he was leaving for Israel—to get fixed.

"After we moved to Cochin, other memories came back. Things I'd forgotten—repressed, more like. I guess I needed a literal change of scene to remember what happened. One time he brought home this board game and asked me to play it with him. We were in my room. He said that if he lost, I could take any one thing of my choice from his house—and the other way around. 'It's our little secret,' he said.

"He beat me at it in a heartbeat. He was thirty and I was twelve."

Marc wondered what he would lose: his Walkman, his stamp collection? His uncle reached for the laundry basket, sitting in one corner, rummaged through it, and picked up a pair of Marc's underwear. Black. He pressed it to his nose and breathed. Then he neatly folded them, like they were freshly washed, and put them in his pocket. His parents, Marc said, were down in the living room.

"That's why my early days in India were hard," Marc said, his voice, like his expression, distant, as if he wasn't sharing a realization but acknowledging it to himself.

Marc and I were on our sides, facing each other. I leaned into him and wrapped myself around him. Tight. His heartbeat drummed my chest. He buried his face, warm and wet, in the hollow of my neck. His toe curled against my foot. It was a gesture not of intimacy but of comfort. My body allowed it.

"I'll get rid of it," I said. "The doll."

"No," Marc said, turning to me again. "Your pure love for him is good for me."

"Ken," "pure," "love": Who thought those words would be used in the same sentence? Can any object, with devotion, become sacred?

His toe uncurled against my bone, his heartbeat softened, he raised his head. I moved away but cradled an elbow in my palm.

"Sleep awhile longer," I said.

He closed his eyes and I waited until his breath slowed to the cadence of sleep. And I felt the need to clean his clothes. So I took them out of his bag and washed them with well water and soap. I pegged them to the clothesline, water dripping and producing a steady rhythm of droplets on mud.

Then I swept and mopped the kitchen, foyer, living room, and stairs. I left four cups of rice to boil and sat on the staircase with a mug of tea.

Marc came and sat behind me. His bare knees looked like custard apples next to my waist. I felt his stubble as he planted his chin on my neck. He said, his voice still groggy, "Thief! Give me back my things."

"You feel rested?" I asked.

There rose from the kitchen a sharp hiss before he responded. He jumped to his feet.

"Relax. It's just the pressure cooker whistling."

"That thing's no whistle. It's a scream."

We got into the kitchen. The pressure cooker's knob lifted and a jet of steam shot out.

"I'm not eating anything made inside that . . . thing."

"Well, I'm hungry and I'm eating yogurt rice."

"Yogurt rice? For breakfast?"

"Relax. For you I have butter-and-jam sandwiches with chips in between."

His eyes widened with surprise. He didn't ask where I'd extracted this knowledge from, in fact he didn't say a word as we sat on the kitchen floor and ate our separate breakfasts: my yogurt rice, squelchy, spiced with lemon pickle, served on a banana leaf, his sandwiches served on a steel plate, his silence broken only by an arrhythmic crunch.

As I washed the dishes and Marc dried them, standing next to me, a knock broke through our companionable silence. My heartbeat quickened. No one knew I was here. What if it was Vikrant? Or Ajay?

"I'll get it," Marc said.

I heard him open the door. I heard a flurry of voices: Marc's, a woman's. Marc returned to the kitchen, followed by Radha and a man.

"You," I said, relieved, genuinely happy to see her.

"Your boyfriend is nicer to me than you, husband," she said.

"I called and told her we were coming home," Marc said. "When I was waiting for you to get out of Hanuman."

"You must be Rupin," I said. "I was telling Radha you have a nice name."

"Liar," Radha exclaimed.

Radha and I made a pot of chai. I crushed a mixture of ginger, black pepper, and cardamom as she brought milk and four spoons of Assam tea to a boil.

"They bother you because I stopped calling?" I asked.

I scooped the paste into the milk tea. She lowered the flame, lidded the pot.

"I told them you were traveling," she said. "You'll have to go with me to the temple, though. That was my pretext for leaving home today."

We joined Marc and Rupin in the living room with cups of tea and a plate lined with tie biscuits. They sat on the first piece of furniture my father had purchased for our family.

"This is good," Rupin said, raising his cup. "The ginger gives it a good bite."

"I'm sure Shagun agrees," Radha said.

Marc blushed. He braided his laughter to ours after a moment.

"We have to give the priest our attendance," I said.

"So I heard," Marc said. "I have things to do too. Rupin said he'll take me."

"Aren't you a gentleman," Radha said.

"Where are you boys off to?" I asked.

"First to the studio to drop off some reels," Marc said.

"From Hanuman?" I asked.

"Yeah. Then I've got to submit my application at the local railway office."

"There's an opening?" Radha asked.

"Not sure, but they try to accommodate you once you've worked with them."

We stepped out together. I opened the gate and watched as Rupin drove Marc past me on his scooter: Marc's back erect, his rich red hair whisked by my hometown's breeze. Rupin turned a corner, and they were out of sight. Radha tapped my shoulder.

"Show's over, let's go," she said.

A SOLUTION

After the priest offered the goddess the nine-flamed candelabrum, after each devotee offered her kumkum powder, one fistful left at her feet, the other cast in the air, Radha introduced me to the priest as her fiancé and a performer of Hindu myths. He blessed me with a spoonful of the sacred water in my cupped palm. He pressed the sacred copper crown, shaped like a temple dome, to my head. He told me about an upcoming event: four weeks from now, in the last week of August, the temple would celebrate a full moon's lunar eclipse. At dusk, people would gather at the Lawson's Street beach. There were two items on the agenda: the priest would lead the devotees through a ritual prayer, propitiating the moon god in the hours preceding the eclipse, and right before the eclipse started, some local musicians would sing a few lively numbers to welcome the celestial event on a celebratory note.

"Perform something for us that evening?" he said.

It was in that moment when I found the solution: to rid my senses of their affliction and become fully present to Marc—to realize the promise of us. After almost a year of being surrounded by the fog of uncertainty, it felt like a concrete possibility with a date to it: the day of the eclipse. Its simplicity and the fact that it came to me when I wasn't expecting it made me regard it with suspicion. It felt impossibly good. What if I was wrong again, what if I failed Marc and myself? I turned my attention to the priest, who was waiting for my response.

"I'd like that," I said. "Can you fit it in after your ritual and before the singers do their piece?"

"You got it," he said, sounding surprisingly trendy for a temple priest.

Over the last seven years, after every performance, I heard my lines in the voices of Mud and Milk, and in my mind, they came back to life. Now theater would help me not forget but outgrow the boy who let his sisters drown and become fully the man who loved Marc.

"You remember Rusty?" Radha asked as we left the temple.

Her face was guileless as she posed the question. It contained no pity, no inkling of my history with Rusty.

"Why do you ask?"

"His family knows mine. His dad came to invite us to the wedding. Mom told him about us, and he said his son Rusty knew you from Magpies."

"My mother told me about his wedding. When's that happening?"

I came home, took out the itinerary Nandi gave me, and called the post office in Gorakhpur to make a phone appointment. When I called back, Nandi answered. I told him about the performance I hoped to mount, four weeks hence. Its story, its structure.

"Will you help?" I asked.

"What do you need?"

"Could I borrow Rooh and Saaya? I'm not supposed to participate in your theater, I get that, but they can participate in mine."

"You're sneaky, boy. Anyone ever tell you that?" he said.

We finalized the logistics: their date of arrival, the duration of their stay. I didn't tell him Marc was with me.

He said, "You know I've been thinking about what you said—about our responsibility to stories. It hasn't changed my perspective, or how I'll run things, not yet."

"Of course it hasn't," I said. "There's a reason we called you Nandi the Bull."

"What!" he exclaimed and exploded with laughter.

I heard Marc come in as I was almost done making dinner. Aloo-gobi and rice.

"Come here, taste this curry, and tell me what you think," I hollered.

He placed on the kitchen countertop a newspaper and an envelope. I knew they contained the photographs. I washed and dried my hands, then opened it.

My former fellow inmates, standing before Hanuman as Servants whipped their exposed crotches. Two photographs, the same scene: inmates watching porn in an auditorium, one taken from behind, their heads blobs of black against the screen where a man leaned over a woman, both naked, the other taken from the side, the men's faces, washed in the adult film's blue light, expressionless. Next picture: Praneet, his penis shriveled, leaning over a woman, behind him the statue of Hanuman imposing.

"When do we start?" I asked.

"How about right now? I'm starving," Marc said.

"I meant the article."

"My role's done. The photos, the tapes, they're yours. Do with them as you please."

I cupped his face. "You risked it. Shouldn't you have some say?"

"I never faced what you did. I wasn't on the run. I can never do with this material what you can. This is your story to tell."

SAI PHOTO STUDIO, the cover of the envelope said. It was where Pita-jee had developed my peeing photos.

"I meant to ask," Marc said. "The final test at Hanuman: What was it like for you?"

"I zoned out during," I said. "But when it was done, it hit me that I lost my virginity not to the man I loved, but to a stranger I'd never again meet, and—"

I paused to give the grief that surfaced the expression it sought, wondering why tears contained salt when salt stings your eyes.

Marc sat next to me, waiting with a patience that I'd come to see as the highest form of love.

When I was ready to speak, I said, "I was numb that day, after it happened, and relieved, and I had a room full of men watching, but only now, as I'm talking to you, I figured out what bothered me about the whole thing."

"What's that?"

"I'm supposed to be with a woman. That's what they said. Dad, Vikrant, Mom. And for the short duration of that test I gave in to what they wanted. I did it to get out, I know."

"But knowing that doesn't make the experience feel any less icky."

I shook my head.

"It may be hard to receive this now but I hope you can remember it for whenever you're ready," Marc said. "You're incredibly brave, Shagun."

"Brave?"

"Despite everything, here you are, choosing us. So no, you didn't let them define you. Far from it."

I took his hand in mine and kissed his palm. "Is there a world out there where being who we are won't make our lives difficult?"

"Maybe. Or maybe you'll help change the world we've inherited so we leave it a better place for ourselves and those who come after."

Marc and I turned the staircase into our study that night. Marc, who decided to apply to more jobs as he waited to hear from the railways, circled two positions in the newspaper's classified list—port scheduler, lighthouse keeper—and started to craft his cover letters. I studied the photographs, listened to the recordings, and made a bullet-point outline. Then I began, in earnest, writing the article.

Two days before Rusty's wedding, I went to his house. A maid ushered me in and asked me to sit. A moment later, Rusty joined me. Shirtless, barefoot, in khaki shorts. Over the years his face had neither gained nor lost any of its weight. Its sharp edges, which once shone through his adolescent beauty, now formed a fitting architecture to his youthful face. His long, fluffy hair, combed back, added several inches to his height.

He sat before me and spread his legs wide, his shorts, cinched up as a result, revealing trunk-like thighs. As if he knew the effect he'd have on me.

"I know why you're here," Rusty said.

"You do?"

He scratched his chin. "You're after something, and if I don't give it to you, you'll show up at my wedding with those photos your manboy took of me."

"And what's it you think I want?"

"An apology? A quickie someplace private? Everyone knew you had the hots for me."

I took an envelope from my trouser pocket and placed it on the table. He didn't look at it. His expression didn't shift. But beads of sweat dotted his forehead.

"You got the blackmail part wrong." I pointed to the envelope. "That's all of them."

I still carried the impact of the photos Pita-jee took of me. I'd resolved not to reenact that pattern of harm.

"As for my intent—wrong as well," I said. "Aren't you a big shot in some fancy financial outfit in Bombay? You're supposed to be good at this negotiation game."

I looked away. I was in the room where Rohit-jee insulted Ma.

"I want the dowry my father paid your dad," I said. "You can afford it—I bet your dad milked your wife's family for dowry."

I turned to him, aware that my eyes had filled with a film of water. My father couldn't attend my sisters' funeral because your family kept his money, I didn't add.

"You know Viren also got in trouble with the boys? Right before you got to Magpies," he asked. "Doesn't matter how. Important thing is he came to me. Had the same pleading look in his eyes that you got now." He pressed his wrist to his forehead. "When the boys made your life hell"—he mimed a soundless gag—"I would've protected you too. If you requested."

I hadn't sought his protection, I recalled. I'd tried talking to him—tried being his friend, an equal.

"What did you do after you left Magpies?" he asked. "You were quite the talk of our grade. A scholarship boy who absconds? How often does that happen?"

"I joined a street theater troupe," I said.

He smirked. Then, he got up, left the room. I heard a muffled conversation.

Rusty returned with a folder. He took out a checkbook and a pen. My heart lurched as he scribbled away. I imagined him writing it In Favor of Bitch Bags. He cut the check and held it out. I leaned forward. It slipped from his hand.

"Oops," he said. "You want to get that?"

As I squatted to pick it up, he said, "Good choice." I looked up at him. "If you pulled blackmail on me, I would've kicked your ass." He sniffed and looked down at me. "All that intelligence and you're a circus kid? Well, better cash that check before they cut your power."

The check was in my name. He held his hand out. I took it. With a powerful tug he got me to my feet.

He said, "If only you respected my power all along. You would've made things easier on yourself. But hey, all that's behind us now. No hard feelings."

He led me out of the room with a hand to my back. Rohit-jee stood in a shadowed corridor with no windows. He watched us, the white of his eyes like enamel. I remembered what he'd said about my sisters. The posthumous shame he pinned on them.

I told Rusty I needed to use the restroom. I went in, locked the door behind me, and turned on the light. On the sink sat a bottle of Rohit-jee's favorite handwash. In the cabinet under the sink: four more bottles. I squirted a generous portion on my hand, smelled it, washed it off. One after the other, I emptied them into the sink's drain hole, picturing

Rohit-jee's face when tomorrow, Sunday morning, he found his bottles empty after he took a shit.

I went to the post office and sent the money to Ma through a cash transfer service. It was my parents' hard-earned money and it belonged to her now. That, I believed, was the reason I had shown up at Rohit-jee's house. On the solitary walk back home, I realized I also wanted to see Rusty, to test if his presence exacted on me the same effect. And I understood that my unreturned feelings for Rusty, despite what he'd done to me, like my pretense that Senior was my lover, had tangled me up in ways that I had to someday parse and release. It would be essential to keeping my relationship with Marc—and myself—healthy.

When I opened the door to my home, Marc, who was sitting on the steps leading upstairs, hollered, "Where were you? I missed you. I know it's not even been a day."

"But it felt longer than that, I know," I said, sitting next to him.

"You smell nice," he said, breathing deep.

I broke into a laughter, reveling in my minor victory, forgetting, momentarily, the sting of Rusty's words. Next to me, Marc looked confused. Understandably.

THE RISE OF THE SEA ELEPHANTS

Between dinner and midnight we worked on the stairs and then took a chai break. We worked another hour or two before turning in for the night. Between applying for more jobs, Marc edited what I wrote.

We took the steaming mugs of chai to the backyard the night I completed the article and basked in the light of the nearly full moon. Marc brought Saaya up.

He said, "I ran into him, the day I came to meet you and you weren't there."

"The day you saw me at the dhaba? That's the day you two flirted."

"Something followed the flirting. Saaya told me I looked stressed."

"What did you say?"

"Usual relationship stuff, is all I said that day. 'If you need an ear, I'm here,' he offered. Later, a little after New Year's—"

"The day the No Contact rule was put in place. Go on."

"I took Saaya up on his offer. Had him over. He heard me out and said, 'Shagun loves you enough to want your babies.' We laughed about it. Things were innocent until we got alcohol in the mix.

"We decided that if I could get some, it would actually help us—you and me. I can't remember how we came to the conclusion. If it was him or me or maybe both."

"Thank you for telling me," I said.

"Let's be honest to a fault from now on," Marc said.

I read my essay after our chai break. What appeared on the page felt dull compared to my lived experience of the facility, stripped of something essential and urgent I couldn't name. So I was restless when I went to sleep. I woke up in the dark with an idea that couldn't wait until morning. I returned to the article and interspersed the paragraphs with everyday anecdotes about Marc and me: our drives, conversations, travels. What about us needed to be fixed or warranted violence? The juxtaposition posed this implicit question.

I revised the paragraphs that detailed the morning ritual and dinnertime, describing bodies huddled together to evoke the intimacy that we celebrated despite the situation to which we were condemned.

"My people will not be erased," I wrote, and felt, for the first time, the weight of that phrase, "my people." The voices of Saaya, Praneet, and Kumar buzzed through my veins.

The sky started to lighten by the time I was done. I knew the writing was far from perfect. But I was satisfied with the content. I made some chai, poured it into a flask, and woke Marc up. He rubbed his eyes with the heel of his hand as he sat up grumbling.

We walked to the train station and followed the tracks. We passed the flask back and forth. The morning air was crisp. When we reached the abandoned factory, I pointed to it.

"My father built that," I said.

We walked down a short slope to get to the building. There was a hole in the boundary wall. We ducked and crossed it. The building revealed its age and the fact of its abandonment: its plaster crumbling, its facade faded, the bricks underneath bared. To our right was an oak tree, its branches busy with leaves, the leaves from last year heaped in the cart that stood underneath.

We lifted the cart together and brought it out, leaving a trail of brittle brown-golden leaves. We heaved it up the short slope and placed it on the tracks. We sat down, a little breathless from the effort. I told Marc about the leaves inside the cauldron at Magpies, the friend I gave chalk faces to. He smiled when I told him that Kumar was that cauldron friend. We were quiet for a moment.

Then, I asked, "Did you photograph any elephants in your hometown?"

"That's random," he said. "Several. But the reels are all at home. Why?"

"I'd like your work to be a part of the play. I'll call Giti and ask her to bring them. If that's okay?"

"Sure. But how will you use photos in a performance?"

"I'll show you. And if you don't like what you see, we won't include them."

He sat in the cart. I pushed him, slowly, then fast. He held on to the sides of the cart and sat back. My face was pressed to his cheek. His laughter drowned my squeals. Tears streamed down my face and, whipped by the wind, by our speed, landed on his forehead like raindrops. We took turns pushing each other. We were exhausted by noon and sat in the shade of the hole in the wall. Two kinds of heat on my face. The sun, his skin.

Once, Nandi and I sat by the Ganga and spoke about time. On the opposite bank, priests offered aarti to the river goddess. The flowing waters reflected the sizzling camphor flames. Boys with shorn heads and saffron robes chanted in tandem to the handheld bells they clanged. Water lapped at stone steps and our feet and released the scent of silt. Time, Nandi said, is a rocking horse. When Krishna was a child, he pulled its ear, released it, and walked away, laughing. It creaked, back and forth, back and forth, back and forth. Noisy nonstop. We worship Krishna in the child form because we want him to come and grab that Time Horse by its tail; when he does, the horse's grinning face will come to a halt and silence will descend. Peace, at last, from the noise of time. Isn't that the need at the heart of our every prayer, whatever our material demands, whatever words we choose? Peace from the noise of time.

When we got back home, Marc went up to sleep a little longer and I called Giti. I presented two requests: one for Marc's reels, the other for the Canon. Marc took photographs that he had put to use, for my article. Wasn't that what David had wanted?

On our way to the railway station, we faxed the article to Giti. I had revised it six times by then, and on the last iteration, I decided to make it anonymous and stripped it of all identifying markers. I forsook the act of defiance—claiming authorship, because we lived in a country where homosexuality was illegal and resulted in ten years in prison. I had already decided to blur out the faces of the men from the photographs for the same reason.

We got to the station just as Konark Express was pulling in. Rooh and Saaya disembarked from the train before it fully came to a stop. They spotted me easily.

I said, "Group hug," as an announcement from the speakers above roared: Konark Express is ready to depart from platform number one. The train puffed, creaked, and lurched to life. Rooh, Saaya, and Marc formed a circle around me, the hands of one on the shoulder of another. I breathed in their heat, the smell of them.

Walking back home, Rooh and Marc fell into one line, Saaya and I into another.

"You made the call?" I asked.

I had asked him to call Kumar.

Saaya said, "Told him to leave right away."

"Thank you," I said.

"Are you sure?" Saaya whispered. "Me? Here?"

"You gave him what I couldn't," I said.

He held my shoulder, drew me toward himself. The bone of my shoulder met his chest.

"You aren't coming back to us," Saaya said. "Your home is here, and your boy."

That evening, we sat in the treehouse and discussed our upcoming performance: a sea elephant story. From *The Dravidian Book of Seas and Stargazing, Volume 2.*

The grief of the sea elephants, over time, becomes potent enough to curse a god: Indra, the one who took Iravat. His blessings start to fail. He bestows upon the king of Magadha the boon of an all-male progeny, but the king's fourth child is born a girl. Chitrangada. Indra uses his celestial vision to understand what has come to pass. So he travels to earth and beseeches the sea elephants for a meeting. Their chief rises to the surface and stands still on the sinuously moving waves, his glistening white body reflecting the starry night. Indra asks for forgiveness. While he cannot replace their ancestor, he offers two gifts: a direct line of communication between them, in the sea, and Iravat, up in heaven; heaven's ambrosia to heal the deep scars of generational trauma. The elephant chief accepts Indra's apology and his gifts. Two generations of sea elephants come of age before their trauma heals. Their songs, thereafter, start to contain the full octave. All seven notes. The elephant songs now sound complete.

Rooh, we decided, would deliver the backstory: the churning of the ocean, Iravat's departure to heaven, his descendants' longing, which makes them steal kids. I would play the sea elephant, Saaya would be our narrator, and Rooh the god Indra.

When our discussion ended, Rooh and Marc started climbing down the ladder. I was about to follow them, when Saaya said, "Wait, Nandi has a gift for you."

He picked up a plastic bag that I hadn't seen him bring with him. He pulled Nandi's gift out of it and gave it to me. I held it in both my hands, then buried my face in it.

It was the green Chitrangada costume.

Two days before the performance, Marc went to bring Giti to our home from the railway station and I sat on the staircase. When the door opened, I stood up, precarious as a rope walker, on the edge of a tread. A smile filled all of Giti's face when she saw me. I couldn't smile back. As I stood stiffly where I was and Marc closed the door, dimming the light that filled the foyer, Giti unzipped her purse and took out a rolled-up magazine. *Newsweek.*

"Fresh off the press," she said, giving it to me.

I took it with me to Ma's room, where I sat on the floor with my back to the bed and gazed fixedly at the cover: Marc's photo of gay men in saffron. The title of the article: "The Inhumanity of Conversion Therapy: An Insider Story."

I turned to page forty-five and found my words surrounding a constellation of Marc's photographs and transcribed excerpts of the audio he recorded. I started to read it, but those words that I had composed were marbles in my head: they rattled about and found no purchase. Perhaps I wasn't prepared yet to digest the fact of its public appearance. I tucked it under the bed and sat there awhile longer.

When I went back downstairs, I found Marc and Giti sitting on the kitchen floor cross-legged. Marc excitedly brandished his first camera, the Canon. Giti set aside the glass of water she was nursing and stood up.

"Marc likes the surprise you planned for him," she said.

"I wanted to apologize in person," I said, "Marc went to exactly the kind of place you wanted to keep him from."

Giti said, "Back then he would've gone to further the agenda of a sick man. This time he went for love, and that makes all the difference."

I hugged them both at once. They released identical gasps of surprise before they returned the gesture. I pressed my head to their joined shoulders and cried. Neither made an attempt to end the hug.

They had identical ears, mother and son, I noticed when I finally stepped back.

"Where is Furniture's shop?" Marc asked.

"Why do you ask?"

"To get you a dining table," Giti said. "My housewarming gift to you two."

"Find him," Marc said, his grin impish. He held the camera out to Giti. "Will you photograph us, Ma, Shagun and me?"

The day before my performance, I left home without telling anyone and returned with Su.

"Why didn't you tell me she was coming?" Marc asked, bringing his hands together for a soundless clap.

I put down her bag and circled his face with a finger. "To see this," I said.

That evening Su, Radha, and I walked the brumous beach with our slippers in our hands. Cold waves rushed over our feet. White froth foamed over my toes. The sand was cold.

We sat down. Radha updated us about her plans: three months from now, when she and Rupin were done with college, they would make their escape to Delhi, where they could find jobs, where they'd be safe in the thicket of the metropolis.

Su said, "And I thought I had it hard because I'll have to bring Sagar up with my parents. Dad will be a pain, but he won't hurt me. The worst he'll do is cut me off for a while."

Radha said, "Talking to your dad about something that deeply matters to you when you know he won't be receptive? That *is* hard, Su. It went well with Sagar's parents though?"

"Better than I thought it would," Su said.

"I told you it's humanly impossible to dislike you," I said.

She rested her head on my shoulder. "His mom's a sweetheart. We're taking a little trip together next month."

"Where are you going?" Radha asked.

"Goa. She wants to have coconut margaritas with me on the beach and I'm here for it."

Radha and I let out cheerful yelps. I spotted a muri mixture seller in the distance. The kerosene lamp on his trolley flickered against the sinuous hush of evening waves. I ran up to him and bought us a paper cone full of puffed rice, dampened by lemon juice, sharpened by shredded chilies, turned tangy by raw cut mangoes. Radha, Su, and I passed around the cone, gulping greedy breaths between mouthfuls to mitigate the bite of the spice. After we were finished, and the burn on our tongues had settled, Su cleared her throat and sang a song about rainfall, its melody heightened by the rhythm of the retreating waves. I thought of those evenings when Ma took us out for a stroll by the sea, my sisters and me, all of us fresh from an evening shower, smelling of talcum powder, soap, and the Parachute oil she slicked our hair with. The twins and I would run off, our chins tucked into our necks, laughing, swinging our fists by our bodies. "Not so far!" Ma cried. "You're little, I cannot see you, come back, I'll buy you muri mixture." And we arranged ourselves once more, one next to the other, the twins holding each other's hands and mine, I holding Ma's, carrying cushions of warm air between my palms.

By the time we returned home, Marc, Saaya, and Rooh had finished work on the props for our performance. Marc's photos of the elephants, six of them, developed in black-and-white and blown up, eleven-by-sixteen inches each, were stitched onto two fabrics, midnight-blue cotton, six feet by two feet. There were three photos per fabric, the eyes of the elephants cold-stamped in copper, their tails in silver. A loop stitched at the top of each fabric accommodated a curtain rod.

"Anything happen between you two?" Su asked, looking from Marc to me.

My silence gave her the response she sought. It was ruptured by a knock on the door. Rupin came home with the photograph Giti had taken, enlarged and framed.

"Want to do the honors?" I asked Su.

We went to the living room. Su suspended the frame from one of the many available hooks.

"Giti, Marc, Saaya. Everyone. Here, now," I hollered.

They filed into the room. Their murmurs scattered and fell away as we observed the picture: Marc and me on the floor, my hand on Marc's knee, his hand on my shoulder, my head tilted toward him, grazing his chin. Twenty years from now, we might look impossibly young to the eyes of our older selves, but now the photograph mirrored who we were. For the first time in decades, the Wall of the Living had an addition. And the people I loved, all but Ma and Nandi, were here, in the room, witnessing the wall's revival.

"I have an idea that'll help Romeo and Romeo," Su whispered. "Leave it to me."

OTHER USES FOR EARTHEN LAMPS

The performance began. I was underwater. A bamboo reed, pressed between my lips, rose beyond the water's surface. It was my source of oxygen. As I waited for my cue to rise as the sea elephant king, I recollected that last fatal excursion my sisters and I took to the port, beguiled by the possibility of spotting a gora.

Did they in fact sit on the boat before bringing it onto the beach sand, or did the waves tip them into the boat as they tried to drag it ashore? Why did I dare them?

I spread my fingers, as if to touch my sisters' drowned breaths. Neither did I sense my tears' heat nor taste the salt of the sea. I relived, instead, my final sighting of my sisters in present tense: their legs going knee-deep into the cold, churning waters; then their identical faces submerged; their hands shooting into the air; their fingers, trembling, sinking out of view. I freed my mouth. I'm sorry, I said, into the waters that had devoured them. I held the reed between my lips again. To breathe. To live. And not be ashamed about it.

My cue arrived: the bellow of a conch, the sea elephant deciding to accept Indra's request for a meeting. I spat the reed. My head, then my shoulders tore the surface of the waters. I stood up.

I found him then: a child whose careless dare had soured. A child reduced to his helplessness. A child, rain-drenched, his fists clenched against his chest.

A child.

I saw Rooh, dressed as Indra: white kurta, white dhoti. He raised the midnight-blue fabrics high, one in each hand, gripping them from behind with their curtain rods. They shivered lightly in the breeze and the metal on Marc's elephants caught sunlight: copper wink of an eye, silver wink of a tail. They symbolized the line of communication that had opened up between Iravat and his sea elephant family.

I stepped out of the waters and closed my eyes. When I opened them, I became the sea elephant.

As our performance ended, the eclipse began. We had planned on that. A crescent of black creased the white surface of the moon that hovered over the sea's abundant waters. What surprised me was the spectacle closer at hand: Su pushed a cart on the beach sand, toward the circle of devotees. Set on it were earthen lamps, wicks burning, flickering in the sea breeze.

I looked to Rooh, who took his mask off, and to Saaya, who pulled off his wig.

"Take a lamp each," Su announced. "Set it afloat in the sea."

I changed out of my wet clothes. Marc waited for me. Together we joined the line of devotees. We walked toward the radiant halo that emanated from the cart. Every step contained a multitude.

We collected an earthen lamp each. I thumbed its warm underbelly. Across a wavering glow, Marc stood still.

In the last few months, how many times had Marc relived our last evening in Chamba?

As we made our way to the sea, I held my palm above the flame. My flesh turned warm. Someone burned incense. Sandalwood infused the smell of sea breeze.

We set our lamps afloat and stepped back. From a distance we watched them. Gradually, they joined thirty or forty lamps. They swam away like a shoal of fish made up of flames. I pictured the hands of Mud and Milk rising to cup the flames, to keep them safe from the wind.

"I forgive you," I said. To me, to Marc.

Su came and stood next to me. Marc turned away, with his wrists pressed to his eyes.

"What did I do to deserve you?" I asked her.

"You don't," she said. "This is just charity."

Around us devotees started to sing bhajans and clap and dance.

"Never asked," Su said. "Mud, Milk—what are their real names?"

I told her. Spoke them out loud for what felt like the first time in my life. Riddhi. Siddhi. After the consorts of Ganesha, the deity of good beginnings.

"Mud wasn't a fan of her name," I said. "Said it made her sound like a conservative grandmother from the turn of the century with a beehive hairdo." Su and Marc lurched forward and exploded with laughter, their joy spilling from their open mouths into the seawater. "So her classmates called her Riddle, and I Mud."

Marc tapped my shoulder. "Look," he said.

Standing next to Giti was Ma: she set an oil lamp afloat and joined her hands as she said a prayer. I ran to her.

She touched her hair and said, "They didn't take away my hair. Happy?"

I laughed and cried as I held her against myself.

"I liked it," she said, gesturing to the space where the play took place.

I was thrilled. It was my first performance she'd seen. It was she who brought the sea elephants into our lives: mine, Mud's, Milk's. A question came to mind.

"How did you know I was performing today?" I asked.

"Marc told me," she said.

"*He* called and you came?" I said.

"He said something that changed my mind."

"Let's hear them, the magic words."

"He quoted the *Gita*. The part where Krishna says the body is an earthly suit. Underneath, the soul is without gender. He told me, 'If you worship Krishna, then how does it matter what the gender of your son's soul mate is?'"

I couldn't help it. I laughed.

"What?" she said, and as I shook my head, Marc and Su came up to us.

"Why didn't you tell me?" I asked Marc.

"For this," he said, circling my face with his finger.

"I read your article," Ma said. She cupped my cheek. "That man? They put him away."

"Vikrant?" I said.

"It was on the news. I saw it on the railway station TV."

"Marc helped me, Ma. He took a risk and got in, he took all those pictures. He learned their stories. Giti helped me edit it, she gave the piece a home."

Ma smiled, and the tears in her eyes spilled over. She hugged Marc, tentatively at first, then tight. She pressed a hand to his head. Filling him with all the blessings she contained. She stepped back and held out her hand toward me. I clasped it.

"I'm happy you took your father's money back from Rohit-jee," she said. "But I'd like you to have it." She looked at Marc and me. I opened my mouth to protest. "Think of it as my blessing—and your father's. For your future together."

"You wanted a celebration," Su said, pointing to the dancing devotees. "You wanted a performance with your theater buddies. You wanted me and your mom to see you run off into your special night."

I nodded, my throat heavy, tight.

"Time to go," Su said. "There's a second surprise."

"Are you coming home?" I asked Ma.

"I told you I can't stay at home anymore," Ma said.

"You still want to live in the ashram," I said, dismayed.

"I'm here now," she said.

"Your future wife is hosting her," Su said.

She gestured with her eyebrows. I turned around and saw Radha waving at me.

"We have things to catch up on," Giti said, placing a hand on Ma's shoulder. "I go where she goes."

"Don't tell Radha's parents," I said. "They can't know."

"Shagun, I know," Ma said.

"What's next?" Su said. "You'll come to each of us and take attendance?"

"Yeah, where will you guys stay? You, Saaya—"

"Oh God. Are you going or do I have to push you?" Su demanded.

Marc and I left the beach. I turned and watched my people still standing there: Rooh, Saaya, Su, Ma. The light of a hundred oil lamps came ashore, washing them in an ochre glow. They were surrounded by throngs of devotees, clapping, dancing, singing.

On the road was our flower man. He cocked an eyebrow at me.

"Your friend was right! Here you are. Two cubits? I'll add extra."

"How many cubits do you have?"

"Thirty, maybe?"

I took it all, paid him, and asked him to come collect his basket next morning.

"I'm highly confused," Marc said.

I said nothing. A draft sent papery bougainvillea flying into our faces. The air carried the tangy scent of pickled mangoes.

The moon was quartered by shadow by the time we got home.

I turned to Marc at the foot of the staircase and said, "Stay. I'll call you when it's time."

Looking at his wrist, where there was no watch, Marc said, "Your time starts now. One, two, three. Go!"

I bounded up the stairs, two at a time, got into our room, and shut the door.

When the totality of the eclipse was four minutes away, I hollered, "You can come in."

His footsteps drummed the stairs. He threw the door open, came running in, but stopped abruptly short.

Marc collected his breath as he surveyed the room: the bed readied in the manner of a bridal night, the stringed jasmine spread from one end to the other. I stood next to the bedpost, wearing a white cotton shirt over blue trousers.

Marc bridged the last leg between us in slow, soundless steps. He pinched my collar. He leaned his head into my neck and breathed hard. I smelled of new fabric. He smelled of incense smoke and sesame.

I felt the need, I told him, to decorate myself. Not to turn into a princess or a king but into the best possible version of me. He pressed his body to mine. I caressed his hair. Even the seagulls flying past the house were quiet that evening. I felt like the rightful bearer of my name. Shagun. The harbinger of good times.

When the window was nearly dark, the eclipse erasing the remainder of moonlight, I smeared his lips with saffron and leaned forward. It wasn't an urgent kiss. It claimed its place as the beginning of a rhythm, a routine. What all can a kiss contain? An apology. Its forgiveness. A statement. Its acknowledgment. A memory. Its healing. An understanding. Its reception. Gratitude. Its return. I tasted it all on the salt of his lips.

When we unlocked our mouths, my lips were wet with his saffron.

"What do you want?" he asked.

I unbuckled his belt and freed his legs from his trousers. Then, I lay down on the bed, waiting. The petals under my flesh released a jasmine breath. He fumbled with the belt of my trousers, he pulled it down to my knees along with my underwear. He leaned over me and his foot pushed them loose of my legs. He slipped a pillow under the small of my back. With his hands on my thighs, he spread my legs, he made room for himself. I clenched my teeth and took a breath, prepared to receive him.

My bones felt his bones as he ground me against the jasmine. I carried the gorgeous burden of his body. He cupped one hand on top of my head as his heart thrummed wildly against mine. I gripped the nape of his neck.

I belonged to him. There was no greater pleasure I'd known.

Later that night, when we lay spent, his sweat gluing his belly to mine, his arm wrapped around me, his chin nestled into my neck, his stubble pricking my skin, our clothes on the floor in a heap, the flowers releasing their fragrance, I wept and wept and wept. Marc didn't ask me why, he didn't say "stop." Slowly, slowly the moon claimed his place back in the sky. From all that distance he washed us in the white of his flesh.

At six in the morning, Marc said, "Will you become a princess for me?"

"Only if you become a god for me," I said.

I changed into Chitrangada's costume. Green blouse, green skirt. With the few rudimentary paints that Rooh and Saaya brought with them, I turned Marc into Krishna: blue cheeks, lips burgundy.

I made a decision: my life as I lived it would reflect who I was, complete, uncensored.

I can be whomever I want, Chitrangada declares. Myth is told in the present tense, Nandi said.

On our way out, I paused outside the living room. Then, I went in, stood before the Wall of the Dead, and cupped the Dabur Dalda can with my palms. My face was embossed on my father's. The distance between our faces grew smaller, it seemed, with each passing year.

Marc stood at the threshold, his patience, the freedom of it, a gift that I reminded myself to treasure.

I raised my arms, lowered my head, and wiped my eyes, my shirt rough against my face, my palms never leaving the can. It was time, I decided.

From the treehouse, as we passed by, came a duet of snores. Saaya, Rooh. A pair of feet was sticking out the open door. Su.

We walked through the fish basti, vacant in this hour, the thatched roofs of shops, lowered, bobbing in the morning breeze against bamboo pillars. The air was thick with the smell of fish. My feet, bare, remembered running down this street with my sisters. In my hands, the can filled with my father's ashes grew heavy.

On the beach, wind whipped his red hair, my green gown. The sound of the waves was a breath in our ears. I stepped into the surf. I called Marc by his name. He joined me, unscrewed the lid, and pressed his palms to mine. We tilted the can, and my father's ashes, gray, fine as sand, made a sound like a whisper upon contact with water. The retreating waves took them away.

The can had emptied. My father was home. Resting. With daughters he'd never met in his lifetime. Peace, at last, from the noise of time.

I looked up and found Marc's face. Blue, smiling, sun-washed. The sea around us bottle green; beyond the sea, on the other side, a distant land where, I was certain, the child who I wanted would be allowed to exist, even welcomed.

I leaned into Marc, and my forehead met the warmth of his neck. I breathed, filled with a great sense of possibility. Our story had just begun, our time together a landscape undreamed.

AUTHOR'S NOTE

India decriminalized homosexuality in 2018. But queer acceptance is still the exception, rather than the norm. Some variation of the reeducation centers described in these pages is the lived reality of many queer men. If you're interested in knowing more stories of queer lives as they are lived in South Asia, here and now, I encourage you to follow Yes, We Exist (@yesweexistindia) on Instagram.

ACKNOWLEDGMENTS

This is a novel that's born from the mouths of many stories.

I applied to the UMass MFA program to work with Sabina Murray on an early draft of *The Sea Elephants*. She read it and said that she felt the ache of desire between the asexual Shagun and his "friend" Marc Singer. The ache she felt on the page had throbbed through my life, but I was unaware of it. I was twenty-seven years old. Six months later, I came out at a potluck Sabina invited her class to.

Gay conversion therapy centers are a place I nearly got sent to when *The Sea Elephants* got outed as a gay novel. I learned from men who survived such spaces, the stories of their experiences.

Many of these pages were written over the course of an unpaid summer vacation during grad school, a time in which my mother and my sisters, Kamakshi and Surekha, housed me, fed me, gave me the gift of their time and support.

Subhadra, the first friend I came out to, is who I think of when I hear the phrase "soul tribe." I wouldn't have quit my Google job and joined an MFA program without her aggressive encouragement, nor would I have embraced queerness in my writing.

When I came out and was still figuring out what it means to be queer in the world, my friend Andrew took me to my first queer dance night and gave me company. He also read six drafts of this novel with the same degree of empathy and attention and let me bribe his cats, the inimitable George and Beaker, into being my writing companions.

Seventeen years back, Grace, my former boss, became my friend because of our shared loved for books. When I had to travel to Canada to get my visa extended under trying circumstances, she drove me and stayed with me. She and Prayathna are wholly responsible for the evolution of my taste in literature: they introduced me to works by Michael Cunningham, Alice Walker, Milan Kundera, and Ben Okri, among others.

My UMass professors went above and beyond being excellent, empathetic teachers. Parker and Edie read my novel in their first year as fiction faculty at UMass and in the seven years that followed, they've been champions of my work. I was Parker's tenant for three years, which is where I wrote a bulk of this book; from waiving my summer rent to keeping my Dominos secret to letting me hang out with Sharik, aka best-doggo-in-the-world, he's the most generous landlord I could've asked for. My PhD adviser, Moira, became my family. We cooked together, traded playlists, and I went to her place in Ipswich when I felt homesick for the sea and wrote pages of my novel. I will always remember the car ride where we listened to Lucinda Williams and remembered our dads.

The birthday party where Callum invited me to read my novel, the wonderfully rendered recordings he sent me of passages from it, the New York trip we took to celebrate its completion; the long conversations I had with Sagari and Kritika; the shared love for horror and film that Spencer and I have; the entirely nonjudgmental conversations I have with Freddie and his indulgence of my love for tacos; my yoga and writing sessions with Daniel; my friendship with Bükem, forged in the COVID summer, evolving into nightlong writing sessions and a shared love for Starbucks, Kate McKinnon, and *Outlander*: all of them nourished my soul and my writing.

Three weeks after my novel sold, my father passed away. Even when he didn't read my novel or agree with what I wrote about, he championed and supported me to pursue my dream and took great pride in my successes. As did my mother, who encouraged me to keep writing through every rejection I received, brought me the first novel I ever read when I was twelve, and read to me the myths that appear in *The Sea Elephants*.

I looked for an agent for two years before Chris Clemans found my novel in his slush pile. What followed is one of the most memorable calls of my life. I had sought him out because I loved the fiction written by the eclectic authors he represents. So I felt very fortunate when he signed me on as his client. His keen, patient editorial gaze has helped the novel and its characters to evolve to heights I had never envisioned for them, and his support, during the challenging summer of 2022, which went above and beyond an agent's responsibility, meant the world to me. I would like to acknowledge, as well, the support I received from Chris's assistant, Roma Panganiban, at both an editorial and a logistical level.

Caroline Bleeke was the first editor I spoke to, a call that lasted over an hour. Her warmth and brilliance that I felt in our conversation were apparent in the feedback she gave me, feedback that, among other things, allowed the novel to finally find the structure that was perfectly suited to its telling. I feel deeply fortunate that as a computer science graduate writing fiction in my third language, I get to work with a brilliant mind like Caroline's.

I would also like to express my gratitude to the entire team at Flatiron for the time and energy they devoted to *The Sea Elephants*: SVP Megan Lynch; president Bob Miller; associate publisher Malati Chavali; Katherine Turro from marketing; publicist Christopher Smith; art director Keith Hayes; managing editor Emily Walters; production editor Morgan Mitchell; production manager Eva Diaz; copy editor Shelly Perron; interior designer Michelle McMillian; the audio team of Elishia Merricks, Emily Dyer, and Drew Kilman; and the wonderful Sydney Jeon, assistant editor.

This is a novel born from the mouth of a thousand stories and manifested by the love and generosity of my family and found family. My words, in this novel and beyond, are my expression of gratitude for their generosity of spirit and big hearts.

ABOUT THE AUTHOR

Shastri Akella holds an MFA in creative writing and a PhD in comparative literature from the University of Massachusetts Amherst. He is a former fellow of the Fine Arts Works Center. His writing has appeared in *Guernica*, *Fairy Tale Review*, *The Masters Review*, *Electric Literature*, *The Rumpus*, and *World Literature Today*, among others. *The Sea Elephants* is his debut novel.